# Heart:

## Cuore

Edmondo de Amicis

*Translated by Isabel F. Hapgood*

Lits © 2010

De Amicis, Edmondo

Heart: Cuore / Edmondo de Amicis – 1st ed.

   1.  Fiction - Classics

# AUTHOR'S PREFACE

This book is especially dedicated to the boys of the elementary schools between the ages of nine and thirteen years, and might be entitled: "The Story of a Scholastic Year written by a Pupil of the Third Class of an Italian Municipal School." In saying written by a pupil of the third class, I do not mean to say that it was written by him exactly as it is printed. He noted day by day in a copy-book, as well as he knew how, what he had seen, felt, thought in the school and outside the school; his father at the end of the year wrote these pages on those notes, taking care not to alter the thought, and preserving, when it was possible, the words of his son. Four years later the boy, being then in the lyceum, read over the MSS. and added something of his own, drawing on his memories, still fresh, of persons and of things.

Now read this book, boys; I hope that you will be pleased with it, and that it may do you good.

Edmondo de Amicis

# CONTENTS

## OCTOBER

## NOVEMBER

## DECEMBER

## JANUARY

## FEBRUARY

## MARCH

## APRIL

## MAY

## JUNE

## JULY

# INTRODUCTION

*I read this book in Italy when I was seven years old and was ill. Since then I have never forgotten it - this was more than thirty years ago. When it was published in 1886, this book had a huge success in Italy and soon, after a few months, about forty editions were printed. It became a classic in the Italian literature for children. The story represents values that are still taught today, such as solidarity, honesty, goodness etc. It also represents a fragmented Italy, divided in social classes. In the book there are many events showing how the social differences characterized the learning, including the difficulties connected to it. For example, in the 1800s, the poorer boys studied in the morning and worked in the afternoon. The school year began in October in Italy at that time, and this is why the book begins in this month. The public schools were good ones and it was common to have children from superior classes studying in the public schools. Since the book was published just a few years after the Italian unification, a few segments in the book are nationalists and refer to the Italian unification. So this book carries a historic aspect. In a general way, this is an amusing book, including adventures and surprises, and a few imaginary events. I hope you enjoy it.*

*Maria Caterina Puddu, Italian Teacher*

*Bologna - Italy, 2010*

# OCTOBER

FIRST DAY OF SCHOOL

Monday, 17th.

TODAY is the first day of school. These three months of vacation in the country have passed like a dream. This morning my mother conducted me to the Baretti schoolhouse to have me enter for the third elementary course: I was thinking of the country and went unwillingly. All the streets were swarming with boys: the two book-shops were thronged with fathers and mothers who were purchasing bags, portfolios, and copy-books, and in front of the school so many people had collected, that the beadle and the policeman found it difficult to keep the entrance disencumbered. Near the door, I felt myself touched on the shoulder: it was my master of the second class, cheerful, as usual, and with his red hair ruffled, and he said to me:

"So we are separated forever, Enrico?"

I knew it perfectly well, yet these words pained me. We made our way in with difficulty. Ladies, gentlemen, women of the people, workmen, officials, nuns, servants, all leading boys with one hand, and holding the promotion books in the other, filled the anteroom and the stairs, making such a buzzing, that it seemed as though one were entering a theatre. I beheld again with pleasure that large room on the ground floor, with the doors leading to the seven classes, where I had passed nearly every day for three years. There was a throng; the teachers were going and coming. My schoolmistress of the first upper class greeted me from the door of the class-room, and said:

"Enrico, you are going to the floor above this year. I shall never see you pass by any more!" and she gazed sadly at me. The director was surrounded by women in distress because there was no room for their sons, and it struck me that his beard was a little whiter than it had been last year. I found the boys had grown taller and stouter. On the ground floor, where the divisions had already been made, there were little children of the first and lowest section, who did not want to enter the class-rooms, and who resisted like donkeys: it was necessary to drag them in by force, and some escaped from the benches; others, when they saw their parents depart, began to cry, and the parents had to go back and comfort and reprimand them, and the teachers were in despair.

My little brother was placed in the class of Mistress Delcati: I was put with Master Perboni, up stairs on the first floor. At ten o'clock we were all in our classes: fifty-four of us; only fifteen or sixteen of my companions of the second class, among them, Derossi, the one who always gets the first prize. The school seemed to me so small and gloomy when I thought of the woods and the mountains where I had passed the summer! I thought again, too, of my master in the second class, who was so good, and who always smiled at us, and was so small that he seemed to be one of us, and I grieved that I should no longer see him there, with his tumbled red hair. Our teacher is tall; he has no beard; his hair is gray and long; and he has a perpendicular wrinkle on his forehead: he has a big voice, and he looks at us fixedly, one after the other, as though he were reading our inmost thoughts; and he never smiles. I said to myself: "This is my first day. There are nine months more. What toil, what monthly examinations, what fatigue!" I really needed to see my mother when I came out, and I ran to kiss her hand. She said to me:

"Courage, Enrico! we will study together." And I returned home content. But I no longer have my master, with his kind, merry smile, and school does not seem pleasant to me as it did before.


OUR MASTER

Tuesday, 18th.

My new teacher pleases me also, since this morning. While we were coming in, and when he was already seated at his post, some one of his scholars of last year every now and then peeped in at the door to salute him; they would present themselves and greet him:

"Good morning, Signor Teacher!" "Good morning, Signor Perboni!" Some entered, touched his hand, and ran away. It was evident that they liked him, and would have liked to return to him. He responded, "Good morning," and shook the hands which were extended to him, but he looked at no one; at every greeting his smile remained serious, with that perpendicular wrinkle on his brow, with his face turned towards the window, and staring at the roof of the house opposite; and instead of being cheered by these greetings, he seemed to suffer from them. Then he surveyed us attentively, one after the other. While he was dictating, he descended and walked among the benches, and, catching sight of a boy whose face was all red with little pimples, he stopped dictating, took the lad's face between his hands and examined it; then he asked him what was the matter with him, and laid his hand on his forehead, to feel if it was hot. Meanwhile, a boy behind him got up on the bench, and began to play the marionette. The teacher turned round suddenly; the boy resumed his seat at one dash, and remained there, with head hanging, in expectation of being punished. The master placed one hand on his head and said to him:

"Don't do so again." Nothing more.

Then he returned to his table and finished the dictation. When he had finished dictating, he looked at us a moment in silence; then he said, very, very slowly, with his big but kind voice:

"Listen. We have a year to pass together; let us see that we pass it well. Study and be good. I have no family; you are my family. Last year I had still a mother: she is dead. I am left alone. I have no one but you in all the world; I have no other affection, no other thought than you: you must be my sons. I wish you well, and you must like me too. I do not wish to be obliged to punish any one. Show me that you are boys of heart: our school shall be a family, and you shall be my consolation and my pride. I do not ask you to give me a promise on your word of honor; I am sure that in your hearts you have already answered me 'yes,' and I thank you."

At that moment the beadle entered to announce the close of school. We all left our seats very, very quietly. The boy who had stood up on the bench approached the master, and said to him, in a trembling voice:

"Forgive me, Signor Master."

The master kissed him on the brow, and said, "Go, my son."

## AN ACCIDENT

Friday, 21st.

The year has begun with an accident. On my way to school this morning I was repeating to my father these words of our teacher, when we perceived that the street was full of people, who were pressing close to the door of the schoolhouse. Suddenly my father said: "An accident! The year is beginning badly!"

We entered with great difficulty. The big hall was crowded with parents and children, whom the teachers had not succeeded in drawing off into the class-rooms, and all were turning towards the director's room, and we heard the words, "Poor boy! Poor Robetti!"

Over their heads, at the end of the room, we could see the helmet of a policeman, and the bald head of the director; then a gentleman with a tall hat entered, and all said, "That is the doctor." My father inquired of a master, "What has happened?"--"A wheel has passed over his foot," replied the latter. "His foot has been crushed," said another. He was a boy belonging to the second class, who, on his way to school through the Via Dora Grossa, seeing a little child of the lowest class, who had run away from its mother, fall down in the middle of the street, a few paces from an omnibus which was bearing down upon it, had hastened boldly forward, caught up the child, and placed it in safety; but, as he had not withdrawn his own foot quickly enough, the wheel of the omnibus had passed over it. He is the son of a captain of artillery. While we were being told this, a woman entered the big hall, like a lunatic, and forced her way through the crowd: she was Robetti's mother, who had been sent for. Another woman hastened towards her, and flung her arms about her neck, with sobs: it was the mother of the baby who had been saved. Both flew into the room, and a desperate cry made itself heard: "Oh my Giulio! My child!"

At that moment a carriage stopped before the door, and a little later the director made his appearance, with the boy in his arms; the latter leaned his head on his shoulder, with pallid face and closed eyes. Every one stood very still; the sobs of the mother were audible. The director paused a moment, quite pale, and raised the boy up a little in his arms, in order to show him to the people. And then the masters, mistresses, parents, and boys all murmured together: "Bravo, Robetti! Bravo, poor child!" and they threw kisses to him; the mistresses and boys who were near him kissed his hands and his arms. He opened his eyes and said, "My portfolio!" The mother of the little boy whom he had saved showed it to him and said, amid her tears, "I will carry it for you, my dear little angel; I will carry it for you." And in the meantime, the mother of the wounded boy smiled, as she covered her face with her hands. They went out, placed the lad comfortably in the carriage, and the carriage drove away. Then we all entered school in silence.

## THE CALABRIAN BOY

Saturday, 22d.

Yesterday afternoon, while the master was telling us the news of poor Robetti, who will have to go on crutches, the director entered with a new pupil, a lad with a very brown face, black hair, large black eyes, and thick eyebrows which met on his forehead: he was dressed entirely in dark clothes, with a black morocco belt round his waist. The director went away, after speaking a few words in the master's ear, leaving beside the latter the boy, who glanced about with his big black eyes as though frightened. The master took him by the hand, and said to the class: "You ought to be glad. Today there enters our school a little Italian born in Reggio, in Calabria, more than five hundred miles from here. Love your brother who has come from so far away. He was born in a glorious land, which has given illustrious men to Italy, and which now furnishes her with stout laborers and brave soldiers; in one of the most beautiful lands of our country, where there are great forests, and great mountains, inhabited by people full of talent and courage. Treat him well, so that he shall not perceive that he is far away from the city in which he was born; make him see that an Italian boy, in whatever Italian school he sets his foot, will find brothers there." So saying, he rose and pointed out on the wall map of Italy the spot where lay Reggio, in Calabria. Then he called loudly:

"Ernesto Derossi!"--the boy who always has the first prize. Derossi rose.

"Come here," said the master. Derossi left his bench and stepped up to the little table, facing the Calabrian.

"As the head boy in the school," said the master to him, "bestow the embrace of welcome on this new companion, in the name of the whole class--the embrace of the sons of Piedmont to the son of Calabria."

Derossi embraced the Calabrian, saying in his clear voice, "Welcome!" and the other kissed him impetuously on the cheeks. All clapped their hands. "Silence!" cried the master; "don't clap your hands in school!" But it was evident that he was pleased. And the Calabrian was pleased also. The master assigned him a place, and accompanied him to the bench. Then he said again:

"Bear well in mind what I have said to you. In order that this case might occur, that a Calabrian boy should be as though in his own house at Turin, and that a boy from Turin should be at home in

Calabria, our country fought for fifty years, and thirty thousand Italians died. You must all respect and love each other; but any one of you who should give offence to this comrade, because he was not born in our province, would render himself unworthy of ever again raising his eyes from the earth when he passes the tricolored flag."

Hardly was the Calabrian seated in his place, when his neighbors presented him with pens and a *print*; and another boy, from the last bench, sent him a Swiss postage-stamp.

MY COMRADES

Tuesday, 25th.

The boy who sent the postage-stamp to the Calabrian is the one who pleases me best of all. His name is Garrone: he is the biggest boy in the class: he is about fourteen years old; his head is large, his shoulders broad; he is good, as one can see when he smiles; but it seems as though he always thought like a man. I already know many of my comrades. Another one pleases me, too, by the name of Coretti, and he wears chocolate-colored trousers and a catskin cap: he is always jolly; he is the son of a huckster of wood, who was a soldier in the war of 1866, in the squadron of Prince Umberto, and they say that he has three medals. There is little Nelli, a poor hunchback, a weak boy, with a thin face. There is one who is very well dressed, who always wears fine Florentine plush, and is named Votini. On the bench in front of me there is a boy who is called "the little mason" because his father is a mason: his face is as round as an apple, with a nose like a small ball; he possesses a special talent: he knows how to make *a hare's face*, and they all get him to make a hare's face, and then they laugh. He wears a little ragged cap, which he carries rolled up in his pocket like a handkerchief. Beside the little mason there sits Garoffi, a long, thin, silly fellow, with a nose and beak of a screech owl, and very small eyes, who is always trafficking in little pens and images and match-boxes, and who writes the lesson on his nails, in order that he may read it on the sly. Then there is a young gentleman, Carlo Nobis, who seems very haughty; and he is between two boys who are sympathetic to me,--the son of a blacksmith-ironmonger, clad in a jacket which reaches to his knees, who is pale, as though from illness, who always has a frightened air, and who never laughs; and one with red hair, who has a useless arm, and wears it suspended from his neck; his father has gone away to America, and his mother goes about peddling pot-herbs. And there is another curious type,--my neighbor on the left,--Stardi--small and thickset, with no neck,--a gruff fellow, who speaks to no one, and seems not to understand much, but stands attending to the master without winking, his brow corrugated with wrinkles, and his teeth clenched; and if he is questioned when the master is speaking, he makes no reply the first and second times, and the third time he gives a kick: and beside him there is a bold, cunning face, belonging to a boy named Franti, who has already been expelled from another district. There are, in addition, two brothers who are dressed exactly alike, who resemble each other to a hair, and both of whom wear caps of Calabrian cut, with a peasant's plume. But handsomer than all the rest, the one who has the most talent, who will surely be the head this year also, is Derossi; and the master, who has already perceived this, always questions him. But I like Precossi, the son of the blacksmith-ironmonger, the one with the long jacket, who seems sickly. They say that his father beats him; he is very timid, and every time that he addresses or touches any one, he says, "Excuse me," and gazes at them with his kind, sad eyes. But Garrone is the biggest and the nicest.

A GENEROUS DEED

Wednesday, 26th.

It was this very morning that Garrone let us know what he is like. When I entered the school a little late, because the mistress of the upper first had stopped me to inquire at what hour she could find me at home, the master had not yet arrived, and three or four boys were tormenting poor Crossi, the one with the red hair, who has a dead arm, and whose mother sells vegetables. They were poking him with rulers, hitting him in the face with chestnut shells, and were making him out to be a cripple and a monster, by mimicking him, with his arm hanging from his neck. And he, alone on the end of the bench, and quite pale, began to be affected by it, gazing now at one and now at another with beseeching eyes, that they might leave him in peace. But the others mocked him worse than ever, and he began to tremble and to turn crimson with rage. All at once, Franti, the boy with the repulsive face, sprang upon a bench, and pretending that he was carrying a basket on each arm, he aped the mother of Crossi, when she used to come to wait for her son at the door; for she is ill now. Many began to laugh loudly. Then Crossi lost his head, and seizing an inkstand, he hurled it at the other's head with all his strength; but Franti dodged, and the inkstand struck the master, who entered at the moment, full in the breast.

All flew to their places, and became silent with terror.

The master, quite pale, went to his table, and said in a constrained voice:

"Who did it?"

No one replied.

The master cried out once more, raising his voice still louder, "Who is it?"

Then Garrone, moved to pity for poor Crossi, rose abruptly and said, resolutely, "It was I."

The master looked at him, looked at the stupefied scholars; then said in a tranquil voice, "It was not you."

And, after a moment: "The culprit shall not be punished. Let him rise!"

Crossi rose and said, weeping, "They were striking me and insulting me, and I lost my head, and threw it."

"Sit down," said the master. "Let those who provoked him rise."

Four rose, and hung their heads.

"You," said the master, "have insulted a companion who had given you no provocation; you have scoffed at an unfortunate lad, you have struck a weak person who could not defend himself. You have committed one of the basest, the most shameful acts with which a human creature can stain himself. Cowards!"

Having said this, he came down among the benches, put his hand under Garrone's chin, as the latter stood with drooping head, and having made him raise it, he looked him straight in the eye, and said to him, "You are a noble soul."

Garrone profited by the occasion to murmur some words, I know not what, in the ear of the master; and he, turning towards the four culprits, said, abruptly, "I forgive you."

## MY SCHOOLMISTRESS OF THE UPPER FIRST

Thursday, 27th.

My schoolmistress has kept her promise which she made, and came today just as I was on the point of going out with my mother to carry some linen to a poor woman recommended by the *Gazette*. It was a year since I had seen her in our house. We all made a great deal of her. She is just the same as ever, a little thing, with a green veil wound about her bonnet, carelessly dressed, and with untidy hair, because she has not time to keep herself nice; but with a little less color than last year, with some white hairs, and a constant cough. My mother said to her:

"And your health, my dear mistress? You do not take sufficient care of yourself!"

"It does not matter," the other replied, with her smile, at once cheerful and melancholy.

"You speak too loud," my mother added; "you exert yourself too much with your boys."

That is true; her voice is always to be heard; I remember how it was when I went to school to her; she talked and talked all the time, so that the boys might not divert their attention, and she did not remain seated a moment. I felt quite sure that she would come, because she never forgets her pupils; she remembers their names for years; on the days of the monthly examination, she runs to ask the director what marks they have won; she waits for them at the entrance, and makes them show her their compositions, in order that she may see what progress they have made; and many still come from the gymnasium to see her, who already wear long trousers and a watch. Today she had come back in a great state of excitement, from the picture-gallery, whither she had taken her boys, just as she had conducted them all to a museum every Thursday in years gone by, and explained everything to them. The poor mistress has grown still thinner than of old. But she is always brisk, and always becomes animated when she speaks of her school. She wanted to have a peep at the bed on which she had seen me lying very ill two years ago, and which is now occupied by my brother; she gazed at it for a while, and could not speak. She was obliged to go away soon to visit a boy belonging to her class, the son of a saddler, who is ill with the measles; and she had besides a package of sheets to correct, a whole evening's work, and she has still a private lesson in arithmetic to give to the mistress of a shop before nightfall.

"Well, Enrico," she said to me as she was going, "are you still fond of your schoolmistress, now that you solve difficult problems and write long compositions?" She kissed me, and called up once more from the foot of the stairs: "You are not to forget me, you know, Enrico!" Oh, my kind teacher, never, never will I forget thee! Even when I grow up I will remember thee and will go to seek thee among thy boys; and every time that I pass near a school and hear the voice of a schoolmistress, I shall think that I hear thy voice, and I shall recall the two years that I passed in thy school, where I learned so many things, where I so often saw thee ill and weary, but always earnest, always indulgent, in despair when any one acquired a bad trick in the writing-fingers, trembling when the examiners interrogated us, happy when we made a good appearance, always kind and loving as a mother. Never, never shall I forget thee, my teacher!


IN AN ATTIC

Friday, 28th.

Yesterday afternoon I went with my mother and my sister Sylvia, to carry the linen to the poor woman recommended by the newspaper: I carried the bundle; Sylvia had the paper with the initials of the name and the address. We climbed to the very roof of a tall house, to a long corridor with many doors. My mother knocked at the last; it was opened by a woman who was still young, blond and thin, and it instantly struck me that I had seen her many times before, with that very same blue kerchief that she wore on her head.

"Are you the person of whom the newspaper says so and so?" asked my mother.

"Yes, signora, I am."

"Well, we have brought you a little linen." Then the woman began to thank us and bless us, and could not make enough of it. Meanwhile I espied in one corner of the bare, dark room, a boy kneeling in front of a chair, with his back turned towards us, who appeared to be writing; and he really was writing, with his paper on the chair and his inkstand on the floor. How did he manage to write thus in the dark? While I was saying this to myself, I suddenly recognized the red hair and the coarse jacket of Crossi, the son of the vegetable-pedler, the boy with the useless arm. I told my mother softly, while the woman was putting away the things.

"Hush!" replied my mother; "perhaps he will feel ashamed to see you giving alms to his mother: don't speak to him."

But at that moment Crossi turned round; I was embarrassed; he smiled, and then my mother gave me a push, so that I should run to him and embrace him. I did embrace him: he rose and took me by the hand.

"Here I am," his mother was saying in the meantime to my mother, "alone with this boy, my husband in America these seven years, and I sick in addition, so that I can no longer make my rounds with my vegetables, and earn a few cents. We have not even a table left for my poor Luigino to do his work on. When there was a bench down at the door, he could, at least, write on the bench; but that has been taken away. He has not even a little light so that he can study without ruining his eyes. And it is a mercy that I can send him to school, since the city provides him with books and copy-books. Poor Luigino, who would be so glad to study! Unhappy woman, that I am!"

My mother gave her all that she had in her purse, kissed the boy, and almost wept as we went out. And she had good cause to say to me: "Look at that poor boy; see how he is forced to work, when you have every comfort, and yet study seems hard to you! Ah! Enrico, there is more merit in the work which he does in one day, than in your work for a year. It is to such that the first prizes should be given!"


THE SCHOOL

Friday, 28th.

Yes, study comes hard to you, my dear Enrico, as your mother says: I do not yet see you set out for school with that resolute mind and that smiling face which I should like. You are still intractable. But listen; reflect a little! What a miserable, despicable thing your day would be if you did not go to school! At the end of a week you would beg with clasped hands that you might return there, for you would be eaten up with weariness and shame; disgusted with your sports and with your existence. Everybody, everybody studies now, my child. Think of the workmen who go to school in the evening after having toiled all the day; think of the women, of the girls of the people, who go to school on Sunday, after having worked all the week; of the soldiers who turn to their books and copy-books when they return exhausted from their drill! Think of the dumb and of the boys who are blind, but who study, nevertheless; and last of all, think of the prisoners, who also learn to read and write. Reflect in the morning, when you set out, that at that very moment, in your own city, thirty thousand other boys are going like yourself, to shut themselves up in a room for three hours and study. Think of the innumerable boys who, at nearly this precise hour, are going to school in all countries. Behold them with your imagination, going, going, through the lanes of quiet villages; through the streets of the noisy towns, along the shores of rivers and lakes; here beneath a burning sun; there amid fogs, in boats, in countries which are intersected with canals; on horseback on the far-reaching plains; in sledges over the snow; through valleys and over hills; across forests and torrents, over the solitary paths of mountains; alone, in couples, in groups, in long files, all with their books under their arms, clad in a thousand ways, speaking a thousand tongues, from the most remote schools in Russia. Almost lost in the ice to the furthermost schools of Arabia, shaded by palm-trees, millions and millions, all going to learn the same things, in a hundred varied forms. Imagine this vast, vast throng of boys of a hundred races, this immense movement of which you form a part, and think, if this movement were to cease, humanity would fall back into barbarism; this movement is the progress, the hope, the glory of the world. Courage, then, little soldier of the immense army. Your books are your arms, your class is your squadron, the field of battle is the whole earth, and the victory is human civilization. Be not a cowardly soldier, my Enrico.

THY FATHER

## THE LITTLE PATRIOT OF PADUA

(*The Monthly Story.*)

Saturday, 29th.

I will not be a *cowardly soldier*, no; but I should be much more willing to go to school if the master would tell us a story every day, like the one he told us this morning. "Every month," said he, "I shall tell you one; I shall give it to you in writing, and it will always be the tale of a fine and noble deed performed by a boy. This one is called *The Little Patriot of Padua*. Here it is. A French steamer set out from Barcelona, a city in Spain, for Genoa; there were on board Frenchmen, Italians, Spaniards, and Swiss. Among the rest was a lad of eleven, poorly clad, and alone, who always held himself aloof, like a wild animal, and stared at all with gloomy eyes. He had good reasons for looking at every one with forbidding eyes. Two years previous to this time his parents, peasants in the neighborhood of Padua, had sold him to a company of mountebanks, who, after they had taught him how to perform tricks, by dint of blows and kicks and starving, had carried him all over France and Spain, beating him continually and never giving him enough to eat. On his arrival in Barcelona, being no longer able to endure ill treatment and hunger, and being reduced to a pitiable condition, he had fled from his slave-master and had betaken himself for protection to the Italian consul, who, moved with compassion, had placed him on board of this steamer, and had given him a letter to the treasurer of Genoa, who was to send the boy back to his parents--to the parents who had sold him like a beast. The poor lad was lacerated and weak. He had been assigned to the second-class cabin. Every one stared at him; some questioned him, but he made no reply, and seemed to hate and despise every one, to such an extent had privation and affliction saddened and irritated him. Nevertheless, three travellers, by dint of persisting in their questions, succeeded in making him unloose his tongue; and in a few rough words, a mixture of Venetian, French, and Spanish, he related his story. These three travellers were not Italians, but they understood him; and partly out of compassion, partly because they were excited with wine, they gave him soldi, jesting with him and urging him on to tell them other things; and as several ladies entered the saloon at the moment, they gave him some more money for the purpose of making a show, and cried: 'Take this! Take this, too!' as they made the money rattle on the table.

"The boy pocketed it all, thanking them in a low voice, with his surly mien, but with a look that was for the first time smiling and affectionate. Then he climbed into his berth, drew the curtain, and lay quiet, thinking over his affairs. With this money he would be able to purchase some good food on board, after having suffered for lack of bread for two years; he could buy a jacket as soon as he landed in Genoa, after having gone about clad in rags for two years; and he could also, by carrying it home, insure for himself from his father and mother a more humane reception than would have fallen to his lot if he had arrived with empty pockets. This money was a little fortune for him; and he was taking comfort out of this thought behind the curtain of his berth, while the three travellers chatted away, as they sat round the dining-table in the second-class saloon. They were drinking and discussing their travels and the countries which they had seen; and from one topic to another they began to discuss Italy. One of them began to complain of the inns, another of the railways, and then, growing warmer, they all began to speak evil of everything. One would have preferred a trip in Lapland; another declared that he had found nothing but swindlers and brigands in Italy; the third said that Italian officials do not know how to read.

"'It's an ignorant nation,' repeated the first. 'A filthy nation,' added the second. 'Ro--' exclaimed the third, meaning to say 'robbers'; but he was not allowed to finish the word: a tempest of soldi and half-lire descended upon their heads and shoulders, and leaped upon the table and the floor with a demoniacal noise. All three sprang up in a rage, looked up, and received another handful of coppers in their faces.

"'Take back your soldi!' said the lad, disdainfully, thrusting his head between the curtains of his berth; 'I do not accept alms from those who insult my country.'"

## THE CHIMNEY-SWEEP

November 1st.

Yesterday afternoon I went to the girls' school building, near ours, to give the story of the boy from Padua to Silvia's teacher, who wished to read it. There are seven hundred girls there. Just as I arrived, they began to come out, all greatly rejoiced at the holiday of All Saints and All Souls; and here is a beautiful thing that I saw: Opposite the door of the school, on the other side of the street, stood a very small chimney-sweep, his face entirely black, with his sack and scraper, with one arm resting against the wall, and his head supported on his arm, weeping copiously and sobbing. Two or three of the girls of the second grade approached him and said, "What is the matter, that you weep like this?" But he made no reply, and went on crying.

"Come, tell us what is the matter with you and why you are crying," the girls repeated. And then he raised his face from his arm,--a baby face,--and said through his tears that he had been to several houses to sweep the chimneys, and had earned thirty soldi, and that he had lost them, that they had slipped through a hole in his pocket,--and he showed the hole,--and he did not dare to return home without the money.

"The master will beat me," he said, sobbing; and again dropped his head upon his arm, like one in despair. The children stood and stared at him very seriously. In the meantime, other girls, large and small, poor girls and girls of the upper classes, with their portfolios under their arms, had come up; and one large girl, who had a blue feather in her hat, pulled two soldi from her pocket, and said:

"I have only two soldi; let us make a collection."

"I have two soldi, also," said another girl, dressed in red; "we shall certainly find thirty soldi among the whole of us"; and then they began to call out:

"Amalia! Luigia! Annina!--A soldo. Who has any soldi? Bring your soldi here!"

Several had soldi to buy flowers or copy-books, and they brought them; some of the smaller girls gave centesimi; the one with the blue feather collected all, and counted them in a loud voice:

"Eight, ten, fifteen!" But more was needed. Then one larger than any of them, who seemed to be an assistant mistress, made her appearance, and gave half a lira; and all made much of her. Five soldi were still lacking.

"The girls of the fourth class are coming; they will have it," said one girl. The members of the fourth class came, and the soldi showered down. All hurried forward eagerly; and it was beautiful to see that poor chimney-sweep in the midst of all those many-colored dresses, of all that whirl of feathers, ribbons, and curls. The thirty soldi were already obtained, and more kept pouring in; and the very smallest who had no money made their way among the big girls, and offered their bunches of flowers, for the sake of giving something. All at once the portress made her appearance, screaming:

"The Signora Directress!" The girls made their escape in all directions, like a flock of sparrows; and then the little chimney-sweep was visible, alone, in the middle of the street, wiping his eyes in perfect content, with his hands full of money, and the button-holes of his jacket, his pockets, his hat, were full of flowers; and there were even flowers on the ground at his feet.


THE DAY OF THE DEAD

(*All-Souls-Day.*)

November 2d.

This day is consecrated to the commemoration of the dead. Do you know, Enrico, that all you boys should, on this day, devote a thought to those who are dead? To those who have died for you,--for boys and little children. How many have died, and how many are dying continually! Have you ever reflected how many fathers have worn out their lives in toil? how many mothers have descended to the grave before their time, exhausted by the privations to which they have condemned themselves for the sake of sustaining their children? Do you know how many men have planted a knife in their hearts in despair at beholding their children in misery? how many women have drowned themselves or have died of sorrow, or have gone mad, through having lost a child? Think of all these dead on this day, Enrico. Think of how many schoolmistresses have died young, have pined away through the fatigues of the school, through love of the children, from whom they had not the heart to tear themselves away; think of the doctors who have perished of contagious diseases, having courageously sacrificed themselves to cure the children; think of all those who in shipwrecks, in conflagrations, in famines, in moments of supreme danger, have yielded to infancy the last morsel of bread, the last place of safety, the last rope of escape from the flames, to expire content with their sacrifice, since they preserved the life of a little innocent. Such dead as these are innumerable, Enrico; every graveyard contains hundreds of these sainted beings, who, if they could rise for a moment from their graves, would cry the name of a child to whom they sacrificed the pleasures of youth, the peace of old age, their affections, their intelligence, their life: wives of twenty, men in the flower of their strength, octogenarians, youths,--heroic and obscure martyrs of infancy,--so grand and so noble, that the earth does not produce as many flowers as should strew their graves. To such a degree are ye loved, O children! Think today on those dead with gratitude, and you will be kinder and more affectionate to all those who love you, and who toil for you, my dear, fortunate son, who, on the day of the dead, have, as yet, no one to grieve for.

THY MOTHER.

# NOVEMBER

## MY FRIEND GARRONE

Friday, 4th.

THERE had been but two days of vacation, yet it seemed to me as though I had been a long time without seeing Garrone. The more I know him, the better I like him; and so it is with all the rest, except with the overbearing, who have nothing to say to him, because he does not permit them to exhibit their oppression. Every time that a big boy raises his hand against a little one, the little one shouts, "Garrone!" and the big one stops striking him. His father is an engine-driver on the railway; he has begun school late, because he was ill for two years. He is the tallest and the strongest of the class; he lifts a bench with one hand; he is always eating; and he is good. Whatever he is asked for,--a pencil, rubber, paper, or penknife,--he lends or gives it; and he neither talks nor laughs in school: he always sits perfectly motionless on a bench that is too narrow for him, with his spine curved forward, and his big head between his shoulders; and when I look at him, he smiles at me with his eyes half closed, as much as to say, "Well, Enrico, are we friends?" He makes me laugh, because, tall and broad as he is, he has a jacket, trousers, and sleeves which are too small for him, and too short; a cap which will not stay on his head; a threadbare cloak; coarse shoes; and a necktie which is always twisted into a cord. Dear Garrone! it needs but one glance in thy face to inspire love for thee. All the little boys would like to be near his bench. He knows arithmetic well. He carries his books bound together with a strap of red leather. He has a knife, with a mother-of-pearl handle, which he found in the field for military manoeuvres, last year, and one day he cut his finger to the bone; but no one in school envies him it, and no one breathes a word about it at home, for fear of alarming his parents. He lets us say anything to him in jest, and he never takes it ill; but woe to any one who says to him, "That is not true," when he affirms a thing: then fire flashes from his eyes, and he hammers down blows enough to split the bench. Saturday morning he gave a soldo to one of the upper first class, who was crying in the middle of the street, because his own had been taken from him, and he could not buy his copy-book. For the last three days he has been working over a letter of eight pages, with pen ornaments on the margins, for the saint's day of his mother, who often comes to get him, and who, like himself, is tall and large and sympathetic. The master is always glancing at him, and every time that he passes near him he taps him on the neck with his hand, as though he were a good, peaceable young bull. I am very fond of him. I am happy when I press his big hand, which seems to be the hand of a man, in mine. I am almost certain that he would risk his life to save that of a comrade; that he would allow himself to be killed in his defence, so clearly can I read his eyes; and although he always seems to be grumbling with that big voice of his, one feels that it is a voice that comes from a gentle heart.

THE CHARCOAL-MAN AND THE GENTLEMAN

Monday, 7th.

Garrone would certainly never have uttered the words which Carlo Nobis spoke yesterday morning to Betti. Carlo Nobis is proud, because his father is a great gentleman; a tall gentleman, with a black beard, and very serious, who accompanies his son to school nearly every day. Yesterday morning Nobis quarrelled with Betti, one of the smallest boys, and the son of a charcoal-man, and not knowing what retort to make, because he was in the wrong, said to him vehemently, "Your father is a tattered beggar!" Betti reddened up to his very hair, and said nothing, but the tears came to his eyes; and when he returned home, he repeated the words to his father; so the charcoal-dealer, a little man, who was black all over, made his appearance at the afternoon session, leading his boy by the hand, in order to complain to the master. While he was making his complaint, and every one was silent, the father of Nobis, who was taking off his son's coat at the entrance, as usual, entered on hearing his name pronounced, and demanded an explanation.

"This workman has come," said the master, "to complain that your son Carlo said to his boy, 'Your father is a tattered beggar.'"

Nobis's father frowned and reddened slightly. Then he asked his son, "Did you say that?"

His son, who was standing in the middle of the school, with his head hanging, in front of little Betti, made no reply.

Then his father grasped him by one arm and pushed him forward, facing Betti, so that they nearly touched, and said to him, "Beg his pardon."

The charcoal-man tried to interpose, saying, "No, no!" but the gentleman paid no heed to him, and repeated to his son, "Beg his pardon. Repeat my words. 'I beg your pardon for the insulting, foolish, and ignoble words which I uttered against your father, whose hand my father would feel himself honored to press.'"

The charcoal-man made a resolute gesture, as though to say, "I will not allow it." The gentleman did not second him, and his son said slowly, in a very thread of a voice, without raising his eyes from the ground, "I beg your pardon--for the insulting--foolish--ignoble--words which I uttered against your father, whose hand my father--would feel himself honored--to press."

Then the gentleman offered his hand to the charcoal-man, who shook it vigorously, and then, with a sudden push, he thrust his son into the arms of Carlo Nobis.

"Do me the favor to place them next each other," said the gentleman to the master. The master put Betti on Nobis's bench. When they were seated, the father of Nobis bowed and went away.

The charcoal-man remained standing there in thought for several moments, gazing at the two boys side by side; then he approached the bench, and fixed upon Nobis a look expressive of affection and regret, as though he were desirous of saying something to him, but he did not say anything; he stretched out his hand to bestow a caress upon him, but he did not dare, and merely stroked his brow with his large fingers. Then he made his way to the door, and turning round for one last look, he disappeared.

"Fix what you have just seen firmly in your minds, boys," said the master; "this is the finest lesson of the year."

## MY BROTHER'S SCHOOLMISTRESS

Thursday, 10th.

The son of the charcoal-man had been a pupil of that schoolmistress Delcati who had come to see my brother when he was ill, and who had made us laugh by telling us how, two years ago, the mother of this boy had brought to her house a big apronful of charcoal, out of gratitude for her having given the medal to her son; and the poor woman had persisted, and had not been willing to carry the coal home again, and had wept when she was obliged to go away with her apron quite full. And she told us, also, of another good woman, who had brought her a very heavy bunch of flowers, inside of which there was a little hoard of soldi. We had been greatly diverted in listening to her, and so my brother had swallowed his medicine, which he had not been willing to do before. How much patience is necessary with those boys of the lower first, all toothless, like old men, who cannot pronounce their r's and s's; and one coughs, and another has the nosebleed, and another loses his shoes under the bench, and another bellows because he has pricked himself with his pen, and another one cries because he has bought copy-book No. 2 instead of No. 1. Fifty in a class, who know nothing, with those flabby little hands, and all of them must be taught to write; they carry in their pockets bits of licorice, buttons, phial corks, pounded brick,--all sorts of little things, and the teacher has to search them; but they conceal these objects even in their shoes. And they are not attentive: a fly enters through the window, and throws them all into confusion; and in summer they bring grass into school, and horn-bugs, which fly round in circles or fall into the inkstand, and then streak the copy-books all over with ink. The schoolmistress has to play mother to all of them, to help them dress themselves, bandage up their pricked fingers, pick up their caps when they drop them, watch to see that they do not exchange coats, and that they do not indulge in cat-calls and shrieks. Poor schoolmistresses! And then the mothers come to complain: "How comes it, signorina, that my boy has lost his pen? How does it happen that mine learns nothing? Why is not my boy mentioned honorably, when he knows so much? Why don't you have that nail which tore my Piero's trousers, taken out of the bench?"

Sometimes my brother's teacher gets into a rage with the boys; and when she can resist no longer, she bites her finger, to keep herself from dealing a blow; she loses patience, and then she repents, and caresses the child whom she has scolded; she sends a little rogue out of school, and then swallows her tears, and flies into a rage with parents who make the little ones fast by way of punishment. Schoolmistress Delcati is young and tall, well-dressed, brown of complexion, and restless; she does everything vivaciously, as though on springs, is affected by a mere trifle, and at such times speaks with great tenderness.

"But the children become attached to you, surely," my mother said to her.

"Many do," she replied; "but at the end of the year the majority of them pay no further heed to us. When they are with the masters, they are almost ashamed of having been with us--with a woman teacher. After two years of cares, after having loved a child so much, it makes us feel sad to part from him; but we say to ourselves, 'Oh, I am sure of that one; he is fond of me.' But the vacation over, he comes back to school. I run to meet him; 'Oh, my child, my child!' And he turns his head away." Here the teacher interrupted herself. "But you will not do so, little one?" she said, raising her humid eyes, and kissing my brother. "You will not turn aside your head, will you? You will not deny your poor friend?"

## MY MOTHER

Thursday, November 10th.

In the presence of your brother's teacher you failed in respect to your mother! Let this never happen again, my Enrico, never again! Your irreverent word pierced my heart like a point of steel. I thought of your mother when, years ago, she bent the whole of one night over your little bed, measuring your breathing, weeping blood in her anguish, and with her teeth chattering with terror, because she thought that she had lost you, and I feared that she would lose her reason; and at this thought I felt a sentiment of horror at you. You, to offend your mother! your mother, who would give a year of happiness to spare you one hour of pain, who would beg for you, who would allow herself to be killed to save your life! Listen, Enrico. Fix this thought well in your mind. Reflect that you are destined to experience many terrible days in the course of your life: the most terrible will be that on which you lose your mother. A thousand times, Enrico, after you are a man, strong, and inured to all fates, you will invoke her, oppressed with an intense desire to hear her voice, if but for a moment, and to see once more her open arms, into which you can throw yourself sobbing, like a poor child bereft of comfort and protection. How you will then recall every bitterness that you have caused her, and with what remorse you will pay for all, unhappy wretch! Hope for no peace in your life, if you have caused your mother grief. You will repent, you will beg her forgiveness, you will venerate her memory--in vain; conscience will give you no rest; that sweet and gentle image will always wear for you an expression of sadness and of reproach which will put your soul to torture. Oh, Enrico, beware; this is the most sacred of human affections; unhappy he who tramples it under foot. The assassin who respects his mother has still something honest and noble in his heart; the most glorious of men who grieves and offends her is but a vile creature. Never again let a harsh word issue from your lips, for the being who gave you life. And if one should ever escape you, let it not be the fear of your father, but let it be the impulse of your soul, which casts you at her feet, to beseech her that she will cancel from your brow, with the kiss of forgiveness, the stain of ingratitude. I love you, my son; you are the dearest hope of my life; but I would rather see you dead than ungrateful to your mother. Go away, for a little space; offer me no more of your caresses; I should not be able to return them from my heart.

THY FATHER.

## MY COMPANION CORETTI

Sunday, 13th.

My father forgave me; but I remained rather sad and then my mother sent me, with the porter's big son, to take a walk on the Corso. Half-way down the Corso, as we were passing a cart which was standing in front of a shop, I heard some one call me by name: I turned round; it was Coretti, my schoolmate, with chocolate-colored clothes and his catskin cap, all in a perspiration, but merry, with a big load of wood on his shoulders. A man who was standing in the cart was handing him an armful of wood at a time, which he took and carried into his father's shop, where he piled it up in the greatest haste.

"What are you doing, Coretti?" I asked him.

"Don't you see?" he answered, reaching out his arms to receive the load; "I am reviewing my lesson."

I laughed; but he seemed to be serious, and, having grasped the armful of wood, he began to repeat as he ran, "*The conjugation of the verb--consists in its variations according to number--according to number and person--*"

And then, throwing down the wood and piling it, "*according to the time--according to the time to which the action refers.*"

And turning to the cart for another armful, "*according to the mode in which the action is enunciated.*"

It was our grammar lesson for the following day. "What would you have me do?" he said. "I am putting my time to use. My father has gone off with the man on business; my mother is ill. It falls to me to do the unloading. In the meantime, I am going over my grammar lesson. It is a difficult lesson today; I cannot succeed in getting it into my head.--My father said that he would be here at seven o'clock to give you your money," he said to the man with the cart.

The cart drove off. "Come into the shop a minute," Coretti said to me. I went in. It was a large apartment, full of piles of wood and fagots, with a steelyard on one side.

"This is a busy day, I can assure you," resumed Coretti; "I have to do my work by fits and starts. I was writing my phrases, when some customers came in. I went to writing again, and behold, that cart arrived. I have already made two trips to the wood market in the Piazza Venezia this morning. My legs are so tired that I cannot stand, and my hands are all swollen. I should be in a pretty pickle if I had to draw!" And as he spoke he set about sweeping up the dry leaves and the straw which covered the brick-paved floor.

"But where do you do your work, Coretti?" I inquired.

"Not here, certainly," he replied. "Come and see"; and he led me into a little room behind the shop, which serves as a kitchen and dining-room, with a table in one corner, on which there were books and copy-books, and work which had been begun. "Here it is," he said; "I left the second answer unfinished: *with which shoes are made, and belts.* Now I will add, *and valises.*" And, taking his pen, he began to write in his fine hand.

"Is there any one here?" sounded a call from the shop at that moment. It was a woman who had come to buy some little fagots.

"Here I am!" replied Coretti; and he sprang out, weighed the fagots, took the money, ran to a corner to enter the sale in a shabby old account-book, and returned to his work, saying, "Let's see if I can finish that sentence." And he wrote, *travelling-bags, and knapsacks for soldiers.* "Oh, my poor coffee is boiling over!" he exclaimed, and ran to the stove to take the coffee-pot from the fire. "It is coffee for mamma," he said; "I had to learn how to make it. Wait a while, and we will carry it to her; you'll see what pleasure it will give her. She has been in bed a whole week.--Conjugation of the verb! I always scald my fingers with this coffee-pot. What is there that I can add after the soldiers' knapsacks? Something more is needed, and I can think of nothing. Come to mamma."

He opened a door, and we entered another small room: there Coretti's mother lay in a big bed, with a white kerchief wound round her head.

"Ah, brave little master!" said the woman to me; "you have come to visit the sick, have you not?"

Meanwhile, Coretti was arranging the pillows behind his mother's back, readjusting the bedclothes, brightening up the fire, and driving the cat off the chest of drawers.

"Do you want anything else, mamma?" he asked, as he took the cup from her. "Have you taken the two spoonfuls of syrup? When it is all gone, I will make a trip to the apothecary's. The wood is unloaded. At four o'clock I will put the meat on the stove, as you told me; and when the butter-woman passes, I will give her those eight soldi. Everything will go on well; so don't give it a thought."

"Thanks, my son!" replied the woman. "Go, my poor boy!--he thinks of everything."

She insisted that I should take a lump of sugar; and then Coretti showed me a little picture,--the photograph portrait of his father dressed as a soldier, with the medal for bravery which he had won in 1866, in the troop of Prince Umberto: he had the same face as his son, with the same vivacious eyes and his merry smile.

We went back to the kitchen. "I have found the thing," said Coretti; and he added on his copy-book, *horse-trappings are also made of it.* "The rest I will do this evening; I shall sit up later. How happy you are, to have time to study and to go to walk, too!" And still gay and active, he re-entered the shop, and began to place pieces of wood on the horse and to saw them, saying: "This is gymnastics; it is quite different from the *throw your arms forwards.* I want my father to find all this wood sawed when he gets home; how glad he will be! The worst part of it is that after sawing I make T's and L's which look like snakes, so the teacher says. What am I to do? I will tell him that I have to move my arms about. The important thing is to have mamma get well quickly. She is better today, thank Heaven! I will study my grammar tomorrow morning at cock-crow. Oh, here's the cart with logs! To work!"

A small cart laden with logs halted in front of the shop. Coretti ran out to speak to the man, then returned: "I cannot keep your company any longer now," he said; "farewell until tomorrow. You did right to come and hunt me up. A pleasant walk to you! happy fellow!"

And pressing my hand, he ran to take the first log, and began once more to trot back and forth between the cart and the shop, with a face as fresh as a rose beneath his catskin cap, and so alert that it was a pleasure to see him.

"Happy fellow!" he had said to me. Ah, no, Coretti, no; you are the happier, because you study and work too; because you are of use to your father and your mother; because you are better--a hundred times better--and more courageous than I, my dear schoolmate.

THE HEAD-MASTER

Friday, 18th.

Coretti was pleased this morning, because his master of the second class, Coatti, a big man, with a huge head of curly hair, a great black beard, big dark eyes, and a voice like a cannon, had come to assist in the work of the monthly examination. He is always threatening the boys that he will break them in pieces and carry them by the nape of the neck to the quæstor, and he makes all sorts of frightful faces; but he never punishes any one, but always smiles the while behind his beard, so that no one can see it. There are eight masters in all, including Coatti, and a little, beardless assistant, who looks like a boy. There is one master of the fourth class, who is lame and always wrapped up in a big woollen scarf, and who is always suffering from pains which he contracted when he was a teacher in the country, in a damp school, where the walls were dripping with moisture. Another of the teachers of the fourth is old and perfectly white-haired, and has been a teacher of the blind. There is one well-dressed master, with eye-glasses, and a blond mustache, who is called the *little lawyer*, because, while he was teaching, he studied law and took his diploma; and he is also making a book to teach how to write letters. On the other hand, the one who teaches gymnastics is of a soldierly type, and was with Garibaldi, and has on his neck a scar from a sabre wound received at the battle of Milazzo. Then there is the head-master, who is tall and bald, and wears gold spectacles, with a gray beard that flows down upon his breast; he dresses entirely in black, and is always buttoned up to the chin. He is so kind to the boys, that when they enter the director's room, all in a tremble, because they have been summoned to receive a reproof, he does not scold them, but takes them by the hand, and tells them so many reasons why they ought not to behave so, and why they should be sorry, and promise to be good, and he speaks in such a kind manner, and in so gentle a voice, that they all come out with red eyes, more confused than if they had been punished. Poor head-master! he is always the first at his post in the morning, waiting for the scholars and lending an ear to the parents; and when the other masters are already on their way home, he is still hovering about the school, and looking out that the boys do not get under the carriage-wheels, or hang about the streets to stand on their heads, or fill their bags with sand or stones; and the moment he makes his appearance at a corner, so tall and black, flocks of boys scamper off in all directions, abandoning their games of coppers and marbles, and he threatens them from afar with his forefinger, with his sad and loving air. No one has ever seen him smile, my mother says, since the death of his son, who was a volunteer in the army: he always keeps the latter's portrait before his eyes, on a little table in the head-master's room. He wanted to go away after this misfortune; he prepared his application for retirement to the Municipal Council, and kept it always on his table, putting off sending it from day to day, because it grieved him to leave the boys. But the other day he seemed undecided; and my father, who was in the director's room with him, was just saying to him, "What a shame it is that you are going away, Signor Director!" when a man entered for the purpose of inscribing the name of a boy who was to be transferred from another schoolhouse to ours, because he had changed his residence. At the sight of this boy, the head-master made a gesture of astonishment, gazed at him for a while, gazed at the portrait that he keeps on his little table, and then stared at the boy again, as he drew him between his knees, and made him hold up his head. This boy resembled his dead son. The head-master said, "It is all right," wrote down his name, dismissed the father and son, and remained absorbed in thought. "What a pity that you are going away!" repeated my father. And then the head-master took up his application for retirement, tore it in two, and said, "I shall remain."

## THE SOLDIERS

Tuesday, 22d.

His son had been a volunteer in the army when he died: this is the reason why the head-master always goes to the Corso to see the soldiers pass, when we come out of school. Yesterday a regiment of infantry was passing, and fifty boys began to dance around the band, singing and beating time with their rulers on their bags and portfolios. We were standing in a group on the sidewalk, watching them: Garrone, squeezed into his clothes, which were too tight for him, was biting at a large piece of bread; Votini, the well-dressed boy, who always wears Florence plush; Precossi, the son of the blacksmith, with his father's jacket; and the Calabrian; and the "little mason"; and Crossi, with his red head; and Franti, with his bold face; and Robetti, too, the son of the artillery captain, the boy who saved the child from the omnibus, and who now walks on crutches. Franti burst into a derisive laugh, in the face of a soldier who was limping. But all at once he felt a man's hand on his shoulder: he turned round; it was the head-master. "Take care," said the master to him; "jeering at a soldier when he is in the ranks, when he can neither avenge himself nor reply, is like insulting a man who is bound: it is baseness."

Franti disappeared. The soldiers were marching by fours, all perspiring and covered with dust, and their guns were gleaming in the sun. The head-master said:

"You ought to feel kindly towards soldiers, boys. They are our defenders, who would go to be killed for our sakes, if a foreign army were to menace our country tomorrow. They are boys too; they are not many years older than you; and they, too, go to school; and there are poor men and gentlemen among them, just as there are among you, and they come from every part of Italy. See if you cannot recognize them by their faces; Sicilians are passing, and Sardinians, and Neapolitans, and Lombards. This is an old regiment, one of those which fought in 1848. They are not the same soldiers, but the flag is still the same. How many have already died for our country around that banner twenty years before you were born!"

"Here it is!" said Garrone. And in fact, not far off, the flag was visible, advancing, above the heads of the soldiers.

"Do one thing, my sons," said the head-master; "make your scholar's salute, with your hand to your brow, when the tricolor passes."

The flag, borne by an officer, passed before us, all tattered and faded, and with the medals attached to the staff. We put our hands to our foreheads, all together. The officer looked at us with a smile, and returned our salute with his hand.

"Bravi, boys!" said some one behind us. We turned to look; it was an old man who wore in his button-hole the blue ribbon of the Crimean campaign--a pensioned officer. "Bravi!" he said; "you have done a fine deed."

In the meantime, the band of the regiment had made a turn at the end of the Corso, surrounded by a throng of boys, and a hundred merry shouts accompanied the blasts of the trumpets, like a war-song.

"Bravi!" repeated the old officer, as he gazed upon us; "he who respects the flag when he is little will know how to defend it when he is grown up."


## NELLI'S PROTECTOR

Wednesday, 23d.

Nelli, too, poor little hunchback! was looking at the soldiers yesterday, but with an air as though he were thinking, "I can never be a soldier!" He is good, and he studies; but he is so puny and wan, and he breathes with difficulty. He always wears a long apron of shining black cloth. His mother is a little blond woman who dresses in black, and always comes to get him at the end of school, so that he may not come out in the confusion with the others, and she caresses him. At first many of the boys ridiculed him, and thumped him on the back with their bags, because he is so unfortunate as to be a hunchback; but he never offered any resistance, and never said anything to his mother, in order not to give her the pain of knowing that her son was the laughing-stock of his companions: they derided him, and he held his peace and wept, with his head laid against the bench.

But one morning Garrone jumped up and said, "The first person who touches Nelli will get such a box on the ear from me that he will spin round three times!"

Franti paid no attention to him; the box on the ear was delivered: the fellow spun round three times, and from that time forth no one ever touched Nelli again. The master placed Garrone near him, on the same bench. They have become friends. Nelli has grown very fond of Garrone. As soon as he enters the schoolroom he looks to see if Garrone is there. He never goes away without saying, "Good by, Garrone," and Garrone does the same with him.

When Nelli drops a pen or a book under the bench, Garrone stoops quickly, to prevent his stooping and tiring himself, and hands him his book or his pen, and then he helps him to put his things in his bag and to twist himself into his coat. For this Nelli loves him, and gazes at him constantly; and when the master praises Garrone he is pleased, as though he had been praised himself. Nelli must at last have told his mother all about the ridicule of the early days, and what they made him suffer; and about the comrade who defended him, and how he had grown fond of the latter; for this is what happened this morning. The master had sent me to carry to the director, half an hour before the close of school, a programme of the lesson, and I entered the office at the same moment with a small blond woman dressed in black, the mother of Nelli, who said, "Signor Director, is there in the class with my son a boy named Garrone?"

"Yes," replied the head-master.

"Will you have the goodness to let him come here for a moment, as I have a word to say to him?"

The head-master called the beadle and sent him to the school, and after a minute Garrone appeared on the threshold, with his big, close-cropped head, in perfect amazement. No sooner did she catch sight of him than the woman flew to meet him, threw her arms on his shoulders, and kissed him a great many times on the head, saying:

"You are Garrone, the friend of my little son, the protector of my poor child; it is you, my dear, brave boy; it is you!" Then she searched hastily in all her pockets, and in her purse, and finding nothing, she detached a chain from her neck, with a small cross, and put it on Garrone's neck, underneath his necktie, and said to him:

"Take it! wear it in memory of me, my dear boy; in memory of Nelli's mother, who thanks and blesses you."

## THE HEAD OF THE CLASS

Friday, 25th.

Garrone attracts the love of all; Derossi, the admiration. He has taken the first medal; he will always be the first, and this year also; no one can compete with him; all recognize his superiority in all points. He is the first in arithmetic, in grammar, in composition, in drawing; he understands everything on the instant; he has a marvellous memory; he succeeds in everything without effort; it seems as though study were play to him. The teacher said to him yesterday:

"You have received great gifts from God; all you have to do is not to squander them." He is, moreover, tall and handsome, with a great crown of golden curls; he is so nimble that he can leap over a bench by resting one hand on it; and he already understands fencing. He is twelve years old, and the son of a merchant; he is always dressed in blue, with gilt buttons; he is always lively, merry, gracious to all, and helps all he can in examinations; and no one has ever dared to do anything disagreeable to him, or to say a rough word to him. Nobis and Franti alone look askance at him, and Votini darts envy from his eyes; but he does not even perceive it. All smile at him, and take his hand or his arm, when he goes about, in his graceful way, to collect the work. He gives away illustrated papers, drawings, everything that is given him at home; he has made a little geographical chart of Calabria for the Calabrian lad; and he gives everything with a smile, without paying any heed to it, like a grand gentleman, and without favoritism for any one. It is impossible not to envy him, not to feel smaller than he in everything. Ah! I, too, envy him, like Votini. And I feel a bitterness, almost a certain scorn, for him, sometimes, when I am striving to accomplish my work at home, and think that he has already finished his, at this same moment, extremely well, and without fatigue. But then, when I return to school, and behold him so handsome, so smiling and triumphant, and hear how frankly and confidently he replies to the master's questions, and how courteous he is, and how the others all like him, then all bitterness, all scorn, departs from my heart, and I am ashamed of having experienced these sentiments. I should like to be always near him at such times; I should like to be able to do all my school tasks with him: his presence, his voice, inspire me with courage, with a will to work, with cheerfulness and pleasure.

The teacher has given him the monthly story, which will be read tomorrow, to copy,--*The Little Vidette of Lombardy*. He copied it this morning, and was so much affected by that heroic deed, that his face was all aflame, his eyes humid, and his lips trembling; and I gazed at him: how handsome and noble he was! With what pleasure would I not have said frankly to his face: "Derossi, you are worth more than I in everything! You are a man in comparison with me! I respect you and I admire you!"


## THE LITTLE VIDETTE OF LOMBARDY

(*Monthly Story.*)

Saturday, 26th.

In 1859, during the war for the liberation of Lombardy, a few days after the battle of Solfarino and San Martino, won by the French and Italians over the Austrians, on a beautiful morning in the month of June, a little band of cavalry of Saluzzo was proceeding at a slow pace along a retired path, in the direction of the enemy, and exploring the country attentively. The troop was commanded by an officer and a sergeant, and all were gazing into the distance ahead of them, with eyes fixed, silent, and prepared at any moment to see the uniforms of the enemy's advance-posts gleam white before them through the trees. In this order they arrived at a rustic cabin, surrounded by ash-trees, in front of which stood a solitary boy, about twelve years old, who was removing the bark from a small branch with a knife, in order to make himself a stick of it. From one window of the little house floated a large tricolored flag; there was no one inside: the peasants had fled, after hanging out the flag, for fear of the Austrians. As soon as the lad saw the cavalry, he flung aside his stick and raised his cap. He was a handsome boy, with a bold face and large blue eyes and long golden hair: he was in his shirt-sleeves and his breast was bare.

"What are you doing here?" the officer asked him, reining in his horse. "Why did you not flee with your family?"

"I have no family," replied the boy. "I am a foundling. I do a little work for everybody. I remained here to see the war."

"Have you seen any Austrians pass?"

"No; not for these three days."

The officer paused a while in thought; then he leaped from his horse, and leaving his soldiers there, with their faces turned towards the foe, he entered the house and mounted to the roof. The house was low; from the roof only a small tract of country was visible. "It will be necessary to climb the trees," said the officer, and descended. Just in front of the garden plot rose a very lofty and slender ash-tree, which was rocking its crest in the azure. The officer stood a brief space in thought, gazing now at the tree, and again at the soldiers; then, all of a sudden, he asked the lad:

"Is your sight good, you monkey?"

"Mine?" replied the boy. "I can spy a young sparrow a mile away."

"Are you good for a climb to the top of this tree?"

"To the top of this tree? I? I'll be up there in half a minute."

"And will you be able to tell me what you see up there--if there are Austrian soldiers in that direction, clouds of dust, gleaming guns, horses?"

"Certainly I shall."

"What do you demand for this service?"

"What do I demand?" said the lad, smiling. "Nothing. A fine thing, indeed! And then--if it were for the *Germans*, I wouldn't do it on any terms; but for our men! I am a Lombard!"

"Good! Then up with you."

"Wait a moment, until I take off my shoes."

He pulled off his shoes, tightened the girth of his trousers, flung his cap on the grass, and clasped the trunk of the ash.

"Take care, now!" exclaimed the officer, making a movement to hold him back, as though seized with a sudden terror.

The boy turned to look at him, with his handsome blue eyes, as though interrogating him.

"No matter," said the officer; "up with you."

Up went the lad like a cat.

"Keep watch ahead!" shouted the officer to the soldiers.

In a few moments the boy was at the top of the tree, twined around the trunk, with his legs among the leaves, but his body displayed to view, and the sun beating down on his blond head, which seemed to be of gold. The officer could hardly see him, so small did he seem up there.

"Look straight ahead and far away!" shouted the officer.

The lad, in order to see better, removed his right hand from the tree, and shaded his eyes with it.

"What do you see?" asked the officer.

The boy inclined his head towards him, and making a speaking-trumpet of his hand, replied, "Two men on horseback, on the white road."

"At what distance from here?"

"Half a mile."

"Are they moving?"

"They are standing still."

"What else do you see?" asked the officer, after a momentary silence. "Look to the right." The boy looked to the right.

Then he said: "Near the cemetery, among the trees, there is something glittering. It seems to be bayonets."

"Do you see men?"

"No. They must be concealed in the grain."

At that moment a sharp whiz of a bullet passed high up in the air, and died away in the distance, behind the house.

"Come down, my lad!" shouted the officer. "They have seen you. I don't want anything more. Come down."

"I'm not afraid," replied the boy.

"Come down!" repeated the officer. "What else do you see to the left?"

"To the left?"

"Yes, to the left."

The lad turned his head to the left: at that moment, another whistle, more acute and lower than the first, cut the air. The boy was thoroughly aroused. "Deuce take them!" he exclaimed. "They actually are aiming at me!" The bullet had passed at a short distance from him.

"Down!" shouted the officer, imperious and irritated.

"I'll come down presently," replied the boy. "But the tree shelters me. Don't fear. You want to know what there is on the left?"

"Yes, on the left," answered the officer; "but come down."

"On the left," shouted the lad, thrusting his body out in that direction, "yonder, where there is a chapel, I think I see--"

A third fierce whistle passed through the air, and almost instantaneously the boy was seen to descend, catching for a moment at the trunk and branches, and then falling headlong with arms outspread.

"Curse it!" exclaimed the officer, running up.

The boy landed on the ground, upon his back, and remained stretched out there, with arms outspread and supine; a stream of blood flowed from his breast, on the left. The sergeant and two soldiers leaped from their horses; the officer bent over and opened his shirt: the ball had entered his left lung. "He is dead!" exclaimed the officer.

"No, he still lives!" replied the sergeant.--"Ah, poor boy! brave boy!" cried the officer. "Courage, courage!" But while he was saying "courage," he was pressing his handkerchief on the wound. The boy rolled his eyes wildly and dropped his head back. He was dead. The officer turned pale and stood for a moment gazing at him; then he laid him down carefully on his cloak upon the grass; then rose and stood looking at him; the sergeant and two soldiers also stood motionless, gazing upon him: the rest were facing in the direction of the enemy.

"Poor boy!" repeated the officer. "Poor, brave boy!"

Then he approached the house, removed the tricolor from the window, and spread it in guise of a funeral pall over the little dead boy, leaving his face uncovered. The sergeant collected the dead boy's shoes, cap, his little stick, and his knife, and placed them beside him.

They stood for a few moments longer in silence; then the officer turned to the sergeant and said to him, "We will send the ambulance for him: he died as a soldier; the soldiers shall bury him." Having said this, he wafted a kiss with his hand to the dead boy, and shouted "To horse!" All sprang into the saddle, the troop drew together and resumed its road.

And a few hours later the little dead boy received the honors of war.

At sunset the whole line of the Italian advance-posts marched forward towards the foe, and along the same road which had been traversed in the morning by the detachment of cavalry, there proceeded, in two files, a heavy battalion of sharpshooters, who, a few days before, had valiantly watered the hill of San Martino with blood. The news of the boy's death had already spread among the soldiers before they left the encampment. The path, flanked by a rivulet, ran a few paces distant from the house. When the first officers of the battalion caught sight of the little body stretched at the foot of the ash-tree and covered with the tricolored banner, they made the salute to it with their swords, and one of them bent over the bank of the streamlet, which was covered with flowers at that spot, plucked a couple of blossoms and threw them on it. Then all the sharpshooters, as they passed, plucked flowers and threw them on the body. In a few minutes the boy was covered with flowers, and officers and soldiers all saluted him as they passed by: "Bravo, little Lombard!" "Farewell, my lad!" "I salute thee, gold locks!" "Hurrah!" "Glory!" "Farewell!" One officer tossed him his medal for valor; another went and kissed his brow. And flowers continued to rain down on his bare feet, on his blood-stained breast, on his golden head. And there he lay asleep on the grass, enveloped in his flag, with a white and almost smiling face, poor boy! as though he heard these salutes and was glad that he had given his life for his Lombardy.


THE POOR

Tuesday, 29th.

To give one's life for one's country as the Lombard boy did, is a great virtue; but you must not neglect the lesser virtues, my son. This morning as you walked in front of me, when we were returning from school, you passed near a poor woman who was holding between her knees a thin, pale child, and who asked alms of you. You looked at her and gave her nothing, and yet you had some coppers in your pocket. Listen, my son. Do not accustom yourself to pass indifferently before misery which stretches out its hand to you and far less before a mother who asks a copper for her child. Reflect that the child may be hungry; think of the agony of that poor woman. Picture to yourself the sob of despair of your mother, if she were some day forced to say, "Enrico, I cannot give you any bread even today!" When I give a soldo to a beggar, and he says to me, "God preserve your health, and the health of all belonging to you!" you cannot understand the sweetness which these words produce in my heart, the gratitude that I feel for that poor man. It seems to me certain that such a good wish must keep one in good health for a long time, and I return home content, and think, "Oh, that poor man has returned to me very much more than I gave him!" Well, let me sometimes feel that good wish called forth, merited by you; draw a soldo from your little purse now and then, and let it fall into the hand of a blind man without means of subsistence, of a mother without bread, of a child without a mother. The poor love the alms of boys, because it does not humiliate them, and because boys, who stand in need of everything, resemble themselves: you see that there are always poor people around the schoolhouses. The alms of a man is an act of charity; but that of a child is at one and the same time an act of charity and a caress--do you understand? It is as though a soldo and a flower fell from your hand together. Reflect that you lack nothing, and that they lack everything, that while you aspire to be happy, they are content simply with not dying. Reflect, that it is a horror, in the midst of so many palaces, along the streets thronged with carriages, and children clad in velvet, that there should be women and children who have nothing to eat. To have nothing to eat! O God! Boys like you, as good as you, as intelligent as you, who, in the midst of a great city, have nothing to eat, like wild beasts lost in a desert! Oh, never again, Enrico, pass a mother who is begging, without placing a soldo in her hand!

THY FATHER.

# DECEMBER

THE TRADER

Thursday, 1st.

MY father wishes me to have some one of my companions come to the house every holiday, or that I should go to see one of them, in order that I may gradually become friends with all of them. Sunday I shall go to walk with Votini, the well-dressed boy who is always polishing himself up, and who is so envious of Derossi. In the meantime, Garoffi came to the house today,--that long, lank boy, with the nose like an owl's beak, and small, knavish eyes, which seem to be ferreting everywhere. He is the son of a grocer; he is an eccentric fellow; he is always counting the soldi that he has in his pocket; he reckons them on his fingers very, very rapidly, and goes through some process of multiplication without any tables; and he hoards his money, and already has a book in the Scholars' Savings Bank. He never spends a soldo, I am positive; and if he drops a centesimo under the benches, he is capable of hunting for it for a week. He does as magpies do, so Derossi says. Everything that he finds--worn-out pens, postage-stamps that have been used, pins, candle-ends--he picks up. He has been collecting postage-stamps for more than two years now; and he already has hundreds of them from every country, in a large album, which he will sell to a bookseller later on, when he has got it quite full. Meanwhile, the bookseller gives him his copy-books gratis, because he takes a great many boys to the shop. In school, he is always bartering; he effects sales of little articles every day, and lotteries and exchanges; then he regrets the exchange, and wants his stuff back; he buys for two and gets rid of it for four; he plays at pitch-penny, and never loses; he sells old newspapers over again to the tobacconist; and he keeps a little blank-book, in which he sets down his transactions, which is completely filled with sums and subtractions. At school he studies nothing but arithmetic; and if he desires the medal, it is only that he may have a free entrance into the puppet-show. But he pleases me; he amuses me. We played at keeping a market, with weights and scales. He knows the exact price of everything; he understands weighing, and makes handsome paper horns, like shopkeepers, with great expedition. He declares that as soon as he has finished school he shall set up in business--in a new business which he has invented himself. He was very much pleased when I gave him some foreign postage-stamps; and he informed me exactly how each one sold for collections. My father pretended to be reading the newspaper; but he listened to him, and was greatly diverted. His pockets are bulging, full of his little wares; and he covers them up with a long black cloak, and always appears thoughtful and preoccupied with business, like a merchant. But the thing that he has nearest his heart is his collection of postage-stamps. This is his treasure; and he always speaks of it as though he were going to get a fortune out of it. His companions accuse him of miserliness and usury. I do not know: I like him; he teaches me a great many things; he seems a man to me. Coretti, the son of the wood-merchant, says that he would not give him his postage-stamps to save his mother's life. My father does not believe it.

"Wait a little before you condemn him," he said to me; "he has this passion, but he has heart as well."

VANITY

Monday, 5th.

Yesterday I went to take a walk along the Rivoli road with Votini and his father. As we were passing through the Via Dora Grossa we saw Stardi, the boy who kicks disturbers, standing stiffly in front of the window of a book-shop, with his eyes fixed on a geographical map; and no one knows how long he had been there, because he studies even in the street. He barely returned our salute, the rude fellow! Votini was well dressed--even too much so. He had on morocco boots embroidered in red, an embroidered coat, small silken frogs, a white beaver hat, and a watch; and he strutted. But his vanity was destined to come to a bad end on this occasion. After having run a tolerably long distance up the Rivoli road, leaving his father, who was walking slowly, a long way in the rear, we halted at a stone seat, beside a modestly clad boy, who appeared to be weary, and was meditating, with drooping head. A man, who must have been his father, was walking to and fro under the trees, reading the newspaper. We sat down. Votini placed himself between me and the boy. All at once he recollected that he was well dressed, and wanted to make his neighbor admire and envy him.

He lifted one foot, and said to me, "Have you seen my officer's boots?" He said this in order to make the other boy look at them; but the latter paid no attention to them.

Then he dropped his foot, and showed me his silk frogs, glancing askance at the boy the while, and said that these frogs did not please him, and that he wanted to have them changed to silver buttons; but the boy did not look at the frogs either.

Then Votini fell to twirling his very handsome white castor hat on the tip of his forefinger; but the boy--and it seemed as though he did it on purpose--did not deign even a glance at the hat.

Votini, who began to become irritated, drew out his watch, opened it, and showed me the wheels; but the boy did not turn his head. "Is it of silver gilt?" I asked him.

"No," he replied; "it is gold."

"But not entirely of gold," I said; "there must be some silver with it."

"Why, no!" he retorted; and, in order to compel the boy to look, he held the watch before his face, and said to him, "Say, look here! isn't it true that it is entirely of gold?"

The boy replied curtly, "I don't know."

"Oh! oh!" exclaimed Votini, full of wrath, "what pride!"

As he was saying this, his father came up, and heard him; he looked steadily at the lad for a moment, then said sharply to his son, "Hold your tongue!" and, bending down to his ear, he added, "he is blind!"

Votini sprang to his feet, with a shudder, and stared the boy in the face: the latter's eyeballs were glassy, without expression, without sight.

Votini stood humbled,--speechless,--with his eyes fixed on the ground. At length he stammered, "I am sorry; I did not know."

But the blind boy, who had understood it all, said, with a kind and melancholy smile, "Oh, it's no matter!"

Well, he is vain; but Votini has not at all a bad heart. He never laughed again during the whole of the walk.


THE FIRST SNOW-STORM

Saturday, 10th.

Farewell, walks to Rivoli! Here is the beautiful friend of the boys! Here is the first snow! Ever since yesterday evening it has been falling in thick flakes as large as gillyflowers. It was a pleasure this morning at school to see it beat against the panes and pile up on the window-sills; even the master watched it, and rubbed his hands; and all were glad, when they thought of making snowballs, and of the ice which will come later, and of the hearth at home. Stardi, entirely absorbed in his lessons, and with his fists pressed to his temples, was the only one who paid no attention to it. What beauty, what a celebration there was when we left school! All danced down the streets, shouting and tossing their arms, catching up handfuls of snow, and dashing about in it, like poodles in water. The umbrellas of the parents, who were waiting for them outside, were all white; the policeman's helmet was white; all our satchels were white in a few moments. Every one appeared to be beside himself with joy-- even Precossi, the son of the blacksmith, that pale boy who never laughs; and Robetti, the lad who saved the little child from the omnibus, poor fellow! he jumped about on his crutches. The Calabrian, who had never touched snow, made himself a little ball of it, and began to eat it, as though it had been a peach; Crossi, the son of the vegetable-vendor, filled his satchel with it; and the little mason made us burst with laughter, when my father invited him to come to our house tomorrow. He had his mouth full of snow, and, not daring either to spit it out or to swallow it, he stood there choking and staring at us, and made no answer. Even the schoolmistress came out of school on a run, laughing; and my mistress of the first upper class, poor little thing! ran through the drizzling snow, covering her face with her green veil, and coughing; and meanwhile, hundreds of girls from the neighboring schoolhouse passed by, screaming and frolicking on that white carpet; and the masters and the beadles and the policemen shouted, "Home! home!" swallowing flakes of snow, and whitening their moustaches and beards. But they, too, laughed at this wild hilarity of the scholars, as they celebrated the winter.

You hail the arrival of winter; but there are boys who have neither clothes nor shoes nor fire. There are thousands of them, who descend to their villages, over a long road, carrying in hands bleeding from chilblains a bit of wood to warm the schoolroom. There are hundreds of schools almost buried in the snow, bare and dismal as caves, where the boys suffocate with smoke or chatter their teeth with cold as they gaze in terror at the white flakes which descend unceasingly, which pile up without cessation on their distant cabins threatened by avalanches. You rejoice in the winter, boys. Think of the thousands of creatures to whom winter brings misery and death.

THY FATHER.

## THE LITTLE MASON

Sunday, 11th.

The little mason came today, in a hunting-jacket, entirely dressed in the cast-off clothes of his father, which were still white with lime and plaster. My father was even more anxious than I that he should come. How much pleasure he gives us! No sooner had he entered than he pulled off his ragged cap, which was all soaked with snow, and thrust it into one of his pockets; then he advanced with his listless gait, like a weary workman, turning his face, as smooth as an apple, with its ball-like nose, from side to side; and when he entered the dining-room, he cast a glance round at the furniture and fixed his eyes on a small picture of Rigoletto, a hunchbacked jester, and made a "hare's face."

It is impossible to refrain from laughing when one sees him make that hare's face. We went to playing with bits of wood: he possesses an extraordinary skill at making towers and bridges, which seem to stand as though by a miracle, and he works at it quite seriously, with the patience of a man. Between one tower and another he told me about his family: they live in a garret; his father goes to the evening school to learn to read, and his mother is a washerwoman. And they must love him, of course, for he is clad like a poor boy, but he is well protected from the cold, with neatly mended clothes, and with his necktie nicely tied by his mother's hands. His father, he told me, is a fine man,-- a giant, who has trouble in getting through doors, but he is kind, and always calls his son "hare's face": the son, on the contrary, is rather small.

At four o'clock we lunched on bread and goat's-milk cheese, as we sat on the sofa; and when we rose, I do not know why, but my father did not wish me to brush off the back, which the little mason had spotted with white, from his jacket: he restrained my hand, and then rubbed it off himself on the sly. While we were playing, the little mason lost a button from his hunting-jacket, and my mother sewed it on, and he grew quite red, and began to watch her sew, in perfect amazement and confusion, holding his breath the while. Then we gave him some albums of caricatures to look at, and he, without being aware of it himself, imitated the grimaces of the faces there so well, that even my father laughed. He was so much pleased when he went away that he forgot to put on his tattered cap; and when we reached the landing, he made a hare's face at me once more in sign of his gratitude. His name is Antonio Rabucco, and he is eight years and eight months old.

Do you know, my son, why I did not wish you to wipe off the sofa? Because to wipe it while your companion was looking on would have been almost the same as administering a reproof to him for having soiled it. And this was not well, in the first place, because he did not do it intentionally, and in the next, because he did it with the clothes of his father, who had covered them with plaster while at work; and what is contracted while at work is not dirt; it is dust, lime, varnish, whatever you like, but it is not dirt. Labor does not engender dirt. Never say of a laborer coming from his work, "He is filthy." You should say, "He has on his garments the signs, the traces, of his toil." Remember this. And you must love the little mason, first, because he is your comrade; and next, because he is the son of a workingman.

THY FATHER.

A SNOWBALL

Friday, 16th.

It is still snow, snow. A shameful thing happened in connection with the snow this morning when we came out of school. A flock of boys had no sooner got into the Corso than they began to throw balls of that watery snow which makes missiles as solid and heavy as stones. Many persons were passing along the sidewalks. A gentleman called out, "Stop that, you little rascals!" and just at that moment a sharp cry rose from another part of the street, and we saw an old man who had lost his hat and was staggering about, covering his face with his hands, and beside him a boy who was shouting, "Help! help!"

People instantly ran from all directions. He had been struck in the eye with a ball. All the boys dispersed, fleeing like arrows. I was standing in front of the bookseller's shop, into which my father had gone, and I saw several of my companions approaching at a run, mingling with others near me, and pretending to be engaged in staring at the windows: there was Garrone, with his penny roll in his pocket, as usual; Coretti, the little mason; and Garoffi, the boy with the postage-stamps. In the meantime a crowd had formed around the old man, and a policeman and others were running to and fro, threatening and demanding: "Who was it? Who did it? Was it you? Tell me who did it!" and they looked at the boys' hands to see whether they were wet with snow.

Garoffi was standing beside me. I perceived that he was trembling all over, and that his face was as white as that of a corpse. "Who was it? Who did it?" the crowd continued to cry.

Then I overheard Garrone say in a low voice to Garoffi, "Come, go and present yourself; it would be cowardly to allow any one else to be arrested."

"But I did not do it on purpose," replied Garoffi, trembling like a leaf.

"No matter; do your duty," repeated Garrone.

"But I have not the courage."

"Take courage, then; I will accompany you."

And the policeman and the other people were crying more loudly than ever: "Who was it? Who did it? One of his glasses has been driven into his eye! He has been blinded! The ruffians!"

I thought that Garoffi would fall to the earth. "Come," said Garrone, resolutely, "I will defend you;" and grasping him by the arm, he thrust him forward, supporting him as though he had been a sick man. The people saw, and instantly understood, and several persons ran up with their fists raised; but Garrone thrust himself between, crying:

"Do ten men of you set on one boy?"

Then they ceased, and a policeman seized Garoffi by the hand and led him, pushing aside the crowd as he went, to a pastry-cook's shop, where the wounded man had been carried. On catching sight of him, I suddenly recognized him as the old employee who lives on the fourth floor of our house with his grandnephew. He was stretched out on a chair, with a handkerchief over his eyes.

"I did not do it intentionally!" sobbed Garoffi, half dead with terror; "I did not do it intentionally!"

Two or three persons thrust him violently into the shop, crying, "Your face to the earth! Beg his pardon!" and they threw him to the ground. But all at once two vigorous arms set him on his feet again, and a resolute voice said:

"No, gentlemen!" It was our head-master, who had seen it all. "Since he has had the courage to present himself," he added, "no one has the right to humiliate him." All stood silent. "Ask his forgiveness," said the head-master to Garoffi. Garoffi, bursting into tears, embraced the old man's knees, and the latter, having felt for the boy's head with his hand, caressed his hair. Then all said:

"Go away, boy! go, return home."

And my father drew me out of the crowd, and said to me as we passed along the street, "Enrico, would you have had the courage, under similar circumstances, to do your duty,--to go and confess your fault?"

I told him that I should. And he said, "Give me your word, as a lad of heart and honor, that you would do it." "I give thee my word, father mine!"

## THE MISTRESSES

Saturday, 17th.

Garoffi was thoroughly terrified today, in the expectation of a severe punishment from the teacher; but the master did not make his appearance; and as the assistant was also missing, Signora Cromi, the oldest of the schoolmistresses, came to teach the school; she has two grown-up children, and she has taught several women to read and write, who now come to accompany their sons to the Baretti schoolhouse.

She was sad today, because one of her sons is ill. No sooner had they caught sight of her, than they began to make an uproar. But she said, in a slow and tranquil tone, "Respect my white hair; I am not only a school-teacher, I am also a mother"; and then no one dared to speak again, in spite of that brazen face of Franti, who contented himself with jeering at her on the sly.

Signora Delcati, my brother's teacher, was sent to take charge of Signora Cromi's class, and to Signora Delcati's was sent the teacher who is called "the little nun," because she always dresses in dark colors, with a black apron, and has a small white face, hair that is always smooth, very bright eyes, and a delicate voice, that seems to be forever murmuring prayers. And it is incomprehensible, my mother says; she is so gentle and timid, with that thread of a voice, which is always even, which is hardly audible, and she never speaks loud nor flies into a passion; but, nevertheless, she keeps the boys so quiet that you cannot hear them, and the most roguish bow their heads when she merely admonishes them with her finger, and her school seems like a church; and it is for this reason, also, that she is called "the little nun."

But there is another one who pleases me,--the young mistress of the first lower, No. 3, that young girl with the rosy face, who has two pretty dimples in her cheeks, and who wears a large red feather on her little bonnet, and a small cross of yellow glass on her neck. She is always cheerful, and keeps her class cheerful; she is always calling out with that silvery voice of hers, which makes her seem to be singing, and tapping her little rod on the table, and clapping her hands to impose silence; then, when they come out of school, she runs after one and another like a child, to bring them back into line: she pulls up the cape of one, and buttons the coat of another, so that they may not take cold; she follows them even into the street, in order that they may not fall to quarrelling; she beseeches the parents not to whip them at home; she brings lozenges to those who have coughs; she lends her muff to those who are cold; and she is continually tormented by the smallest children, who caress her and demand kisses, and pull at her veil and her mantle; but she lets them do it, and kisses them all with a smile, and returns home all rumpled and with her throat all bare, panting and happy, with her beautiful dimples and her red feather. She is also the girls' drawing-teacher, and she supports her mother and a brother by her own labor.

IN THE HOUSE OF THE WOUNDED MAN

Sunday, 18th.

The grandnephew of the old employee who was struck in the eye by Garoffi's snowball is with the schoolmistress who has the red feather: we saw him today in the house of his uncle, who treats him like a son. I had finished writing out the monthly story for the coming week,--*The Little Florentine Scribe*,--which the master had given to me to copy; and my father said to me:

"Let us go up to the fourth floor, and see how that old gentleman's eye is."

We entered a room which was almost dark, where the old man was sitting up in bed, with a great many pillows behind his shoulders; by the bedside sat his wife, and in one corner his nephew was amusing himself. The old man's eye was bandaged. He was very glad to see my father; he made us sit down, and said that he was better, that his eye was not only not ruined, but that he should be quite well again in a few days.

"It was an accident," he added. "I regret the terror which it must have caused that poor boy." Then he talked to us about the doctor, whom he expected every moment to attend him. Just then the door-bell rang.

"There is the doctor," said his wife.

The door opened--and whom did I see? Garoffi, in his long cloak, standing, with bowed head, on the threshold, and without the courage to enter.

"Who is it?" asked the sick man.

"It is the boy who threw the snowball," said my father. And then the old man said:

"Oh, my poor boy! come here; you have come to inquire after the wounded man, have you not? But he is better; be at ease; he is better and almost well. Come here."

Garoffi, who did not perceive us in his confusion, approached the bed, forcing himself not to cry; and the old man caressed him, but could not speak.

"Thanks," said the old man; "go and tell your father and mother that all is going well, and that they are not to think any more about it."

But Garoffi did not move, and seemed to have something to say which he dared not utter.

"What have you to say to me? What is it that you want?"

"I!--Nothing."

"Well, good by, until we meet again, my boy; go with your heart in peace."

Garoffi went as far as the door; but there he halted, turned to the nephew, who was following him, and gazed curiously at him. All at once he pulled some object from beneath his cloak, put it in the boy's hand, and whispered hastily to him, "It is for you," and away he went like a flash.

The boy carried the object to his uncle; we saw that on it was written, *I give you this*; we looked inside, and uttered an exclamation of surprise. It was the famous album, with his collection of postage-stamps, which poor Garoffi had brought, the collection of which he was always talking, upon which he had founded so many hopes, and which had cost him so much trouble; it was his treasure, poor boy! it was the half of his very blood, which he had presented in exchange for his pardon.

## THE LITTLE FLORENTINE SCRIBE

(*Monthly Story.*)

He was in the fourth elementary class. He was a graceful Florentine lad of twelve, with black hair and a white face, the eldest son of an employee on the railway, who, having a large family and but small pay, lived in straitened circumstances. His father loved him and was tolerably kind and indulgent to him--indulgent in everything except in that which referred to school: on this point he required a great deal, and showed himself severe, because his son was obliged to attain such a rank as would enable him to soon obtain a place and help his family; and in order to accomplish anything quickly, it was necessary that he should work a great deal in a very short time. And although the lad studied, his father was always exhorting him to study more.

His father was advanced in years, and too much toil had aged him before his time. Nevertheless, in order to provide for the necessities of his family, in addition to the toil which his occupation imposed upon him, he obtained special work here and there as a copyist, and passed a good part of the night at his writing-table. Lately, he had undertaken, in behalf of a house which published journals and books in parts, to write upon the parcels the names and addresses of their subscribers, and he earned three lire[1] for every five hundred of these paper wrappers, written in large and regular characters. But this work wearied him, and he often complained of it to his family at dinner.

"My eyes are giving out," he said; "this night work is killing me." One day his son said to him, "Let me work instead of you, papa; you know that I can write like you, and fairly well." But the father answered:

"No, my son, you must study; your school is a much more important thing than my wrappers; I feel remorse at robbing you of a single hour; I thank you, but I will not have it; do not mention it to me again."

The son knew that it was useless to insist on such a matter with his father, and he did not persist; but this is what he did. He knew that exactly at midnight his father stopped writing, and quitted his workroom to go to his bedroom; he had heard him several times: as soon as the twelve strokes of the clock had sounded, he had heard the sound of a chair drawn back, and the slow step of his father. One night he waited until the latter was in bed, then dressed himself very, very softly, and felt his way to the little workroom, lighted the petroleum lamp again, seated himself at the writing-table, where lay a pile of white wrappers and the list of addresses, and began to write, imitating exactly his father's handwriting. And he wrote with a will, gladly, a little in fear, and the wrappers piled up, and

---

[1] Sixty cents.

from time to time he dropped the pen to rub his hands, and then began again with increased alacrity, listening and smiling. He wrote a hundred and sixty--one lira! Then he stopped, placed the pen where he had found it, extinguished the light, and went back to bed on tiptoe.

At noon that day his father sat down to the table in a good humor. He had perceived nothing. He performed the work mechanically, measuring it by the hour, and thinking of something else, and only counted the wrappers he had written on the following day. He seated himself at the table in a fine humor, and slapping his son on one shoulder, he said to him:

"Eh, Giulio! Your father is even a better workman than you thought. In two hours I did a good third more work than usual last night. My hand is still nimble, and my eyes still do their duty." And Giulio, silent but content, said to himself, "Poor daddy, besides the money, I am giving him some satisfaction in the thought that he has grown young again. Well, courage!"

Encouraged by these good results, when night came and twelve o'clock struck, he rose once more, and set to work. And this he did for several nights. And his father noticed nothing; only once, at supper, he uttered this exclamation, "It is strange how much oil has been used in this house lately!" This was a shock to Giulio; but the conversation ceased there, and the nocturnal labor proceeded.

However, by dint of thus breaking his sleep every night, Giulio did not get sufficient rest: he rose in the morning fatigued, and when he was doing his school work in the evening, he had difficulty in keeping his eyes open. One evening, for the first time in his life, he fell asleep over his copy-book.

"Courage! courage!" cried his father, clapping his hands; "to work!"

He shook himself and set to work again. But the next evening, and on the days following, the same thing occurred, and worse: he dozed over his books, he rose later than usual, he studied his lessons in a languid way, he seemed disgusted with study. His father began to observe him, then to reflect seriously, and at last to reprove him. He should never have done it!

"Giulio," he said to him one morning, "you put me quite beside myself; you are no longer as you used to be. I don't like it. Take care; all the hopes of your family rest on you. I am dissatisfied; do you understand?"

At this reproof, the first severe one, in truth, which he had ever received, the boy grew troubled.

"Yes," he said to himself, "it is true; it cannot go on so; this deceit must come to an end."

But at dinner, on the evening of that very same day, his father said with much cheerfulness, "Do you know that this month I have earned thirty-two lire more at addressing those wrappers than last month!" and so saying, he drew from under the table a paper package of sweets which he had bought, that he might celebrate with his children this extraordinary profit, and they all hailed it with clapping of hands. Then Giulio took heart again, courage again, and said in his heart, "No, poor papa, I will not cease to deceive you; I will make greater efforts to work during the day, but I shall continue to work at night for you and for the rest." And his father added, "Thirty-two lire more! I am satisfied. But that boy there," pointing at Giulio, "is the one who displeases me." And Giulio received the reprimand in silence, forcing back two tears which tried to flow; but at the same time he felt a great pleasure in his heart.

And he continued to work by main force; but fatigue added to fatigue rendered it ever more difficult for him to resist. Thus things went on for two months. The father continued to reproach his son, and to gaze at him with eyes which grew constantly more wrathful. One day he went to make inquiries of the teacher, and the teacher said to him: "Yes, he gets along, he gets along, because he is intelligent; but he no longer has the good will which he had at first. He is drowsy, he yawns, his mind is distracted. He writes short compositions, scribbled down in all haste, in bad chirography. Oh, he could do a great deal, a great deal more."

That evening the father took the son aside, and spoke to him words which were graver than any the latter had ever heard. "Giulio, you see how I toil, how I am wearing out my life, for the family. You do not second my efforts. You have no heart for me, nor for your brothers, nor for your mother!"

"Ah no! don't say that, father!" cried the son, bursting into tears, and opening his mouth to confess all. But his father interrupted him, saying:

"You are aware of the condition of the family; you know that good will and sacrifices on the part of all are necessary. I myself, as you see, have had to double my work. I counted on a gift of a hundred lire from the railway company this month, and this morning I have learned that I shall receive nothing!"

At this information, Giulio repressed the confession which was on the point of escaping from his soul, and repeated resolutely to himself: "No, papa, I shall tell you nothing; I shall guard my secret for the sake of being able to work for you; I will recompense you in another way for the sorrow which I occasion you; I will study enough at school to win promotion; the important point is to help you to earn our living, and to relieve you of the fatigue which is killing you."

And so he went on, and two months more passed, of labor by night and weakness by day, of desperate efforts on the part of the son, and of bitter reproaches on the part of the father. But the worst of it was, that the latter grew gradually colder towards the boy, only addressed him rarely, as though he had been a recreant son, of whom there was nothing any longer to be expected, and almost avoided meeting his glance. And Giulio perceived this and suffered from it, and when his father's back was turned, he threw him a furtive kiss, stretching forth his face with a sentiment of sad and dutiful tenderness; and between sorrow and fatigue, he grew thin and pale, and he was constrained to still further neglect his studies. And he understood well that there must be an end to it some day, and every evening he said to himself, "I will not get up to-night"; but when the clock struck twelve, at the moment when he should have vigorously reaffirmed his resolution, he felt remorse: it seemed to him, that by remaining in bed he should be failing in a duty, and robbing his father and the family of a lira. And he rose, thinking that some night his father would wake up and discover him, or that he would discover the deception by accident, by counting the wrappers twice;

and then all would come to a natural end, without any act of his will, which he did not feel the courage to exert. And thus he went on.

But one evening at dinner his father spoke a word which was decisive so far as he was concerned. His mother looked at him, and as it seemed to her that he was more ill and weak than usual, she said to him, "Giulio, you are ill." And then, turning to his father with anxiety: "Giulio is ill. See how pale he is Giulio, my dear, how do you feel?"

His father gave a hasty glance, and said: "It is his bad conscience that produces his bad health. He was not thus when he was a studious scholar and a loving son."

"But he is ill!" exclaimed the mother.

"I don't care anything about him any longer!" replied the father.

This remark was like a stab in the heart to the poor boy. Ah! he cared nothing any more. His father, who once trembled at the mere sound of a cough from him! He no longer loved him; there was no longer any doubt; he was dead in his father's heart. "Ah, no! my father," said the boy to himself, his heart oppressed with anguish, "now all is over indeed; I cannot live without your affection; I must have it all back. I will tell you all; I will deceive you no longer. I will study as of old, come what will, if you will only love me once more, my poor father! Oh, this time I am quite sure of my resolution!"

Nevertheless he rose that night again, by force of habit more than anything else; and when he was once up, he wanted to go and salute and see once more, for the last time, in the quiet of the night, that little chamber where he toiled so much in secret with his heart full of satisfaction and tenderness. And when he beheld again that little table with the lamp lighted and those white wrappers on which he was never more to write those names of towns and persons, which he had come to know by heart, he was seized with a great sadness, and with an impetuous movement he grasped the pen to recommence his accustomed toil. But in reaching out his hand he struck a book, and the book fell. The blood rushed to his heart. What if his father had waked! Certainly he would not have discovered him in the commission of a bad deed: he had himself decided to tell him all, and yet--the sound of that step approaching in the darkness,--the discovery at that hour, in that silence,--his mother, who would be awakened and alarmed,--and the thought, which had occurred to him for the first time, that his father might feel humiliated in his presence on thus discovering all;--all this terrified him almost. He bent his ear, with suspended breath. He heard no sound. He laid his ear to the lock of the door behind him--nothing. The whole house was asleep. His father had not heard. He recovered his composure, and he set himself again to his writing, and wrapper was piled on wrapper. He heard the regular tread of the policeman below in the deserted street; then the rumble of a carriage which gradually died away; then, after an interval, the rattle of a file of carts, which passed slowly by; then a profound silence, broken from time to time by the distant barking of a dog. And he wrote on and on: and meanwhile his father was behind him. He had risen on hearing the fall of the book, and had remained waiting for a long time: the rattle of the carts had drowned the noise of his footsteps and the creaking of the door-casing; and he was there, with his white head bent over Giulio's little black head, and he had seen the pen flying over the wrappers, and in an instant he had divined all, remembered all, understood all, and a despairing penitence, but at the same time an immense tenderness, had taken possession of his mind and had held him nailed to the spot suffocating behind his child. Suddenly Giulio uttered a piercing shriek: two arms had pressed his head convulsively.

"Oh, papa, papa! forgive me, forgive me!" he cried, recognizing his parent by his weeping.

"Do you forgive me!" replied his father, sobbing, and covering his brow with kisses. "I have understood all, I know all; it is I, it is I who ask your pardon, my blessed little creature; come, come with me!" and he pushed or rather carried him to the bedside of his mother, who was awake, and throwing him into her arms, he said:

"Kiss this little angel of a son, who has not slept for three months, but has been toiling for me, while I was saddening his heart, and he was earning our bread!" The mother pressed him to her breast and held him there, without the power to speak; at last she said: "Go to sleep at once, my baby, go to sleep and rest.--Carry him to bed."

The father took him from her arms, carried him to his room, and laid him in his bed, still breathing hard and caressing him, and arranged his pillows and coverlets for him.

"Thanks, papa," the child kept repeating; "thanks; but go to bed yourself now; I am content; go to bed, papa."

But his father wanted to see him fall asleep; so he sat down beside the bed, took his hand, and said to him, "Sleep, sleep, my little son!" and Giulio, being weak, fell asleep at last, and slumbered many hours, enjoying, for the first time in many months, a tranquil sleep, enlivened by pleasant dreams; and as he opened his eyes, when the sun had already been shining for a tolerably long time, he first felt, and then saw, close to his breast, and resting upon the edge of the little bed, the white head of his father, who had passed the night thus, and who was still asleep, with his brow against his son's heart.

WILL

Wednesday, 28th.

There is Stardi in my school, who would have the force to do what the little Florentine did. This morning two events occurred at the school: Garoffi, wild with delight, because his album had been returned to him, with the addition of three postage-stamps of the Republic of Guatemala, which he had been seeking for three months; and Stardi, who took the second medal; Stardi the next in the class after Derossi! All were amazed at it. Who could ever have foretold it, when, in October, his father brought him to school bundled up in that big green coat, and said to the master, in presence of every one:

"You must have a great deal of patience with him, because he is very hard of understanding!"

Every one credited him with a wooden head from the very beginning. But he said, "I will burst or I will succeed," and he set to work doggedly, to studying day and night, at home, at school, while walking, with set teeth and clenched fists, patient as an ox, obstinate as a mule; and thus, by dint of trampling on every one, disregarding mockery, and dealing kicks to disturbers, this big thick-head passed in advance of the rest. He understood not the first thing of arithmetic, he filled his compositions with absurdities, he never succeeded in retaining a phrase in his mind; and now he solves problems, writes correctly, and sings his lessons like a song. And his iron will can be divined from the seeing how he is made, so very thickset and squat, with a square head and no neck, with short, thick hands, and coarse voice. He studies even on scraps of newspaper, and on theatre bills, and every time that he has ten soldi, he buys a book; he has already collected a little library, and in a moment of good humor he allowed the promise to slip from his mouth that he would take me home and show it to me. He speaks to no one, he plays with no one, he is always on hand, on his bench, with his fists pressed to his temples, firm as a rock, listening to the teacher. How he must have toiled, poor Stardi! The master said to him this morning, although he was impatient and in a bad humor, when he bestowed the medals:

"Bravo, Stardi! he who endures, conquers." But the latter did not appear in the least puffed up with pride--he did not smile; and no sooner had he returned to his seat, with the medal, than he planted his fists on his temples again, and became more motionless and more attentive than before. But the finest thing happened when he went out of school; for his father, a blood-letter, as big and squat as himself, with a huge face and a huge voice, was there waiting for him. He had not expected this medal, and he was not willing to believe in it, so that it was necessary for the master to reassure him, and then he began to laugh heartily, and tapped his son on the back of the neck, saying energetically, "Bravo! good! my dear pumpkin; you'll do!" and he stared at him, astonished and smiling. And all the boys around him smiled too, except Stardi. He was already ruminating the lesson for tomorrow morning in that huge head of his.

GRATITUDE

Saturday, 31st.

Your comrade Stardi never complains of his teacher; I am sure of that. "The master was in a bad temper, was impatient,"--you say it in a tone of resentment. Think an instant how often you give way to acts of impatience, and towards whom? towards your father and your mother, towards whom your impatience is a crime. Your master has very good cause to be impatient at times! Reflect that he has been laboring for boys these many years, and that if he has found many affectionate and noble individuals among them, he has also found many ungrateful ones, who have abused his kindness and ignored his toils; and that, between you all, you cause him far more bitterness than satisfaction. Reflect, that the most holy man on earth, if placed in his position, would allow himself to be conquered by wrath now and then. And then, if you only knew how often the teacher goes to give a lesson to a sick boy, all alone, because he is not ill enough to be excused from school and is impatient on account of his suffering, and is pained to see that the rest of you do not notice it, or abuse it! Respect, love, your master, my son. Love him, also, because your father loves and respects him; because he consecrates his life to the welfare of so many boys who will forget him; love him because he opens and enlightens your intelligence and educates your mind; because one of these days, when you have become a man, and when neither I nor he shall be in the world, his image will often present itself to your mind, side by side with mine, and then you will see certain expressions of sorrow and fatigue in his honest countenance to which you now pay no heed: you will recall them, and they will pain you, even after the lapse of thirty years; and you will feel ashamed, you will feel sad at not having loved him, at having behaved badly to him. Love your master; for he belongs to that vast family of fifty thousand elementary instructors, scattered throughout all Italy, who are the intellectual fathers of the millions of boys who are growing up with you; the laborers, hardly recognized and poorly recompensed, who are preparing in our country a people superior to those of the present. I am not content with the affection which you have for me, if you have it not also for all those who are doing you good, and among these, your master stands first, after your parents. Love him as you would love a brother of mine; love him when he caresses and when he reproves you; when he is just, and when he appears to you to be unjust; love him when he is amiable and gracious; and love him even more when you see him sad. Love him always. And always pronounce with reverence that name of "teacher," which, after that of your father, is the noblest, the sweetest name which one man can apply to another man.

THY FATHER.

# JANUARY

## THE ASSISTANT MASTER

Wednesday, 4th.

MY father was right; the master was in a bad humor because he was not well; for the last three days, in fact, the assistant has been coming in his stead,--that little man, without a beard, who seems like a youth. A shameful thing happened this morning. There had been an uproar on the first and second days, in the school, because the assistant is very patient and does nothing but say, "Be quiet, be quiet, I beg of you."

But this morning they passed all bounds. Such a noise arose, that his words were no longer audible, and he admonished and besought; but it was a mere waste of breath. Twice the head-master appeared at the door and looked in; but the moment he disappeared the murmur increased as in a market. It was in vain that Derossi and Garrone turned round and made signs to their comrades to be good, so that it was a shame. No one paid any heed to them. Stardi alone remained quiet, with his elbows on the bench, and his fists to his temples, meditating, perhaps, on his famous library; and Garoffi, that boy with the hooked nose and the postage-stamps, who was wholly occupied in making a catalogue of the subscribers at two centesimi each, for a lottery for a pocket inkstand. The rest chattered and laughed, pounded on the points of pens fixed in the benches, and snapped pellets of paper at each other with the elastics of their garters.

The assistant grasped now one, now another, by the arm, and shook him; and he placed one of them against the wall--time wasted. He no longer knew what to do, and he entreated them. "Why do you behave like this? Do you wish me to punish you by force?" Then he thumped the little table with his fist, and shouted in a voice of wrath and lamentation, "Silence! silence! silence!" It was difficult to hear him. But the uproar continued to increase. Franti threw a paper dart at him, some uttered cat-calls, others thumped each other on the head; the hurly-burly was indescribable; when, all of a sudden, the beadle entered and said:

"Signor Master, the head-master has sent for you." The master rose and went out in haste, with a gesture of despair. Then the tumult began more vigorously than ever. But suddenly Garrone sprang up, his face all convulsed, and his fists clenched, and shouted in a voice choked with rage:

"Stop this! You are brutes! You take advantage of him because he is kind. If he were to bruise your bones for you, you would be as abject as dogs. You are a pack of cowards! The first one of you that jeers at him again, I shall wait for outside, and I will break his teeth,--I swear it,--even under the very eyes of his father!"

All became silent. Ah, what a fine thing it was to see Garrone, with his eyes darting flames! He seemed to be a furious young lion. He stared at the most daring, one after the other, and all hung their heads. When the assistant re-entered, with red eyes, not a breath was audible. He stood in amazement; then, catching sight of Garrone, who was still all fiery and trembling, he understood it all, and he said to him, with accents of great affection, as he might have spoken to a brother, "I thank you, Garrone."

## STARDI'S LIBRARY

I have been home with Stardi, who lives opposite the schoolhouse; and I really experienced a feeling of envy at the sight of his library. He is not at all rich, and he cannot buy many books; but he preserves his schoolbooks with great care, as well as those which his relatives give him; and he lays aside every soldo that is given to him, and spends it at the bookseller's. In this way he has collected a little library; and when his father perceived that he had this passion, he bought him a handsome bookcase of walnut wood, with a green curtain, and he has had most of his volumes bound for him in the colors that he likes. Thus when he draws a little cord, the green curtain runs aside, and three rows of books of every color become visible, all ranged in order, and shining, with gilt titles on their backs,--books of tales, of travels, and of poetry; and some illustrated ones. And he understands how to combine colors well: he places the white volumes next to the red ones, the yellow next the black, the blue beside the white, so that, viewed from a distance, they make a very fine appearance; and he amuses himself by varying the combinations. He has made himself a catalogue. He is like a librarian. He is always standing near his books, dusting them, turning over the leaves, examining the bindings: it is something to see the care with which he opens them, with his big, stubby hands, and blows between the pages: then they seem perfectly new again. I have worn out all of mine. It is a festival for him to polish off every new book that he buys, to put it in its place, and to pick it up again to take another look at it from all sides, and to brood over it as a treasure. He showed me nothing else for a whole hour. His eyes were troubling him, because he had read too much. At a certain time his father, who is large and thickset like himself, with a big head like his, entered the room, and gave him two or three taps on the nape of the neck, saying with that huge voice of his:

"What do you think of him, eh? of this head of bronze? It is a stout head, that will succeed in anything, I assure you!"

And Stardi half closed his eyes, under these rough caresses, like a big hunting-dog. I do not know, I did not dare to jest with him; it did not seem true to me, that he was only a year older than myself; and when he said to me, "Farewell until we meet again," at the door, with that face of his that always seems wrathful, I came very near replying to him, "I salute you, sir," as to a man. I told my father afterwards, at home: "I don't understand it; Stardi has no natural talent, he has not fine manners, and his face is almost ridiculous; yet he suggests ideas to me." And my father answered, "It is because he has character." And I added, "During the hour that I spent with him he did not utter fifty words, he did not show me a single plaything, he did not laugh once; yet I liked to go there."

And my father answered, "That is because you esteem him."

## THE SON OF THE BLACKSMITH-IRONMONGER

Yes, but I also esteem Precossi; and to say that I esteem him is not enough,--Precossi, the son of the blacksmith-ironmonger,--that thin little fellow, who has kind, melancholy eyes and a frightened air; who is so timid that he says to every one, "Excuse me"; who is always sickly, and who, nevertheless, studies so much. His father returns home, intoxicated with brandy, and beats him without the slightest reason in the world, and flings his books and his copy-books in the air with a backward turn of his hand; and he comes to school with the black and blue marks on his face, and sometimes with his face all swollen, and his eyes inflamed with much weeping. But never, never can he be made to acknowledge that his father beats him.

"Your father has been beating you," his companions say to him; and he instantly exclaims, "That is not true! it is not true!" for the sake of not dishonoring his father.

"You did not burn this leaf," the teacher says to him, showing him his work, half burned.

"Yes," he replies, in a trembling voice; "I let it fall on the fire."

But we know very well, nevertheless, that his drunken father overturned the table and the light with a kick, while the boy was doing his work. He lives in a garret of our house, on another staircase. The portress tells my mother everything: my sister Silvia heard him screaming from the terrace one day, when his father had sent him headlong down stairs, because he had asked for a few soldi to buy a grammar. His father drinks, but does not work, and his family suffers from hunger. How often Precossi comes to school with an empty stomach and nibbles in secret at a roll which Garrone has given him, or at an apple brought to him by the schoolmistress with the red feather, who was his teacher in the first lower class. But he never says, "I am hungry; my father does not give me anything to eat." His father sometimes comes for him, when he chances to be passing the schoolhouse,-- pallid, unsteady on his legs, with a fierce face, and his hair over his eyes, and his cap awry; and the poor boy trembles all over when he catches sight of him in the street; but he immediately runs to meet him, with a smile; and his father does not appear to see him, but seems to be thinking of something else. Poor Precossi! He mends his torn copy-books, borrows books to study his lessons, fastens the fragments of his shirt together with pins; and it is a pity to see him performing his gymnastics, with those huge shoes in which he is fairly lost, in those trousers which drag on the ground, and that jacket which is too long, and those huge sleeves turned back to the very elbows. And he studies; he does his best; he would be one of the first, if he were able to work at home in peace. This morning he came to school with the marks of finger-nails on one cheek, and they all began to say to him:

"It is your father, and you cannot deny it this time; it was your father who did that to you. Tell the head-master about it, and he will have him called to account for it."

But he sprang up, all flushed, with a voice trembling with indignation:

"It's not true! it's not true! My father never beats me!"

But afterwards, during lesson time, his tears fell upon the bench, and when any one looked at him, he tried to smile, in order that he might not show it. Poor Precossi! Tomorrow Derossi, Coretti, and Nelli are coming to my house; I want to tell him to come also; and I want to have him take luncheon with me: I want to treat him to books, and turn the house upside down to amuse him, and to fill his pockets with fruit, for the sake of seeing him contented for once, poor Precossi! who is so good and so courageous.


A FINE VISIT

Thursday, 12th.

This has been one of the finest Thursdays of the year for me. At two o'clock, precisely, Derossi and Coretti came to the house, with Nelli, the hunchback: Precossi was not permitted by his father to come. Derossi and Coretti were still laughing at their encounter with Crossi, the son of the vegetable-seller, in the street,--the boy with the useless arm and the red hair,--who was carrying a huge cabbage for sale, and with the soldo which he was to receive for the cabbage he was to go and buy a pen. He was perfectly happy because his father had written from America that they might expect him any day. Oh, the two beautiful hours that we passed together! Derossi and Coretti are the two jolliest boys in the school; my father fell in love with them. Coretti had on his chocolate-colored tights and his catskin cap. He is a lively imp, who wants to be always doing something, stirring up something, setting something in motion. He had already carried on his shoulders half a cartload of wood, early that morning; nevertheless, he galloped all over the house, taking note of everything and talking incessantly, as sprightly and nimble as a squirrel; and passing into the kitchen, he asked the cook how much we had to pay a myriagramme for wood, because his father sells it at forty-five centesimi. He is always talking of his father, of the time when he was a soldier in the 49th regiment, at the battle of Custoza, where he served in the squadron of Prince Umberto; and he is so gentle in his manners! It makes no difference that he was born and brought up surrounded by wood: he has nobility in his blood, in his heart, as my father says. And Derossi amused us greatly; he knows geography like a master: he shut his eyes and said:

"There, I see the whole of Italy; the Apennines, which extend to the Ionian Sea, the rivers flowing here and there, the white cities, the gulfs, the blue bays, the green islands;" and he repeated the names correctly in their order and very rapidly, as though he were reading them on the map; and at the sight of him standing thus, with his head held high, with all his golden curls, with his closed eyes, and all dressed in bright blue with gilt buttons, as straight and handsome as a statue, we were all filled with admiration. In one hour he had learned by heart nearly three pages, which he is to recite the day after tomorrow, for the anniversary of the funeral of King Vittorio. And even Nelli gazed at him in wonder and affection, as he rubbed the folds of his apron of black cloth, and smiled with his clear and mournful eyes. This visit gave me a great deal of pleasure; it left something like sparks in my mind and my heart. And it pleased me, too, when they went away, to see poor Nelli between the other two tall, strong fellows, who carried him home on their arms, and made him laugh as I have never seen him laugh before. On returning to the dining-room, I perceived that the picture representing Rigoletto, the hunchbacked jester, was no longer there. My father had taken it away in order that Nelli might not see it.

## THE FUNERAL OF VITTORIO EMANUELE

January, 17th.

Today, at two o'clock, as soon as we entered the schoolroom, the master called up Derossi, who went and took his place in front of the little table facing us, and began to recite, in his vibrating tones, gradually raising his limpid voice, and growing flushed in the face:

"Four years ago, on this day, at this hour, there arrived in front of the Pantheon at Rome, the funeral car which bore the body of Vittorio Emanuele II., the first king of Italy, dead after a reign of twenty-nine years, during which the great Italian fatherland, broken up into seven states, and oppressed by strangers and by tyrants, had been brought back to life in one single state, free and independent; after a reign of twenty-nine years, which he had made illustrious and beneficent with his valor, with loyalty, with boldness amid perils, with wisdom amid triumphs, with constancy amid misfortunes. The funeral car arrived, laden with wreaths, after having traversed Rome under a rain of flowers, amid the silence of an immense and sorrowing multitude, which had assembled from every part of Italy; preceded by a legion of generals and by a throng of ministers and princes, followed by a retinue of crippled veterans, by a forest of banners, by the envoys of three hundred towns, by everything which represents the power and the glory of a people, it arrived before the august temple where the tomb awaited it. At that moment twelve cuirassiers removed the coffin from the car. At that moment Italy bade her last farewell to her dead king, to her old king whom she had loved so dearly, the last farewell to her soldier, to her father, to the twenty-nine most fortunate and most blessed years in her history. It was a grand and solemn moment. The looks, the souls, of all were quivering at the sight of that coffin and the darkened banners of the eighty regiments of the army of Italy, borne by eighty officers, drawn up in line on its passage: for Italy was there in those eighty tokens, which recalled the thousands of dead, the torrents of blood, our most sacred glories, our most holy sacrifices, our most tremendous griefs. The coffin, borne by the cuirassiers, passed, and then the banners bent forward all together in salute,--the banners of the new regiments, the old, tattered banners of Goito, of Pastrengo, of Santa Lucia, of Novara, of the Crimea, of Palestro, of San Martino, of Castelfidardo; eighty black veils fell, a hundred medals clashed against the staves, and that sonorous and confused uproar, which stirred the blood of all, was like the sound of a thousand human voices saying all together, 'Farewell, good king, gallant king, loyal king! Thou wilt live in the heart of thy people as long as the sun shall shine over Italy.'

"After this, the banners rose heavenward once more, and King Vittorio entered into the immortal glory of the tomb."

## FRANTI EXPELLED FROM SCHOOL

Saturday, 21st.

Only one boy was capable of laughing while Derossi was declaiming the funeral oration of the king, and Franti laughed. I detest that fellow. He is wicked. When a father comes to the school to reprove his son, he enjoys it; when any one cries, he laughs. He trembles before Garrone, and he strikes the little mason because he is small; he torments Crossi because he has a helpless arm; he ridicules Precossi, whom every one respects; he even jeers at Robetti, that boy in the second grade who walks on crutches, through having saved a child. He provokes those who are weaker than himself, and when it comes to blows, he grows ferocious and tries to do harm. There is something beneath that low forehead, in those turbid eyes, which he keeps nearly concealed under the visor of his small cap of waxed cloth, which inspires a shudder. He fears no one; he laughs in the master's face; he steals when he gets a chance; he denies it with an impenetrable countenance; he is always engaged in a quarrel with some one; he brings big pins to school, to prick his neighbors with; he tears the buttons from his own jackets and from those of others, and plays with them: his paper, books, and copy-books are all crushed, torn, dirty; his ruler is jagged, his pens gnawed, his nails bitten, his clothes covered with stains and rents which he has got in his brawls. They say that his mother has fallen ill from the trouble that he causes her, and that his father has driven him from the house three times; his mother comes every now and then to make inquiries, and she always goes away in tears. He hates school, he hates his companions, he hates the teacher. The master sometimes pretends not to see his rascalities, and he behaves all the worse. He tried to get a hold on him by kind treatment, and the boy ridiculed him for it. He said terrible things to him, and the boy covered his face with his hands, as though he were crying; but he was laughing. He was suspended from school for three days, and he returned more perverse and insolent than before. Derossi said to him one day, "Stop it! don't you see how much the teacher suffers?" and the other threatened to stick a nail into his stomach. But this morning, at last, he got himself driven out like a dog. While the master was giving to Garrone the rough draft of *The Sardinian Drummer-Boy*, the monthly story for January, to copy, he threw a petard on the floor, which exploded, making the schoolroom resound as from a discharge of musketry. The whole class was startled by it. The master sprang to his feet, and cried:

"Franti, leave the school!"

The latter retorted, "It wasn't I;" but he laughed. The master repeated:

"Go!"

"I won't stir," he answered.

Then the master lost his temper, and flung himself upon him, seized him by the arms, and tore him from his seat. He resisted, ground his teeth, and made him carry him out by main force. The master bore him thus, heavy as he was, to the head-master, and then returned to the schoolroom alone and seated himself at his little table, with his head clutched in his hands, gasping, and with an expression of such weariness and trouble that it was painful to look at him.

"After teaching school for thirty years!" he exclaimed sadly, shaking his head. No one breathed. His hands were trembling with fury, and the perpendicular wrinkle that he has in the middle of his forehead was so deep that it seemed like a wound. Poor master! All felt sorry for him. Derossi rose and said, "Signor Master, do not grieve. We love you." And then he grew a little more tranquil, and said, "We will go on with the lesson, boys."

## THE SARDINIAN DRUMMER-BOY

(*Monthly Story.*)

On the first day of the battle of Custoza, on the 24th of July, 1848, about sixty soldiers, belonging to an infantry regiment of our army, who had been sent to an elevation to occupy an isolated house, suddenly found themselves assaulted by two companies of Austrian soldiers, who, showering them with bullets from various quarters, hardly gave them time to take refuge in the house and to barricade the doors, after leaving several dead and wounded on the field. Having barred the doors, our men ran in haste to the windows of the ground floor and the first story, and began to fire brisk discharges at their assailants, who, approaching gradually, ranged in a semicircle, made vigorous reply. The sixty Italian soldiers were commanded by two non-commissioned officers and a captain, a tall, dry, austere old man, with white hair and mustache; and with them there was a Sardinian drummer-boy, a lad of a little over fourteen, who did not look twelve, small, with an olive-brown complexion, and two small, deep, sparkling eyes. The captain directed the defence from a room on the first floor, launching commands that seemed like pistol-shots, and no sign of emotion was visible on his iron countenance. The drummer-boy, a little pale, but firm on his legs, had jumped upon a table, and was holding fast to the wall and stretching out his neck in order to gaze out of the windows, and athwart the smoke on the fields he saw the white uniforms of the Austrians, who were slowly advancing. The house was situated at the summit of a steep declivity, and on the side of the slope it had but one high window, corresponding to a chamber in the roof: therefore the Austrians did not threaten the house from that quarter, and the slope was free; the fire beat only upon the front and the two ends.

But it was an infernal fire, a hailstorm of leaden bullets, which split the walls on the outside, ground the tiles to powder, and in the interior cracked ceilings, furniture, window-frames, and door-frames, sending splinters of wood flying through the air, and clouds of plaster, and fragments of kitchen utensils and glass, whizzing, and rebounding, and breaking everything with a noise like the crushing of a skull. From time to time one of the soldiers who were firing from the windows fell crashing back to the floor, and was dragged to one side. Some staggered from room to room, pressing their hands on their wounds. There was already one dead body in the kitchen, with its forehead cleft. The semicircle of the enemy was drawing together.

At a certain point the captain, hitherto impassive, was seen to make a gesture of uneasiness, and to leave the room with huge strides, followed by a sergeant. Three minutes later the sergeant returned on a run, and summoned the drummer-boy, making him a sign to follow. The lad followed him at a quick pace up the wooden staircase, and entered with him into a bare garret, where he saw the captain writing with a pencil on a sheet of paper, as he leaned against the little window; and on the floor at his feet lay the well-rope.

The captain folded the sheet of paper, and said sharply, as he fixed his cold gray eyes, before which all the soldiers trembled, on the boy:

"Drummer!"

The drummer-boy put his hand to his visor.

The captain said, "You have courage."

The boy's eyes flashed.

"Yes, captain," he replied.

"Look down there," said the captain, pushing him to the window; "on the plain, near the houses of Villafranca, where there is a gleam of bayonets. There stand our troops, motionless. You are to take this billet, tie yourself to the rope, descend from the window, get down that slope in an instant, make your way across the fields, arrive at our men, and give the note to the first officer you see. Throw off your belt and knapsack."

The drummer took off his belt and knapsack and thrust the note into his breast pocket; the sergeant flung the rope out of the window, and held one end of it clutched fast in his hands; the captain helped the lad to clamber out of the small window, with his back turned to the landscape.

"Now look out," he said; "the salvation of this detachment lies in your courage and in your legs."

"Trust to me, Signor Captain," replied the drummer-boy, as he let himself down.

"Bend over on the slope," said the captain, grasping the rope, with the sergeant.

"Never fear."

"God aid you!"

In a few moments the drummer-boy was on the ground; the sergeant drew in the rope and disappeared; the captain stepped impetuously in front of the window and saw the boy flying down the slope.

He was already hoping that he had succeeded in escaping unobserved, when five or six little puffs of powder, which rose from the earth in front of and behind the lad, warned him that he had been espied by the Austrians, who were firing down upon him from the top of the elevation: these little clouds were thrown into the air by the bullets. But the drummer continued to run at a headlong speed. All at once he fell to the earth. "He is killed!" roared the captain, biting his fist. But before he had uttered the word he saw the drummer spring up again. "Ah, only a fall," he said to himself, and drew a long breath. The drummer, in fact, set out again at full speed; but he limped. "He has turned his ankle," thought the captain. Again several cloudlets of powder smoke rose here and there about the lad, but ever more distant. He was safe. The captain uttered an exclamation of triumph. But he continued to follow him with his eyes, trembling because it was an affair of minutes: if he did not arrive yonder in the shortest possible time with that billet, which called for instant succor, either all his soldiers would be killed or he should be obliged to surrender himself a prisoner with them.

The boy ran rapidly for a space, then relaxed his pace and limped, then resumed his course, but grew constantly more fatigued, and every little while he stumbled and paused.

"Perhaps a bullet has grazed him," thought the captain, and he noted all his movements, quivering with excitement; and he encouraged him, he spoke to him, as though he could hear him; he measured incessantly, with a flashing eye, the space intervening between the fleeing boy and that gleam of arms which he could see in the distance on the plain amid the fields of grain gilded by the sun. And meanwhile he heard the whistle and the crash of the bullets in the rooms beneath, the imperious and angry shouts of the sergeants and the officers, the piercing laments of the wounded, the ruin of furniture, and the fall of rubbish.

"On! courage!" he shouted, following the far-off drummer with his glance. "Forward! run! He halts, that cursed boy! Ah, he resumes his course!"

An officer came panting to tell him that the enemy, without slackening their fire, were flinging out a white flag to hint at a surrender. "Don't reply to them!" he cried, without detaching his eyes from the boy, who was already on the plain, but who was no longer running, and who seemed to be dragging himself along with difficulty.

"Go! run!" said the captain, clenching his teeth and his fists; "let them kill you; die, you rascal, but go!" Then he uttered a horrible oath. "Ah, the infamous poltroon! he has sat down!" In fact, the boy, whose head he had hitherto been able to see projecting above a field of grain, had disappeared, as though he had fallen; but, after the lapse of a minute, his head came into sight again; finally, it was lost behind the hedges, and the captain saw it no more.

Then he descended impetuously; the bullets were coming in a tempest; the rooms were encumbered with the wounded, some of whom were whirling round like drunken men, and clutching at the furniture; the walls and floor were bespattered with blood; corpses lay across the doorways; the lieutenant had had his arm shattered by a ball; smoke and clouds of dust enveloped everything.

"Courage!" shouted the captain. "Stand firm at your post! Succor is on the way! Courage for a little while longer!"

The Austrians had approached still nearer: their contorted faces were already visible through the smoke, and amid the crash of the firing their savage and offensive shouts were audible, as they uttered insults, suggested a surrender, and threatened slaughter. Some soldiers were terrified, and withdrew from the windows; the sergeants drove them forward again. But the fire of the defence weakened; discouragement made its appearance on all faces. It was not possible to protract the resistance longer. At a given moment the fire of the Austrians slackened, and a thundering voice shouted, first in German and then in Italian, "Surrender!"

"No!" howled the captain from a window.

And the firing recommenced more fast and furious on both sides. More soldiers fell. Already more than one window was without defenders. The fatal moment was near at hand. The captain shouted through his teeth, in a strangled voice, "They are not coming! they are not coming!" and rushed wildly about, twisting his sword about in his convulsively clenched hand, and resolved to die; when a sergeant descending from the garret, uttered a piercing shout, "They are coming!" "They are coming!" repeated the captain, with a cry of joy.

At that cry all, well and wounded, sergeants and officers, rushed to the windows, and the resistance became fierce once more. A few moments later a sort of uncertainty was noticeable, and a beginning of disorder among the foe. Suddenly the captain hastily collected a little troop in the room on the ground floor, in order to make a sortie with fixed bayonets. Then he flew up stairs. Scarcely had he arrived there when they heard a hasty trampling of feet, accompanied by a formidable hurrah, and saw from the windows the two-pointed hats of the Italian carabineers advancing through the smoke, a squadron rushing forward at great speed, and a lightning flash of blades whirling in the air, as they fell on heads, on shoulders, and on backs. Then the troop darted out of the door, with bayonets lowered; the enemy wavered, were thrown into disorder, and turned their backs; the field was left unincumbered, the house was free, and a little later two battalions of Italian infantry and two cannons occupied the eminence.

The captain, with the soldiers that remained to him, rejoined his regiment, went on fighting, and was slightly wounded in the left hand by a bullet on the rebound, in the final assault with bayonets.

The day ended with the victory on our side.

But on the following day, the conflict having begun again, the Italians were overpowered by the overwhelming numbers of the Austrians, in spite of a valorous resistance, and on the morning of the 27th they sadly retreated towards the Mincio.

The captain, although wounded, made the march on foot with his soldiers, weary and silent, and, arrived at the close of the day at Goito, on the Mincio, he immediately sought out his lieutenant, who had been picked up with his arm shattered, by our ambulance corps, and who must have arrived before him. He was directed to a church, where the field hospital had been installed in haste. Thither he betook himself. The church was full of wounded men, ranged in two lines of beds, and on mattresses spread on the floor; two doctors and numerous assistants were going and coming, busily occupied; and suppressed cries and groans were audible.

No sooner had the captain entered than he halted and cast a glance around, in search of his officer.

At that moment he heard himself called in a weak voice,--"Signor Captain!" He turned round. It was his drummer-boy. He was lying on a cot bed, covered to the breast with a coarse window curtain, in red and white squares, with his arms on the outside, pale and thin, but with eyes which still sparkled like black gems.

"Are you here?" asked the captain, amazed, but still sharply. "Bravo! You did your duty."

"I did all that I could," replied the drummer-boy.

"Were you wounded?" said the captain, seeking with his eyes for his officer in the neighboring beds.

"What could one expect?" said the lad, who gained courage by speaking, expressing the lofty satisfaction of having been wounded for the first time, without which he would not have dared to open his mouth in the presence of this captain; "I had a fine run, all bent over, but suddenly they caught sight of me. I should have arrived twenty minutes earlier if they had not hit me. Luckily, I soon came across a captain of the staff, to whom I gave the note. But it was hard work to get down after that caress! I was dying of thirst. I was afraid that I should not get there at all. I wept with rage at the thought that at every moment of delay another man was setting out yonder for the other world. But enough! I did what I could. I am content. But, with your permission, captain, you should look to yourself: you are losing blood."

Several drops of blood had in fact trickled down on the captain's fingers from his imperfectly bandaged palm.

"Would you like to have me give the bandage a turn, captain? Hold it here a minute."

The captain held out his left hand, and stretched out his right to help the lad to loosen the knot and to tie it again; but no sooner had the boy raised himself from his pillow than he turned pale and was obliged to support his head once more.

"That will do, that will do," said the captain, looking at him and withdrawing his bandaged hand, which the other tried to retain. "Attend to your own affairs, instead of thinking of others, for things that are not severe may become serious if they are neglected."

The drummer-boy shook his head.

"But you," said the captain, observing him attentively, "must have lost a great deal of blood to be as weak as this."

"Must have lost a great deal of blood!" replied the boy, with a smile. "Something else besides blood: look here." And with one movement he drew aside the coverlet.

The captain started back a pace in horror.

The lad had but one leg. His left leg had been amputated above the knee; the stump was swathed in blood-stained cloths.

At that moment a small, plump, military surgeon passed, in his shirt-sleeves. "Ah, captain," he said, rapidly, nodding towards the drummer, "this is an unfortunate case; there is a leg that might have been saved if he had not exerted himself in such a crazy manner--that cursed inflammation! It had to be cut off away up here. Oh, but he's a brave lad. I can assure you! He never shed a tear, nor uttered a cry! He was proud of being an Italian boy, while I was performing the operation, upon my word of honor. He comes of a good race, by Heavens!" And away he went, on a run.

The captain wrinkled his heavy white brows, gazed fixedly at the drummer-boy, and spread the coverlet over him again, and slowly, then as though unconsciously, and still gazing intently at him, he raised his hand to his head, and lifted his cap.

"Signor Captain!" exclaimed the boy in amazement. "What are you doing, captain? To me!"

And then that rough soldier, who had never said a gentle word to an inferior, replied in an indescribably sweet and affectionate voice, "I am only a captain; you are a hero."

Then he threw himself with wide-spread arms upon the drummer-boy, and kissed him three times upon the heart.


THE LOVE OF COUNTRY

Tuesday, 24th.

Since the tale of the *Drummer-boy* has touched your heart, it should be easy for you this morning to do your composition for examination--*Why you love Italy*--well. Why do I love Italy? Do not a hundred answers present themselves to you on the instant? I love Italy because my mother is an Italian; because the blood that flows in my veins is Italian; because the soil in which are buried the dead whom my mother mourns and whom my father venerates is Italian; because the town in which I was born, the language that I speak, the books that educate me,--because my brother, my sister, my comrades, the great people among whom I live, and the beautiful nature which surrounds me, and all that I see, that I love, that I study, that I admire, is Italian. Oh, you cannot feel that affection in its entirety! You will feel it when you become a man; when, returning from a long journey, after a prolonged absence, you step up in the morning to the bulwarks of the vessel and see on the distant horizon the lofty blue mountains of your country; you will feel it then in the impetuous flood of tenderness which will fill your eyes with tears and will wrest a cry from your heart. You will feel it in some great and distant city, in that impulse of the soul which will impel you from the strange throng towards a workingman from whom you have heard in passing a word in your own tongue. You will feel it in that sad and proud wrath which will drive the blood to your brow when you hear insults to your country from the mouth of a stranger. You will feel it in more proud and vigorous measure on the day when the menace of a hostile race shall call forth a tempest of fire upon your country, and when you shall behold arms raging on every side, youths thronging in legions, fathers kissing their children and saying, "Courage!" mothers bidding adieu to their young sons and crying, "Conquer!" You will feel it like a joy divine if you have the good fortune to behold the re-entrance to your town of the regiments, weary, ragged, with thinned ranks, yet terrible, with the splendor of victory in their eyes, and their banners torn by bullets, followed by a vast convoy of brave fellows, bearing their bandaged heads and their stumps of arms loftily, amid a wild throng, which covers them with flowers, with blessings, and with kisses. Then you will comprehend the love of country; then you will feel your country, Enrico. It is a grand and sacred thing. May I one day see you return in safety from a battle fought for her, safe,--you who are my flesh and soul; but if I should learn that you have preserved your life because you were concealed from death, your father, who welcomes you with a cry of joy when you return from school, will receive you with a sob of anguish, and I shall never be able to love you again, and I shall die with that dagger in my heart.

THY FATHER.


ENVY

Wednesday, 25th.

The boy who wrote the best composition of all on our country was Derossi, as usual. And Votini, who thought himself sure of the first medal--I like Votini well enough, although he is rather vain and does polish himself up a trifle too much,--but it makes me scorn him, now that I am his neighbor on the bench, to see how envious he is of Derossi. He would like to vie with him; he studies hard, but he cannot do it by any possibility, for the other is ten times as strong as he is on every point; and Votini rails at him. Carlo Nobis envies him also; but he has so much pride in his body that, purely from pride, he does not allow it to be perceived. Votini, on the other hand, betrays himself: he complains of his difficulties at home, and says that the master is unjust to him; and when Derossi replies so promptly and so well to questions, as he always does, his face clouds over, he hangs his head, pretends not to hear, or tries to laugh, but he laughs awkwardly. And thus every one knows about it, so that when the master praises Derossi they all turn to look at Votini, who chews his venom, and the little mason makes a hare's face at him. Today, for instance, he was put to the torture. The head-master entered the school and announced the result of the examination,-- "Derossi ten tenths and the first medal."

Votini gave a huge sneeze. The master looked at him: it was not hard to understand the matter. "Votini," he said, "do not let the serpent of envy enter your body; it is a serpent which gnaws at the brain and corrupts the heart."

Every one stared at him except Derossi. Votini tried to make some answer, but could not; he sat there as though turned to stone, and with a white face. Then, while the master was conducting the lesson, he began to write in large characters on a sheet of paper, "*I am not envious of those who gain the first medal through favoritism and injustice.*" It was a note which he meant to send to Derossi. But, in the meantime, I perceived that Derossi's neighbors were plotting among themselves, and whispering in each other's ears, and one cut with penknife from paper a big medal on which they had drawn a black serpent. But Votini did not notice this. The master went out for a few moments. All at once Derossi's neighbors rose and left their seats, for the purpose of coming and solemnly presenting the paper medal to Votini. The whole class was prepared for a scene. Votini had already begun to quiver all over. Derossi exclaimed:

"Give that to me!"

"So much the better," they replied; "you are the one who ought to carry it."

Derossi took the medal and tore it into bits. At that moment the master returned, and resumed the lesson. I kept my eye on Votini. He had turned as red as a coal. He took his sheet of paper very, very quietly, as though in absence of mind, rolled it into a ball, on the sly, put it into his mouth, chewed it a little, and then spit it out under the bench. When school broke up, Votini, who was a little confused, let fall his blotting-paper, as he passed Derossi. Derossi politely picked it up, put it in his satchel, and helped him to buckle the straps. Votini dared not raise his eyes.

## FRANTI'S MOTHER

Saturday, 28th.

But Votini is incorrigible. Yesterday morning, during the lesson on religion, in the presence of the head-master, the teacher asked Derossi if he knew by heart the two couplets in the reading-book,--

"Where'er I turn my gaze, 'tis Thee, great God, I see."

Derossi said that he did not, and Votini suddenly exclaimed, "I know them!" with a smile, as though to pique Derossi. But he was piqued himself, instead, for he could not recite the poetry, because Franti's mother suddenly flew into the schoolroom, breathless, with her gray hair dishevelled and all wet with snow, and pushing before her her son, who had been suspended from school for a week. What a sad scene we were doomed to witness! The poor woman flung herself almost on her knees before the head-master, with clasped hands, and besought him:

"Oh, Signor Director, do me the favor to put my boy back in school! He has been at home for three days. I have kept him hidden; but God have mercy on him, if his father finds out about this affair: he will murder him! Have pity! I no longer know what to do! I entreat you with my whole soul!"

The director tried to lead her out, but she resisted, still continuing to pray and to weep.

"Oh, if you only knew the trouble that this boy has caused me, you would have compassion! Do me this favor! I hope that he will reform. I shall not live long, Signor Director; I bear death within me; but I should like to see him reformed before my death, because"--and she broke into a passion of weeping--"he is my son--I love him--I shall die in despair! Take him back once more, Signor Director, that a misfortune may not happen in the family! Do it out of pity for a poor woman!" And she covered her face with her hands and sobbed.

Franti stood impassive, and hung his head. The head-master looked at him, reflected a little, then said, "Franti, go to your place."

Then the woman removed her hands from her face, quite comforted, and began to express thanks upon thanks, without giving the director a chance to speak, and made her way towards the door, wiping her eyes, and saying hastily: "I beg of you, my son.--May all have patience.--Thanks, Signor Director; you have performed a deed of mercy.--Be a good boy.--Good day, boys.--Thanks, Signor Teacher; good by, and forgive a poor mother." And after bestowing another supplicating glance at her son from the door, she went away, pulling up the shawl which was trailing after her, pale, bent, with a head which still trembled, and we heard her coughing all the way down the stairs. The head-master gazed intently at Franti, amid the silence of the class, and said to him in accents of a kind to make him tremble:

"Franti, you are killing your mother!"

We all turned to look at Franti; and that infamous boy smiled.


HOPE

Sunday, 29th.

Very beautiful, Enrico, was the impetuosity with which you flung yourself on your mother's heart on your return from your lesson of religion. Yes, your master said grand and consoling things to you. God threw you in each other's arms; he will never part you. When I die, when your father dies, we shall not speak to each other these despairing words, "Mamma, papa, Enrico, I shall never see you again!" We shall see each other again in another life, where he who has suffered much in this life will receive compensation; where he who has loved much on earth will find again the souls whom he has loved, in a world without sin, without sorrow, and without death. But we must all render ourselves worthy of that other life. Reflect, my son. Every good action of yours, every impulse of affection for those who love you, every courteous act towards your companions, every noble thought of yours, is like a leap towards that other world. And every misfortune, also, serves to raise you towards that world; every sorrow, for every sorrow is the expiation of a sin, every tear blots out a stain. Make it your rule to become better and more loving every day than the day before. Say every morning, "Today I will do something for which my conscience will praise me, and with which my father will be satisfied; something which will render me beloved by such or such a comrade, by my teacher, by my brother, or by others." And beseech God to give you the strength to put your resolution into practice. "Lord, I wish to be good, noble, courageous, gentle, sincere; help me; grant that every night, when my mother gives me her last kiss, I may be able to say to her, 'You kiss this night a nobler and more worthy boy than you kissed last night.'" Keep always in your thoughts that other superhuman and blessed Enrico which you may be after this life. And pray. You cannot imagine the sweetness that you experience,--how much better a mother feels when she sees her child with hands clasped in prayer. When I behold you praying, it seems impossible to me that there should not be some one there gazing at you and listening to you. Then I believe more firmly that there is a supreme goodness and an infinite pity; I love you more, I work with more ardor, I endure with more force, I forgive with all my heart, and I think of death with serenity. O great and good God! To hear once more, after death, the voice of my mother, to meet my children again, to see my Enrico once more, my Enrico, blessed and immortal, and to clasp him in an embrace which shall nevermore be loosed, nevermore, nevermore to all eternity! Oh, pray! let us pray, let us love each other, let us be good, let us bear this celestial hope in our hearts and souls, my adored child!

THY MOTHER.

# FEBRUARY

## A MEDAL WELL BESTOWED

Saturday, 4th.

THIS morning the superintendent of the schools, a gentleman with a white beard, and dressed in black, came to bestow the medals. He entered with the head-master a little before the close and seated himself beside the teacher. He questioned a few, then gave the first medal to Derossi, and before giving the second, he stood for a few moments listening to the teacher and the head-master, who were talking to him in a low voice. All were asking themselves, "To whom will he give the second?" The superintendent said aloud:

"Pupil Pietro Precossi has merited the second medal this week,--merited it by his work at home, by his lessons, by his handwriting, by his conduct in every way." All turned to look at Precossi, and it was evident that all took pleasure in it. Precossi rose in such confusion that he did not know where he stood.

"Come here," said the superintendent. Precossi sprang up from his seat and stepped up to the master's table. The superintendent looked attentively at that little waxen face, at that puny body enveloped in turned and ill-fitting garments, at those kind, sad eyes, which avoided his, but which hinted at a story of suffering; then he said to him, in a voice full of affection, as he fastened the medal on his shoulder:

"I give you the medal, Precossi. No one is more worthy to wear it than you. I bestow it not only on your intelligence and your good will; I bestow it on your heart, I give it to your courage, to your character of a brave and good son. Is it not true," he added, turning to the class, "that he deserves it also on that score?"

"Yes, yes!" all answered, with one voice. Precossi made a movement of the throat as though he were swallowing something, and cast upon the benches a very sweet look, which was expressive of immense gratitude.

"Go, my dear boy," said the superintendent; "and may God protect you!"

It was the hour for dismissing the school. Our class got out before the others. As soon as we were outside the door, whom should we espy there, in the large hall, just at the entrance? The father of Precossi, the blacksmith, pallid as was his wont, with fierce face, hair hanging over his eyes, his cap awry, and unsteady on his legs. The teacher caught sight of him instantly, and whispered to the superintendent. The latter sought out Precossi in haste, and taking him by the hand, he led him to his father. The boy was trembling. The boy and the superintendent approached; many boys collected around them.

"Is it true that you are the father of this lad?" demanded the superintendent of the blacksmith, with a cheerful air, as though they were friends. And, without awaiting a reply:

"I rejoice with you. Look: he has won the second medal over fifty-four of his comrades. He has deserved it by his composition, his arithmetic, everything. He is a boy of great intelligence and good will, who will accomplish great things; a fine boy, who possesses the affection and esteem of all. You may feel proud of him, I assure you."

The blacksmith, who had stood there with open mouth listening to him, stared at the superintendent and the head-master, and then at his son, who was standing before him with downcast eyes and trembling; and as though he had remembered and comprehended then, for the first time, all that he had made the little fellow suffer, and all the goodness, the heroic constancy, with which the latter had borne it, he displayed in his countenance a certain stupid wonder, then a sullen remorse, and finally a sorrowful and impetuous tenderness, and with a rapid gesture he caught the boy round the head and strained him to his breast. We all passed before them. I invited him to come to the house on Thursday, with Garrone and Crossi; others saluted him; one bestowed a caress on him, another touched his medal, all said something to him; and his father stared at us in amazement, as he still held his son's head pressed to his breast, while the boy sobbed.

## GOOD RESOLUTIONS

Sunday, 5th.

That medal given to Precossi has awakened a remorse in me. I have never earned one yet! For some time past I have not been studying, and I am discontented with myself, and the teacher, my father and mother are discontented with me. I no longer experience the pleasure in amusing myself that I did formerly, when I worked with a will, and then sprang up from the table and ran to my games full of mirth, as though I had not played for a month. Neither do I sit down to the table with my family with the same contentment as of old. I have always a shadow in my soul, an inward voice, that says to me continually, "It won't do; it won't do."

In the evening I see a great many boys pass through the square on their return from work, in the midst of a group of workingmen, weary but merry. They step briskly along, impatient to reach their homes and suppers, and they talk loudly, laughing and slapping each other on the shoulder with hands blackened with coal, or whitened with plaster; and I reflect that they have been working since daybreak up to this hour. And with them are also many others, who are still smaller, who have been standing all day on the summits of roofs, in front of ovens, among machines, and in the water, and underground, with nothing to eat but a little bread; and I feel almost ashamed, I, who in all that time have accomplished nothing but scribble four small pages, and that reluctantly. Ah, I am discontented, discontented! I see plainly that my father is out of humor, and would like to tell me so; but he is sorry, and he is still waiting. My dear father, who works so hard! all is yours, all that I see around me in the house, all that I touch, all that I wear and eat, all that affords me instruction and diversion,--all is the fruit of your toil, and I do not work; all has cost you thought, privations, trouble, effort; and I make no effort. Ah, no; this is too unjust, and causes me too much pain. I will begin this very day; I will apply myself to my studies, like Stardi, with clenched fists and set teeth. I will set about it with all the strength of my will and my heart. I will conquer my drowsiness in the evening, I will come down promptly in the morning, I will cudgel my brains without ceasing, I will chastise my laziness without mercy. I will toil, suffer, even to the extent of making myself ill; but I will put a stop, once for all, to this languishing and tiresome life, which is degrading me and causing sorrow to others. Courage! to work! To work with all my soul, and all my nerves! To work, which will restore to me sweet repose, pleasing games, cheerful meals! To work, which will give me back again the kindly smile of my teacher, the blessed kiss of my father!

## THE ENGINE

Friday, 10th.

Precossi came to our house today with Garrone. I do not think that two sons of princes would have been received with greater delight. This is the first time that Garrone has been here, because he is rather shy, and then he is ashamed to show himself because he is so large, and is still in the third grade. We all went to open the door when they rang. Crossi did not come, because his father has at last arrived from America, after an absence of seven years. My mother kissed Precossi at once. My father introduced Garrone to her, saying:

"Here he is. This lad is not only a good boy; he is a man of honor and a gentleman."

And the boy dropped his big, shaggy head, with a sly smile at me. Precossi had on his medal, and he was happy, because his father has gone to work again, and has not drunk anything for the last five days, wants him to be always in the workshop to keep him company, and seems quite another man.

We began to play, and I brought out all my things. Precossi was enchanted with my train of cars, with the engine that goes of itself on being wound up. He had never seen anything of the kind. He devoured the little red and yellow cars with his eyes. I gave him the key to play with, and he knelt down to his amusement, and did not raise his head again. I have never seen him so pleased. He kept saying, "Excuse me, excuse me," to everything, and motioning to us with his hands, that we should not stop the engine; and then he picked it up and replaced the cars with a thousand precautions, as though they had been made of glass. He was afraid of tarnishing them with his breath, and he polished them up again, examining them top and bottom, and smiling to himself. We all stood around him and gazed at him. We looked at that slender neck, those poor little ears, which I had seen bleeding one day, that jacket with the sleeves turned up, from which projected two sickly little arms, which had been upraised to ward off blows from his face. Oh! at that moment I could have cast all my playthings and all my books at his feet, I could have torn the last morsel of bread from my lips to give to him, I could have divested myself of my clothing to clothe him, I could have flung myself on my knees to kiss his hand. "I will at least give you the train," I thought; but--was necessary to ask permission of my father. At that moment I felt a bit of paper thrust into my hand. I looked; it was written in pencil by my father; it said:

"Your train pleases Precossi. He has no playthings. Does your heart suggest nothing to you?"

Instantly I seized the engine and the cars in both hands, and placed the whole in his arms, saying:

"Take this; it is yours."

He looked at me, and did not understand. "It is yours," I said; "I give it to you."

Then he looked at my father and mother, in still greater astonishment, and asked me:

"But why?"

My father said to him:

"Enrico gives it to you because he is your friend, because he loves you--to celebrate your medal."

Precossi asked timidly:

"I may carry it away--home?"

"Of course!" we all responded. He was already at the door, but he dared not go out. He was happy! He begged our pardon with a mouth that smiled and quivered. Garrone helped him to wrap up the train in a handkerchief, and as he bent over, he made the things with which his pockets were filled rattle.

"Some day," said Precossi to me, "you shall come to the shop to see my father at work. I will give you some nails."

My mother put a little bunch of flowers into Garrone's buttonhole, for him to carry to his mother in her name. Garrone said, "Thanks," in his big voice, without raising his chin from his breast. But all his kind and noble soul shone in his eyes.


PRIDE

Saturday, 11th.

The idea of Carlo Nobis rubbing off his sleeve affectedly, when Precossi touches him in passing! That fellow is pride incarnate because his father is a rich man. But Derossi's father is rich too. He would like to have a bench to himself; he is afraid that the rest will soil it; he looks down on everybody and always has a scornful smile on his lips: woe to him who stumbles over his foot, when we go out in files two by two! For a mere trifle he flings an insulting word in your face, or a threat to get his father to come to the school. It is true that his father did give him a good lesson when he called the little son of the charcoal-man a ragamuffin. I have never seen so disagreeable a schoolboy! No one speaks to him, no one says good by to him when he goes out; there is not even a dog who would give him a suggestion when he does not know his lesson. And he cannot endure any one, and he pretends to despise Derossi more than all, because he is the head boy; and Garrone, because he is beloved by all. But Derossi pays no attention to him when he is by; and when the boys tell Garrone that Nobis has been speaking ill of him, he says:

"His pride is so senseless that it does not deserve even my passing notice."

But Coretti said to him one day, when he was smiling disdainfully at his catskin cap:

"Go to Derossi for a while, and learn how to play the gentleman!"

Yesterday he complained to the master, because the Calabrian touched his leg with his foot. The master asked the Calabrian:

"Did you do it intentionally?"--"No, sir," he replied, frankly.--"You are too petulant, Nobis."

And Nobis retorted, in his airy way, "I shall tell my father about it." Then the teacher got angry.

"Your father will tell you that you are in the wrong, as he has on other occasions. And besides that, it is the teacher alone who has the right to judge and punish in school." Then he added pleasantly:

"Come, Nobis, change your ways; be kind and courteous to your comrades. You see, we have here sons of workingmen and of gentlemen, of the rich and the poor, and all love each other and treat each other like brothers, as they are. Why do not you do like the rest? It would not cost you much to make every one like you, and you would be so much happier yourself, too!--Well, have you no reply to make me?"

Nobis, who had listened to him with his customary scornful smile, answered coldly:

"No, sir."

"Sit down," said the master to him. "I am sorry for you. You are a heartless boy."

This seemed to be the end of it all; but the little mason, who sits on the front bench, turned his round face towards Nobis, who sits on the back bench, and made such a fine and ridiculous hare's face at him, that the whole class burst into a shout of laughter. The master reproved him; but he was obliged to put his hand over his own mouth to conceal a smile. And even Nobis laughed, but not in a pleasant way.


THE WOUNDS OF LABOR

Monday, 15th.

Nobis can be paired off with Franti: neither of them was affected this morning in the presence of the terrible sight which passed before their eyes. On coming out of school, I was standing with my father and looking at some big rogues of the second grade, who had thrown themselves on their knees and were wiping off the ice with their cloaks and caps, in order to make slides more quickly, when we saw a crowd of people appear at the end of the street, walking hurriedly, all serious and seemingly terrified, and conversing in low tones. In the midst of them were three policemen, and behind the policemen two men carrying a litter. Boys hastened up from all quarters. The crowd advanced towards us. On the litter was stretched a man, pale as a corpse, with his head resting on one shoulder, and his hair tumbled and stained with blood, for he had been losing blood through the mouth and ears; and beside the litter walked a woman with a baby in her arms, who seemed crazy, and who shrieked from time to time, "He is dead! He is dead! He is dead!"

Behind the woman came a boy who had a portfolio under his arm and who was sobbing.

"What has happened?" asked my father. A neighbor replied, that the man was a mason who had fallen from the fourth story while at work. The bearers of the litter halted for a moment. Many turned away their faces in horror. I saw the schoolmistress of the red feather supporting my mistress of the upper first, who was almost in a swoon. At the same moment I felt a touch on the elbow; it was the little mason, who was ghastly white and trembling from head to foot. He was certainly thinking of his father. I was thinking of him, too. I, at least, am at peace in my mind while I am in school: I know that my father is at home, seated at his table, far removed from all danger; but how many of my companions think that their fathers are at work on a very high bridge or close to the wheels of a machine, and that a movement, a single false step, may cost them their lives! They are like so many sons of soldiers who have fathers in the battle. The little mason gazed and gazed, and trembled more and more, and my father noticed it and said:

"Go home, my boy; go at once to your father, and you will find him safe and tranquil; go!"

The little mason went off, turning round at every step. And in the meanwhile the crowd had begun to move again, and the woman to shriek in a way that rent the heart, "He is dead! He is dead! He is dead!"

"No, no; he is not dead," people on all sides said to her. But she paid no heed to them, and tore her hair. Then I heard an indignant voice say, "You are laughing!" and at the same moment I saw a bearded man staring in Franti's face. Then the man knocked his cap to the ground with his stick, saying:

"Uncover your head, you wicked boy, when a man wounded by labor is passing by!"

The crowd had already passed, and a long streak of blood was visible in the middle of the street.


THE PRISONER

Friday, 17th.

Ah, this is certainly the strangest event of the whole year! Yesterday morning my father took me to the suburbs of Moncalieri, to look at a villa which he thought of hiring for the coming summer, because we shall not go to Chieri again this year, and it turned out that the person who had the keys was a teacher who acts as secretary to the owner. He showed us the house, and then he took us to his own room, where he gave us something to drink. On his table, among the glasses, there was a wooden inkstand, of a conical form, carved in a singular manner. Perceiving that my father was looking at it, the teacher said:

"That inkstand is very precious to me: if you only knew, sir, the history of that inkstand!" And he told it.

Years ago he was a teacher at Turin, and all one winter he went to give lessons to the prisoners in the judicial prison. He gave the lessons in the chapel of the prison, which is a circular building, and all around it, on the high, bare walls, are a great many little square windows, covered with two cross-bars of iron, each one of which corresponds to a very small cell inside. He gave his lessons as he paced about the dark, cold chapel, and his scholars stood at the holes, with their copy-books resting against the gratings, showing nothing in the shadow but wan, frowning faces, gray and ragged beards, staring eyes of murderers and thieves. Among the rest there was one, No. 78, who was more attentive than all the others, and who studied a great deal, and gazed at his teacher with eyes full of respect and gratitude. He was a young man, with a black beard, more unfortunate than wicked, a cabinet-maker who, in a fit of rage, had flung a plane at his master, who had been persecuting him for some time, and had inflicted a mortal wound on his head: for this he had been condemned to several years of seclusion. In three months he had learned to read and write, and he read constantly, and the more he learned, the better he seemed to become, and the more remorseful for his crime. One day, at the conclusion of the lesson, he made a sign to the teacher that he should come near to his little window, and he announced to him that he was to leave Turin on the following day, to go and expiate his crime in the prison at Venice; and as he bade him farewell, he begged in a humble and much moved voice, that he might be allowed to touch the master's hand. The master offered him his hand, and he kissed it; then he said:

"Thanks! thanks!" and disappeared. The master drew back his hand; it was bathed with tears. After that he did not see the man again.

Six years passed. "I was thinking of anything except that unfortunate man," said the teacher, "when, the other morning, I saw a stranger come to the house, a man with a large black beard already sprinkled with gray, and badly dressed, who said to me: 'Are you the teacher So-and-So, sir?' 'Who are you?' I asked him. 'I am prisoner No. 78,' he replied; 'you taught me to read and write six years ago; if you recollect, you gave me your hand at the last lesson; I have now expiated my crime, and I have come hither--to beg you to do me the favor to accept a memento of me, a poor little thing which I made in prison. Will you accept it in memory of me, Signor Master?'

"I stood there speechless. He thought that I did not wish to take it, and he looked at me as much as to say, 'So six years of suffering are not sufficient to cleanse my hands!' but with so poignant an expression of pain did he gaze at me, that I instantly extended my hand and took the little object. This is it."

We looked attentively at the inkstand: it seemed to have been carved with the point of a nail, and with, great patience; on its top was carved a pen lying across a copy-book, and around it was written: "*To my teacher. A memento of No. 78. Six years!*" And below, in small letters, "*Study and hope.*"

The master said nothing more; we went away. But all the way from Moncalieri to Turin I could not get that prisoner, standing at his little window, that farewell to his master, that poor inkstand made in prison, which told so much, out of my head; and I dreamed of them all night, and was still thinking of them this morning--far enough from imagining the surprise which awaited me at school! No sooner had I taken my new seat, beside Derossi, and written my problem in arithmetic for the monthly examination, than I told my companion the story of the prisoner and the inkstand, and how the inkstand was made, with the pen across the copy-book, and the inscription around it, "Six years!" Derossi sprang up at these words, and began to look first at me and then at Crossi, the son of the vegetable-vender, who sat on the bench in front, with his back turned to us, wholly absorbed on his problem.

"Hush!" he said; then, in a low voice, catching me by the arm, "don't you know that Crossi spoke to me day before yesterday of having caught a glimpse; of an inkstand in the hands of his father, who has returned from America; a conical inkstand, made by hand, with a copy-book and a pen,--that is the one; six years! He said that his father was in America; instead of that he was in prison: Crossi was a little boy at the time of the crime; he does not remember it; his mother has deceived him; he knows nothing; let not a syllable of this escape!"

I remained speechless, with my eyes fixed on Crossi. Then Derossi solved his problem, and passed it under the bench to Crossi; he gave him a sheet of paper; he took out of his hands the monthly story, *Daddy's Nurse*, which the teacher had given him to copy out, in order that he might copy it in his stead; he gave him pens, and stroked his shoulder, and made me promise on my honor that I would say nothing to any one; and when we left school, he said hastily to me:

"His father came to get him yesterday; he will be here again this morning: do as I do."

We emerged into the street; Crossi's father was there, a little to one side: a man with a black beard sprinkled with gray, badly dressed, with a colorless and thoughtful face. Derossi shook Crossi's hand, in a way to attract attention, and said to him in a loud tone, "Farewell until we meet again, Crossi,"--and passed his hand under his chin. I did the same. But as he did so, Derossi turned crimson, and so did I; and Crossi's father gazed attentively at us, with a kindly glance; but through it shone an expression of uneasiness and suspicion which made our hearts grow cold.

DADDY'S NURSE

(*Monthly Story.*)

One morning, on a rainy day in March, a lad dressed like a country boy, all muddy and saturated with water, with a bundle of clothes under his arm, presented himself to the porter of the great hospital at Naples, and, presenting a letter, asked for his father. He had a fine oval face, of a pale brown hue, thoughtful eyes, and two thick lips, always half open, which displayed extremely white teeth. He came from a village in the neighborhood of Naples. His father, who had left home a year previously to seek work in France, had returned to Italy, and had landed a few days before at Naples, where, having fallen suddenly ill, he had hardly time to write a line to announce his arrival to his family, and to say that he was going to the hospital. His wife, in despair at this news, and unable to leave home because she had a sick child, and a baby at the breast, had sent her eldest son to Naples, with a few soldi, to help his father--his *daddy*, as they called him: the boy had walked ten miles.

The porter, after glancing at the letter, called a nurse and told him to conduct the lad to his father.

"What father?" inquired the nurse.

The boy, trembling with terror, lest he should hear bad news, gave the name.

The nurse did not recall such a name.

"An old laborer, arrived from abroad?" he asked.

"Yes, a laborer," replied the lad, still more uneasy; "not so very old. Yes, arrived from abroad."

"When did he enter the hospital?" asked the nurse.

The lad glanced at his letter; "Five days ago, I think."

The nurse stood a while in thought; then, as though suddenly recalling him; "Ah!" he said, "the furthest bed in the fourth ward."

"Is he very ill? How is he?" inquired the boy, anxiously.

The nurse looked at him, without replying. Then he said, "Come with me."

They ascended two flights of stairs, walked to the end of a long corridor, and found themselves facing the open door of a large hall, wherein two rows of beds were arranged. "Come," repeated the nurse, entering. The boy plucked up his courage, and followed him, casting terrified glances to right and left, on the pale, emaciated faces of the sick people, some of whom had their eyes closed, and seemed to be dead, while others were staring into the air, with their eyes wide open and fixed, as though frightened. Some were moaning like children. The big room was dark, the air was impregnated with an acute odor of medicines. Two sisters of charity were going about with phials in their hands.

Arrived at the extremity of the great room, the nurse halted at the head of a bed, drew aside the curtains, and said, "Here is your father."

The boy burst into tears, and letting fall his bundle, he dropped his head on the sick man's shoulder, clasping with one hand the arm which was lying motionless on the coverlet. The sick man did not move.

The boy rose to his feet, and looked at his father, and broke into a fresh fit of weeping. Then the sick man gave a long look at him, and seemed to recognize him; but his lips did not move. Poor daddy, how he was changed! The son would never have recognized him. His hair had turned white, his beard had grown, his face was swollen, of a dull red hue, with the skin tightly drawn and shining; his eyes were diminished in size, his lips very thick, his whole countenance altered. There was no longer anything natural about him but his forehead and the arch of his eyebrows. He breathed with difficulty.

"Daddy! daddy!" said the boy, "it is I; don't you know me? I am Cicillo, your own Cicillo, who has come from the country: mamma has sent me. Take a good look at me; don't you know me? Say one word to me."

But the sick man, after having looked attentively at him, closed his eyes.

"Daddy! daddy! What is the matter with you? I am your little son--your own Cicillo."

The sick man made no movement, and continued to breathe painfully.

Then the lad, still weeping, took a chair, seated himself and waited, without taking his eyes from his father's face. "A doctor will surely come to pay him a visit," he thought; "he will tell me something." And he became immersed in sad thoughts, recalling many things about his kind father, the day of parting, when he said the last good by to him on board the ship, the hopes which his family had founded on his journey, the desolation of his mother on the arrival of the letter; and he thought of death: he beheld his father dead, his mother dressed in black, the family in misery. And he remained a long time thus. A light hand touched him on the shoulder, and he started up: it was a nun.

"What is the matter with my father?" he asked her quickly.

"Is he your father?" said the sister gently.

"Yes, he is my father; I have come. What ails him?"

"Courage, my boy," replied the sister; "the doctor will be here soon now." And she went away without saying anything more.

Half an hour later he heard the sound of a bell, and he saw the doctor enter at the further end of the hall, accompanied by an assistant; the sister and a nurse followed him. They began the visit, pausing at every bed. This time of waiting seemed an eternity to the lad, and his anxiety increased at every step of the doctor. At length they arrived at the next bed. The doctor was an old man, tall and stooping, with a grave face. Before he left the next bed the boy rose to his feet, and when he approached he began to cry.

The doctor looked at him.

"He is the sick man's son," said the sister; "he arrived this morning from the country."

The doctor placed one hand on his shoulder; then bent over the sick man, felt his pulse, touched his forehead, and asked a few questions of the sister, who replied, "There is nothing new." Then he thought for a while and said, "Continue the present treatment."

Then the boy plucked up courage, and asked in a tearful voice, "What is the matter with my father?"

"Take courage, my boy," replied the doctor, laying his hand on his shoulder once more; "he has erysipelas in his face. It is a serious case, but there is still hope. Help him. Your presence may do him a great deal of good."

"But he does not know me!" exclaimed the boy in a tone of affliction.

"He will recognize you--tomorrow perhaps. Let us hope for the best and keep up our courage."

The boy would have liked to ask some more questions, but he did not dare. The doctor passed on. And then he began his life of nurse. As he could do nothing else, he arranged the coverlets of the sick man, touched his hand every now and then, drove away the flies, bent over him at every groan, and when the sister brought him something to drink, he took the glass or the spoon from her hand, and administered it in her stead. The sick man looked at him occasionally, but he gave no sign of recognition. However, his glance rested longer on the lad each time, especially when the latter put his handkerchief to his eyes.

Thus passed the first day. At night the boy slept on two chairs, in a corner of the ward, and in the morning he resumed his work of mercy. That day it seemed as though the eyes of the sick man revealed a dawning of consciousness. At the sound of the boy's caressing voice a vague expression of gratitude seemed to gleam for an instant in his pupils, and once he moved his lips a little, as though he wanted to say something. After each brief nap he seemed, on opening his eyes, to seek his little nurse. The doctor, who had passed twice, thought he noted a slight improvement. Towards evening, on putting the cup to his lips, the lad fancied that he perceived a very faint smile glide across the swollen lips. Then he began to take comfort and to hope; and with the hope of being understood, confusedly at least, he talked to him--talked to him at great length--of his mother, of his little sisters, of his own return home, and he exhorted him to courage with warm and loving words. And although he often doubted whether he was heard, he still talked; for it seemed to him that even if he did not understand him, the sick man listened with a certain pleasure to his voice,--to that unaccustomed intonation of affection and sorrow. And in this manner passed the second day, and the third, and the fourth, with vicissitudes of slight improvements and unexpected changes for the worse; and the boy was so absorbed in all his cares, that he hardly nibbled a bit of bread and cheese twice a day, when the sister brought it to him, and hardly saw what was going on around him,--the dying patients, the sudden running up of the sisters at night, the moans and despairing gestures of visitors,--all those doleful and lugubrious scenes of hospital life, which on any other occasion would have disconcerted and alarmed him. Hours, days, passed, and still he was there with his daddy; watchful, wistful, trembling at every sigh and at every look, agitated incessantly between a hope which relieved his mind and a discouragement which froze his heart.

On the fifth day the sick man suddenly grew worse. The doctor, on being interrogated, shook his head, as much as to say that all was over, and the boy flung himself on a chair and burst out sobbing. But one thing comforted him. In spite of the fact that he was worse, the sick man seemed to be slowly regaining a little intelligence. He stared at the lad with increasing intentness, and, with an expression which grew in sweetness, would take his drink and medicine from no one but him, and made strenuous efforts with his lips with greater frequency, as though he were trying to pronounce some word; and he did it so plainly sometimes that his son grasped his arm violently, inspired by a sudden hope, and said to him in a tone which was almost that of joy, "Courage, courage, daddy; you will get well, we will go away from here, we will return home with mamma; courage, for a little while longer!"

It was four o'clock in the afternoon, and just when the boy had abandoned himself to one of these outbursts of tenderness and hope, when a sound of footsteps became audible outside the nearest door in the ward, and then a strong voice uttering two words only,--"Farewell, sister!"--which made him spring to his feet, with a cry repressed in his throat.

At that moment there entered the ward a man with a thick bandage on his hand, followed by a sister.

The boy uttered a sharp cry, and stood rooted to the spot.

The man turned round, looked at him for a moment, and uttered a cry in his turn,--"Cicillo!"--and darted towards him.

The boy fell into his father's arms, choking with emotion.

The sister, the nurse, and the assistant ran up, and stood there in amazement.

The boy could not recover his voice.

"Oh, my Cicillo!" exclaimed the father, after bestowing an attentive look on the sick man, as he kissed the boy repeatedly. "Cicillo, my son, how is this? They took you to the bedside of another man. And there was I, in despair at not seeing you after mamma had written, 'I have sent him.' Poor Cicillo! How many days have you been here? How did this mistake occur? I have come out of it easily! I have a good constitution, you know! And how is mamma? And Concettella? And the little baby--how are they all? I am leaving the hospital now. Come, then. Oh, Lord God! Who would have thought it!"

The boy tried to interpolate a few words, to tell the news of the family. "Oh how happy I am!" he stammered. "How happy I am! What terrible days I have passed!" And he could not finish kissing his father.

But he did not stir.

"Come," said his father; "we can get home this evening." And he drew the lad towards him. The boy turned to look at his patient.

"Well, are you coming or not?" his father demanded, in amazement.

The boy cast yet another glance at the sick man, who opened his eyes at that moment and gazed intently at him.

Then a flood of words poured from his very soul. "No, daddy; wait--here--I can't. Here is this old man. I have been here for five days. He gazes at me incessantly. I thought he was you. I love him dearly. He looks at me; I give him his drink; he wants me always beside him; he is very ill now. Have patience; I have not the courage--I don't know--it pains me too much; I will return home tomorrow; let me stay here a little longer; I don't at all like to leave him. See how he looks at me! I don't know who he is, but he wants me; he will die alone: let me stay here, dear daddy!"

"Bravo, little fellow!" exclaimed the attendant.

The father stood in perplexity, staring at the boy; then he looked at the sick man. "Who is he?" he inquired.

"A countryman, like yourself," replied the attendant, "just arrived from abroad, and who entered the hospital on the very day that you entered it. He was out of his senses when they brought him here, and could not speak. Perhaps he has a family far away, and sons. He probably thinks that your son is one of his."

The sick man was still looking at the boy.

The father said to Cicillo, "Stay."

"He will not have to stay much longer," murmured the attendant.

"Stay," repeated his father: "you have heart. I will go home immediately, to relieve mamma's distress. Here is a scudo for your expenses. Good by, my brave little son, until we meet!"

He embraced him, looked at him intently, kissed him again on the brow, and went away.

The boy returned to his post at the bedside, and the sick man appeared consoled. And Cicillo began again to play the nurse, no longer weeping, but with the same eagerness, the same patience, as before; he again began to give the man his drink, to arrange his bedclothes, to caress his hand, to speak softly to him, to exhort him to courage. He attended him all that day, all that night; he remained beside him all the following day. But the sick man continued to grow constantly worse; his face turned a purple color, his breathing grew heavier, his agitation increased, inarticulate cries escaped his lips, the inflammation became excessive. On his evening visit, the doctor said that he would not live through the night. And then Cicillo redoubled his cares, and never took his eyes from him for a minute. The sick man gazed and gazed at him, and kept moving his lips from time to time, with great effort, as though he wanted to say something, and an expression of extraordinary tenderness passed over his eyes now and then, as they continued to grow smaller and more dim. And that night the boy watched with him until he saw the first rays of dawn gleam white through the windows, and the sister appeared. The sister approached the bed, cast a glance at the patient, and then went away with rapid steps. A few moments later she reappeared with the assistant doctor, and with a nurse, who carried a lantern.

"He is at his last gasp," said the doctor.

The boy clasped the sick man's hand. The latter opened his eyes, gazed at him, and closed them once more.

At that moment the lad fancied that he felt his hand pressed. "He pressed my hand!" he exclaimed.

The doctor bent over the patient for an instant, then straightened himself up.

The sister detached a crucifix from the wall.

"He is dead!" cried the boy.

"Go, my son," said the doctor: "your work of mercy is finished. Go, and may fortune attend you! for you deserve it. God will protect you. Farewell!"

The sister, who had stepped aside for a moment, returned with a little bunch of violets which she had taken from a glass on the window-sill, and handed them to the boy, saying:

"I have nothing else to give you. Take these in memory of the hospital."

"Thanks," returned the boy, taking the bunch of flowers with one hand and drying his eyes with the other; "but I have such a long distance to go on foot--I shall spoil them." And separating the violets, he scattered them over the bed, saying: "I leave them as a memento for my poor dead man. Thanks, sister! thanks, doctor!" Then, turning to the dead man, "Farewell--" And while he sought a name to give him, the sweet name which he had applied to him for five days recurred to his lips,--"Farewell, poor daddy!"

So saying, he took his little bundle of clothes under his arm, and, exhausted with fatigue, he walked slowly away. The day was dawning.

## THE WORKSHOP

Saturday, 18th.

Precossi came last night to remind me that I was to go and see his workshop, which is down the street, and this morning when I went out with my father, I got him to take me there for a moment. As we approached the shop, Garoffi issued from it on a run, with a package in his hand, and making his big cloak, with which he covers up his merchandise, flutter. Ah! now I know where he goes to pilfer iron filings, which he sells for old papers, that barterer of a Garoffi! When we arrived in front of the door, we saw Precossi seated on a little pile of bricks, engaged in studying his lesson, with his book resting on his knees. He rose quickly and invited us to enter. It was a large apartment, full of coal-dust, bristling with hammers, pincers, bars, and old iron of every description; and in one corner burned a fire in a small furnace, where puffed a pair of bellows worked by a boy. Precossi, the father, was standing near the anvil, and a young man was holding a bar of iron in the fire.

"Ah! here he is," said the smith, as soon as he caught sight of us, and he lifted his cap, "the nice boy who gives away railway trains! He has come to see me work a little, has he not? I shall be at your service in a moment." And as he said it, he smiled; and he no longer had the ferocious face, the malevolent eyes of former days. The young man handed him a long bar of iron heated red-hot on one end, and the smith placed it on the anvil. He was making one of those curved bars for the rail of terrace balustrades. He raised a large hammer and began to beat it, pushing the heated part now here, now there, between one point of the anvil and the middle, and turning it about in various ways; and it was a marvel to see how the iron curved beneath the rapid and accurate blows of the hammer, and twisted, and gradually assumed the graceful form of a leaf torn from a flower, like a pipe of dough which he had modelled with his hands. And meanwhile his son watched us with a certain air of pride, as much as to say, "See how my father works!"

"Do you see how it is done, little master?" the blacksmith asked me, when he had finished, holding out the bar, which looked like a bishop's crosier. Then he laid it aside, and thrust another into the fire.

"That was very well made, indeed," my father said to him. And he added, "So you are working--eh! You have returned to good habits?"

"Yes, I have returned," replied the workman, wiping away the perspiration, and reddening a little. "And do you know who has made me return to them?" My father pretended not to understand. "This brave boy," said the blacksmith, indicating his son with his finger; "that brave boy there, who studied and did honor to his father, while his father rioted, and treated him like a dog. When I saw that medal--Ah! thou little lad of mine, no bigger than a soldo[2] of cheese, come hither, that I may take a good look at thy phiz!"

The boy ran to him instantly; the smith took him and set him directly on the anvil, holding him under the arms, and said to him:

---

[2] The twentieth part of a cubit; Florentine measure.

"Polish off the frontispiece of this big beast of a daddy of yours a little!"

And then Precossi covered his father's black face with kisses, until he was all black himself.

"That's as it should be," said the smith, and he set him on the ground again.

"That really is as it should be, Precossi!" exclaimed my father, delighted. And bidding the smith and his son good day, he led me away. As I was going out, little Precossi said to me, "Excuse me," and thrust a little packet of nails into my pocket. I invited him to come and view the Carnival from my house.

"You gave him your railway train," my father said to me in the street; "but if it had been made of gold and filled with pearls, it would still have been but a petty gift to that sainted son, who has reformed his father's heart."


## THE LITTLE HARLEQUIN

Monday, 20th.

The whole city is in a tumult over the Carnival, which is nearing its close. In every square rise booths of mountebanks and jesters; and we have under our windows a circus-tent, in which a little Venetian company, with five horses, is giving a show. The circus is in the centre of the square; and in one corner there are three very large vans in which the mountebanks sleep and dress themselves,--three small houses on wheels, with their tiny windows, and a chimney in each of them, which smokes continually; and between window and window the baby's swaddling-bands are stretched. There is one woman who is nursing a child, who prepares the food, and dances on the tight-rope. Poor people! The word *mountebank* is spoken as though it were an insult; but they earn their living honestly, nevertheless, by amusing all the world--and how they work! All day long they run back and forth between the circus-tent and the vans, in tights, in all this cold; they snatch a mouthful or two in haste, standing, between two performances; and sometimes, when they get their tent full, a wind arises, wrenches away the ropes and extinguishes the lights, and then good by to the show! They are obliged to return the money, and to work the entire night at repairing their booth. There are two lads who work; and my father recognized the smallest one as he was traversing the square; and he is the son of the proprietor, the same one whom we saw perform tricks on horseback last year in a circus on the Piazza Vittorio Emanuele. And he has grown; he must be eight years old: he is a handsome boy, with a round and roguish face, with so many black curls that they escape from his pointed cap. He is dressed up like a harlequin, decked out in a sort of sack, with sleeves of white, embroidered with black, and his slippers are of cloth. He is a merry little imp. He charms every one. He does everything. We see him early in the morning, wrapped in a shawl, carrying milk to his wooden house; then he goes to get the horses at the boarding-stable on the Via Bertola. He holds the tiny baby in his arms; he transports hoops, trestles, rails, ropes; he cleans the vans, lights the fire, and in his leisure moments he always hangs about his mother. My father is always watching him from the window, and does nothing but talk about him and his family, who have the air of nice people, and of being fond of their children.

One evening we went to the circus: it was cold; there was hardly any one there; but the little harlequin exerted himself greatly to cheer those few people: he executed precarious leaps; he caught hold of the horses' tails; he walked with his legs in the air, all alone; he sang, always with a smile constantly on his handsome little brown face. And his father, who had on a red vest and white trousers, with tall boots, and a whip in his hand, watched him: but it was melancholy. My father took pity on him, and spoke of him on the following day to Delis the painter, who came to see us. These poor people were killing themselves with hard work, and their affairs were going so badly! The little boy pleased him so much! What could be done for them? The painter had an idea.

"Write a fine article for the *Gazette*," he said: "you know how to write well: relate the miraculous things which the little harlequin does, and I will take his portrait for you. Everybody reads the *Gazette*, and people will flock thither for once."

And thus they did. My father wrote a fine article, full of jests, which told all that we had observed from the window, and inspired a desire to see and caress the little artist; and the painter sketched a little portrait which was graceful and a good likeness, and which was published on Saturday evening. And behold! at the Sunday performance a great crowd rushed to the circus. The announcement was made: *Performance for the Benefit of the Little Harlequin*, as he was styled in the *Gazette*. The circus was crammed; many of the spectators held the *Gazette* in their hands, and showed it to the little harlequin, who laughed and ran from one to another, perfectly delighted. The proprietor was delighted also. Just fancy! Not a single newspaper had ever done him such an honor, and the money-box was filled. My father sat beside me. Among the spectators we found persons of our acquaintance. Near the entrance for the horses stood the teacher of gymnastics--the one who has been with Garibaldi; and opposite us, in the second row, was the little mason, with his little round face, seated beside his gigantic father; and no sooner did he catch sight of me than he made a hare's face at me. A little further on I espied Garoffi, who was counting the spectators, and calculated on his fingers how much money the company had taken in. On one of the chairs in the first row, not far from us, there was also poor Robetti, the boy who saved the child from the omnibus, with his crutches between his knees, pressed close to the side of his father, the artillery captain, who kept one hand on his shoulder. The performance began. The little harlequin accomplished wonders on his horse, on the trapeze, on the tight-rope; and every time that he jumped down, every one clapped their hands, and many pulled his curls. Then several others, rope-dancers, jugglers, and riders, clad in tights, and sparkling with silver, went through their exercises; but when the boy was not performing, the audience seemed to grow weary. At a certain point I saw the teacher of gymnastics, who held his post at the entrance for the horses, whisper in the ear of the proprietor of the circus, and the latter instantly glanced around, as though in search of some one. His glance rested on us. My father perceived it, and understood that the teacher had revealed that he was the author of the article, and in order to escape being thanked, he hastily retreated, saying to me:

"Remain, Enrico; I will wait for you outside."

After exchanging a few words with his father, the little harlequin went through still another trick: erect upon a galloping horse, he appeared in four characters--as a pilgrim, a sailor, a soldier, and an acrobat; and every time that he passed near me, he looked at me. And when he dismounted, he began to make the tour of the circus, with his harlequin's cap in his hand, and everybody threw soldi or sugar-plums into it. I had two soldi ready; but when he got in front of me, instead of offering his cap, he drew it back, gave me a look and passed on. I was mortified. Why had he offered me that affront?

The performance came to an end; the proprietor thanked the audience; and all the people rose also, and thronged to the doors. I was confused by the crowd, and was on the point of going out, when I felt a touch on my hand. I turned round: it was the little harlequin, with his tiny brown face and his black curls, who was smiling at me; he had his hands full of sugar-plums. Then I understood.

"Will you accept these sugar-plums from the little harlequin?" said he to me, in his dialect.

I nodded, and took three or four.

"Then," he added, "please accept a kiss also."

"Give me two," I answered; and held up my face to him. He rubbed off his floury face with his hand, put his arm round my neck, and planted two kisses on my cheek, saying:

"There! take one of them to your father."

## THE LAST DAY OF THE CARNIVAL

Tuesday, 21st.

What a sad scene was that which we witnessed today at the procession of the masks! It ended well; but it might have resulted in a great misfortune. In the San Carlo Square, all decorated with red, white, and yellow festoons, a vast multitude had assembled; masks of every hue were flitting about; cars, gilded and adorned, in the shape of pavilions; little theatres, barks filled with harlequins and warriors, cooks, sailors, and shepherdesses; there was such a confusion that one knew not where to look; a tremendous clash of trumpets, horns, and cymbals lacerated the ears; and the masks on the chariots drank and sang, as they apostrophized the people in the streets and at the windows, who retorted at the top of their lungs, and hurled oranges and sugar-plums at each other vigorously; and above the chariots and the throng, as far as the eye could reach, one could see banners fluttering, helmets gleaming, plumes waving, gigantic pasteboard heads moving, huge head-dresses, enormous trumpets, fantastic arms, little drums, castanets, red caps, and bottles;--all the world seemed to have gone mad. When our carriage entered the square, a magnificent chariot was driving in front of us, drawn by four horses covered with trappings embroidered in gold, and all wreathed in artificial roses, upon which there were fourteen or fifteen gentlemen masquerading as gentlemen at the court of France, all glittering with silk, with huge white wigs, a plumed hat, under the arm a small-sword, and a tuft of ribbons and laces on the breast. They were very gorgeous. They were singing a French canzonette in concert and throwing sweetmeats to the people, and the people clapped their hands and shouted. Suddenly, on our left, we saw a man lift a child of five or six above the heads of the crowd,--a poor little creature, who wept piteously, and flung her arms about as though in a fit of convulsions. The man made his way to the gentlemen's chariot; one of the latter bent down, and the other said aloud:

"Take this child; she has lost her mother in the crowd; hold her in your arms; the mother may not be far off, and she will catch sight of her: there is no other way."

The gentleman took the child in his arms: all the rest stopped singing; the child screamed and struggled; the gentleman removed his mask; the chariot continued to move slowly onwards. Meanwhile, as we were afterwards informed, at the opposite extremity of the square a poor woman, half crazed with despair, was forcing her way through the crowd, by dint of shoves and elbowing, and shrieking:

"Maria! Maria! Maria! I have lost my little daughter! She has been stolen from me! They have suffocated my child!" And for a quarter of an hour she raved and expressed her despair in this manner, straying now a little way in this direction, and then a little way in that, crushed by the throng through which she strove to force her way.

The gentleman on the car was meanwhile holding the child pressed against the ribbons and laces on his breast, casting glances over the square, and trying to calm the poor creature, who covered her face with her hands, not knowing where she was, and sobbed as though she would break her heart. The gentleman was touched: it was evident that these screams went to his soul. All the others offered the child oranges and sugar-plums; but she repulsed them all, and grew constantly more convulsed and frightened.

"Find her mother!" shouted the gentleman to the crowd; "seek her mother!" And every one turned to the right and the left; but the mother was not to be found. Finally, a few paces from the place where the Via Roma enters the square, a woman was seen to rush towards the chariot. Ah, I shall never forget that! She no longer seemed a human creature: her hair was streaming, her face distorted, her garments torn; she hurled herself forward with a rattle in her throat,--one knew not whether to attribute it to either joy, anguish, or rage,--and darted out her hands like two claws to snatch her child. The chariot halted.

"Here she is," said the gentleman, reaching out the child after kissing it; and he placed her in her mother's arms, who pressed her to her breast like a fury. But one of the tiny hands rested a second longer in the hands of the gentleman; and the latter, pulling off of his right hand a gold ring set with a large diamond, and slipping it with a rapid movement upon the finger of the little girl, said:

"Take this; it shall be your marriage dowry."

The mother stood rooted to the spot, as though enchanted; the crowd broke into applause; the gentleman put on his mask again, his companions resumed their song, and the chariot started on again slowly, amid a tempest of hand-clapping and hurrahs.


THE BLIND BOYS

Thursday, 24th.

The master is very ill, and they have sent in his stead the master of the fourth grade, who has been a teacher in the Institute for the Blind. He is the oldest of all the instructors, with hair so white that it looks like a wig made of cotton, and he speaks in a peculiar manner, as though he were chanting a melancholy song; but he does it well, and he knows a great deal. No sooner had he entered the schoolroom than, catching sight of a boy with a bandage on his eye, he approached the bench, and asked him what was the matter.

"Take care of your eyes, my boy," he said to him. And then Derossi asked him:

"Is it true, sir, that you have been a teacher of the blind?"

"Yes, for several years," he replied. And Derossi said, in a low tone, "Tell us something about it."

The master went and seated himself at his table.

Coretti said aloud, "The Institute for the Blind is in the Via Nizza."

"You say blind--blind," said the master, "as you would say poor or ill, or I know not what. But do you thoroughly comprehend the significance of that word? Reflect a little. Blind! Never to see anything! Not to be able to distinguish the day from night; to see neither the sky, nor sun, nor your parents, nor anything of what is around you, and which you touch; to be immersed in a perpetual obscurity, and as though buried in the bowels of the earth! Make a little effort to close your eyes, and to think of being obliged to remain forever thus; you will suddenly be overwhelmed by a mental agony, by terror; it will seem to you impossible to resist, that you must burst into a scream, that you must go mad or die. But, poor boys! when you enter the Institute of the Blind for the first time, during their recreation hour, and hear them playing on violins and flutes in all directions, and talking loudly and laughing, ascending and descending the stairs at a rapid pace, and wandering freely through the corridors and dormitories, you would never pronounce these unfortunates to be the unfortunates that they are. It is necessary to observe them closely. There are lads of sixteen or eighteen, robust and cheerful, who bear their blindness with a certain ease, almost with hardihood; but you understand from a certain proud, resentful expression of countenance that they must have suffered tremendously before they became resigned to this misfortune.

"There are others, with sweet and pallid faces, on which a profound resignation is visible; but they are sad, and one understands that they must still weep at times in secret. Ah, my sons! reflect that some of them have lost their sight in a few days, some after years of martyrdom and many terrible chirurgical operations, and that many were born so,--born into a night that has no dawn for them, that they entered into the world as into an immense tomb, and that they do not know what the human countenance is like. Picture to yourself how they must have suffered, and how they must still suffer, when they think thus confusedly of the tremendous difference between themselves and those who see, and ask themselves, 'Why this difference, if we are not to blame?'

"I who have spent many years among them, when I recall that class, all those eyes forever sealed, all those pupils without sight and without life, and then look at the rest of you, it seems impossible to me that you should not all be happy. Think of it! there are about twenty-six thousand blind persons in Italy! Twenty-six thousand persons who do not see the light--do you understand? An army which would employ four hours in marching past our windows."

The master paused. Not a breath was audible in all the school. Derossi asked if it were true that the blind have a finer sense of feeling than the rest of us.

The master said: "It is true. All the other senses are finer in them, because, since they must replace, among them, that of sight, they are more and better exercised than they are in the case of those who see. In the morning, in the dormitory, one asks another, 'Is the sun shining?' and the one who is the most alert in dressing runs instantly into the yard, and flourishes his hands in the air, to find out whether there is any warmth of the sun perceptible, and then he runs to communicate the good news, 'The sun is shining!' From the voice of a person they obtain an idea of his height. We judge of a man's soul by his eyes; they, by his voice. They remember intonations and accents for years. They perceive if there is more than one person in a room, even if only one speaks, and the rest remain motionless. They know by their touch whether a spoon is more or less polished. Little girls distinguish dyed wools from that which is of the natural color. As they walk two and two along the streets, they recognize nearly all the shops by their odors, even those in which we perceive no odor. They spin top, and by listening to its humming they go straight to it and pick it up without any mistake. They trundle hoop, play at ninepins, jump the rope, build little houses of stones, pick violets as though they saw them, make mats and baskets, weaving together straw of various colors rapidly and well--to such a degree is their sense of touch skilled. The sense of touch is their sight. One of their greatest pleasures is to handle, to grasp, to guess the forms of things by feeling them. It is affecting to see them when they are taken to the Industrial Museum, where they are allowed to handle whatever they please, and to observe with what eagerness they fling themselves on geometrical bodies, on little models of houses, on instruments; with what joy they feel over and rub and turn everything about in their hands, in order to see how it is made. They call this *seeing*!"

Garoffi interrupted the teacher to inquire if it was true that blind boys learn to reckon better than others.

The master replied: "It is true. They learn to reckon and to write. They have books made on purpose for them, with raised characters; they pass their fingers over these, recognize the letters and pronounce the words. They read rapidly; and you should see them blush, poor little things, when they make a mistake. And they write, too, without ink. They write on a thick and hard sort of paper with a metal bodkin, which makes a great many little hollows, grouped according to a special alphabet; these little punctures stand out in relief on the other side of the paper, so that by turning the paper over and drawing their fingers across these projections, they can read what they have written, and also the writing of others; and thus they write compositions: and they write letters to each other. They write numbers in the same way, and they make calculations; and they calculate mentally with an incredible facility, since their minds are not diverted by the sight of surrounding objects, as ours are. And if you could see how passionately fond they are of reading, how attentive they are, how well they remember everything, how they discuss among themselves, even the little ones, of things connected with history and language, as they sit four or five on the same bench, without turning to each other, and converse, the first with the third, the second with the fourth, in a loud voice and all together, without losing a single word, so acute and prompt is their hearing.

"And they attach more importance to the examinations than you do, I assure you, and they are fonder of their teachers. They recognize their teacher by his step and his odor; they perceive whether he is in a good or bad humor, whether he is well or ill, simply by the sound of a single word of his. They want the teacher to touch them when he encourages and praises them, and they feel of his hand and his arms in order to express their gratitude. And they love each other and are good comrades to each other. In play time they are always together, according to their wont. In the girls' school, for instance, they form into groups according to the instrument on which they play,-- violinists, pianists, and flute-players,--and they never separate. When they have become attached to any one, it is difficult for them to break it off. They take much comfort in friendship. They judge correctly among themselves. They have a clear and profound idea of good and evil. No one grows so enthusiastic as they over the narration of a generous action, of a grand deed."

Votini inquired if they played well.

"They are ardently fond of music," replied the master. "It is their delight: music is their life. Little blind children, when they first enter the Institute, are capable of standing three hours perfectly motionless, to listen to playing. They learn easily; they play with fire. When the teacher tells one of them that he has not a talent for music, he feels very sorrowful, but he sets to studying desperately. Ah! if you could hear the music there, if you could see them when they are playing, with their heads thrown back a smile on their lips, their faces aflame, trembling with emotion, in ecstasies at listening to that harmony which replies to them in the obscurity which envelops them, you would feel what a divine consolation is music! And they shout for joy, they beam with happiness when a teacher says to them, "You will become an artist." The one who is first in music, who succeeds the best on the violin or piano, is like a king to them; they love, they venerate him. If a quarrel arises between two of them, they go to him; if two friends fall out, it is he who reconciles them. The smallest pupils, whom he teaches to play, regard him as a father. Then all go to bid him good night before retiring to bed. And they talk constantly of music. They are already in bed, late at night, wearied by study and work, and half asleep, and still they are discussing, in a low tone, operas, masters, instruments, and orchestras. It is so great a punishment for them to be deprived of the reading, or lesson in music, it causes them such sorrow that one hardly ever has the courage to punish them in that way. That which the light is to our eyes, music is to their hearts."

Derossi asked whether we could not go to see them.

"Yes," replied the teacher; "but you boys must not go there now. You shall go there later on, when you are in a condition to appreciate the whole extent of this misfortune, and to feel all the compassion which it merits. It is a sad sight, my boys. You will sometimes see there boys seated in front of an open window, enjoying the fresh air, with immovable countenances, which seem to be gazing at the wide green expanse and the beautiful blue mountains which you can see; and when you remember that they see nothing--that they will never see anything--of that vast loveliness, your soul is oppressed, as though you had yourselves become blind at that moment. And then there are those who were born blind, who, as they have never seen the world, do not complain because they do not possess the image of anything, and who, therefore, arouse less compassion. But there are lads who have been blind but a few months, who still recall everything, who thoroughly understand all that they have lost; and these have, in addition, the grief of feeling their minds obscured, the dearest images grow a little more dim in their minds day by day, of feeling the persons whom they have loved the most die out of their memories. One of these boys said to me one day, with inexpressible sadness, 'I should like to have my sight again, only for a moment, in order to see mamma's face once more, for I no longer remember it!' And when their mothers come to see them, the boys place their hands on her face; they feel her over thoroughly from brow to chin, and her ears, to see how they are made, and they can hardly persuade themselves that they cannot see her, and they call her by name many times, to beseech her that she will allow them, that she will make them see her just once. How many, even hard-hearted men, go away in tears! And when you do go out, your case seems to you to be the exception, and the power to see people, houses, and the sky a hardly deserved privilege. Oh! there is not one of you, I am sure, who, on emerging thence, would not feel disposed to deprive himself of a portion of his own sight, in order to bestow a gleam at least upon all those poor children, for whom the sun has no light, for whom a mother has no face!"

THE SICK MASTER

Saturday, 25th.

Yesterday afternoon, on coming out of school, I went to pay a visit to my sick master. He made himself ill by overworking. Five hours of teaching a day, then an hour of gymnastics, then two hours more of evening school, which is equivalent to saying but little sleep, getting his food by snatches, and working breathlessly from morning till night. He has ruined his health. That is what my mother says. My mother was waiting for me at the big door; I came out alone, and on the stairs I met the teacher with the black beard--Coatti,--the one who frightens every one and punishes no one. He stared at me with wide-open eyes, and made his voice like that of a lion, in jest, but without laughing. I was still laughing when I pulled the bell on the fourth floor; but I ceased very suddenly when the servant let me into a wretched, half-lighted room, where my teacher was in bed. He was lying in a little iron bed. His beard was long. He put one hand to his brow in order to see better, and exclaimed in his affectionate voice:

"Oh, Enrico!"

I approached the bed; he laid one hand on my shoulder and said:

"Good, my boy. You have done well to come and see your poor teacher. I am reduced to a sad state, as you see, my dear Enrico. And how fares the school? How are your comrades getting along? All well, eh? Even without me? You do very well without your old master, do you not?"

I was on the point of saying "no"; he interrupted me.

"Come, come, I know that you do not hate me!" and he heaved a sigh.

I glanced at some photographs fastened to the wall.

"Do you see?" he said to me. "All of them are of boys who gave me their photographs more than twenty years ago. They were good boys. These are my souvenirs. When I die, my last glance will be at them; at those roguish urchins among whom my life has been passed. You will give me your portrait, also, will you not, when you have finished the elementary course?" Then he took an orange from his nightstand, and put it in my hand.

"I have nothing else to give you," he said; "it is the gift of a sick man."

I looked at it, and my heart was sad; I know not why.

"Attend to me," he began again. "I hope to get over this; but if I should not recover, see that you strengthen yourself in arithmetic, which is your weak point; make an effort. It is merely a question of a first effort: because sometimes there is no lack of aptitude; there is merely an absence of a fixed purpose--of stability, as it is called."

But in the meantime he was breathing hard; and it was evident that he was suffering.

"I am feverish," he sighed; "I am half gone; I beseech you, therefore, apply yourself to arithmetic, to problems. If you don't succeed at first, rest a little and begin afresh. And press forward, but quietly without fagging yourself, without straining your mind. Go! My respects to your mamma. And do not mount these stairs again. We shall see each other again in school. And if we do not, you must now and then call to mind your master of the third grade, who was fond of you."

I felt inclined to cry at these words.

"Bend down your head," he said to me.

I bent my head to his pillow; he kissed my hair. Then he said to me, "Go!" and turned his face towards the wall. And I flew down the stairs; for I longed to embrace my mother.

## THE STREET

Saturday, 25th.

I was watching you from the window this afternoon, when you were on your way home from the master's; you came in collision with a woman. Take more heed to your manner of walking in the street. There are duties to be fulfilled even there. If you keep your steps and gestures within bounds in a private house, why should you not do the same in the street, which is everybody's house. Remember this, Enrico. Every time that you meet a feeble old man, a poor person, a woman with a child in her arms, a cripple with his crutches, a man bending beneath a burden, a family dressed in mourning, make way for them respectfully. We must respect age, misery, maternal love, infirmity, labor, death. Whenever you see a person on the point of being run down by a vehicle, drag him away, if it is a child; warn him, if he is a man; always ask what ails the child who is crying all alone; pick up the aged man's cane, when he lets it fall. If two boys are fighting, separate them; if it is two men, go away: do not look on a scene of brutal violence, which offends and hardens the heart. And when a man passes, bound, and walking between a couple of policemen, do not add your curiosity to the cruel curiosity of the crowd; he may be innocent. Cease to talk with your companion, and to smile, when you meet a hospital litter, which is, perhaps, bearing a dying person, or a funeral procession; for one may issue from your own home on the morrow. Look with reverence upon all boys from the asylums, who walk two and two,--the blind, the dumb, those afflicted with the rickets, orphans, abandoned children; reflect that it is misfortune and human charity which is passing by. Always pretend not to notice any one who has a repulsive or laughter-provoking deformity. Always extinguish every match that you find in your path; for it may cost some one his life. Always answer a passer-by who asks you the way, with politeness. Do not look at any one and laugh; do not run without necessity; do not shout. Respect the street. The education of a people is judged first of all by their behavior on the street. Where you find offences in the streets, there you will find offences in the houses. And study the streets; study the city in which you live. If you were to be hurled far away from it tomorrow, you would be glad to have it clearly present in your memory, to be able to traverse it all again in memory. Your own city, and your little country--that which has been for so many years your world; where you took your first steps at your mother's side; where you experienced your first emotions, opened your mind to its first ideas; found your first friends. It has been a mother to you: it has taught you, loved you, protected you. Study it in its streets and in its people, and love it; and when you hear it insulted, defend it.

THY FATHER.

# MARCH

## THE EVENING SCHOOLS

Thursday, 2d.

LAST night my father took me to see the evening schools in our Baretti schoolhouse, which were all lighted up already, and where the workingmen were already beginning to enter. On our arrival we found the head-master and the other masters in a great rage, because a little while before the glass in one window had been broken by a stone. The beadle had darted forth and seized a boy by the hair, who was passing; but thereupon, Stardi, who lives in the house opposite, had presented himself, and said:

"This is not the right one; I saw it with my own eyes; it was Franti who threw it; and he said to me, 'Woe to you if you tell of me!' but I am not afraid."

Then the head-master declared that Franti should be expelled for good. In the meantime I was watching the workingmen enter by twos and threes; and more than two hundred had already entered. I have never seen anything so fine as the evening school. There were boys of twelve and upwards; bearded men who were on their way from their work, carrying their books and copy-books; there were carpenters, engineers with black faces, masons with hands white with plaster, bakers' boys with their hair full of flour; and there was perceptible the odor of varnish, hides, fish, oil,--odors of all the various trades. There also entered a squad of artillery workmen, dressed like soldiers and headed by a corporal. They all filed briskly to their benches, removed the board underneath, on which we put our feet, and immediately bent their heads over their work.

Some stepped up to the teachers to ask explanations, with their open copy-books in their hands. I caught sight of that young and well-dressed master "the little lawyer," who had three or four workingmen clustered round his table, and was making corrections with his pen; and also the lame one, who was laughing with a dyer who had brought him a copy-book all adorned with red and blue dyes. My master, who had recovered, and who will return to school tomorrow, was there also. The doors of the schoolroom were open. I was amazed, when the lessons began, to see how attentive they all were, and how they kept their eyes fixed on their work. Yet the greater part of them, so the head-master said, for fear of being late, had not even been home to eat a mouthful of supper, and they were hungry.

But the younger ones, after half an hour of school, were falling off the benches with sleep; one even went fast asleep with his head on the bench, and the master waked him up by poking his ear with a pen. But the grown-up men did nothing of the sort; they kept awake, and listened, with their mouths wide open, to the lesson, without even winking; and it made a deep impression on me to see all those bearded men on our benches. We also ascended to the story floor above, and I ran to the door of my schoolroom and saw in my seat a man with a big mustache and a bandaged hand, who might have injured himself while at work about some machine; but he was trying to write, though very, very slowly.

But what pleased me most was to behold in the seat of the little mason, on the very same bench and in the very same corner, his father, the mason, as huge as a giant, who sat there all coiled up into a narrow space, with his chin on his fists and his eyes on his book, so absorbed that he hardly breathed. And there was no chance about it, for it was he himself who said to the head-master the first evening he came to the school:

"Signor Director, do me the favor to place me in the seat of 'my hare's face.'" For he always calls his son so.

My father kept me there until the end, and in the street we saw many women with children in their arms, waiting for their husbands; and at the entrance a change was effected: the husbands took the children in their arms, and the women made them surrender their books and copy-books; and in this wise they proceeded to their homes. For several minutes the street was filled with people and with noise. Then all grew silent, and all we could see was the tall and weary form of the head-master disappearing in the distance.

THE FIGHT

Sunday, 5th.

It was what might have been expected. Franti, on being expelled by the head-master, wanted to revenge himself on Stardi, and he waited for Stardi at a corner, when he came out of school, and when the latter was passing with his sister, whom he escorts every day from an institution in the Via Dora Grossa. My sister Silvia, on emerging from her schoolhouse, witnessed the whole affair, and came home thoroughly terrified. This is what took place. Franti, with his cap of waxed cloth canted over one ear, ran up on tiptoe behind Stardi, and in order to provoke him, gave a tug at his sister's braid of hair,--a tug so violent that it almost threw the girl flat on her back on the ground. The little girl uttered a cry; her brother whirled round; Franti, who is much taller and stronger than Stardi, thought:

"He'll not utter a word, or I'll break his skin for him!"

But Stardi never paused to reflect, and small and ill-made as he is, he flung himself with one bound on that big fellow, and began to belabor him with his fists. He could not hold his own, however, and he got more than he gave. There was no one in the street but girls, so there was no one who could separate them. Franti flung him on the ground; but the other instantly got up, and then down he went on his back again, and Franti pounded away as though upon a door: in an instant he had torn away half an ear, and bruised one eye, and drawn blood from the other's nose. But Stardi was tenacious; he roared:

"You may kill me, but I'll make you pay for it!" And down went Franti, kicking and cuffing, and Stardi under him, butting and lungeing out with his heels. A woman shrieked from a window, "Good for the little one!" Others said, "It is a boy defending his sister; courage! give it to him well!" And they screamed at Franti, "You overbearing brute! you coward!" But Franti had grown ferocious; he held out his leg; Stardi tripped and fell, and Franti on top of him.

"Surrender!"--"No!"--"Surrender!"--"No!" and in a flash Stardi recovered his feet, clasped Franti by the body, and, with one furious effort, hurled him on the pavement, and fell upon him with one knee on his breast.

"Ah, the infamous fellow! he has a knife!" shouted a man, rushing up to disarm Franti.

But Stardi, beside himself with rage, had already grasped Franti's arm with both hands, and bestowed on the fist such a bite that the knife fell from it, and the hand began to bleed. More people had run up in the meantime, who separated them and set them on their feet. Franti took to his heels in a sorry plight, and Stardi stood still, with his face all scratched, and a black eye,--but triumphant,--beside his weeping sister, while some of the girls collected the books and copy-books which were strewn over the street.

"Bravo, little fellow!" said the bystanders; "he defended his sister!"

But Stardi, who was thinking more of his satchel than of his victory, instantly set to examining the books and copy-books, one by one, to see whether anything was missing or injured. He rubbed them off with his sleeve, scrutinized his pen, put everything back in its place, and then, tranquil and serious as usual, he said to his sister, "Let us go home quickly, for I have a problem to solve."

THE BOYS' PARENTS

Monday, 6th.

This morning big Stardi, the father, came to wait for his son, fearing lest he should again encounter Franti. But they say that Franti will not be seen again, because he will be put in the penitentiary.

There were a great many parents there this morning. Among the rest there was the retail wood-dealer, the father of Coretti, the perfect image of his son, slender, brisk, with his mustache brought to a point, and a ribbon of two colors in the button-hole of his jacket. I know nearly all the parents of the boys, through constantly seeing them there. There is one crooked grandmother, with her white cap, who comes four times a day, whether it rains or snows or storms, to accompany and to get her little grandson, of the upper primary; and she takes off his little cloak and puts it on for him, adjusts his necktie, brushes off the dust, polishes him up, and takes care of the copy-books. It is evident that she has no other thought, that she sees nothing in the world more beautiful. The captain of artillery also comes frequently, the father of Robetti, the lad with the crutches, who saved a child from the omnibus, and as all his son's companions bestow a caress on him in passing, he returns a caress or a salute to every one, and he never forgets any one; he bends over all, and the poorer and more badly dressed they are, the more pleased he seems to be, and he thanks them.

At times, however, sad sights are to be seen. A gentleman who had not come for a month because one of his sons had died, and who had sent a maidservant for the other, on returning yesterday and beholding the class, the comrades of his little dead boy, retired into a corner and burst into sobs, with both hands before his face, and the head-master took him by the arm and led him to his office.

There are fathers and mothers who know all their sons' companions by name. There are girls from the neighboring schoolhouse, and scholars in the gymnasium, who come to wait for their brothers. There is one old gentleman who was a colonel formerly, and who, when a boy drops a copy-book or a pen, picks it up for him. There are also to be seen well-dressed men, who discuss school matters with others, who have kerchiefs on their heads, and baskets on their arm, and who say:

"Oh! the problem has been a difficult one this time."--"That grammar lesson will never come to an end this morning!"

And when there is a sick boy in the class, they all know it; when a sick boy is convalescent, they all rejoice. And this morning there were eight or ten gentlemen and workingmen standing around Crossi's mother, the vegetable-vender, making inquiries about a poor baby in my brother's class, who lives in her court, and who is in danger of his life. The school seems to make them all equals and friends.


NUMBER 78

Wednesday, 8th.

I witnessed a touching scene yesterday afternoon. For several days, every time that the vegetable-vender has passed Derossi she has gazed and gazed at him with an expression of great affection; for Derossi, since he made the discovery about that inkstand and prisoner Number 78, has acquired a love for her son, Crossi, the red-haired boy with the useless arm; and he helps him to do his work in school, suggests answers to him, gives him paper, pens, and pencils; in short, he behaves to him like a brother, as though to compensate him for his father's misfortune, which has affected him, although he does not know it.

The vegetable-vender had been gazing at Derossi for several days, and she seemed loath to take her eyes from him, for she is a good woman who lives only for her son; and Derossi, who assists him and makes him appear well, Derossi, who is a gentleman and the head of the school, seems to her a king, a saint. She continued to stare at him, and seemed desirous of saying something to him, yet ashamed to do it. But at last, yesterday morning, she took courage, stopped him in front of a gate, and said to him:

"I beg a thousand pardons, little master! Will you, who are so kind to my son, and so fond of him, do me the favor to accept this little memento from a poor mother?" and she pulled out of her vegetable-basket a little pasteboard box of white and gold.

Derossi flushed up all over, and refused, saying with decision:

"Give it to your son; I will accept nothing."

The woman was mortified, and stammered an excuse:

"I had no idea of offending you. It is only caramels."

But Derossi said "no," again, and shook his head. Then she timidly lifted from her basket a bunch of radishes, and said:

"Accept these at least,--they are fresh,--and carry them to your mamma."

Derossi smiled, and said:

"No, thanks: I don't want anything; I shall always do all that I can for Crossi, but I cannot accept anything. I thank you all the same."

"But you are not at all offended?" asked the woman, anxiously.

Derossi said "No, no!" smiled, and went off, while she exclaimed, in great delight:

"Oh, what a good boy! I have never seen so fine and handsome a boy as he!"

And that appeared to be the end of it. But in the afternoon, at four o'clock, instead of Crossi's mother, his father approached, with that gaunt and melancholy face of his. He stopped Derossi, and from the way in which he looked at the latter I instantly understood that he suspected Derossi of knowing his secret. He looked at him intently, and said in his sorrowful, affectionate voice:

"You are fond of my son. Why do you like him so much?"

Derossi's face turned the color of fire. He would have liked to say: "I am fond of him because he has been unfortunate; because you, his father, have been more unfortunate than guilty, and have nobly expiated your crime, and are a man of heart." But he had not the courage to say it, for at bottom he still felt fear and almost loathing in the presence of this man who had shed another's blood, and had been six years in prison. But the latter divined it all, and lowering his voice, he said in Derossi's ear, almost trembling the while:

"You love the son; but you do not hate, do not wholly despise the father, do you?"

"Ah, no, no! Quite the reverse!" exclaimed Derossi, with a soulful impulse. And then the man made an impetuous movement, as though to throw one arm round his neck; but he dared not, and instead he took one of the lad's golden curls between two of his fingers, smoothed it out, and released it;

then he placed his hand on his mouth and kissed his palm, gazing at Derossi with moist eyes, as though to say that this kiss was for him. Then he took his son by the hand, and went away at a rapid pace.


A LITTLE DEAD BOY

Monday, 13th.

The little boy who lived in the vegetable-vender's court, the one who belonged to the upper primary, and was the companion of my brother, is dead. Schoolmistress Delcati came in great affliction, on Saturday afternoon, to inform the master of it; and instantly Garrone and Coretti volunteered to carry the coffin. He was a fine little lad. He had won the medal last week. He was fond of my brother, and he had presented him with a broken money-box. My mother always caressed him when she met him. He wore a cap with two stripes of red cloth. His father is a porter on the railway. Yesterday (Sunday) afternoon, at half-past four o'clock, we went to his house, to accompany him to the church.

They live on the ground floor. Many boys of the upper primary, with their mothers, all holding candles, and five or six teachers and several neighbors were already collected in the courtyard. The mistress with the red feather and Signora Delcati had gone inside, and through an open window we beheld them weeping. We could hear the mother of the child sobbing loudly. Two ladies, mothers of two school companions of the dead child, had brought two garlands of flowers.

Exactly at five o'clock we set out. In front went a boy carrying a cross, then a priest, then the coffin,-- a very, very small coffin, poor child!--covered with a black cloth, and round it were wound the garlands of flowers brought by the two ladies. On the black cloth, on one side, were fastened the medal and honorable mentions which the little boy had won in the course of the year. Garrone, Coretti, and two boys from the courtyard bore the coffin. Behind the coffin, first came Signora Delcati, who wept as though the little dead boy were her own; behind her the other schoolmistresses; and behind the mistresses, the boys, among whom were some very little ones, who carried bunches of violets in one hand, and who stared in amazement at the bier, while their other hand was held by their mothers, who carried candles. I heard one of them say, "And shall I not see him at school again?"

When the coffin emerged from the court, a despairing cry was heard from the window. It was the child's mother; but they made her draw back into the room immediately. On arriving in the street, we met the boys from a college, who were passing in double file, and on catching sight of the coffin with the medal and the schoolmistresses, they all pulled off their hats.

Poor little boy! he went to sleep forever with his medal. We shall never see his red cap again. He was in perfect health; in four days he was dead. On the last day he made an effort to rise and do his little task in nomenclature, and he insisted on keeping his medal on his bed for fear it would be taken from him. No one will ever take it from you again, poor boy! Farewell, farewell! We shall always remember thee at the Baretti School! Sleep in peace, dear little boy!

## THE EVE OF THE FOURTEENTH OF MARCH

Today has been more cheerful than yesterday. The thirteenth of March! The eve of the distribution of prizes at the Theatre Vittorio Emanuele, the greatest and most beautiful festival of the whole year! But this time the boys who are to go upon the stage and present the certificates of the prizes to the gentlemen who are to bestow them are not to be taken at haphazard. The head-master came in this morning, at the close of school, and said:

"Good news, boys!" Then he called, "Coraci!" the Calabrian. The Calabrian rose. "Would you like to be one of those to carry the certificates of the prizes to the authorities in the theatre tomorrow?" The Calabrian answered that he should.

"That is well," said the head-master; "then there will also be a representative of Calabria there; and that will be a fine thing. The municipal authorities are desirous that this year the ten or twelve lads who hand the prizes should be from all parts of Italy, and selected from all the public school buildings. We have twenty buildings, with five annexes--seven thousand pupils. Among such a multitude there has been no difficulty in finding one boy for each region of Italy. Two representatives of the Islands were found in the Torquato Tasso schoolhouse, a Sardinian, and a Sicilian; the Boncompagni School furnished a little Florentine, the son of a wood-carver; there is a Roman, a native of Rome, in the Tommaseo building; several Venetians, Lombards, and natives of Romagna have been found; the Monviso School gives us a Neapolitan, the son of an officer; we furnish a Genoese and a Calabrian,--you, Coraci,--with the Piemontese: that will make twelve. Does not this strike you as nice? It will be your brothers from all quarters of Italy who will give you your prizes. Look out! the whole twelve will appear on the stage together. Receive them with hearty applause. They are only boys, but they represent the country just as though they were men. A small tricolored flag is the symbol of Italy as much as a huge banner, is it not?

"Applaud them warmly, then. Let it be seen that your little hearts are all aglow, that your souls of ten years grow enthusiastic in the presence of the sacred image of your fatherland."

Having spoken thus, he went away, and the master said, with a smile, "So, Coraci, you are to be the deputy from Calabria."

And then all clapped their hands and laughed; and when we got into the street, we surrounded Coraci, seized him by the legs, lifted him on high, and set out to carry him in triumph, shouting, "Hurrah for the Deputy of Calabria!" by way of making a noise, of course; and not in jest, but quite the contrary, for the sake of making a celebration for him, and with a good will, for he is a boy who pleases every one; and he smiled. And thus we bore him as far as the corner, where we ran into a gentleman with a black beard, who began to laugh. The Calabrian said, "That is my father." And then the boys placed his son in his arms and ran away in all directions.


## THE DISTRIBUTION OF PRIZES

March 14th.

Towards two o'clock the vast theatre was crowded,--pit, gallery, boxes, stage, all were thronged; thousands of faces,--boys, gentlemen, teachers, workingmen, women of the people, babies. There was a moving of heads and hands, a flutter of feathers, ribbons, and curls, and loud and merry murmur which inspired cheerfulness. The theatre was all decorated with festoons of white, red, and green cloth. In the pit two little stairways had been erected: one on the right, which the winners of prizes were to ascend in order to reach the stage; the other, on the left, which they were to descend after receiving their prizes. On the front of the platform there was a row of red chairs; and from the back of the one in the centre hung two laurel crowns. At the back of the stage was a trophy of flags; on one side stood a small green table, and upon it lay all the certificates of premiums, tied with tricolored ribbons. The band of music was stationed in the pit, under the stage; the schoolmasters and mistresses filled all one side of the first balcony, which had been reserved for them; the benches and passages of the pit were crammed with hundreds of boys, who were to sing, and who had written music in their hands. At the back and all about, masters and mistresses could be seen going to and fro, arranging the prize scholars in lines; and it was full of parents who were giving a last touch to their hair and the last pull to their neckties.

No sooner had I entered my box with my family than I perceived in the opposite box the young mistress with the red feather, who was smiling and showing all the pretty dimples in her cheeks, and with her my brother's teacher and "the little nun," dressed wholly in black, and my kind mistress of the upper first; but she was so pale, poor thing! and coughed so hard, that she could be heard all over the theatre. In the pit I instantly espied Garrone's dear, big face and the little blond head of Nelli, who was clinging close to the other's shoulder. A little further on I saw Garoffi, with his owl's-beak nose, who was making great efforts to collect the printed catalogues of the prize-winners; and he already had a large bundle of them which he could put to some use in his bartering--we shall find out what it is tomorrow. Near the door was the wood-seller with his wife,--both dressed in festive attire,--together with their boy, who has a third prize in the second grade. I was amazed at no longer beholding the catskin cap and the chocolate-colored tights: on this occasion he was dressed like a little gentleman. In one balcony I caught a momentary glimpse of Votini, with a large lace collar; then he disappeared. In a proscenium box, filled with people, was the artillery captain, the father of Robetti, the boy with the crutches who saved the child from the omnibus.

On the stroke of two the band struck up, and at the same moment the mayor, the prefect, the judge, the *provveditore*, and many other gentlemen, all dressed in black, mounted the stairs on the right, and seated themselves on the red chairs at the front of the platform. The band ceased playing. The director of singing in the schools advanced with a *baton* in his hand. At a signal from him all the boys in the pit rose to their feet; at another sign they began to sing. There were seven hundred singing a very beautiful song,--seven hundred boys' voices singing together; how beautiful! All listened motionless: it was a slow, sweet, limpid song which seemed like a church chant. When they ceased, every one applauded; then they all became very still. The distribution of the prizes was about to begin. My little master of the second grade, with his red head and his quick eyes, who was to read the names of the prize-winners, had already advanced to the front of the stage. The entrance of the twelve boys who were to present the certificates was what they were waiting for. The newspapers had already stated that there would be boys from all the provinces of Italy. Every one knew it, and was watching for them and gazing curiously towards the spot where they were to enter, and the mayor and the other gentlemen gazed also, and the whole theatre was silent.

All at once the whole twelve arrived on the stage at a run, and remained standing there in line, with a smile. The whole theatre, three thousand persons, sprang up simultaneously, breaking into applause which sounded like a clap of thunder. The boys stood for a moment as though disconcerted. "Behold Italy!" said a voice on the stage. All at once I recognized Coraci, the Calabrian, dressed in black as usual. A gentleman belonging to the municipal government, who was with us and who knew them all, pointed them out to my mother. "That little blond is the representative of Venice. The Roman is that tall, curly-haired lad, yonder." Two or three of them were dressed like gentlemen; the others were sons of workingmen, but all were neatly clad and clean. The Florentine, who was the smallest, had a blue scarf round his body. They all passed in front of the mayor, who kissed them, one after the other, on the brow, while a gentleman seated next to him smilingly told him the names of their cities: "Florence, Naples, Bologna, Palermo." And as each passed by, the whole theatre clapped. Then they all ran to the green table, to take the certificates. The master began to read the list, mentioning the schoolhouses, the classes, the names; and the prize-winners began to mount the stage and to file past.

The foremost ones had hardly reached the stage, when behind the scenes there became audible a very, very faint music of violins, which did not cease during the whole time that they were filing past--a soft and always even air, like the murmur of many subdued voices, the voices of all the mothers, and all the masters and mistresses, giving counsel in concert, and beseeching and administering loving reproofs. And meanwhile, the prize-winners passed one by one in front of the seated gentlemen, who handed them their certificates, and said a word or bestowed a caress on each.

The boys in the pit and the balconies applauded loudly every time that there passed a very small lad, or one who seemed, from his garments, to be poor; and also for those who had abundant curly hair, or who were clad in red or white. Some of those who filed past belonged to the upper primary, and once arrived there, they became confused and did not know where to turn, and the whole theatre laughed. One passed, three spans high, with a big knot of pink ribbon on his back, so that he could hardly walk, and he got entangled in the carpet and tumbled down; and the prefect set him on his feet again, and all laughed and clapped. Another rolled headlong down the stairs, when descending again to the pit: cries arose, but he had not hurt himself. Boys of all sorts passed,--boys with roguish faces, with frightened faces, with faces as red as cherries; comical little fellows, who laughed in every one's face: and no sooner had they got back into the pit, than they were seized upon by their fathers and mothers, who carried them away.

When our schoolhouse's turn came, how amused I was! Many whom I knew passed. Coretti filed by, dressed in new clothes from head to foot, with his fine, merry smile, which displayed all his white teeth; but who knows how many myriagrammes of wood he had already carried that morning! The mayor, on presenting him with his certificate, inquired the meaning of a red mark on his forehead, and as he did so, laid one hand on his shoulder. I looked in the pit for his father and mother, and saw them laughing, while they covered their mouths with one hand. Then Derossi passed, all dressed in bright blue, with shining buttons, with all those golden curls, slender, easy, with his head held high, so handsome, so sympathetic, that I could have blown him a kiss; and all the gentlemen wanted to speak to him and to shake his hand.

Then the master cried, "Giulio Robetti!" and we saw the captain's son come forward on his crutches. Hundreds of boys knew the occurrence; a rumor ran round in an instant; a salvo of applause broke forth, and of shouts, which made the theatre tremble: men sprang to their feet, the ladies began to wave their handkerchiefs, and the poor boy halted in the middle of the stage, amazed and trembling. The mayor drew him to him, gave him his prize and a kiss, and removing the two laurel crowns which were hanging from the back of the chair, he strung them on the cross-bars of his crutches. Then he accompanied him to the proscenium box, where his father, the captain, was seated; and the latter lifted him bodily and set him down inside, amid an indescribable tumult of bravos and hurrahs.

Meanwhile, the soft and gentle music of the violins continued, and the boys continued to file by,-- those from the Schoolhouse della Consolata, nearly all the sons of petty merchants; those from the Vanchiglia School, the sons of workingmen; those from the Boncompagni School, many of whom were the sons of peasants; those of the Rayneri, which was the last. As soon as it was over, the seven hundred boys in the pit sang another very beautiful song; then the mayor spoke, and after him the judge, who terminated his discourse by saying to the boys:

"But do not leave this place without sending a salute to those who toil so hard for you; who have consecrated to you all the strength of their intelligence and of their hearts; who live and die for you. There they are; behold them!" And he pointed to the balcony of teachers. Then, from the balconies, from the pit, from the boxes, the boys rose, and extended their arms towards the masters and mistresses, with a shout, and the latter responded by waving their hands, their hats, and handkerchiefs, as they all stood up, in their emotion. After this, the band played once more, and the audience sent a last noisy salute to the twelve lads of all the provinces of Italy, who presented themselves at the front of the stage, all drawn up in line, with their hands interlaced, beneath a shower of flowers.

STRIFE

Monday, 26th.

However, it is not out of envy, because he got the prize and I did not, that I quarrelled with Coretti this morning. It was not out of envy. But I was in the wrong. The teacher had placed him beside me, and I was writing in my copy-book for calligraphy; he jogged my elbow and made me blot and soil the monthly story, *Blood of Romagna*, which I was to copy for the little mason, who is ill. I got angry, and said a rude word to him. He replied, with a smile, "I did not do it intentionally." I should have believed him, because I know him; but it displeased me that he should smile, and I thought:

"Oh! now that he has had a prize, he has grown saucy!" and a little while afterwards, to revenge myself, I gave him a jog which made him spoil his page. Then, all crimson with wrath, "You did that on purpose," he said to me, and raised his hand: the teacher saw it; he drew it back. But he added:

"I shall wait for you outside!" I felt ill at ease; my wrath had simmered away; I repented. No; Coretti could not have done it intentionally. He is good, I thought. I recalled how I had seen him in his own home; how he had worked and helped his sick mother; and then how heartily he had been welcomed in my house; and how he had pleased my father. What would I not have given not to have said that word to him; not to have insulted him thus! And I thought of the advice that my father had given to me: "Have you done wrong?"--"Yes."--"Then beg his pardon." But this I did not dare to do; I was ashamed to humiliate myself. I looked at him out of the corner of my eye, and I saw his coat ripped on the shoulder,--perhaps because he had carried too much wood,--and I felt that I loved him; and I said to myself, "Courage!" But the words, "excuse me," stuck in my throat. He looked at me askance from time to time, and he seemed to me to be more grieved than angry. But at such times I looked malevolently at him, to show him that I was not afraid.

He repeated, "We shall meet outside!" And I said, "We shall meet outside!" But I was thinking of what my father had once said to me, "If you are wronged, defend yourself, but do not fight."

And I said to myself, "I will defend myself, but I will not fight." But I was discontented, and I no longer listened to the master. At last the moment of dismissal arrived. When I was alone in the street I perceived that he was following me. I stopped and waited for him, ruler in hand. He approached; I raised my ruler.

"No, Enrico," he said, with his kindly smile, waving the ruler aside with his hand; "let us be friends again, as before."

I stood still in amazement, and then I felt what seemed to be a hand dealing a push on my shoulders, and I found myself in his arms. He kissed me, and said:

"We'll have no more altercations between us, will we?"

"Never again! never again!" I replied. And we parted content. But when I returned home, and told my father all about it, thinking to give him pleasure, his face clouded over, and he said:

"You should have been the first to offer your hand, since you were in the wrong." Then he added, "You should not raise your ruler at a comrade who is better than you are--at the son of a soldier!" and snatching the ruler from my hand, he broke it in two, and hurled it against the wall.

MY SISTER

Friday, 24th.

Why, Enrico, after our father has already reproved you for having behaved badly to Coretti, were you so unkind to me? You cannot imagine the pain that you caused me. Do you not know that when you were a baby, I stood for hours and hours beside your cradle, instead of playing with my companions, and that when you were ill, I got out of bed every night to feel whether your forehead was burning? Do you not know, you who grieve your sister, that if a tremendous misfortune should overtake us, I should be a mother to you and love you like my son? Do you not know that when our father and mother are no longer here, I shall be your best friend, the only person with whom you can talk about our dead and your infancy, and that, should it be necessary, I shall work for you, Enrico, to earn your bread and to pay for your studies, and that I shall always love you when you are grown up, that I shall follow you in thought when you go far away, always because we grew up together and have the same blood? O Enrico, be sure of this when you are a man, that if misfortune happens to you, if you are alone, be very sure that you will seek me, that you will come to me and say: "Silvia, sister, let me stay with you; let us talk of the days when we were happy--do you remember? Let us talk of our mother, of our home, of those beautiful days that are so far away." O Enrico, you will always find your sister with her arms wide open. Yes, dear Enrico; and you must forgive me for the reproof that I am administering to you now. I shall never recall any wrong of yours; and if you should give me other sorrows, what matters it? You will always be my brother, the same brother; I shall never recall you otherwise than as having held you in my arms when a baby, of having loved our father and mother with you, of having watched you grow up, of having been for years your most faithful companion. But do you write me a kind word in this same copy-book, and I will come for it and read it before the evening. In the meanwhile, to show you that I am not angry with you, and perceiving that you are weary, I have copied for you the monthly story, *Blood of Romagna*, which you were to have copied for the little sick mason. Look in the left drawer of your table; I have been writing all night, while you were asleep. Write me a kind word, Enrico, I beseech you.

THY SISTER SILVIA.

I am not worthy to kiss your hands.--ENRICO.

BLOOD OF ROMAGNA.

(*Monthly Story.*)

That evening the house of Ferruccio was more silent than was its wont. The father, who kept a little haberdasher's shop, had gone to Forli to make some purchases, and his wife had accompanied him, with Luigina, a baby, whom she was taking to a doctor, that he might operate on a diseased eye; and they were not to return until the following morning. It was almost midnight. The woman who came to do the work by day had gone away at nightfall. In the house there was only the grandmother with the paralyzed legs, and Ferruccio, a lad of thirteen. It was a small house of but one story, situated on the highway, at a gunshot's distance from a village not far from Forli, a town of Romagna; and there was near it only an uninhabited house, ruined two months previously by fire, on which the sign of an inn was still to be seen. Behind the tiny house was a small garden surrounded by a hedge, upon which a rustic gate opened; the door of the shop, which also served as the house door, opened on the highway. All around spread the solitary campagna, vast cultivated fields, planted with mulberry-trees.

It was nearly midnight; it was raining and blowing. Ferruccio and his grandmother, who was still up, were in the dining-room, between which and the garden there was a small, closet-like room, encumbered with old furniture. Ferruccio had only returned home at eleven o'clock, after an absence of many hours, and his grandmother had watched for him with eyes wide open, filled with anxiety, nailed to the large arm-chair, upon which she was accustomed to pass the entire day, and often the whole night as well, since a difficulty of breathing did not allow her to lie down in bed.

It was raining, and the wind beat the rain against the window-panes: the night was very dark. Ferruccio had returned weary, muddy, with his jacket torn, and the livid mark of a stone on his forehead. He had engaged in a stone fight with his comrades; they had come to blows, as usual; and in addition he had gambled, and lost all his soldi, and left his cap in a ditch.

Although the kitchen was illuminated only by a small oil lamp, placed on the corner of the table, near the arm-chair, his poor grandmother had instantly perceived the wretched condition of her grandson, and had partly divined, partly brought him to confess, his misdeeds.

She loved this boy with all her soul. When she had learned all, she began to cry.

"Ah, no!" she said, after a long silence, "you have no heart for your poor grandmother. You have no feeling, to take advantage in this manner of the absence of your father and mother, to cause me sorrow. You have left me alone the whole day long. You had not the slightest compassion. Take care, Ferruccio! You are entering on an evil path which will lead you to a sad end. I have seen others begin like you, and come to a bad end. If you begin by running away from home, by getting into brawls with the other boys, by losing soldi, then, gradually, from stone fights you will come to knives, from gambling to other vices, and from other vices to--theft."

Ferruccio stood listening three paces away, leaning against a cupboard, with his chin on his breast and his brows knit, being still hot with wrath from the brawl. A lock of fine chestnut hair fell across his forehead, and his blue eyes were motionless.

"From gambling to theft!" repeated his grandmother, continuing to weep. "Think of it, Ferruccio!

Think of that scourge of the country about here, of that Vito Mozzoni, who is now playing the vagabond in the town; who, at the age of twenty-four, has been twice in prison, and has made that poor woman, his mother, die of a broken heart--I knew her; and his father has fled to Switzerland in despair. Think of that bad fellow, whose salute your father is ashamed to return: he is always roaming with miscreants worse than himself, and some day he will go to the galleys. Well, I knew him as a boy, and he began as you are doing. Reflect that you will reduce your father and mother to the same end as his."

Ferruccio held his peace. He was not at all remorseful at heart; quite the reverse: his misdemeanors arose rather from superabundance of life and audacity than from an evil mind; and his father had managed him badly in precisely this particular, that, holding him capable, at bottom, of the finest sentiments, and also, when put to the proof, of a vigorous and generous action, he left the bridle loose upon his neck, and waited for him to acquire judgment for himself. The lad was good rather than perverse, but stubborn; and it was hard for him, even when his heart was oppressed with repentance, to allow those good words which win pardon to escape his lips, "If I have done wrong, I will do so no more; I promise it; forgive me." His soul was full of tenderness at times; but pride would not permit it to manifest itself.

"Ah, Ferruccio," continued his grandmother, perceiving that he was thus dumb, "not a word of penitence do you utter to me! You see to what a condition I am reduced, so that I am as good as actually buried. You ought not to have the heart to make me suffer so, to make the mother of your mother, who is so old and so near her last day, weep; the poor grandmother who has always loved you so, who rocked you all night long, night after night, when you were a baby a few months old, and who did not eat for amusing you,--you do not know that! I always said, 'This boy will be my consolation!' And now you are killing me! I would willingly give the little life that remains to me if I could see you become a good boy, and an obedient one, as you were in those days when I used to lead you to the sanctuary--do you remember, Ferruccio? You used to fill my pockets with pebbles and weeds, and I carried you home in my arms, fast asleep. You used to love your poor grandma then. And now I am a paralytic, and in need of your affection as of the air to breathe, since I have no one else in the world, poor, half-dead woman that I am: my God!"

Ferruccio was on the point of throwing himself on his grandmother, overcome with emotion, when he fancied that he heard a slight noise, a creaking in the small adjoining room, the one which opened on the garden. But he could not make out whether it was the window-shutters rattling in the wind, or something else.

He bent his head and listened.

The rain beat down noisily.

The sound was repeated. His grandmother heard it also.

"What is it?" asked the grandmother, in perturbation, after a momentary pause.

"The rain," murmured the boy.

"Then, Ferruccio," said the old woman, drying her eyes, "you promise me that you will be good, that you will not make your poor grandmother weep again--"

Another faint sound interrupted her.

"But it seems to me that it is not the rain!" she exclaimed, turning pale. "Go and see!"

But she instantly added, "No; remain here!" and seized Ferruccio by the hand.

Both remained as they were, and held their breath. All they heard was the sound of the water.

Then both were seized with a shivering fit.

It seemed to both that they heard footsteps in the next room.

"Who's there?" demanded the lad, recovering his breath with an effort.

No one replied.

"Who is it?" asked Ferruccio again, chilled with terror.

But hardly had he pronounced these words when both uttered a shriek of terror. Two men sprang into the room. One of them grasped the boy and placed one hand over his mouth; the other clutched the old woman by the throat. The first said:

"Silence, unless you want to die!"

The second:

"Be quiet!" and raised aloft a knife.

Both had dark cloths over their faces, with two holes for the eyes.

For a moment nothing was audible but the gasping breath of all four, the patter of the rain; the old woman emitted frequent rattles from her throat, and her eyes were starting from her head.

The man who held the boy said in his ear, "Where does your father keep his money?"

The lad replied in a thread of a voice, with chattering teeth, "Yonder--in the cupboard."

"Come with me," said the man.

And he dragged him into the closet room, holding him securely by the throat. There was a dark lantern standing on the floor.

"Where is the cupboard?" he demanded.

The suffocating boy pointed to the cupboard.

Then, in order to make sure of the boy, the man flung him on his knees in front of the cupboard, and, pressing his neck closely between his own legs, in such a way that he could throttle him if he shouted, and holding his knife in his teeth and his lantern in one hand, with the other he pulled from his pocket a pointed iron, drove it into the lock, fumbled about, broke it, threw the doors wide open, tumbled everything over in a perfect fury of haste, filled his pockets, shut the cupboard again, opened it again, made another search; then he seized the boy by the windpipe again, and pushed him to where the other man was still grasping the old woman, who was convulsed, with her head thrown back and her mouth open.

The latter asked in a low voice, "Did you find it?"

His companion replied, "I found it."

And he added, "See to the door."

The one that was holding the old woman ran to the door of the garden to see if there were any one there, and called in from the little room, in a voice that resembled a hiss, "Come!"

The one who remained behind, and who was still holding Ferruccio fast, showed his knife to the boy and the old woman, who had opened her eyes again, and said, "Not a sound, or I'll come back and cut your throat."

And he glared at the two for a moment.

At this juncture, a song sung by many voices became audible far off on the highway.

The robber turned his head hastily toward the door, and the violence of the movement caused the cloth to fall from his face.

The old woman gave vent to a shriek; "Mozzoni!"

"Accursed woman," roared the robber, on finding himself recognized, "you shall die!"

And he hurled himself, with his knife raised, against the old woman, who swooned on the spot.

The assassin dealt the blow.

But Ferruccio, with an exceedingly rapid movement, and uttering a cry of desperation, had rushed to his grandmother, and covered her body with his own. The assassin fled, stumbling against the table and overturning the light, which was extinguished.

The boy slipped slowly from above his grandmother, fell on his knees, and remained in that attitude, with his arms around her body and his head upon her breast.

Several moments passed; it was very dark; the song of the peasants gradually died away in the campagna. The old woman recovered her senses.

"Ferruccio!" she cried, in a voice that was barely intelligible, with chattering teeth.

"Grandmamma!" replied the lad.

The old woman made an effort to speak; but terror had paralyzed her tongue.

She remained silent for a while, trembling violently.

Then she succeeded in asking:

"They are not here now?"

"No."

"They did not kill me," murmured the old woman in a stifled voice.

"No; you are safe," said Ferruccio, in a weak voice. "You are safe, dear grandmother. They carried off the money. But daddy had taken nearly all of it with him."

His grandmother drew a deep breath.

"Grandmother," said Ferruccio, still kneeling, and pressing her close to him, "dear grandmother, you love me, don't you?"

"O Ferruccio! my poor little son!" she replied, placing her hands on his head; "what a fright you must have had!--O Lord God of mercy!--Light the lamp. No; let us still remain in the dark! I am still afraid."

"Grandmother," resumed the boy, "I have always caused you grief."

"No, Ferruccio, you must not say such things; I shall never think of that again; I have forgotten everything, I love you so dearly!"

"I have always caused you grief," pursued Ferruccio, with difficulty, and his voice quivered; "but I have always loved you. Do you forgive me?--Forgive me, grandmother."

"Yes, my son, I forgive you with all my heart. Think, how could I help forgiving you! Rise from your knees, my child. I will never scold you again. You are so good, so good! Let us light the lamp. Let us take courage a little. Rise, Ferruccio."

"Thanks, grandmother," said the boy, and his voice was still weaker. "Now--I am content. You will remember me, grandmother--will you not? You will always remember me--your Ferruccio?"

"My Ferruccio!" exclaimed his grandmother, amazed and alarmed, as she laid her hands on his shoulders and bent her head, as though to look him in his face.

"Remember me," murmured the boy once more, in a voice that seemed like a breath. "Give a kiss to my mother--to my father--to Luigina.--Good by, grandmother."

"In the name of Heaven, what is the matter with you?" shrieked the old woman, feeling the boy's head anxiously, as it lay upon her knees; and then with all the power of voice of which her throat was capable, and in desperation: "Ferruccio! Ferruccio! Ferruccio! My child! My love! Angels of Paradise, come to my aid!"

But Ferruccio made no reply. The little hero, the saviour of the mother of his mother, stabbed by a blow from a knife in the back, had rendered up his beautiful and daring soul to God.


## THE LITTLE MASON ON HIS SICK-BED

Tuesday, 18th.

The poor little mason is seriously ill; the master told us to go and see him; and Garrone, Derossi, and I agreed to go together. Stardi would have come also, but as the teacher had assigned us the description of *The Monument to Cavour*, he told us that he must go and see the monument, in order that his description might be more exact. So, by way of experiment, we invited that puffed-up fellow, Nobis, who replied "No," and nothing more. Votini also excused himself, perhaps because he was afraid of soiling his clothes with plaster.

We went there when we came out of school at four o'clock. It was raining in torrents. On the street Garrone halted, and said, with his mouth full of bread:

"What shall I buy?" and he rattled a couple of soldi in his pocket. We each contributed two soldi, and purchased three huge oranges. We ascended to the garret. At the door Derossi removed his medal and put it in his pocket. I asked him why.

"I don't know," he answered; "in order not to have the air: it strikes me as more delicate to go in without my medal." We knocked; the father, that big man who looks like a giant, opened to us; his face was distorted so that he appeared terrified.

"Who are you?" he demanded. Garrone replied:

"We are Antonio's schoolmates, and we have brought him three oranges."

"Ah, poor Tonino!" exclaimed the mason, shaking his head, "I fear that he will never eat your oranges!" and he wiped his eyes with the back of his hand. He made us come in. We entered an attic room, where we saw "the little mason" asleep in a little iron bed; his mother hung dejectedly over the bed, with her face in her hands, and she hardly turned to look at us; on one side hung brushes, a trowel, and a plaster-sieve; over the feet of the sick boy was spread the mason's jacket, white with lime. The poor boy was emaciated; very, very white; his nose was pointed, and his breath was short. O dear Tonino, my little comrade! you who were so kind and merry, how it pains me! what would I not give to see you make the hare's face once more, poor little mason! Garrone laid an orange on his pillow, close to his face; the odor waked him; he grasped it instantly; then let go of it, and gazed intently at Garrone.

"It is I," said the latter; "Garrone: do you know me?" He smiled almost imperceptibly, lifted his stubby hand with difficulty from the bed and held it out to Garrone, who took it between his, and laid it against his cheek, saying:

"Courage, courage, little mason; you are going to get well soon and come back to school, and the master will put you next to me; will that please you?"

But the little mason made no reply. His mother burst into sobs: "Oh, my poor Tonino! My poor Tonino! He is so brave and good, and God is going to take him from us!"

"Silence!" cried the mason; "silence, for the love of God, or I shall lose my reason!"

Then he said to us, with anxiety: "Go, go, boys, thanks; go! what do you want to do here? Thanks; go home!" The boy had closed his eyes again, and appeared to be dead.

"Do you need any assistance?" asked Garrone.

"No, my good boy, thanks," the mason answered. And so saying, he pushed us out on the landing, and shut the door. But we were not half-way down the stairs, when we heard him calling, "Garrone! Garrone!"

We all three mounted the stairs once more in haste.

"Garrone!" shouted the mason, with a changed countenance, "he has called you by name; it is two days since he spoke; he has called you twice; he wants you; come quickly! Ah, holy God, if this is only a good sign!"

"Farewell for the present," said Garrone to us; "I shall remain," and he ran in with the father. Derossi's eyes were full of tears. I said to him:

"Are you crying for the little mason? He has spoken; he will recover."

"I believe it," replied Derossi; "but I was not thinking of him. I was thinking how good Garrone is, and what a beautiful soul he has."


COUNT CAVOUR

Wednesday, 29th.

You are to make a description of the monument to Count Cavour. You can do it. But who was Count Cavour? You cannot understand at present. For the present this is all you know: he was for many years the prime minister of Piemont. It was he who sent the Piemontese army to the Crimea to raise once more, with the victory of the Cernaia, our military glory, which had fallen with the defeat at Novara; it was he who made one hundred and fifty thousand Frenchmen descend from the Alps to chase the Austrians from Lombardy; it was he who governed Italy in the most solemn period of our revolution; who gave, during those years, the most potent impulse to the holy enterprise of the unification of our country,--he with his luminous mind, with his invincible perseverance, with his more than human industry. Many generals have passed terrible hours on the field of battle; but he passed more terrible ones in his cabinet, when his enormous work might suffer destruction at any moment, like a fragile edifice at the tremor of an earthquake. Hours, nights of struggle and anguish did he pass, sufficient to make him issue from it with reason distorted and death in his heart. And it was this gigantic and stormy work which shortened his life by twenty years. Nevertheless, devoured by the fever which was to cast him into his grave, he yet contended desperately with the malady in order to accomplish something for his country. "It is strange," he said sadly on his death-bed, "I no longer know how to read; I can no longer read."

While they were bleeding him, and the fever was increasing, he was thinking of his country, and he said imperiously: "Cure me; my mind is clouding over; I have need of all my faculties to manage important affairs." When he was already reduced to extremities, and the whole city was in a tumult, and the king stood at his bedside, he said anxiously, "I have many things to say to you, Sire, many things to show you; but I am ill; I cannot, I cannot;" and he was in despair.

And his feverish thoughts hovered ever round the State, round the new Italian provinces which had been united with us, round the many things which still remained to be done. When delirium seized him, "Educate the children!" he exclaimed, between his gasps for breath,--"educate the children and the young people--govern with liberty!"

His delirium increased; death hovered over him, and with burning words he invoked General Garibaldi, with whom he had had disagreements, and Venice and Rome, which were not yet free: he had vast visions of the future of Italy and of Europe; he dreamed of a foreign invasion; he inquired where the corps of the army were, and the generals; he still trembled for us, for his people. His great sorrow was not, you understand, that he felt that his life was going, but to see himself fleeing his country, which still had need of him, and for which he had, in a few years, worn out the measureless forces of his miraculous organism. He died with the battle-cry in his throat, and his death was as great as his life. Now reflect a little, Enrico, what sort of a thing is our labor, which nevertheless so weighs us down; what are our griefs, our death itself, in the face of the toils, the terrible anxieties, the tremendous agonies of these men upon whose hearts rests a world! Think of this, my son, when you pass before that marble image, and say to it, "Glory!" in your heart.

THY FATHER.

# APRIL

SPRING

Saturday, 1st.

THE first of April! Only three months more! This has been one of the most beautiful mornings of the year. I was happy in school because Coretti told me to come day after tomorrow to see the king make his entrance with his father, *who knows him*, and because my mother had promised to take me the same day to visit the Infant Asylum in the Corso Valdocco. I was pleased, too, because the little mason is better, and because the teacher said to my father yesterday evening as he was passing, "He is doing well; he is doing well."

And then it was a beautiful spring morning. From the school windows we could see the blue sky, the trees of the garden all covered with buds, and the wide-open windows of the houses, with their boxes and vases already growing green. The master did not laugh, because he never laughs; but he was in a good humor, so that that perpendicular wrinkle hardly ever appeared on his brow; and he explained a problem on the blackboard, and jested. And it was plain that he felt a pleasure in breathing the air of the gardens which entered through the open window, redolent with the fresh odor of earth and leaves, which suggested thoughts of country rambles.

While he was explaining, we could hear in a neighboring street a blacksmith hammering on his anvil, and in the house opposite, a woman singing to lull her baby to sleep; far away, in the Cernaia barracks, the trumpets were sounding. Every one appeared pleased, even Stardi. At a certain moment the blacksmith began to hammer more vigorously, the woman to sing more loudly. The master paused and lent an ear. Then he said, slowly, as he gazed out of the window:

"The smiling sky, a singing mother, an honest man at work, boys at study,--these are beautiful things."

When we emerged from the school, we saw that every one else was cheerful also. All walked in a line, stamping loudly with their feet, and humming, as though on the eve of a four days' vacation; the schoolmistresses were playful; the one with the red feather tripped along behind the children like a schoolgirl; the parents of the boys were chatting together and smiling, and Crossi's mother, the vegetable-vender, had so many bunches of violets in her basket, that they filled the whole large hall with perfume.

I have never felt such happiness as this morning on catching sight of my mother, who was waiting for me in the street. And I said to her as I ran to meet her:

"Oh, I am happy! what is it that makes me so happy this morning?" And my mother answered me with a smile that it was the beautiful season and a good conscience.

KING UMBERTO

Monday, 3d.

At ten o'clock precisely my father saw from the window Coretti, the wood-seller, and his son waiting for me in the square, and said to me:

"There they are, Enrico; go and see your king."

I went like a flash. Both father and son were even more alert than usual, and they never seemed to me to resemble each other so strongly as this morning. The father wore on his jacket the medal for valor between two commemorative medals, and his mustaches were curled and as pointed as two pins.

We at once set out for the railway station, where the king was to arrive at half-past ten. Coretti, the father, smoked his pipe and rubbed his hands. "Do you know," said he, "I have not seen him since the war of 'sixty-six? A trifle of fifteen years and six months. First, three years in France, and then at Mondovì, and here, where I might have seen him, I have never had the good luck of being in the city when he came. Such a combination of circumstances!"

He called the King "Umberto," like a comrade. Umberto commanded the 16th division; Umberto was twenty-two years and so many days old; Umberto mounted a horse thus and so.

"Fifteen years!" he said vehemently, accelerating his pace. "I really have a great desire to see him again. I left him a prince; I see him once more, a king. And I, too, have changed. From a soldier I have become a hawker of wood." And he laughed.

His son asked him, "If he were to see you, would he remember you?"

He began to laugh.

"You are crazy!" he answered. "That's quite another thing. He, Umberto, was one single man; we were as numerous as flies. And then, he never looked at us one by one."

We turned into the Corso Vittorio Emanuele; there were many people on their way to the station. A company of Alpine soldiers passed with their trumpets. Two armed policemen passed by on horseback at a gallop. The day was serene and brilliant.

"Yes!" exclaimed the elder Coretti, growing animated, "it is a real pleasure to me to see him once more, the general of my division. Ah, how quickly I have grown old! It seems as though it were only the other day that I had my knapsack on my shoulders and my gun in my hands, at that affair of the 24th of June, when we were on the point of coming to blows. Umberto was going to and fro with his officers, while the cannon were thundering in the distance; and every one was gazing at him and saying, 'May there not be a bullet for him also!' I was a thousand miles from thinking that I should soon find myself so near him, in front of the lances of the Austrian uhlans; actually, only four paces from each other, boys. That was a fine day; the sky was like a mirror; but so hot! Let us see if we can get in."

We had arrived at the station; there was a great crowd,--carriages, policemen, carabineers, societies with banners. A regimental band was playing. The elder Coretti attempted to enter the portico, but he was stopped. Then it occurred to him to force his way into the front row of the crowd which formed an opening at the entrance; and making way with his elbow, he succeeded in thrusting us forward also. But the undulating throng flung us hither and thither a little. The wood-seller got his eye upon the first pillar of the portico, where the police did not allow any one to stand; "Come with me," he said suddenly, dragging us by the hand; and he crossed the empty space in two bounds, and went and planted himself there, with his back against the wall.

A police brigadier instantly hurried up and said to him, "You can't stand here."

"I belong to the fourth battalion of forty-nine," replied Coretti, touching his medal.

The brigadier glanced at it, and said, "Remain."

"Didn't I say so!" exclaimed Coretti triumphantly; "it's a magic word, that fourth of the forty-ninth! Haven't I the right to see my general with some little comfort,--I, who was in that squadron? I saw him close at hand then; it seems right that I should see him close at hand now. And I say general! He was my battalion commander for a good half-hour; for at such moments he commanded the battalion himself, while it was in the heart of things, and not Major Ubrich, by Heavens!"

In the meantime, in the reception-room and outside, a great mixture of gentlemen and officers was visible, and in front of the door, the carriages, with the lackeys dressed in red, were drawn up in a line.

Coretti asked his father whether Prince Umberto had his sword in his hand when he was with the regiment.

"He would certainly have had his sword in his hand," the latter replied, "to ward off a blow from a lance, which might strike him as well as another. Ah! those unchained demons! They came down on us like the wrath of God; they descended on us. They swept between the groups, the squadrons, the cannon, as though tossed by a hurricane, crushing down everything. There was a whirl of light cavalry of Alessandria, of lancers of Foggia, of infantry, of sharpshooters, a pandemonium in which nothing could any longer be understood. I heard the shout, 'Your Highness! your Highness!' I saw the lowered lances approaching; we discharged our guns; a cloud of smoke hid everything. Then the smoke cleared away. The ground was covered with horses and uhlans, wounded and dead. I turned round, and beheld in our midst Umberto, on horseback, gazing tranquilly about, with the air of demanding, 'Have any of my lads received a scratch?' And we shouted to him, 'Hurrah!' right in his face, like madmen. Heavens, what a moment that was! Here's the train coming!"

The band struck up; the officers hastened forward; the crowd elevated themselves on tiptoe.

"Eh, he won't come out in a hurry," said a policeman; "they are presenting him with an address now."

The elder Coretti was beside himself with impatience.

"Ah! when I think of it," he said, "I always see him there. Of course, there is cholera and there are earthquakes; and in them, too, he bears himself bravely; but I always have him before my mind as I saw him then, among us, with that tranquil face. I am sure that he too recalls the fourth of the forty-ninth, even now that he is King; and that it would give him pleasure to have for once, at a table together, all those whom he saw about him at such moments. Now, he has generals, and great gentlemen, and courtiers; then, there was no one but us poor soldiers. If we could only exchange a few words alone! Our general of twenty-two; our prince, who was intrusted to our bayonets! I have not seen him for fifteen years. Our Umberto! that's what he is! Ah! that music stirs my blood, on my word of honor."

An outburst of shouts interrupted him; thousands of hats rose in the air; four gentlemen dressed in black got into the first carriage.

"'Tis he!" cried Coretti, and stood as though enchanted.

Then he said softly, "Madonna mia, how gray he has grown!"

We all three uncovered our heads; the carriage advanced slowly through the crowd, who shouted and waved their hats. I looked at the elder Coretti. He seemed to me another man; he seemed to have become taller, graver, rather pale, and fastened bolt upright against the pillar.

The carriage arrived in front of us, a pace distant from the pillar. "Hurrah!" shouted many voices.

"Hurrah!" shouted Coretti, after the others.

The King glanced at his face, and his eye dwelt for a moment on his three medals.

Then Coretti lost his head, and roared, "The fourth battalion of the forty-ninth!"

The King, who had turned away, turned towards us again, and looking Coretti straight in the eye, reached his hand out of the carriage.

Coretti gave one leap forwards and clasped it. The carriage passed on; the crowd broke in and separated us; we lost sight of the elder Coretti. But it was only for a moment. We found him again directly, panting, with wet eyes, calling for his son by name, and holding his hand on high. His son flew towards him, and he said, "Here, little one, while my hand is still warm!" and he passed his hand over the boy's face, saying, "This is a caress from the King."

And there he stood, as though in a dream, with his eyes fixed on the distant carriage, smiling, with his pipe in his hand, in the centre of a group of curious people, who were staring at him. "He's one of the fourth battalion of the forty-ninth!" they said. "He is a soldier that knows the King." "And the

King recognized him." "And he offered him his hand." "He gave the King a petition," said one, more loudly.

"No," replied Coretti, whirling round abruptly; "I did not give him any petition. There is something else that I would give him, if he were to ask it of me."

They all stared at him.

And he said simply, "My blood."

THE INFANT ASYLUM

Tuesday, 4th.

After breakfast yesterday my mother took me, as she had promised, to the Infant Asylum in the Corso Valdocco, in order to recommend to the directress a little sister of Precossi. I had never seen an asylum. How much amused I was! There were two hundred of them, boy-babies and girl-babies, and so small that the children in our lower primary schools are men in comparison.

We arrived just as they were entering the refectory in two files, where there were two very long tables, with a great many round holes, and in each hole a black bowl filled with rice and beans, and a tin spoon beside it. On entering, some grew confused and remained on the floor until the mistresses ran and picked them up. Many halted in front of a bowl, thinking it was their proper place, and had already swallowed a spoonful, when a mistress arrived and said, "Go on!" and then they advanced three or four paces and got down another spoonful, and then advanced again, until they reached their own places, after having fraudulently disposed of half a portion. At last, by dint of pushing and crying, "Make haste! make haste!" they were all got into order, and the prayer was begun. But all those on the inner line, who had to turn their backs on the bowls for the prayer, twisted their heads round so that they could keep an eye on them, lest some one might meddle; and then they said their prayer thus, with hands clasped and their eyes on the ceiling, but with their hearts on their food. Then they set to eating. Ah, what a charming sight it was! One ate with two spoons, another with his hands; many picked up the beans one by one, and thrust them into their pockets; others wrapped them tightly in their little aprons, and pounded them to reduce them to a paste. There were even some who did not eat, because they were watching the flies flying, and others coughed and sprinkled a shower of rice all around them. It resembled a poultry-yard. But it was charming. The two rows of babies formed a pretty sight, with their hair all tied on the tops of their heads with red, green, and blue ribbons. One teacher asked a row of eight children, "Where does rice grow?" The whole eight opened their mouths wide, filled as they were with the pottage, and replied in concert, in a sing-song, "It grows in the water." Then the teacher gave the order, "Hands up!" and it was pretty to see all those little arms fly up, which a few months ago were all in swaddling-clothes, and all those little hands flourishing, which looked like so many white and pink butterflies.

Then they all went to recreation; but first they all took their little baskets, which were hanging on the wall with their lunches in them. They went out into the garden and scattered, drawing forth their provisions as they did so,--bread, stewed plums, a tiny bit of cheese, a hard-boiled egg, little apples, a handful of boiled vetches, or a wing of chicken. In an instant the whole garden was strewn with crumbs, as though they had been scattered from their feed by a flock of birds. They ate in all the queerest ways,--like rabbits, like rats, like cats, nibbling, licking, sucking. There was one child who held a bit of rye bread hugged closely to his breast, and was rubbing it with a medlar, as though he were polishing a sword. Some of the little ones crushed in their fists small cheeses, which trickled between their fingers like milk, and ran down inside their sleeves, and they were utterly unconscious of it. They ran and chased each other with apples and rolls in their teeth, like dogs. I saw three of them excavating a hard-boiled egg with a straw, thinking to discover treasures, and they spilled half of it on the ground, and then picked the crumbs up again one by one with great patience, as though they had been pearls. And those who had anything extraordinary were surrounded by eight or ten, who stood staring at the baskets with bent heads, as though they were looking at the moon in a well. There were twenty congregated round a mite of a fellow who had a paper horn of sugar, and they were going through all sorts of ceremonies with him for the privilege of dipping their bread in it, and he accorded it to some, while to others, after many prayers, he only granted his finger to suck.

In the meantime, my mother had come into the garden and was caressing now one and now another. Many hung about her, and even on her back, begging for a kiss, with faces upturned as though to a third story, and with mouths that opened and shut as though asking for the breast. One offered her the quarter of an orange which had been bitten, another a small crust of bread; one little girl gave her a leaf; another showed her, with all seriousness, the tip of her forefinger, a minute examination of which revealed a microscopic swelling, which had been caused by touching the flame of a candle on the preceding day. They placed before her eyes, as great marvels, very tiny insects, which I cannot understand their being able to see and catch, the halfs of corks, shirt-buttons, and flowerets pulled from the vases. One child, with a bandaged head, who was determined to be heard at any cost, stammered out to her some story about a head-over-heels tumble, not one word of which was intelligible; another insisted that my mother should bend down, and then whispered in her ear, "My father makes brushes."

And in the meantime a thousand accidents were happening here and there which caused the teachers to hasten up. Children wept because they could not untie a knot in their handkerchiefs; others disputed, with scratches and shrieks, the halves of an apple; one child, who had fallen face downward over a little bench which had been overturned, wept amid the ruins, and could not rise.

Before her departure my mother took three or four of them in her arms, and they ran up from all quarters to be taken also, their faces smeared with yolk of egg and orange juice; and one caught her hands; another her finger, to look at her ring; another tugged at her watch chain; another tried to seize her by the hair.

"Take care," the teacher said to her; "they will tear your clothes all to pieces."

But my mother cared nothing for her dress, and she continued to kiss them, and they pressed closer and closer to her: those who were nearest, with their arms extended as though they were desirous of climbing; the more distant endeavoring to make their way through the crowd, and all screaming:

"Good by! good by! good by!"

At last she succeeded in escaping from the garden. And they all ran and thrust their faces through the railings to see her pass, and to thrust their arms through to greet her, offering her once more bits of bread, bites of apple, cheese-rinds, and all screaming in concert:

"Good by! good by! good by! Come back tomorrow! Come again!"

As my mother made her escape, she passed her hand once more over those hundreds of tiny outstretched hands as over a garland of living roses, and finally arrived safely in the street, covered with crumbs and spots, rumpled and dishevelled, with one hand full of flowers and her eyes swelling with tears, and happy as though she had come from a festival. And inside there was still audible a sound like the twittering of birds, saying:

"Good by! good by! Come again, *madama*!"

GYMNASTICS

Tuesday, 5th.

As the weather continues extremely fine, they have made us pass from chamber gymnastics to gymnastics with apparatus in the garden.

Garrone was in the head-master's office yesterday when Nelli's mother, that blond woman dressed in black, came in to get her son excused from the new exercises. Every word cost her an effort; and as she spoke, she held one hand on her son's head.

"He is not able to do it," she said to the head-master. But Nelli showed much grief at this exclusion from the apparatus, at having this added humiliation imposed upon him.

"You will see, mamma," he said, "that I shall do like the rest."

His mother gazed at him in silence, with an air of pity and affection. Then she remarked, in a hesitating way, "I fear lest his companions--"

What she meant to say was, "lest they should make sport of him." But Nelli replied:

"They will not do anything to me--and then, there is Garrone. It is sufficient for him to be present, to prevent their laughing."

And then he was allowed to come. The teacher with the wound on his neck, who was with Garibaldi, led us at once to the vertical bars, which are very high, and we had to climb to the very top, and stand upright on the transverse plank. Derossi and Coretti went up like monkeys; even little Precossi mounted briskly, in spite of the fact that he was embarrassed with that jacket which extends to his knees; and in order to make him laugh while he was climbing, all the boys repeated to him his constant expression, "Excuse me! excuse me!" Stardi puffed, turned as red as a turkey-cock, and set his teeth until he looked like a mad dog; but he would have reached the top at the expense of bursting, and he actually did get there; and so did Nobis, who, when he reached the summit, assumed the attitude of an emperor; but Votini slipped back twice, notwithstanding his fine new suit with azure stripes, which had been made expressly for gymnastics.

In order to climb the more easily, all the boys had daubed their hands with resin, which they call colophony, and as a matter of course it is that trader of a Garoffi who provides every one with it, in a powdered form, selling it at a soldo the paper hornful, and turning a pretty penny.

Then it was Garrone's turn, and up he went, chewing away at his bread as though it were nothing out of the common; and I believe that he would have been capable of carrying one of us up on his shoulders, for he is as muscular and strong as a young bull.

After Garrone came Nelli. No sooner did the boys see him grasp the bars with those long, thin hands of his, than many of them began to laugh and to sing; but Garrone crossed his big arms on his breast, and darted round a glance which was so expressive, which so clearly said that he did not mind dealing out half a dozen punches, even in the master's presence, that they all ceased laughing on the instant. Nelli began to climb. He tried hard, poor little fellow; his face grew purple, he breathed with difficulty, and the perspiration poured from his brow. The master said, "Come down!" But he would not. He strove and persisted. I expected every moment to see him fall headlong, half dead. Poor Nelli! I thought, what if I had been like him, and my mother had seen me! How she would have suffered, poor mother! And as I thought of that I felt so tenderly towards Nelli that I could have given, I know not what, to be able, for the sake of having him climb those bars, to give him a push from below without being seen.

Meanwhile Garrone, Derossi, and Coretti were saying: "Up with you, Nelli, up with you!" "Try--one effort more--courage!" And Nelli made one more violent effort, uttering a groan as he did so, and found himself within two spans of the plank.

"Bravo!" shouted the others. "Courage--one dash more!" and behold Nelli clinging to the plank.

All clapped their hands. "Bravo!" said the master. "But that will do now. Come down."

But Nelli wished to ascend to the top like the rest, and after a little exertion he succeeded in getting his elbows on the plank, then his knees, then his feet; at last he stood upright, panting and smiling, and gazed at us.

We began to clap again, and then he looked into the street. I turned in that direction, and through the plants which cover the iron railing of the garden I caught sight of his mother, passing along the sidewalk without daring to look. Nelli descended, and we all made much of him. He was excited and rosy, his eyes sparkled, and he no longer seemed like the same boy.

Then, at the close of school, when his mother came to meet him, and inquired with some anxiety, as she embraced him, "Well, my poor son, how did it go? how did it go?" all his comrades replied, in concert, "He did well--he climbed like the rest of us--he's strong, you know--he's active--he does exactly like the others."

And then the joy of that woman was a sight to see. She tried to thank us, and could not; she shook hands with three or four, bestowed a caress on Garrone, and carried off her son; and we watched them for a while, walking in haste, and talking and gesticulating, both perfectly happy, as though no one were looking at them.

## MY FATHER'S TEACHER

Tuesday, 11th.

What a beautiful excursion I took yesterday with my father! This is the way it came about.

Day before yesterday, at dinner, as my father was reading the newspaper, he suddenly uttered an exclamation of astonishment. Then he said:

"And I thought him dead twenty years ago! Do you know that my old first elementary teacher, Vincenzo Crosetti, is eighty-four years old? I see here that the minister has conferred on him the medal of merit for sixty years of teaching. Six-ty ye-ars, you understand! And it is only two years since he stopped teaching school. Poor Crosetti! He lives an hour's journey from here by rail, at Condove, in the country of our old gardener's wife, of the town of Chieri." And he added, "Enrico, we will go and see him."

And the whole evening he talked of nothing but him. The name of his primary teacher recalled to his mind a thousand things which had happened when he was a boy, his early companions, his dead mother. "Crosetti!" he exclaimed. "He was forty when I was with him. I seem to see him now. He was a small man, somewhat bent even then, with bright eyes, and always cleanly shaved. Severe, but in a good way; for he loved us like a father, and forgave us more than one offence. He had risen from the condition of a peasant by dint of study and privations. He was a fine man. My mother was attached to him, and my father treated him like a friend. How comes it that he has gone to end his days at Condove, near Turin? He certainly will not recognize me. Never mind; I shall recognize him. Forty-four years have elapsed,--forty-four years, Enrico! and we will go to see him tomorrow."

And yesterday morning, at nine o'clock, we were at the Susa railway station. I should have liked to have Garrone come too; but he could not, because his mother is ill.

It was a beautiful spring day. The train ran through green fields and hedgerows in blossom, and the air we breathed was perfumed. My father was delighted, and every little while he would put his arm round my neck and talk to me like a friend, as he gazed out over the country.

"Poor Crosetti!" he said; "he was the first man, after my father, to love me and do me good. I have never forgotten certain of his good counsels, and also certain sharp reprimands which caused me to return home with a lump in my throat. His hands were large and stubby. I can see him now, as he used to enter the schoolroom, place his cane in a corner and hang his coat on the peg, always with the same gesture. And every day he was in the same humor,--always conscientious, full of good will, and attentive, as though each day he were teaching school for the first time. I remember him as well as though I heard him now when he called to me: 'Bottini! eh, Bottini! The fore and middle fingers on that pen!' He must have changed greatly in these four and forty years."

As soon as we reached Condove, we went in search of our old gardener's wife of Chieri, who keeps a stall in an alley. We found her with her boys: she made much of us and gave us news of her husband, who is soon to return from Greece, where he has been working these three years; and of her eldest daughter, who is in the Deaf-mute Institute in Turin. Then she pointed out to us the street which led to the teacher's house,--for every one knows him.

We left the town, and turned into a steep lane flanked by blossoming hedges.

My father no longer talked, but appeared entirely absorbed in his reminiscences; and every now and then he smiled, and then shook his head.

Suddenly he halted and said: "Here he is. I will wager that this is he." Down the lane towards us a little old man with a white beard and a large hat was descending, leaning on a cane. He dragged his feet along, and his hands trembled.

"It is he!" repeated my father, hastening his steps.

When we were close to him, we stopped. The old man stopped also and looked at my father. His face was still fresh colored, and his eyes were clear and vivacious.

"Are you," asked my father, raising his hat, "Vincenzo Crosetti, the schoolmaster?"

The old man raised his hat also, and replied: "I am," in a voice that was somewhat tremulous, but full.

"Well, then," said my father, taking one of his hands, "permit one of your old scholars to shake your hand and to inquire how you are. I have come from Turin to see you."

The old man stared at him in amazement. Then he said: "You do me too much honor. I do not know--When were you my scholar? Excuse me; your name, if you please."

My father mentioned his name, Alberto Bottini, and the year in which he had attended school, and where, and he added: "It is natural that you should not remember me. But I recollect you so perfectly!"

The master bent his head and gazed at the ground in thought, and muttered my father's name three or four times; the latter, meanwhile, observed him with intent and smiling eyes.

All at once the old man raised his face, with his eyes opened widely, and said slowly: "Alberto Bottini? the son of Bottini, the engineer? the one who lived in the Piazza della Consolata?"

"The same," replied my father, extending his hands.

"Then," said the old man, "permit me, my dear sir, permit me"; and advancing, he embraced my father: his white head hardly reached the latter's shoulder. My father pressed his cheek to the other's brow.

"Have the goodness to come with me," said the teacher. And without speaking further he turned about and took the road to his dwelling.

In a few minutes we arrived at a garden plot in front of a tiny house with two doors, round one of which there was a fragment of whitewashed wall.

The teacher opened the second and ushered us into a room. There were four white walls: in one corner a cot bed with a blue and white checked coverlet; in another, a small table with a little library; four chairs, and one ancient geographical map nailed to the wall. A pleasant odor of apples was perceptible.

We seated ourselves, all three. My father and his teacher remained silent for several minutes.

"Bottini!" exclaimed the master at length, fixing his eyes on the brick floor where the sunlight formed a checker-board. "Oh! I remember well! Your mother was such a good woman! For a while, during your first year, you sat on a bench to the left near the window. Let us see whether I do not recall it. I can still see your curly head." Then he thought for a while longer. "You were a lively lad, eh? Very. The second year you had an attack of croup. I remember when they brought you back to school, emaciated and wrapped up in a shawl. Forty years have elapsed since then, have they not? You are very kind to remember your poor teacher. And do you know, others of my old pupils have come hither in years gone by to seek me out: there was a colonel, and there were some priests, and several gentlemen." He asked my father what his profession was. Then he said, "I am glad, heartily glad. I thank you. It is quite a while now since I have seen any one. I very much fear that you will be the last, my dear sir."

"Don't say that," exclaimed my father. "You are well and still vigorous. You must not say that."

"Eh, no!" replied the master; "do you see this trembling?" and he showed us his hands. "This is a bad sign. It seized on me three years ago, while I was still teaching school. At first I paid no attention to it; I thought it would pass off. But instead of that, it stayed and kept on increasing. A day came when I could no longer write. Ah! that day on which I, for the first time, made a blot on the copy-book of one of my scholars was a stab in the heart for me, my dear sir. I did drag on for a while longer; but I was at the end of my strength. After sixty years of teaching I was forced to bid farewell to my school, to my scholars, to work. And it was hard, you understand, hard. The last time that I gave a lesson, all the scholars accompanied me home, and made much of me; but I was sad; I understood that my life was finished. I had lost my wife the year before, and my only son. I had only two peasant grandchildren left. Now I am living on a pension of a few hundred lire. I no longer do anything; it seems to me as though the days would never come to an end. My only occupation, you see, is to turn over my old schoolbooks, my scholastic journals, and a few volumes that have been given to me. There they are," he said, indicating his little library; "there are my reminiscences, my whole past; I have nothing else remaining to me in the world."

Then in a tone that was suddenly joyous, "I want to give you a surprise, my dear Signor Bottini."

He rose, and approaching his desk, he opened a long casket which contained numerous little parcels, all tied up with a slender cord, and on each was written a date in four figures.

After a little search, he opened one, turned over several papers, drew forth a yellowed sheet, and handed it to my father. It was some of his school work of forty years before.

At the top was written, *Alberto Bottini, Dictation, April 3, 1838.* My father instantly recognized his own large, schoolboy hand, and began to read it with a smile. But all at once his eyes grew moist. I rose and inquired the cause.

He threw one arm around my body, and pressing me to his side, he said: "Look at this sheet of paper. Do you see? These are the corrections made by my poor mother. She always strengthened my *l*'s and my *t*'s. And the last lines are entirely hers. She had learned to imitate my characters; and when I was tired and sleepy, she finished my work for me. My sainted mother!"

And he kissed the page.

"See here," said the teacher, showing him the other packages; "these are my reminiscences. Each year I laid aside one piece of work of each of my pupils; and they are all here, dated and arranged in order. Every time that I open them thus, and read a line here and there, a thousand things recur to my mind, and I seem to be living once more in the days that are past. How many of them have passed, my dear sir! I close my eyes, and I see behind me face after face, class after class, hundreds and hundreds of boys, and who knows how many of them are already dead! Many of them I remember well. I recall distinctly the best and the worst: those who gave me the greatest pleasure, and those who caused me to pass sorrowful moments; for I have had serpents, too, among that vast number! But now, you understand, it is as though I were already in the other world, and I love them all equally."

He sat down again, and took one of my hands in his.

"And tell me," my father said, with a smile, "do you not recall any roguish tricks?"

"Of yours, sir?" replied the old man, also with a smile. "No; not just at this moment. But that does not in the least mean that you never played any. However, you had good judgment; you were serious for your age. I remember the great affection of your mother for you. But it is very kind and polite of you to have come to seek me out. How could you leave your occupations, to come and see a poor old schoolmaster?"

"Listen, Signor Crosetti," responded my father with vivacity. "I recollect the first time that my poor mother accompanied me to school. It was to be her first parting from me for two hours; of letting me out of the house alone, in other hands than my father's; in the hands of a stranger, in short. To this good creature my entrance into school was like my entrance into the world, the first of a long series of necessary and painful separations; it was society which was tearing her son from her for the first time, never again to return him to her intact. She was much affected; so was I. I bade her farewell with a trembling voice, and then, as she went away, I saluted her once more through the glass in the door, with my eyes full of tears. And just at that point you made a gesture with one hand, laying the other on your breast, as though to say, 'Trust me, signora.' Well, the gesture, the glance, from which I perceived that you had comprehended all the sentiments, all the thoughts of my mother; that look which seemed to say, 'Courage!' that gesture which was an honest promise of protection, of affection, of indulgence, I have never forgotten; it has remained forever engraved on my heart; and it is that memory which induced me to set out from Turin. And here I am, after the lapse of four and forty years, for the purpose of saying to you, 'Thanks, dear teacher.'"

The master did not reply; he stroked my hair with his hand, and his hand trembled, and glided from my hair to my forehead, from my forehead to my shoulder.

In the meanwhile, my father was surveying those bare walls, that wretched bed, the morsel of bread and the little phial of oil which lay on the window-sill, and he seemed desirous of saying, "Poor master! after sixty years of teaching, is this all thy recompense?"

But the good old man was content, and began once more to talk with vivacity of our family, of the other teachers of that day, and of my father's schoolmates; some of them he remembered, and some of them he did not; and each told the other news of this one or of that one. When my father interrupted the conversation, to beg the old man to come down into the town and lunch with us, he replied effusively, "I thank you, I thank you," but he seemed undecided. My father took him by both hands, and besought him afresh. "But how shall I manage to eat," said the master, "with these poor hands which shake in this way? It is a penance for others also."

"We will help you, master," said my father. And then he accepted, as he shook his head and smiled.

"This is a beautiful day," he said, as he closed the outer door, "a beautiful day, dear Signor Bottini! I assure you that I shall remember it as long as I live."

My father gave one arm to the master, and the latter took me by the hand, and we descended the lane. We met two little barefooted girls leading some cows, and a boy who passed us on a run, with a huge load of straw on his shoulders. The master told us that they were scholars of the second grade;

that in the morning they led the cattle to pasture, and worked in the fields barefoot; and in the afternoon they put on their shoes and went to school. It was nearly mid-day. We encountered no one else. In a few minutes we reached the inn, seated ourselves at a large table, with the master between us, and began our breakfast at once. The inn was as silent as a convent. The master was very merry, and his excitement augmented his palsy: he could hardly eat. But my father cut up his meat, broke his bread, and put salt on his plate. In order to drink, he was obliged to hold the glass with both hands, and even then he struck his teeth. But he talked constantly, and with ardor, of the reading-books of his young days; of the notaries of the present day; of the commendations bestowed on him by his superiors; of the regulations of late years: and all with that serene countenance, a trifle redder than at first, and with that gay voice of his, and that laugh which was almost the laugh of a young man. And my father gazed and gazed at him, with that same expression with which I sometimes catch him gazing at me, at home, when he is thinking and smiling to himself, with his face turned aside.

The teacher allowed some wine to trickle down on his breast; my father rose, and wiped it off with his napkin. "No, sir; I cannot permit this," the old man said, and smiled. He said some words in Latin. And, finally, he raised his glass, which wavered about in his hand, and said very gravely, "To your health, my dear engineer, to that of your children, to the memory of your good mother!"

"To yours, my good master!" replied my father, pressing his hand. And at the end of the room stood the innkeeper and several others, watching us, and smiling as though they were pleased at this attention which was being shown to the teacher from their parts.

At a little after two o'clock we came out, and the master wanted to escort us to the station. My father gave him his arm once more, and he again took me by the hand: I carried his cane for him. The people paused to look on, for they all knew him: some saluted him. At one point in the street we heard, through an open window, many boys' voices, reading together, and spelling. The old man halted, and seemed to be saddened by it.

"This, my dear Signor Bottini," he said, "is what pains me. To hear the voices of boys in school, and not be there any more; to think that another man is there. I have heard that music for sixty years, and I have grown to love it. Now I am deprived of my family. I have no sons."

"No, master," my father said to him, starting on again; "you still have many sons, scattered about the world, who remember you, as I have always remembered you."

"No, no," replied the master sadly; "I have no longer a school; I have no longer any sons. And without sons, I shall not live much longer. My hour will soon strike."

"Do not say that, master; do not think it," said my father. "You have done so much good in every way! You have put your life to such a noble use!"

The aged master inclined his hoary head for an instant on my father's shoulder, and pressed my hand.

We entered the station. The train was on the point of starting.

"Farewell, master!" said my father, kissing him on both cheeks.

"Farewell! thanks! farewell!" replied the master, taking one of my father's hands in his two trembling hands, and pressing it to his heart.

Then I kissed him and felt that his face was bathed in tears. My father pushed me into the railway carriage, and at the moment of starting he quickly removed the coarse cane from the schoolmaster's hand, and in its place he put his own handsome one, with a silver handle and his initials, saying, "Keep it in memory of me."

The old man tried to return it and to recover his own; but my father was already inside and had closed the door.

"Farewell, my kind master!"

"Farewell, my son!" responded the master as the train moved off; "and may God bless you for the consolation which you have afforded to a poor old man!"

"Until we meet again!" cried my father, in a voice full of emotion.

But the master shook his head, as much as to say, "We shall never see each other more."

"Yes, yes," repeated my father, "until we meet again!"

And the other replied by raising his trembling hand to heaven, "Up there!"

And thus he disappeared from our sight, with his hand on high.


CONVALESCENCE

Thursday, 20th.

Who could have told me, when I returned from that delightful excursion with my father, that for ten days I should not see the country or the sky again? I have been very ill--in danger of my life. I have heard my mother sobbing--I have seen my father very, very pale, gazing intently at me; and my sister Silvia and my brother talking in a low voice; and the doctor, with his spectacles, who was there every moment, and who said things to me that I did not understand. In truth, I have been on the verge of saying a final farewell to every one. Ah, my poor mother! I passed three or four days at least, of which I recollect almost nothing, as though I had been in a dark and perplexing dream. I thought I beheld at my bedside my kind schoolmistress of the upper primary, who was trying to stifle her cough in her handkerchief in order not to disturb me. In the same manner I confusedly recall my master, who bent over to kiss me, and who pricked my face a little with his beard; and I saw, as in a mist, the red head of Crossi, the golden curls of Derossi, the Calabrian clad in black, all pass by, and

Garrone, who brought me a mandarin orange with its leaves, and ran away in haste because his mother is ill.

Then I awoke as from a very long dream, and understood that I was better from seeing my father and mother smiling, and hearing Silvia singing softly. Oh, what a sad dream it was! Then I began to improve every day. The little mason came and made me laugh once more for the first time, with his hare's face; and how well he does it, now that his face is somewhat elongated through illness, poor fellow! And Coretti came; and Garoffi came to present me with two tickets in his new lottery of "a penknife with five surprises," which he purchased of a second-hand dealer in the Via Bertola. Then, yesterday, while I was asleep, Precossi came and laid his cheek on my hand without waking me; and as he came from his father's workshop, with his face covered with coal dust, he left a black print on my sleeve, the sight of which caused me great pleasure when I awoke.

How green the trees have become in these few days! And how I envy the boys whom I see running to school with their books when my father carries me to the window! But I shall go back there soon myself. I am so impatient to see all the boys once more, and my seat, the garden, the streets; to know all that has taken place during the interval; to apply myself to my books again, and to my copy-books, which I seem not to have seen for a year! How pale and thin my poor mother has grown! Poor father! how weary he looks! And my kind companions who came to see me and walked on tiptoe and kissed my brow! It makes me sad, even now, to think that one day we must part. Perhaps I shall continue my studies with Derossi and with some others; but how about all the rest? When the fourth grade is once finished, then good by! we shall never see each other again: I shall never see them again at my bedside when I am ill,--Garrone, Precossi, Coretti, who are such fine boys and kind and dear comrades,--never more!

## FRIENDS AMONG THE WORKINGMEN

Thursday, 20th.

Why "never more," Enrico? That will depend on yourself. When you have finished the fourth grade, you will go to the Gymnasium, and they will become workingmen; but you will remain in the same city for many years, perhaps. Why, then, will you never meet again? When you are in the University or the Lyceum, you will seek them out in their shops or their workrooms, and it will be a great pleasure for you to meet the companions of your youth once more, as men at work.

I should like to see you neglecting to look up Coretti or Precossi, wherever they may be! And you will go to them, and you will pass hours in their company, and you will see, when you come to study life and the world, how many things you can learn from them, which no one else is capable of teaching you, both about their arts and their society and your own country. And have a care; for if you do not preserve these friendships, it will be extremely difficult for you to acquire other similar ones in the future,--friendships, I mean to say, outside of the class to which you belong; and thus you will live in one class only; and the man who associates with but one social class is like the student who reads but one book.

Let it be your firm resolve, then, from this day forth, that you will keep these good friends even after you shall be separated, and from this time forth, cultivate precisely these by preference because they are the sons of workingmen. You see, men of the upper classes are the officers, and men of the lower classes are the soldiers of toil; and thus in society as in the army, not only is the soldier no less noble than the officer, since nobility consists in work and not in wages, in valor and not in rank; but if there is also a superiority of merit, it is on the side of the soldier, of the workmen, who draw the lesser profit from the work. Therefore love and respect above all others, among your companions, the sons of the soldiers of labor; honor in them the toil and the sacrifices of their parents; disregard the differences of fortune and of class, upon which the base alone regulate their sentiments and courtesy; reflect that from the veins of laborers in the shops and in the country issued nearly all that blessed blood which has redeemed your country; love Garrone, love Coretti, love Precossi, love your little mason, who, in their little workingmen's breasts, possess the hearts of princes; and take an oath to yourself that no change of fortune shall ever eradicate these friendships of childhood from your soul. Swear to yourself that forty years hence, if, while passing through a railway station, you recognize your old Garrone in the garments of an engineer, with a black face,--ah! I cannot think what to tell you to swear. I am sure that you will jump upon the engine and fling your arms round his neck, though you were even a senator of the kingdom.

THY FATHER.


## GARRONE'S MOTHER

Saturday, 29th.

On my return to school, the first thing I heard was some bad news. Garrone had not been there for several days because his mother was seriously ill. She died on Saturday. Yesterday morning, as soon as we came into school, the teacher said to us:

"The greatest misfortune that can happen to a boy has happened to poor Garrone: his mother is dead. He will return to school tomorrow. I beseech you now, boys, respect the terrible sorrow that is now rending his soul. When he enters, greet him with affection, and gravely; let no one jest, let no one laugh at him, I beg of you."

And this morning poor Garrone came in, a little later than the rest; I felt a blow at my heart at the sight of him. His face was haggard, his eyes were red, and he was unsteady on his feet; it seemed as though he had been ill for a month. I hardly recognized him; he was dressed all in black; he aroused our pity. No one even breathed; all gazed at him. No sooner had he entered than at the first sight of that schoolroom whither his mother had come to get him nearly every day, of that bench over which she had bent on so many examination days to give him a last bit of advice, and where he had so many times thought of her, in his impatience to run out and meet her, he burst into a desperate fit of weeping. The teacher drew him aside to his own place, and pressed him to his breast, and said to him:

"Weep, weep, my poor boy; but take courage. Your mother is no longer here; but she sees you, she still loves you, she still lives by your side, and one day you will behold her once again, for you have a good and upright soul like her own. Take courage!"

Having said this, he accompanied him to the bench near me. I dared not look at him. He drew out his copy-books and his books, which he had not opened for many days, and as he opened the reading-book at a place where there was a cut representing a mother leading her son by the hand, he burst out crying again, and laid his head on his arm. The master made us a sign to leave him thus, and began the lesson. I should have liked to say something to him, but I did not know what. I laid one hand on his arm, and whispered in his ear:

"Don't cry, Garrone."

He made no reply, and without raising his head from the bench he laid his hand on mine and kept it there a while. At the close of school, no one addressed him; all the boys hovered round him respectfully, and in silence. I saw my mother waiting for me, and ran to embrace her; but she repulsed me, and gazed at Garrone. For the moment I could not understand why; but then I perceived that Garrone was standing apart by himself and gazing at me; and he was gazing at me with a look of indescribable sadness, which seemed to say: "You are embracing your mother, and I shall never embrace mine again! You have still a mother, and mine is dead!" And then I understood why my mother had thrust me back, and I went out without taking her hand.

GIUSEPPE MAZZINI

Saturday, 29th.

This morning, also, Garrone came to school with a pale face and his eyes swollen with weeping, and he hardly cast a glance at the little gifts which we had placed on his desk to console him. But the teacher had brought a page from a book to read to him in order to encourage him. He first informed us that we are to go tomorrow at one o'clock to the town-hall to witness the award of the medal for civic valor to a boy who has saved a little child from the Po, and that on Monday he will dictate the description of the festival to us instead of the monthly story. Then turning to Garrone, who was standing with drooping head, he said to him:

"Make an effort, Garrone, and write down what I dictate to you as well as the rest."

We all took our pens, and the teacher dictated.

"Giuseppe Mazzini, born in Genoa in 1805, died in Pisa in 1872, a grand, patriotic soul, the mind of a great writer, the first inspirer and apostle of the Italian Revolution; who, out of love for his country, lived for forty years poor, exiled, persecuted, a fugitive heroically steadfast in his principles and in his resolutions. Giuseppe Mazzini, who adored his mother, and who derived from her all that there was noblest and purest in her strong and gentle soul, wrote as follows to a faithful friend of his, to console him in the greatest of misfortunes. These are almost his exact words:

"'My friend, thou wilt never more behold thy mother on this earth. That is the terrible truth. I do not attempt to see thee, because thine is one of those solemn and sacred sorrows which each must suffer and conquer for himself. Dost thou understand what I mean to convey by these words, *It is necessary to conquer sorrow*--to conquer the least sacred, the least purifying part of sorrow, that which, instead of rendering the soul better, weakens and debases it? But the other part of sorrow, the noble part-- that which enlarges and elevates the soul--that must remain with thee and never leave thee more. Nothing here below can take the place of a good mother. In the griefs, in the consolations which life may still bring to thee, thou wilt never forget her. But thou must recall her, love her, mourn her death, in a manner which is worthy of her. O my friend, hearken to me! Death exists not; it is nothing. It cannot even be understood. Life is life, and it follows the law of life--progress. Yesterday thou hadst a mother on earth; today thou hast an angel elsewhere. All that is good will survive the life of earth with increased power. Hence, also, the love of thy mother. She loves thee now more than ever. And thou art responsible for thy actions to her more, even, than before. It depends upon thee, upon thy actions, to meet her once more, to see her in another existence. Thou must, therefore, out of love and reverence for thy mother, grow better and cause her joy for thee. Henceforth thou must say to thyself at every act of thine, "Would my mother approve this?" Her transformation has placed a guardian angel in the world for thee, to whom thou must refer in all thy affairs, in everything that pertains to thee. Be strong and brave; fight against desperate and vulgar grief; have the tranquillity of great suffering in great souls; and that it is what she would have.'"

"Garrone," added the teacher, "*be strong and tranquil, for that is what she would have*. Do you understand?"

Garrone nodded assent, while great and fast-flowing tears streamed over his hands, his copy-book, and his desk.


CIVIC VALOR

(*Monthly Story.*)

At one o'clock we went with our schoolmaster to the front of the town-hall, to see the medal for civic valor bestowed on the lad who saved one of his comrades from the Po.

On the front terrace waved a huge tricolored flag.

We entered the courtyard of the palace.

It was already full of people. At the further end of it there was visible a table with a red cover, and papers on it, and behind it a row of gilded chairs for the mayor and the council; the ushers of the municipality were there, with their under-waistcoats of sky-blue and their white stockings. To the right of the courtyard a detachment of policemen, who had a great many medals, was drawn up in line; and beside them a detachment of custom-house officers; on the other side were the firemen in festive array; and numerous soldiers not in line, who had come to look on,--cavalrymen, sharpshooters, artillery-men. Then all around were gentlemen, country people, and some officers and women and boys who had assembled. We crowded into a corner where many scholars from other buildings were already collected with their teachers; and near us was a group of boys belonging to the common people, between ten and eighteen years of age, who were talking and laughing loudly; and we made out that they were all from Borgo Po, comrades or acquaintances of the boy who was to receive the medal. Above, all the windows were thronged with the employees of the city government; the balcony of the library was also filled with people, who pressed against the balustrade; and in the one on the opposite side, which is over the entrance gate, stood a crowd of girls from the public schools, and many *Daughters of military men*, with their pretty blue veils. It looked like a theatre. All were talking merrily, glancing every now and then at the red table, to see whether any one had made his appearance. A band of music was playing softly at the extremity of the portico. The sun beat down on the lofty walls. It was beautiful.

All at once every one began to clap their hands, from the courtyard, from the balconies, from the windows.

I raised myself on tiptoe to look.

The crowd which stood behind the red table had parted, and a man and woman had come forward. The man was leading a boy by the hand.

This was the lad who had saved his comrade.

The man was his father, a mason, dressed in his best. The woman, his mother, small and blond, had on a black gown. The boy, also small and blond, had on a gray jacket.

At the sight of all those people, and at the sound of that thunder of applause, all three stood still, not daring to look nor to move. A municipal usher pushed them along to the side of the table on the right.

All remained quiet for a moment, and then once more the applause broke out on all sides. The boy glanced up at the windows, and then at the balcony with the *Daughters of military men*; he held his cap in his hand, and did not seem to understand very thoroughly where he was. It struck me that he looked a little like Coretti, in the face; but he was redder. His father and mother kept their eyes fixed on the table.

In the meantime, all the boys from Borgo Po who were near us were making motions to their comrade, to attract his attention, and hailing him in a low tone: *Pin! Pin! Pinot!* By dint of calling they made themselves heard. The boy glanced at them, and hid his smile behind his cap.

At a certain moment the guards put themselves in the attitude of *attention*.

The mayor entered, accompanied by numerous gentlemen.

The mayor, all white, with a big tricolored scarf, placed himself beside the table, standing; all the others took their places behind and beside him.

The band ceased playing; the mayor made a sign, and every one kept quiet.

He began to speak. I did not understand the first words perfectly; but I gathered that he was telling the story of the boy's feat. Then he raised his voice, and it rang out so clear and sonorous through the whole court, that I did not lose another word: "When he saw, from the shore, his comrade struggling in the river, already overcome with the fear of death, he tore the clothes from his back, and hastened to his assistance, without hesitating an instant. They shouted to him, 'You will be drowned!'--he made no reply; they caught hold of him--he freed himself; they called him by name-- he was already in the water. The river was swollen; the risk terrible, even for a man. But he flung himself to meet death with all the strength of his little body and of his great heart; he reached the unfortunate fellow and seized him just in time, when he was already under water, and dragged him to the surface; he fought furiously with the waves, which strove to overwhelm him, with his companion who tried to cling to him; and several times he disappeared beneath the water, and rose again with a desperate effort; obstinate, invincible in his purpose, not like a boy who was trying to save another boy, but like a man, like a father who is struggling to save his son, who is his hope and his life. In short, God did not permit so generous a prowess to be displayed in vain. The child swimmer tore the victim from the gigantic river, and brought him to land, and with the assistance of others, rendered him his first succor; after which he returned home quietly and alone, and ingenuously narrated his deed.

"Gentlemen, beautiful, and worthy of veneration is heroism in a man! But in a child, in whom there can be no prompting of ambition or of profit whatever; in a child, who must have all the more ardor in proportion as he has less strength; in a child, from whom we require nothing, who is bound to nothing, who already appears to us so noble and lovable, not when he acts, but when he merely understands, and is grateful for the sacrifices of others;--in a child, heroism is divine! I will say nothing more, gentlemen. I do not care to deck, with superfluous praises, such simple grandeur. Here before you stands the noble and valorous rescuer. Soldier, greet him as a brother; mothers, bless him like a son; children, remember his name, engrave on your minds his visage, that it may nevermore be erased from your memories and from your hearts. Approach, my boy. In the name of the king of Italy, I give you the medal for civic valor."

An extremely loud hurrah, uttered at the same moment by many voices, made the palace ring.

The mayor took the medal from the table, and fastened it on the boy's breast. Then he embraced and kissed him. The mother placed one hand over her eyes; the father held his chin on his breast.

The mayor shook hands with both; and taking the decree of decoration, which was bound with a ribbon, he handed it to the woman.

Then he turned to the boy again, and said: "May the memory of this day, which is such a glorious one for you, such a happy one for your father and mother, keep you all your life in the path of virtue and honor! Farewell!"

The mayor withdrew, the band struck up, and everything seemed to be at an end, when the detachment of firemen opened, and a lad of eight or nine years, pushed forwards by a woman who instantly concealed herself, rushed towards the boy with the decoration, and flung himself in his arms.

Another outburst of hurrahs and applause made the courtyard echo; every one had instantly understood that this was the boy who had been saved from the Po, and who had come to thank his rescuer. After kissing him, he clung to one arm, in order to accompany him out. These two, with the father and mother following behind, took their way towards the door, making a path with difficulty among the people who formed in line to let them pass,--policemen, boys, soldiers, women, all mingled together in confusion. All pressed forwards and raised on tiptoe to see the boy. Those who stood near him as he passed, touched his hand. When he passed before the schoolboys, they all waved their caps in the air. Those from Borgo Po made a great uproar, pulling him by the arms and by his jacket and shouting. "*Pin! hurrah for Pin! bravo, Pinot!*" I saw him pass very close to me. His face was all aflame and happy; his medal had a red, white, and green ribbon. His mother was crying and smiling; his father was twirling his mustache with one hand, which trembled violently, as though he had a fever. And from the windows and the balconies the people continued to lean out and applaud. All at once, when they were on the point of entering the portico, there descended from the balcony of the *Daughters of military men* a veritable shower of pansies, of bunches of violets and daisies, which fell upon the head of the boy, and of his father and mother, and scattered over the ground. Many people stooped to pick them up and hand them to the mother. And the band at the further end of the courtyard played, very, very softly, a most entrancing air, which seemed like a song by a great many silver voices fading slowly into the distance on the banks of a river.

# MAY

## CHILDREN WITH THE RICKETS

Friday, 5th.

TODAY I took a vacation, because I was not well, and my mother took me to the Institution for Children with the Rickets, whither she went to recommend a child belonging to our porter; but she did not allow me to go into the school.

You did not understand, Enrico, why I did not permit you to enter? In order not to place before the eyes of those unfortunates, there in the midst of the school, as though on exhibition, a healthy, robust boy: they have already but too many opportunities for making melancholy comparisons. What a sad thing! Tears rushed from my heart when I entered. There were sixty of them, boys and girls. Poor tortured bones! Poor hands, poor little shrivelled and distorted feet! Poor little deformed bodies! I instantly perceived many charming faces, with eyes full of intelligence and affection. There was one little child's face with a pointed nose and a sharp chin, which seemed to belong to an old woman; but it wore a smile of celestial sweetness. Some, viewed from the front, are handsome, and appear to be without defects: but when they turn round--they cast a weight upon your soul. The doctor was there, visiting them. He set them upright on their benches and pulled up their little garments, to feel their little swollen stomachs and enlarged joints; but they felt not the least shame, poor creatures! it was evident that they were children who were used to being undressed, examined, turned round on all sides. And to think that they are now in the best stage of their malady, when they hardly suffer at all any more! But who can say what they suffered during the first stage, while their bodies were undergoing the process of deformation, when with the increase of their infirmity, they saw affection decrease around them, poor children! saw themselves left alone for hour after hour in a corner of the room or the courtyard, badly nourished, and at times scoffed at, or tormented for months by bandages and by useless orthopedic apparatus! Now, however, thanks to care and good food and gymnastic exercises, many are improving. Their schoolmistress makes them practise gymnastics. It was a pitiful sight to see them, at a certain command, extend all those bandaged legs under the benches, squeezed as they were between splints, knotty and deformed; legs which should have been covered with kisses! Some could not rise from the bench, and remained there, with their heads resting on their arms, caressing their crutches with their hands; others, on making the thrust with their arms, felt their breath fail them, and fell back on their seats, all pale; but they smiled to conceal their panting. Ah, Enrico! you other children do not prize your good health, and it seems to you so small a thing to be well! I thought of the strong and thriving lads, whom their mothers carry about in triumph, proud of their beauty; and I could have clasped all those poor little heads, I could have pressed them to my heart, in despair; I could have said, had I been alone, "I will never stir from here again; I wish to consecrate my life to you, to serve you, to be a mother to you all, to my last day." And in the meantime, they sang; sang in peculiar, thin, sweet, sad voices, which penetrated the soul; and when their teacher praised them, they looked happy; and as she passed among the benches, they kissed her hands and wrists; for they are very grateful for what is done for them, and very affectionate. And these little angels have good minds, and study well, the teacher told me. The teacher is young and gentle, with a face full of kindness, a certain expression of sadness, like a reflection of the misfortunes which she caresses and comforts. The dear girl! Among all the human creatures who earn their livelihood by toil, there is not one who earns it more holily than thou, my daughter!

THY MOTHER.


SACRIFICE

Tuesday, 9th.

My mother is good, and my sister Silvia is like her, and has a large and noble heart. Yesterday evening I was copying a part of the monthly story, *From the Apennines to the Andes,*--which the teacher has distributed among us all in small portions to copy, because it is so long,--when Silvia entered on tiptoe, and said to me hastily, and in a low voice: "Come to mamma with me. I heard them talking together this morning: some affair has gone wrong with papa, and he was sad; mamma was encouraging him: we are in difficulties--do you understand? We have no more money. Papa said that it would be necessary to make some sacrifices in order to recover himself. Now we must make sacrifices, too, must we not? Are you ready to do it? Well, I will speak to mamma, and do you nod assent, and promise her on your honor that you will do everything that I shall say."

Having said this, she took me by the hand and led me to our mother, who was sewing, absorbed in thought. I sat down on one end of the sofa, Silvia on the other, and she immediately said:

"Listen, mamma, I have something to say to you. Both of us have something to say to you." Mamma stared at us in surprise, and Silvia began:

"Papa has no money, has he?"

"What are you saying?" replied mamma, turning crimson. "Has he not indeed! What do you know about it? Who has told you?"

"I know it," said Silvia, resolutely. "Well, then, listen, mamma; we must make some sacrifices, too. You promised me a fan at the end of May, and Enrico expected his box of paints; we don't want anything now; we don't want to waste a soldo; we shall be just as well pleased--you understand?"

Mamma tried to speak; but Silvia said: "No; it must be thus. We have decided. And until papa has money again, we don't want any fruit or anything else; broth will be enough for us, and we will eat bread in the morning for breakfast: thus we shall spend less on the table, for we already spend too much; and we promise you that you will always find us perfectly contented. Is it not so, Enrico?"

I replied that it was. "Always perfectly contented," repeated Silvia, closing mamma's mouth with one hand. "And if there are any other sacrifices to be made, either in the matter of clothing or anything else, we will make them gladly; and we will even sell our presents; I will give up all my things, I will serve you as your maid, we will not have anything done out of the house any more, I will work all day long with you, I will do everything you wish, I am ready for anything! For anything!" she exclaimed, throwing her arms around my mother's neck, "if papa and mamma can only be saved further troubles, if I can only behold you both once more at ease, and in good spirits, as in former days, between your Silvia and your Enrico, who love you so dearly, who would give their lives for you!"

Ah! I have never seen my mother so happy as she was on hearing these words; she never before kissed us on the brow in that way, weeping and laughing, and incapable of speech. And then she assured Silvia that she had not understood rightly; that we were not in the least reduced in circumstances, as she imagined; and she thanked us a hundred times, and was cheerful all the evening, until my father came in, when she told him all about it. He did not open his mouth, poor father! But this morning, as we sat at the table, I felt at once both a great pleasure and a great sadness: under my napkin I found my box of colors, and under hers, Silvia found her fan.


THE FIRE

Thursday, 11th.

This morning I had finished copying my share of the story, *From the Apennines to the Andes*, and was seeking for a theme for the independent composition which the teacher had assigned us to write, when I heard an unusual talking on the stairs, and shortly after two firemen entered the house, and asked permission of my father to inspect the stoves and chimneys, because a smoke-pipe was on fire on the roof, and they could not tell to whom it belonged.

My father said, "Pray do so." And although we had no fire burning anywhere, they began to make the round of our apartments, and to lay their ears to the walls, to hear if the fire was roaring in the flues which run up to the other floors of the house.

And while they were going through the rooms, my father said to me, "Here is a theme for your composition, Enrico,--the firemen. Try to write down what I am about to tell you.

"I saw them at work two years ago, one evening, when I was coming out of the Balbo Theatre late at night. On entering the Via Roma, I saw an unusual light, and a crowd of people collecting. A house was on fire. Tongues of flame and clouds of smoke were bursting from the windows and the roof; men and women appeared at the windows and then disappeared, uttering shrieks of despair. There was a dense throng in front of the door: the crowd was shouting: 'They will be burned alive! Help!

The firemen!' At that moment a carriage arrived, four firemen sprang out of it--the first who had reached the town-hall--and rushed into the house. They had hardly gone in when a horrible thing happened: a woman ran to a window of the third story, with a yell, clutched the balcony, climbed down it, and remained suspended, thus clinging, almost suspended in space, with her back outwards, bending beneath the flames, which flashed out from the room and almost licked her head. The crowd uttered a cry of horror. The firemen, who had been stopped on the second floor by mistake by the terrified lodgers, had already broken through a wall and precipitated themselves into a room, when a hundred shouts gave them warning:

"'On the third floor! On the third floor!'

"They flew to the third floor. There there was an infernal uproar,--beams from the roof crashing in, corridors filled with a suffocating smoke. In order to reach the rooms where the lodgers were imprisoned, there was no other way left but to pass over the roof. They instantly sprang upon it, and a moment later something which resembled a black phantom appeared on the tiles, in the midst of the smoke. It was the corporal, who had been the first to arrive. But in order to get from the roof to the small set of rooms cut off by the fire, he was forced to pass over an extremely narrow space comprised between a dormer window and the eavestrough: all the rest was in flames, and that tiny space was covered with snow and ice, and there was no place to hold on to.

"'It is impossible for him to pass!' shouted the crowd below.

"The corporal advanced along the edge of the roof. All shuddered, and began to observe him with bated breath. He passed. A tremendous hurrah rose towards heaven. The corporal resumed his way, and on arriving at the point which was threatened, he began to break away, with furious blows of his axe, beams, tiles, and rafters, in order to open a hole through which he might descend within.

"In the meanwhile, the woman was still suspended outside the window. The fire raged with increased violence over her head; another moment, and she would have fallen into the street.

"The hole was opened. We saw the corporal pull off his shoulder-belt and lower himself inside: the other firemen, who had arrived, followed.

"At that instant a very lofty Porta ladder, which had just arrived, was placed against the entablature of the house, in front of the windows whence issued flames, and howls, as of maniacs. But it seemed as though they were too late.

"'No one can be saved now!' they shouted. 'The firemen are burning! The end has come! They are dead!'

"All at once the black form of the corporal made its appearance at the window with the balcony, lighted up by the flames overhead. The woman clasped him round the neck; he caught her round the body with both arms, drew her up, and laid her down inside the room.

"The crowd set up a shout a thousand voices strong, which rose above the roar of the conflagration.

"But the others? And how were they to get down? The ladder which leaned against the roof on the front of another window was at a good distance from them. How could they get hold of it?

"While the people were saying this to themselves, one of the firemen stepped out of the window, set his right foot on the window-sill and his left on the ladder, and standing thus upright in the air, he grasped the lodgers, one after the other, as the other men handed them to him from within, passed them on to a comrade, who had climbed up from the street, and who, after securing a firm grasp for them on the rungs, sent them down, one after the other, with the assistance of more firemen.

"First came the woman of the balcony, then a baby, then another woman, then an old man. All were saved. After the old man, the fireman who had remained inside descended. The last to come down was the corporal who had been the first to hasten up. The crowd received them all with a burst of applause; but when the last made his appearance, the vanguard of the rescuers, the one who had faced the abyss in advance of the rest, the one who would have perished had it been fated that one should perish, the crowd saluted him like a conqueror, shouting and stretching out their arms, with an affectionate impulse of admiration and of gratitude, and in a few minutes his obscure name-- Giuseppe Robbino--rang from a thousand throats.

"Have you understood? That is courage--the courage of the heart, which does not reason, which does not waver, which dashes blindly on, like a lightning flash, wherever it hears the cry of a dying man. One of these days I will take you to the exercises of the firemen, and I will point out to you Corporal Robbino; for you would be very glad to know him, would you not?"

I replied that I should.

"Here he is," said my father.

I turned round with a start. The two firemen, having completed their inspection, were traversing the room in order to reach the door.

My father pointed to the smaller of the men, who had straps of gold braid, and said, "Shake hands with Corporal Robbino."

The corporal halted, and offered me his hand; I pressed it; he made a salute and withdrew.

"And bear this well in mind," said my father; "for out of the thousands of hands which you will shake in the course of your life there will probably not be ten which possess the worth of his."


## FROM THE APENNINES TO THE ANDES

(*Monthly Story.*)

Many years ago a Genoese lad of thirteen, the son of a workingman, went from Genoa to America all alone to seek his mother.

His mother had gone two years before to Buenos Ayres, a city, the capital of the Argentine Republic, to take service in a wealthy family, and to thus earn in a short time enough to place her family once more in easy circumstances, they having fallen, through various misfortunes, into poverty and debt. There are courageous women--not a few--who take this long voyage with this object in view, and who, thanks to the large wages which people in service receive there, return home at the end of a few years with several thousand lire. The poor mother had wept tears of blood at parting from her children,--the one aged eighteen, the other, eleven; but she had set out courageously and filled with hope.

The voyage was prosperous: she had no sooner arrived at Buenos Ayres than she found, through a Genoese shopkeeper, a cousin of her husband, who had been established there for a very long time, a good Argentine family, which gave high wages and treated her well. And for a short time she kept up a regular correspondence with her family. As it had been settled between them, her husband addressed his letters to his cousin, who transmitted them to the woman, and the latter handed her replies to him, and he despatched them to Genoa, adding a few lines of his own. As she was earning eighty lire a month and spending nothing for herself, she sent home a handsome sum every three months, with which her husband, who was a man of honor, gradually paid off their most urgent debts, and thus regained his good reputation. And in the meantime, he worked away and was satisfied with the state of his affairs, since he also cherished the hope that his wife would shortly return; for the house seemed empty without her, and the younger son in particular, who was extremely attached to his mother, was very much depressed, and could not resign himself to having her so far away.

But a year had elapsed since they had parted; after a brief letter, in which she said that her health was not very good, they heard nothing more. They wrote twice to the cousin; the cousin did not reply. They wrote to the Argentine family where the woman was at service; but it is possible that the letter never reached them, for they had distorted the name in addressing it: they received no answer. Fearing a misfortune, they wrote to the Italian Consulate at Buenos Ayres to have inquiries made, and after a lapse of three months they received a response from the consul, that in spite of advertisements in the newspapers no one had presented herself nor sent any word. And it could not have happened otherwise, for this reason if for no other: that with the idea of sparing the good name of her family, which she fancied she was discrediting by becoming a servant, the good woman had not given her real name to the Argentine family.

Several months more passed by; no news. The father and sons were in consternation; the youngest was oppressed by a melancholy which he could not conquer. What was to be done? To whom should they have recourse? The father's first thought had been to set out, to go to America in search of his wife. But his work? Who would support his sons? And neither could the eldest son go, for he had just then begun to earn something, and he was necessary to the family. And in this anxiety they lived, repeating each day the same sad speeches, or gazing at each other in silence; when, one evening, Marco, the youngest, declared with decision, "I am going to America to look for my mother."

His father shook his head sadly and made no reply. It was an affectionate thought, but an impossible thing. To make a journey to America, which required a month, alone, at the age of thirteen! But the boy patiently insisted. He persisted that day, the day after, every day, with great calmness, reasoning with the good sense of a man. "Others have gone thither," he said; "and smaller boys than I, too. Once on board the ship, I shall get there like anybody else. Once arrived there, I only have to hunt up our cousin's shop. There are plenty of Italians there who will show me the street. After finding our cousin, my mother is found; and if I do not find him, I will go to the consul: I will search out that Argentine family. Whatever happens, there is work for all there; I shall find work also; sufficient, at least, to earn enough to get home." And thus little by little he almost succeeded in persuading his father. His father esteemed him; he knew that he had good judgment and courage; that he was inured to privations and to sacrifices; and that all these good qualities had acquired double force in his heart in consequence of the sacred project of finding his mother, whom he adored. In addition to this, the captain of a steamer, the friend of an acquaintance of his, having heard the plan mentioned, undertook to procure a free third-class passage for the Argentine Republic.

And then, after a little hesitation, the father gave his consent. The voyage was decided on. They filled a sack with clothes for him, put a few crowns in his pocket, and gave him the address of the cousin; and one fine evening in April they saw him on board.

"Marco, my son," his father said to him, as he gave him his last kiss, with tears in his eyes, on the steps of the steamer, which was on the point of starting, "take courage. Thou hast set out on a holy undertaking, and God will aid thee."

Poor Marco! His heart was strong and prepared for the hardest trials of this voyage; but when he beheld his beautiful Genoa disappear on the horizon, and found himself on the open sea on that huge steamer thronged with emigrating peasants, alone, unacquainted with any one, with that little bag which held his entire fortune, a sudden discouragement assailed him. For two days he remained crouching like a dog on the bows, hardly eating, and oppressed with a great desire to weep. Every description of sad thoughts passed through his mind, and the saddest, the most terrible, was the one which was the most persistent in its return,--the thought that his mother was dead. In his broken and painful slumbers he constantly beheld a strange face, which surveyed him with an air of compassion, and whispered in his ear, "Your mother is dead!" And then he awoke, stifling a shriek.

Nevertheless, after passing the Straits of Gibraltar, at the first sight of the Atlantic Ocean he recovered his spirits a little, and his hope. But it was only a brief respite. That vast but always smooth sea, the increasing heat, the misery of all those poor people who surrounded him, the consciousness of his own solitude, overwhelmed him once more. The empty and monotonous days which succeeded each other became confounded in his memory, as is the case with sick people. It seemed to him that he had been at sea a year. And every morning, on waking, he felt surprised afresh at finding himself there alone on that vast watery expanse, on his way to America. The beautiful flying fish which fell on deck every now and then, the marvelous sunsets of the tropics, with their enormous clouds colored like flame and blood, and those nocturnal phosphorescences which make the ocean seem all on fire like a sea of lava, did not produce on him the effect of real things, but of marvels beheld in a dream. There were days of bad weather, during which he remained constantly in the dormitory, where everything was rolling and crashing, in the midst of a terrible chorus of lamentations and imprecations, and he thought that his last hour had come. There were other days, when the sea was calm and yellowish, of insupportable heat, of infinite tediousness; interminable and wretched hours, during which the enervated passengers, stretched motionless on the planks, seemed all dead. And the voyage was endless: sea and sky, sky and sea; today the same as yesterday, tomorrow like today, and so on, always, eternally.

And for long hours he stood leaning on the bulwarks, gazing at that interminable sea in amazement, thinking vaguely of his mother, until his eyes closed and his head was drooping with sleep; and then again he beheld that unknown face which gazed upon him with an air of compassion, and repeated in his ear, "Your mother is dead!" and at the sound of that voice he awoke with a start, to resume his dreaming with wide-open eyes, and to gaze at the unchanging horizon.

The voyage lasted twenty-seven days. But the last days were the best. The weather was fine, and the air cool. He had made the acquaintance of a good old man, a Lombard, who was going to America to find his son, an agriculturist in the vicinity of the town of Rosario; he had told him his whole story, and the old man kept repeating every little while, as he tapped him on the nape of the neck with his hand, "Courage, my lad; you will find your mother well and happy."

This companionship comforted him; his sad presentiments were turned into joyous ones. Seated on the bow, beside the aged peasant, who was smoking his pipe, beneath the beautiful starry heaven, in the midst of a group of singing peasants, he imagined to himself in his own mind a hundred times his arrival at Buenos Ayres; he saw himself in a certain street; he found the shop, he flew to his cousin. "How is my mother? Come, let us go at once! Let us go at once!" They hurried on together; they ascended a staircase; a door opened. And here his mute soliloquy came to an end; his imagination was swallowed up in a feeling of inexpressible tenderness, which made him secretly pull forth a little medal that he wore on his neck, and murmur his prayers as he kissed it.

On the twenty-seventh day after their departure they arrived. It was a beautiful, rosy May morning, when the steamer cast anchor in the immense river of the Plata, near the shore along which stretches the vast city of Buenos Ayres, the capital of the Argentine Republic. This splendid weather seemed to him to be a good augury. He was beside himself with joy and impatience. His mother was only a few miles from him! In a few hours more he would have seen her! He was in America, in the new world, and he had had the daring to come alone! The whole of that extremely long voyage now seemed to him to have passed in an instant. It seemed to him that he had flown hither in a dream, and that he had that moment waked. And he was so happy, that he hardly experienced any surprise or distress when he felt in his pockets and found only one of the two little heaps into which he had divided his little treasure, in order to be the more sure of not losing the whole of it. He had been robbed; he had only a few lire left; but what mattered that to him, when he was near his mother? With his bag in his hand, he descended, in company with many other Italians, to the tug-boat which carried him within a short distance of the shore; clambered down from the tug into a boat which bore the name of *Andrea Doria*; was landed on the wharf; saluted his old Lombard friend, and directed his course, in long strides, towards the city.

On arriving at the entrance of the first street, he stopped a man who was passing by, and begged him to show him in what direction he should go in order to reach the street of *los Artes*. He chanced to have stopped an Italian workingman. The latter surveyed him with curiosity, and inquired if he knew how to read. The lad nodded, "Yes."

"Well, then," said the laborer, pointing to the street from which he had just emerged, "keep straight on through there, reading the names of all the streets on the corners; you will end by finding the one you want."

The boy thanked him, and turned into the street which opened before him.

It was a straight and endless but narrow street, bordered by low white houses, which looked like so many little villas, filled with people, with carriages, with carts which made a deafening noise; here and there floated enormous banners of various hues, with announcements as to the departure of steamers for strange cities inscribed upon them in large letters. At every little distance along the street, on the right and left, he perceived two other streets which ran straight away as far as he could see, also bordered by low white houses, filled with people and vehicles, and bounded at their extremity by the level line of the measureless plains of America, like the horizon at sea. The city seemed infinite to him; it seemed to him that he might wander for days or weeks, seeing other streets like these, on one hand and on the other, and that all America must be covered with them. He looked attentively at the names of the streets: strange names which cost him an effort to read. At every fresh street, he felt his heart beat, at the thought that it was the one he was in search of. He stared at all the women, with the thought that he might meet his mother. He caught sight of one in front of him who made his blood leap; he overtook her: she was a negro. And accelerating his pace, he walked on and on. On arriving at the cross-street, he read, and stood as though rooted to the sidewalk. It was the street *del los Artes*. He turned into it, and saw the number 117; his cousin's shop was No. 175. He quickened his pace still more, and almost ran; at No. 171 he had to pause to regain his breath. And he said to himself, "O my mother! my mother! It is really true that I shall see you in another moment!" He ran on; he arrived at a little haberdasher's shop. This was it. He stepped up close to it. He saw a woman with gray hair and spectacles.

"What do you want, boy?" she asked him in Spanish.

"Is not this," said the boy, making an effort to utter a sound, "the shop of Francesco Merelli?"

"Francesco Merelli is dead," replied the woman in Italian.

The boy felt as though he had received a blow on his breast.

"When did he die?"

"Eh? quite a while ago," replied the woman. "Months ago. His affairs were in a bad state, and he ran away. They say he went to Bahia Blanca, very far from here. And he died just after he reached there. The shop is mine."

The boy turned pale.

Then he said quickly, "Merelli knew my mother; my mother who was at service with Signor Mequinez. He alone could tell me where she is. I have come to America to find my mother. Merelli sent her our letters. I must find my mother."

"Poor boy!" said the woman; "I don't know. I can ask the boy in the courtyard. He knew the young man who did Merelli's errands. He may be able to tell us something."

She went to the end of the shop and called the lad, who came instantly. "Tell me," asked the shopwoman, "do you remember whether Merelli's young man went occasionally to carry letters to a woman in service, in the house of the *son of the country*?"

"To Signor Mequinez," replied the lad; "yes, signora, sometimes he did. At the end of the street *del los Artes*."

"Ah! thanks, signora!" cried Marco. "Tell me the number; don't you know it? Send some one with me; come with me instantly, my boy; I have still a few soldi."

And he said this with so much warmth, that without waiting for the woman to request him, the boy replied, "Come," and at once set out at a rapid pace.

They proceeded almost at a run, without uttering a word, to the end of the extremely long street, made their way into the entrance of a little white house, and halted in front of a handsome iron gate, through which they could see a small yard, filled with vases of flowers. Marco gave a tug at the bell.

A young lady made her appearance.

"The Mequinez family lives here, does it not?" demanded the lad anxiously.

"They did live here," replied the young lady, pronouncing her Italian in Spanish fashion. "Now we, the Zeballos, live here."

"And where have the Mequinez gone?" asked Marco, his heart palpitating.

"They have gone to Cordova."

"Cordova!" exclaimed Marco. "Where is Cordova? And the person whom they had in their service? The woman, my mother! Their servant was my mother! Have they taken my mother away, too?"

The young lady looked at him and said: "I do not know. Perhaps my father may know, for he knew them when they went away. Wait a moment."

She ran away, and soon returned with her father, a tall gentleman, with a gray beard. He looked intently for a minute at this sympathetic type of a little Genoese sailor, with his golden hair and his aquiline nose, and asked him in broken Italian, "Is your mother a Genoese?"

Marco replied that she was.

"Well then, the Genoese maid went with them; that I know for certain."

"And where have they gone?"

"To Cordova, a city."

The boy gave vent to a sigh; then he said with resignation, "Then I will go to Cordova."

"Ah, poor child!" exclaimed the gentleman in Spanish; "poor boy! Cordova is hundreds of miles from here."

Marco turned as white as a corpse, and clung with one hand to the railings.

"Let us see, let us see," said the gentleman, moved to pity, and opening the door; "come inside a moment; let us see if anything can be done." He sat down, gave the boy a seat, and made him tell his story, listened to it very attentively, meditated a little, then said resolutely, "You have no money, have you?"

"I still have some, a little," answered Marco.

The gentleman reflected for five minutes more; then seated himself at a desk, wrote a letter, sealed it, and handing it to the boy, he said to him:

"Listen to me, little Italian. Take this letter to Boca. That is a little city which is half Genoese, and lies two hours' journey from here. Any one will be able to show you the road. Go there and find the gentleman to whom this letter is addressed, and whom every one knows. Carry the letter to him. He will send you off to the town of Rosario tomorrow, and will recommend you to some one there, who will think out a way of enabling you to pursue your journey to Cordova, where you will find the Mequinez family and your mother. In the meanwhile, take this." And he placed in his hand a few lire. "Go, and keep up your courage; you will find fellow-countrymen of yours in every direction, and you will not be deserted. *Adios!*"

The boy said, "Thanks," without finding any other words to express himself, went out with his bag, and having taken leave of his little guide, he set out slowly in the direction of Boca, filled with sorrow and amazement, across that great and noisy town.

Everything that happened to him from that moment until the evening of that day ever afterwards lingered in his memory in a confused and uncertain form, like the wild vagaries of a person in a fever, so weary was he, so troubled, so despondent. And at nightfall on the following day, after having slept over night in a poor little chamber in a house in Boca, beside a harbor porter, after having passed nearly the whole of that day seated on a pile of beams, and, as in delirium, in sight of thousands of ships and boats and tugs, he found himself on the poop of a large sailing vessel, loaded with fruit, which was setting out for the town of Rosario, managed by three robust Genoese, who were bronzed by the sun; and their voices and the dialect which they spoke put a little comfort into his heart once more.

They set out, and the voyage lasted three days and four nights, and it was a continual amazement to the little traveller. Three days and four nights on that wonderful river Paranà, in comparison with which our great Po is but a rivulet; and the length of Italy quadrupled does not equal that of its course. The barge advanced slowly against this immeasurable mass of water. It threaded its way among long islands, once the haunts of serpents and tigers, covered with orange-trees and willows, like floating coppices; now they passed through narrow canals, from which it seemed as though they could never issue forth; now they sailed out on vast expanses of water, having the aspect of great tranquil lakes; then among islands again, through the intricate channels of an archipelago, amid enormous masses of vegetation. A profound silence reigned. For long stretches the shores and very vast and solitary waters produced the impression of an unknown stream, upon which this poor little sail was the first in all the world to venture itself. The further they advanced, the more this monstrous river dismayed him. He imagined that his mother was at its source, and that their navigation must last for years. Twice a day he ate a little bread and salted meat with the boatmen, who, perceiving that he was sad, never addressed a word to him. At night he slept on deck and woke every little while with a start, astounded by the limpid light of the moon, which silvered the immense expanse of water and the distant shores; and then his heart sank within him. "Cordova!" He repeated that name, "Cordova!" like the name of one of those mysterious cities of which he had heard in fables. But then he thought, "My mother passed this spot; she saw these islands, these shores;" and then these places upon which the glance of his mother had fallen no longer seemed strange and solitary to him. At night one of the boatmen sang. That voice reminded him of his mother's songs, when she had lulled him to sleep as a little child. On the last night, when he heard that song, he sobbed. The boatman interrupted his song. Then he cried, "Courage, courage, my son! What the deuce! A Genoese crying because he is far from home! The Genoese make the circuit of the world, glorious and triumphant!"

And at these words he shook himself, he heard the voice of the Genoese blood, and he raised his head aloft with pride, dashing his fist down on the rudder. "Well, yes," he said to himself; "and if I am also obliged to travel for years and years to come, all over the world, and to traverse hundreds of miles on foot, I will go on until I find my mother, were I to arrive in a dying condition, and fall dead at her feet! If only I can see her once again! Courage!" And with this frame of mind he arrived at daybreak, on a cool and rosy morning, in front of the city of Rosario, situated on the high bank of the Paranà, where the beflagged yards of a hundred vessels of every land were mirrored in the waves.

Shortly after landing, he went to the town, bag in hand, to seek an Argentine gentleman for whom his protector in Boca had intrusted him with a visiting-card, with a few words of recommendation. On entering Rosario, it seemed to him that he was coming into a city with which he was already familiar. There were the straight, interminable streets, bordered with low white houses, traversed in all directions above the roofs by great bundles of telegraph and telephone wires, which looked like enormous spiders' webs; and a great confusion of people, of horses, and of vehicles. His head grew confused; he almost thought that he had got back to Buenos Ayres, and must hunt up his cousin once more. He wandered about for nearly an hour, making one turn after another, and seeming always to come back to the same street; and by dint of inquiring, he found the house of his new protector. He pulled the bell. There came to the door a big, light-haired, gruff man, who had the air of a steward, and who demanded awkwardly, with a foreign accent:

"What do you want?"

The boy mentioned the name of his patron.

"The master has gone away," replied the steward; "he set out yesterday afternoon for Buenos Ayres, with his whole family."

The boy was left speechless. Then he stammered, "But I--I have no one here! I am alone!" and he offered the card.

The steward took it, read it, and said surlily: "I don't know what to do for you. I'll give it to him when he returns a month hence."

"But I, I am alone; I am in need!" exclaimed the lad, in a supplicating voice.

"Eh? come now," said the other; "just as though there were not a plenty of your sort from your country in Rosario! Be off, and do your begging in Italy!" And he slammed the door in his face.

The boy stood there as though he had been turned to stone.

Then he picked up his bag again slowly, and went out, his heart torn with anguish, with his mind in a whirl, assailed all at once by a thousand anxious thoughts. What was to be done? Where was he to go? From Rosario to Cordova was a day's journey, by rail. He had only a few lire left. After deducting what he should be obliged to spend that day, he would have next to nothing left. Where was he to find the money to pay his fare? He could work--but how? To whom should he apply for work? Ask alms? Ah, no! To be repulsed, insulted, humiliated, as he had been a little while ago? No; never, never more--rather would he die! And at this idea, and at the sight of the very long street which was lost in the distance of the boundless plain, he felt his courage desert him once more, flung his bag on the sidewalk, sat down with his back against the wall, and bent his head between his hands, in an attitude of despair.

People jostled him with their feet as they passed; the vehicles filled the road with noise; several boys stopped to look at him. He remained thus for a while. Then he was startled by a voice saying to him in a mixture of Italian and Lombard dialect, "What is the matter, little boy?"

He raised his face at these words, and instantly sprang to his feet, uttering an exclamation of wonder: "You here!"

It was the old Lombard peasant with whom he had struck up a friendship during the voyage.

The amazement of the peasant was no less than his own; but the boy did not leave him time to question him, and he rapidly recounted the state of his affairs.

"Now I am without a soldo. I must go to work. Find me work, that I may get together a few lire. I will do anything; I will carry rubbish, I will sweep the streets; I can run on errands, or even work in the country; I am content to live on black bread; but only let it be so that I may set out quickly, that I may find my mother once more. Do me this charity, and find me work, find me work, for the love of God, for I can do no more!"

"The deuce! the deuce!" said the peasant, looking about him, and scratching his chin. "What a story is this! To work, to work!--that is soon said. Let us look about a little. Is there no way of finding thirty lire among so many fellow-countrymen?"

The boy looked at him, consoled by a ray of hope.

"Come with me," said the peasant.

"Where?" asked the lad, gathering up his bag again.

"Come with me."

The peasant started on; Marco followed him. They traversed a long stretch of street together without speaking. The peasant halted at the door of an inn which had for its sign a star, and an inscription beneath, *The Star of Italy*. He thrust his face in, and turning to the boy, he said cheerfully, "We have arrived at just the right moment."

They entered a large room, where there were numerous tables, and many men seated, drinking and talking loudly. The old Lombard approached the first table, and from the manner in which he saluted the six guests who were gathered around it, it was evident that he had been in their company until a short time previously. They were red in the face, and were clinking their glasses, and vociferating and laughing.

"Comrades," said the Lombard, without any preface, remaining on his feet, and presenting Marco, "here is a poor lad, our fellow-countryman, who has come alone from Genoa to Buenos Ayres to seek his mother. At Buenos Ayres they told him, 'She is not here; she is in Cordova.' He came in a bark to Rosario, three days and three nights on the way, with a couple of lines of recommendation. He presents the card; they make an ugly face at him: he hasn't a centesimo to bless himself with. He is here alone and in despair. He is a lad full of heart. Let us see a bit. Can't we find enough to pay for his ticket to go to Cordova in search of his mother? Are we to leave him here like a dog?"

"Never in the world, by Heavens! That shall never be said!" they all shouted at once, hammering on the table with their fists. "A fellow-countryman of ours! Come hither, little fellow! We are emigrants! See what a handsome young rogue! Out with your coppers, comrades! Bravo! Come alone! He has daring! Drink a sup, *patriotta*! We'll send you to your mother; never fear!" And one pinched his cheek, another slapped him on the shoulder, a third relieved him of his bag; other emigrants rose from the neighboring tables, and gathered about; the boy's story made the round of the inn; three Argentine guests hurried in from the adjoining room; and in less than ten minutes the Lombard peasant, who was passing round the hat, had collected forty-two lire.

"Do you see," he then said, turning to the boy, "how fast things are done in America?"

"Drink!" cried another to him, offering him a glass of wine; "to the health of your mother!"

All raised their glasses, and Marco repeated, "To the health of my--" But a sob of joy choked him, and, setting the glass on the table, he flung himself on the old man's neck.

At daybreak on the following morning he set out for Cordova, ardent and smiling, filled with presentiments of happiness. But there is no cheerfulness that rules for long in the face of certain sinister aspects of nature. The weather was close and dull; the train, which was nearly empty, ran through an immense plain, destitute of every sign of habitation. He found himself alone in a very long car, which resembled those on trains for the wounded. He gazed to the right, he gazed to the left, and he saw nothing but an endless solitude, strewn with tiny, deformed trees, with contorted trunks and branches, in attitudes such as were never seen before, almost of wrath and anguish, and a sparse and melancholy vegetation, which gave to the plain the aspect of a ruined cemetery.

He dozed for half an hour; then resumed his survey: the spectacle was still the same. The railway stations were deserted, like the dwellings of hermits; and when the train stopped, not a sound was heard; it seemed to him that he was alone in a lost train, abandoned in the middle of a desert. It seemed to him as though each station must be the last, and that he should then enter the mysterious regions of the savages. An icy breeze nipped his face. On embarking at Genoa, towards the end of April, it had not occurred to him that he should find winter in America, and he was dressed for summer.

After several hours of this he began to suffer from cold, and in connection with the cold, from the fatigue of the days he had recently passed through, filled as they had been with violent emotions, and from sleepless and harassing nights. He fell asleep, slept a long time, and awoke benumbed; he felt ill. Then a vague terror of falling ill, of dying on the journey, seized upon him; a fear of being thrown out there, in the middle of that desolate prairie, where his body would be torn in pieces by dogs and birds of prey, like the corpses of horses and cows which he had caught sight of every now and then beside the track, and from which he had turned aside his eyes in disgust. In this state of anxious illness, in the midst of that dark silence of nature, his imagination grew excited, and looked on the dark side of things.

Was he quite sure, after all, that he should find his mother at Cordova? And what if she had not gone there? What if that gentleman in the Via del los Artes had made a mistake? And what if she were dead? Thus meditating, he fell asleep again, and dreamed that he was in Cordova, and it was night, and that he heard cries from all the doors and all the windows: "She is not here! She is not here! She is not here!" This roused him with a start, in terror, and he saw at the other end of the car three bearded men enveloped in shawls of various colors who were staring at him and talking together in a low tone; and the suspicion flashed across him that they were assassins, and that they wanted to kill him for the sake of stealing his bag. Fear was added to his consciousness of illness and to the cold; his fancy, already perturbed, became distorted: the three men kept on staring at him; one of them moved towards him; then his reason wandered, and rushing towards him with arms wide open, he shrieked, "I have nothing; I am a poor boy; I have come from Italy; I am in quest of my mother; I am alone: do not do me any harm!"

They instantly understood the situation; they took compassion on him, caressed and soothed him, speaking to him many words which he did not hear nor comprehend; and perceiving that his teeth were chattering with cold, they wrapped one of their shawls around him, and made him sit down again, so that he might go to sleep. And he did fall asleep once more, when the twilight was descending. When they aroused him, he was at Cordova.

Ah, what a deep breath he drew, and with what impetuosity he flew from the car! He inquired of one of the station employees where the house of the engineer Mequinez was situated; the latter mentioned the name of a church; it stood beside the church: the boy hastened away.

It was night. He entered the city, and it seemed to him that he was entering Rosario once more; that he again beheld those straight streets, flanked with little white houses, and intersected by other very long and straight streets. But there were very few people, and under the light of the rare street lanterns, he encountered strange faces of a hue unknown to him, between black and greenish; and raising his head from time to time, he beheld churches of bizarre architecture which were outlined black and vast against the sky. The city was dark and silent, but after having traversed that immense desert, it appeared lively to him. He inquired his way of a priest, speedily found the church and the house, pulled the bell with one trembling hand, and pressed the other on his breast to repress the beating of his heart, which was leaping into his throat.

An old woman, with a light in her hand, opened the door.

The boy could not speak at once.

"Whom do you want?" demanded the dame in Spanish.

"The engineer Mequinez," replied Marco.

The old woman made a motion to cross her arms on her breast, and replied, with a shake of the head: "So you, too, have dealings with the engineer Mequinez! It strikes me that it is time to stop this. We have been worried for the last three months. It is not enough that the newspapers have said it. We shall have to have it printed on the corner of the street, that Signor Mequinez has gone to live at Tucuman!"

The boy gave way to a gesture of despair. Then he gave way to an outburst of passion.

"So there is a curse upon me! I am doomed to die on the road, without having found my mother! I shall go mad! I shall kill myself! My God! what is the name of that country? Where is it? At what distance is it situated?"

"Eh, poor boy," replied the old woman, moved to pity; "a mere trifle! We are four or five hundred miles from there, at least."

The boy covered his face with his hands; then he asked with a sob, "And now what am I to do!"

"What am I to say to you, my poor child?" responded the dame: "I don't know."

But suddenly an idea struck her, and she added hastily: "Listen, now that I think of it. There is one thing that you can do. Go down this street, to the right, and at the third house you will find a courtyard; there there is a *capataz*, a trader, who is setting out tomorrow for Tucuman, with his wagons and his oxen. Go and see if he will take you, and offer him your services; perhaps he will give you a place on his wagons: go at once."

The lad grasped his bag, thanked her as he ran, and two minutes later found himself in a vast courtyard, lighted by lanterns, where a number of men were engaged in loading sacks of grain on certain enormous carts which resembled the movable houses of mountebanks, with rounded tops, and very tall wheels; and a tall man with mustaches, enveloped in a sort of mantle of black and white check, and with big boots, was directing the work.

The lad approached this man, and timidly proffered his request, saying that he had come from Italy, and that he was in search of his mother.

The *capataz*, which signifies the head (the head conductor of this convoy of wagons), surveyed him from head to foot with a keen glance, and replied drily, "I have no place."

"I have fifteen lire," answered the boy in a supplicating tone; "I will give you my fifteen lire. I will work on the journey; I will fetch the water and fodder for the animals; I will perform all sorts of services. A little bread will suffice for me. Make a little place for me, signor."

The *capataz* looked him over again, and replied with a better grace, "There is no room; and then, we are not going to Tucuman; we are going to another town, Santiago dell'Estero. We shall have to leave you at a certain point, and you will still have a long way to go on foot."

"Ah, I will make twice as long a journey!" exclaimed Marco; "I can walk; do not worry about that; I shall get there by some means or other: make a little room for me, signor, out of charity; for pity's sake, do not leave me here alone!"

"Beware; it is a journey of twenty days."

"It matters nothing to me."

"It is a hard journey."

"I will endure everything."

"You will have to travel alone."

"I fear nothing, if I can only find my mother. Have compassion!"

The *capataz* drew his face close to a lantern, and scrutinized him. Then he said, "Very well."

The lad kissed his hand.

"You shall sleep in one of the wagons to-night," added the *capataz*, as he quitted him; "tomorrow morning, at four o'clock, I will wake you. Good night."

At four o'clock in the morning, by the light of the stars, the long string of wagons was set in motion with a great noise; each cart was drawn by six oxen, and all were followed by a great number of spare animals for a change.

The boy, who had been awakened and placed in one of the carts, on the sacks, instantly fell again into a deep sleep. When he awoke, the convoy had halted in a solitary spot, full in the sun, and all the men--the *peones*--were seated round a quarter of calf, which was roasting in the open air, beside a large fire, which was flickering in the wind. They all ate together, took a nap, and then set out again; and thus the journey continued, regulated like a march of soldiers. Every morning they set out on the road at five o'clock, halted at nine, set out again at five o'clock in the evening, and halted again at ten. The *peones* rode on horseback, and stimulated the oxen with long goads. The boy lighted the fire for the roasting, gave the beasts their fodder, polished up the lanterns, and brought water for drinking.

The landscape passed before him like an indistinct vision: vast groves of little brown trees; villages consisting of a few scattered houses, with red and battlemented façades; very vast tracts, possibly the ancient beds of great salt lakes, which gleamed white with salt as far as the eye could reach; and on every hand, and always, the prairie, solitude, silence. On very rare occasions they encountered two or three travellers on horseback, followed by a herd of picked horses, who passed them at a gallop, like a whirlwind. The days were all alike, as at sea, wearisome and interminable; but the weather was fine. But the *peones* became more and more exacting every day, as though the lad were their bond slave; some of them treated him brutally, with threats; all forced him to serve them without mercy: they made him carry enormous bundles of forage; they sent him to get water at great distances; and he, broken with fatigue, could not even sleep at night, continually tossed about as he was by the violent jolts of the wagon, and the deafening groaning of the wheels and wooden axles. And in addition to this, the wind having risen, a fine, reddish, greasy dust, which enveloped everything, penetrated the wagon, made its way under the covers, filled his eyes and mouth, robbed him of sight and breath, constantly, oppressively, insupportably. Worn out with toil and lack of sleep, reduced to rags and dirt, reproached and ill treated from morning till night, the poor boy grew every day more dejected, and would have lost heart entirely if the *capataz* had not addressed a kind word to him now and then. He often wept, unseen, in a corner of the wagon, with his face against his bag, which no longer contained anything but rags. Every morning he rose weaker and more discouraged, and as he looked out over the country, and beheld always the same boundless and implacable plain, like a terrestrial ocean, he said to himself: "Ah, I shall not hold out until to-night! I shall not hold out until to-night! Today I shall die on the road!" And his toil increased, his ill treatment was redoubled. One morning, in the absence of the *capataz*, one of the men struck him, because he had delayed in fetching the water. And then they all began to take turns at it, when they gave him an order, dealing him a kick, saying: "Take that, you vagabond! Carry that to your mother!"

His heart was breaking. He fell ill; for three days he remained in the wagon, with a coverlet over him, fighting a fever, and seeing no one except the *capataz*, who came to give him his drink and feel his pulse. And then he believed that he was lost, and invoked his mother in despair, calling her a hundred times by name: "O my mother! my mother! Help me! Come to me, for I am dying! Oh, my poor mother, I shall never see you again! My poor mother, who will find me dead beside the way!" And he folded his hands over his bosom and prayed. Then he grew better, thanks to the care of the *capataz*, and recovered; but with his recovery arrived the most terrible day of his journey, the day on which he was to be left to his own devices. They had been on the way for more than two weeks; when they arrived at the point where the road to Tucuman parted from that which leads to Santiago dell'Estero, the *capataz* announced to him that they must separate. He gave him some instructions with regard to the road, tied his bag on his shoulders in a manner which would not annoy him as he walked, and, breaking off short, as though he feared that he should be affected, he bade him farewell. The boy had barely time to kiss him on one arm. The other men, too, who had treated him so harshly, seemed to feel a little pity at the sight of him left thus alone, and they made signs of farewell to him as they moved away. And he returned the salute with his hand, stood watching the convoy until it was lost to sight in the red dust of the plain, and then set out sadly on his road.

One thing, on the other hand, comforted him a little from the first. After all those days of travel across that endless plain, which was forever the same, he saw before him a chain of mountains very high and blue, with white summits, which reminded him of the Alps, and gave him the feeling of having drawn near to his own country once more. They were the Andes, the dorsal spine of the American continent, that immense chain which extends from Tierra del Fuego to the glacial sea of the Arctic pole, through a hundred and ten degrees of latitude. And he was also comforted by the fact that the air seemed to him to grow constantly warmer; and this happened, because, in ascending towards the north, he was slowly approaching the tropics. At great distances apart there were tiny groups of houses with a petty shop; and he bought something to eat. He encountered men on horseback; every now and then he saw women and children seated on the ground, motionless and grave, with faces entirely new to him, of an earthen hue, with oblique eyes and prominent cheek-bones, who looked at him intently, and accompanied him with their gaze, turning their heads slowly like automatons. They were Indians.

The first day he walked as long as his strength would permit, and slept under a tree. On the second day he made considerably less progress, and with less spirit. His shoes were dilapidated, his feet wounded, his stomach weakened by bad food. Towards evening he began to be alarmed. He had heard, in Italy, that in this land there were serpents; he fancied that he heard them crawling; he halted, then set out on a run, and with cold chills in all his bones. At times he was seized with a profound pity for himself, and he wept silently as he walked. Then he thought, "Oh, how much my mother would suffer if she knew that I am afraid!" and this thought restored his courage. Then, in order to distract his thoughts from fear, he meditated much of her; he recalled to mind her words when she had set out from Genoa, and the movement with which she had arranged the coverlet beneath his chin when he was in bed, and when he was a baby; for every time that she took him in her arms, she said to him, "Stay here a little while with me"; and thus she remained for a long time, with her head resting on his, thinking, thinking.

And he said to himself: "Shall I see thee again, dear mother? Shall I arrive at the end of my journey, my mother?" And he walked on and on, among strange trees, vast plantations of sugar-cane, and fields without end, always with those blue mountains in front of him, which cut the sky with their exceedingly lofty crests. Four days, five days--a week, passed. His strength was rapidly declining, his feet were bleeding. Finally, one evening at sunset, they said to him:

"Tucuman is fifty miles from here."

He uttered a cry of joy, and hastened his steps, as though he had, in that moment, regained all his lost vigor. But it was a brief illusion. His forces suddenly abandoned him, and he fell upon the brink of a ditch, exhausted. But his heart was beating with content. The heaven, thickly sown with the most brilliant stars, had never seemed so beautiful to him. He contemplated it, as he lay stretched out on the grass to sleep, and thought that, perhaps, at that very moment, his mother was gazing at him. And he said:

"O my mother, where art thou? What art thou doing at this moment? Dost thou think of thy son? Dost thou think of thy Marco, who is so near to thee?"

Poor Marco! If he could have seen in what a case his mother was at that moment, he would have made a superhuman effort to proceed on his way, and to reach her a few hours earlier. She was ill in bed, in a ground-floor room of a lordly mansion, where dwelt the entire Mequinez family. The latter had become very fond of her, and had helped her a great deal. The poor woman had already been ailing when the engineer Mequinez had been obliged unexpectedly to set out far from Buenos Ayres, and she had not benefited at all by the fine air of Cordova. But then, the fact that she had received no response to her letters from her husband, nor from her cousin, the presentiment, always lively, of some great misfortune, the continual anxiety in which she had lived, between the parting and staying, expecting every day some bad news, had caused her to grow worse out of all proportion. Finally, a very serious malady had declared itself,--a strangled internal rupture. She had not risen from her bed for a fortnight. A surgical operation was necessary to save her life. And at precisely the moment when Marco was apostrophizing her, the master and mistress of the house were standing beside her bed, arguing with her, with great gentleness, to persuade her to allow herself to be operated on, and she was persisting in her refusal, and weeping. A good physician of Tucuman had come in vain a week before.

"No, my dear master," she said; "do not count upon it; I have not the strength to resist; I should die under the surgeon's knife. It is better to allow me to die thus. I no longer cling to life. All is at an end for me. It is better to die before learning what has happened to my family."

And her master and mistress opposed, and said that she must take courage, that she would receive a reply to the last letters, which had been sent directly to Genoa; that she must allow the operation to be performed; that it must be done for the sake of her family. But this suggestion of her children only aggravated her profound discouragement, which had for a long time prostrated her, with increasing anguish. At these words she burst into tears.

"O my sons! my sons!" she exclaimed, wringing her hands; "perhaps they are no longer alive! It is better that I should die also. I thank you, my good master and mistress; I thank you from my heart. But it is better that I should die. At all events, I am certain that I shall not be cured by this operation. Thanks for all your care, my good master and mistress. It is useless for the doctor to come again after tomorrow. I wish to die. It is my fate to die here. I have decided."

And they began again to console her, and to repeat, "Don't say that," and to take her hand and beseech her.

But she closed her eyes then in exhaustion, and fell into a doze, so that she appeared to be dead. And her master and mistress remained there a little while, by the faint light of a taper, watching with great compassion that admirable mother, who, for the sake of saving her family, had come to die six thousand miles from her country, to die after having toiled so hard, poor woman! and she was so honest, so good, so unfortunate.

Early on the morning of the following day, Marco, bent and limping, with his bag on his back, entered the city of Tucuman, one of the youngest and most flourishing towns of the Argentine Republic. It seemed to him that he beheld again Cordova, Rosario, Buenos Ayres: there were the same straight and extremely long streets, the same low white houses, but on every hand there was a new and magnificent vegetation, a perfumed air, a marvellous light, a sky limpid and profound, such as he had never seen even in Italy. As he advanced through the streets, he experienced once more the feverish agitation which had seized on him at Buenos Ayres; he stared at the windows and doors of all the houses; he stared at all the women who passed him, with an anxious hope that he might meet his mother; he would have liked to question every one, but did not dare to stop any one. All the people who were standing at their doors turned to gaze after the poor, tattered, dusty lad, who showed that he had come from afar. And he was seeking, among all these people, a countenance which should inspire him with confidence, in order to direct to its owner that tremendous query, when his eyes fell upon the sign of an inn upon which was inscribed an Italian name. Inside were a man with spectacles, and two women. He approached the door slowly, and summoning up a resolute spirit, he inquired:

"Can you tell me, signor, where the family Mequinez is?"

"The engineer Mequinez?" asked the innkeeper in his turn.

"The engineer Mequinez," replied the lad in a thread of a voice.

"The Mequinez family is not in Tucuman," replied the innkeeper.

A cry of desperate pain, like that of one who has been stabbed, formed an echo to these words.

The innkeeper and the women rose, and some neighbors ran up.

"What's the matter? what ails you, my boy?" said the innkeeper, drawing him into the shop and making him sit down. "The deuce! there's no reason for despairing! The Mequinez family is not here, but at a little distance off, a few hours from Tucuman."

"Where? where?" shrieked Marco, springing up like one restored to life.

"Fifteen miles from here," continued the man, "on the river, at Saladillo, in a place where a big sugar factory is being built, and a cluster of houses; Signor Mequinez's house is there; every one knows it: you can reach it in a few hours."

"I was there a month ago," said a youth, who had hastened up at the cry.

Marco stared at him with wide-open eyes, and asked him hastily, turning pale as he did so, "Did you see the servant of Signor Mequinez--the Italian?"

"The Genoese? Yes; I saw her."

Marco burst into a convulsive sob, which was half a laugh and half a sob. Then, with a burst of violent resolution: "Which way am I to go? quick, the road! I shall set out instantly; show me the way!"

"But it is a day's march," they all told him, in one breath. "You are weary; you should rest; you can set out tomorrow."

"Impossible! impossible!" replied the lad. "Tell me the way; I will not wait another instant; I shall set out at once, were I to die on the road!"

On perceiving him so inflexible, they no longer opposed him. "May God accompany you!" they said to him. "Look out for the path through the forest. A fair journey to you, little Italian!" A man accompanied him outside of the town, pointed out to him the road, gave him some counsel, and stood still to watch him start. At the expiration of a few minutes, the lad disappeared, limping, with his bag on his shoulders, behind the thick trees which lined the road.

That night was a dreadful one for the poor sick woman. She suffered atrocious pain, which wrung from her shrieks that were enough to burst her veins, and rendered her delirious at times. The women waited on her. She lost her head. Her mistress ran in, from time to time, in affright. All began to fear that, even if she had decided to allow herself to be operated on, the doctor, who was not to come until the next day, would have arrived too late. During the moments when she was not raving, however, it was evident that her most terrible torture arose not from her bodily pains, but from the thought of her distant family. Emaciated, wasted away, with changed visage, she thrust her hands through her hair, with a gesture of desperation, and shrieked:

"My God! My God! To die so far away, to die without seeing them again! My poor children, who will be left without a mother, my poor little creatures, my poor darlings! My Marco, who is still so small! only as tall as this, and so good and affectionate! You do not know what a boy he was! If you only knew, signora! I could not detach him from my neck when I set out; he sobbed in a way to move your pity; he sobbed; it seemed as though he knew that he would never behold his poor mother again. Poor Marco, my poor baby! I thought that my heart would break! Ah, if I had only died then, died while they were bidding me farewell! If I had but dropped dead! Without a mother, my poor child, he who loved me so dearly, who needed me so much! without a mother, in misery, he will be forced to beg! He, Marco, my Marco, will stretch out his hand, famishing! O eternal God! No! I will not die! The doctor! Call him at once I let him come, let him cut me, let him cleave my breast, let him drive me mad; but let him save my life! I want to recover; I want to live, to depart, to flee, tomorrow, at once! The doctor! Help! help!"

And the women seized her hands and soothed her, and made her calm herself little by little, and spoke to her of God and of hope. And then she fell back again into a mortal dejection, wept with her hands clutched in her gray hair, moaned like an infant, uttering a prolonged lament, and murmuring from time to time:

"O my Genoa! My house! All that sea!--O my Marco, my poor Marco! Where is he now, my poor darling?"

It was midnight; and her poor Marco, after having passed many hours on the brink of a ditch, his strength exhausted, was then walking through a forest of gigantic trees, monsters of vegetation, huge boles like the pillars of a cathedral, which interlaced their enormous crests, silvered by the moon, at a wonderful height. Vaguely, amid the half gloom, he caught glimpses of myriads of trunks of all forms, upright, inclined, contorted, crossed in strange postures of menace and of conflict; some overthrown on the earth, like towers which had fallen bodily, and covered with a dense and confused mass of vegetation, which seemed like a furious throng, disputing the ground span by span; others collected in great groups, vertical and serrated, like trophies of titanic lances, whose tips touched the clouds; a superb grandeur, a prodigious disorder of colossal forms, the most majestically terrible spectacle which vegetable nature ever presented.

At times he was overwhelmed by a great stupor. But his mind instantly took flight again towards his mother. He was worn out, with bleeding feet, alone in the middle of this formidable forest, where it was only at long intervals that he saw tiny human habitations, which at the foot of these trees seemed like the ant-hills, or some buffalo asleep beside the road; he was exhausted, but he was not conscious of his exhaustion; he was alone, and he felt no fear. The grandeur of the forest rendered his soul grand; his nearness to his mother gave him the strength and the hardihood of a man; the memory of the ocean, of the alarms and the sufferings which he had undergone and vanquished, of the toil which he had endured, of the iron constancy which he had displayed, caused him to uplift his brow. All his strong and noble Genoese blood flowed back to his heart in an ardent tide of joy and audacity. And a new thing took place within him; while he had, up to this time, borne in his mind an image of his mother, dimmed and paled somewhat by the two years of absence, at that moment the image grew clear; he again beheld her face, perfect and distinct, as he had not beheld it for a long time; he beheld it close to him, illuminated, speaking; he again beheld the most fleeting motions of her eyes, and of her lips, all her attitudes, all the shades of her thoughts; and urged on by these pursuing recollections, he hastened his steps; and a new affection, an unspeakable tenderness, grew in him, grew in his heart, making sweet and quiet tears to flow down his face; and as he advanced through the gloom, he spoke to her, he said to her the words which he would murmur in her ear in a little while more:

"I am here, my mother; behold me here. I will never leave you again; we will return home together, and I will remain always beside you on board the ship, close beside you, and no one shall ever part me from you again, no one, never more, so long as I have life!"

And in the meantime he did not observe how the silvery light of the moon was dying away on the summits of the gigantic trees in the delicate whiteness of the dawn.

At eight o'clock on that morning, the doctor from Tucuman, a young Argentine, was already by the bedside of the sick woman, in company with an assistant, endeavoring, for the last time, to persuade her to permit herself to be operated on; and the engineer Mequinez and his wife added their warmest persuasions to those of the former. But all was in vain. The woman, feeling her strength exhausted, had no longer any faith in the operation; she was perfectly certain that she should die under it, or that she should only survive it a few hours, after having suffered in vain pains that were more atrocious than those of which she should die in any case. The doctor lingered to tell her once more:

"But the operation is a safe one; your safety is certain, provided you exercise a little courage! And your death is equally certain if you refuse!" It was a sheer waste of words.

"No," she replied in a faint voice, "I still have courage to die; but I no longer have any to suffer uselessly. Leave me to die in peace."

The doctor desisted in discouragement. No one said anything more. Then the woman turned her face towards her mistress, and addressed to her her last prayers in a dying voice.

"Dear, good signora," she said with a great effort, sobbing, "you will send this little money and my poor effects to my family--through the consul. I hope that they may all be alive. My heart presages well in these, my last moments. You will do me the favor to write--that I have always thought of them, that I have always toiled for them--for my children--that my sole grief was not to see them once more--but that I died courageously--with resignation--blessing them; and that I recommend to my husband--and to my elder son--the youngest, my poor Marco--that I bore him in my heart until the last moment--" And suddenly she became excited, and shrieked, as she clasped her hands: "My Marco, my baby, my baby! My life!--" But on casting her tearful eyes round her, she perceived that her mistress was no longer there; she had been secretly called away. She sought her master; he had disappeared. No one remained with her except the two nurses and the assistant. She heard in the adjoining room the sound of hurried footsteps, a murmur of hasty and subdued voices, and repressed exclamations. The sick woman fixed her glazing eyes on the door, in expectation. At the end of a few minutes she saw the doctor appear with an unusual expression on his face; then her mistress and master, with their countenances also altered. All three gazed at her with a singular expression, and exchanged a few words in a low tone. She fancied that the doctor said to her mistress, "Better let it be at once." She did not understand.

"Josefa," said her mistress to the sick woman, in a trembling voice, "I have some good news for you. Prepare your heart for good news."

The woman observed her intently.

"News," pursued the lady, with increasing agitation, "which will give you great joy."

The sick woman's eyes dilated.

"Prepare yourself," continued her mistress, "to see a person--of whom you are very fond."

The woman raised her head with a vigorous movement, and began to gaze in rapid succession, first at the lady and then at the door, with flashing eyes.

"A person," added the lady, turning pale, "who has just arrived--unexpectedly."

"Who is it?" shrieked the woman, with a strange and choked voice, like that of a person in terror. An instant later she gave vent to a shrill scream, sprang into a sitting posture in her bed, and remained motionless, with starting eyes, and her hands pressed to her temples, as in the presence of a supernatural apparition.

Marco, tattered and dusty, stood there on the threshold, held back by the doctor's hand on one arm.

The woman uttered three shrieks: "God! God! My God!"

Marco rushed forward; she stretched out to him her fleshless arms, and straining him to her heart with the strength of a tiger, she burst into a violent laugh, broken by deep, tearless sobs, which caused her to fall back suffocating on her pillow.

But she speedily recovered herself, and mad with joy, she shrieked as she covered his head with kisses: "How do you come here? Why? Is it you? How you have grown! Who brought you? Are you alone? You are not ill? It is you, Marco! It is not a dream! My God! Speak to me!"

Then she suddenly changed her tone: "No! Be silent! Wait!" And turning to the doctor, she said with precipitation: "Quick, doctor! this instant! I want to get well. I am ready. Do not lose a moment. Take Marco away, so that he may not hear.--Marco, my love, it is nothing. I will tell you about it. One more kiss. Go!--Here I am, doctor."

Marco was taken away. The master, mistress, and women retired in haste; the surgeon and his assistant remained behind, and closed the door.

Signor Mequinez attempted to lead Marco to a distant room, but it was impossible; he seemed rooted to the pavement.

"What is it?" he asked. "What is the matter with my mother? What are they doing to her?"

And then Mequinez said softly, still trying to draw him away: "Here! Listen to me. I will tell you now. Your mother is ill; she must undergo a little operation; I will explain it all to you: come with me."

"No," replied the lad, resisting; "I want to stay here. Explain it to me here."

The engineer heaped words on words, as he drew him away; the boy began to grow terrified and to tremble.

Suddenly an acute cry, like that of one wounded to the death, rang through the whole house.

The boy responded with another desperate shriek, "My mother is dead!"

The doctor appeared on the threshold and said, "Your mother is saved."

The boy gazed at him for a moment, and then flung himself at his feet, sobbing, "Thanks, doctor!"

But the doctor raised him with a gesture, saying: "Rise! It is you, you heroic child, who have saved your mother!"


SUMMER

Wednesday, 24th.

Marco, the Genoese, is the last little hero but one whose acquaintance we shall make this year; only one remains for the month of June. There are only two more monthly examinations, twenty-six days of lessons, six Thursdays, and five Sundays. The air of the end of the year is already perceptible. The trees of the garden, leafy and in blossom, cast a fine shade on the gymnastic apparatus. The scholars are already dressed in summer clothes. And it is beautiful, at the close of school and the exit of the classes, to see how different everything is from what it was in the months that are past. The long locks which touched the shoulders have disappeared; all heads are closely shorn; bare legs and throats are to be seen; little straw hats of every shape, with ribbons that descend even on the backs of the wearers; shirts and neckties of every hue; all the little children with something red or blue about them, a facing, a border, a tassel, a scrap of some vivid color tacked on somewhere by the mother, so that even the poorest may make a good figure; and many come to school without any hats, as though they had run away from home. Some wear the white gymnasium suit. There is one of Schoolmistress Delcati's boys who is red from head to foot, like a boiled crab. Several are dressed like sailors.

But the finest of all is the little mason, who has donned a big straw hat, which gives him the appearance of a half-candle with a shade over it; and it is ridiculous to see him make his hare's face beneath it. Coretti, too, has abandoned his catskin cap, and wears an old travelling-cap of gray silk. Votini has a sort of Scotch dress, all decorated; Crossi displays his bare breast; Precossi is lost inside of a blue blouse belonging to the blacksmith-ironmonger.

And Garoffi? Now that he has been obliged to discard the cloak beneath which he concealed his wares, all his pockets are visible, bulging with all sorts of huckster's trifles, and the lists of his lotteries force themselves out. Now all his pockets allow their contents to be seen,--fans made of half a newspaper, knobs of canes, darts to fire at birds, herbs, and maybugs which creep out of his pockets and crawl gradually over the jackets.

Many of the little fellows carry bunches of flowers to the mistresses. The mistresses are dressed in summer garments also, of cheerful tints; all except the "little nun," who is always in black; and the mistress with the red feather still has her red feather, and a knot of red ribbon at her neck, all tumbled with the little paws of her scholars, who always make her laugh and flee.

It is the season, too, of cherry-trees, of butterflies, of music in the streets, and of rambles in the country; many of the fourth grade run away to bathe in the Po; all have their hearts already set on the vacation; each day they issue forth from school more impatient and content than the day before. Only it pains me to see Garrone in mourning, and my poor mistress of the primary, who is thinner and whiter than ever, and who coughs with ever-increasing violence. She walks all bent over now, and salutes me so sadly!

POETRY

Friday, 26th.

You are now beginning to comprehend the poetry of school, Enrico; but at present you only survey the school from within. It will seem much more beautiful and more poetic to you twenty years from now, when you go thither to escort your own boys; and you will then survey it from the outside, as I do. While waiting for school to close, I wander about the silent street, in the vicinity of the edifice, and lay my ear to the windows of the ground floor, which are screened by Venetian blinds. At one window I hear the voice of a schoolmistress saying:

"Ah, what a shape for a *t*! It won't do, my dear boy! What would your father say to it?"

At the next window there resounds the heavy voice of a master, which is saying:

"I will buy fifty metres of stuff--at four lire and a half the metre--and sell it again--"

Further on there is the mistress with the red feather, who is reading aloud:

"Then Pietro Micca, with the lighted train of powder--"

From the adjoining class-room comes the chirping of a thousand birds, which signifies that the master has stepped out for a moment. I proceed onward, and as I turn the corner, I hear a scholar weeping, and the voice of the mistress reproving and comforting him. From the lofty windows issue verses, names of great and good men, fragments of sentences which inculcate virtue, the love of country, and courage. Then ensue moments of silence, in which one would declare that the edifice is empty, and it does not seem possible that there should be seven hundred boys within; noisy outbursts of hilarity become audible, provoked by the jest of a master in a good humor. And the people who are passing halt, and all direct a glance of sympathy towards that pleasing building, which contains so much youth and so many hopes. Then a sudden dull sound is heard, a clapping to of books and portfolios, a shuffling of feet, a buzz which spreads from room to room, and from the lower to the higher, as at the sudden diffusion of a bit of good news: it is the beadle, who is making his rounds, announcing the dismissal of school. And at that sound a throng of women, men, girls, and youths press closer from this side and that of the door, waiting for their sons, brothers, or grandchildren; while from the doors of the class-rooms little boys shoot forth into the big hall, as from a spout, seize their little capes and hats, creating a great confusion with them on the floor, and dancing all about, until the beadle chases them forth one after the other. And at length they come forth, in long files, stamping their feet. And then from all the relatives there descends a shower of questions: "Did you know your lesson?--How much work did they give you?--What have you to do for tomorrow!--When does the monthly examination come?"

And then even the poor mothers who do not know how to read, open the copy-books, gaze at the problems, and ask particulars: "Only eight?--Ten with commendation?--Nine for the lesson?"

And they grow uneasy, and rejoice, and interrogate the masters, and talk of prospectuses and examinations. How beautiful all this is, and how great and how immense is its promise for the world!

THY FATHER.

THE DEAF-MUTE

Sunday, 28th.

The month of May could not have had a better ending than my visit of this morning. We heard a jingling of the bell, and all ran to see what it meant. I heard my father say in a tone of astonishment:

"You here, Giorgio?"

Giorgio was our gardener in Chieri, who now has his family at Condove, and who had just arrived from Genoa, where he had disembarked on the preceding day, on his return from Greece, where he has been working on the railway for the last three years. He had a big bundle in his arms. He has grown a little older, but his face is still red and jolly.

My father wished to have him enter; but he refused, and suddenly inquired, assuming a serious expression:

"How is my family? How is Gigia?"

"She was well a few days ago," replied my mother.

Giorgio uttered a deep sigh.

"Oh, God be praised! I had not the courage to present myself at the Deaf-mute Institution until I had heard about her. I will leave my bundle here, and run to get her. It is three years since I have seen my poor little daughter! Three years since I have seen any of my people!"

My father said to me, "Accompany him."

"Excuse me; one word more," said the gardener, from the landing.

My father interrupted him, "And your affairs?"

"All right," the other replied. "Thanks to God, I have brought back a few soldi. But I wanted to inquire. Tell me how the education of the little dumb girl is getting on. When I left her, she was a poor little animal, poor thing! I don't put much faith in those colleges. Has she learned how to make signs? My wife did write to me, to be sure, 'She is learning to speak; she is making progress.' But I said to myself, What is the use of her learning to talk if I don't know how to make the signs myself? How shall we manage to understand each other, poor little thing? That is well enough to enable them to understand each other, one unfortunate to comprehend another unfortunate. How is she getting on, then? How is she?"

My father smiled, and replied:

"I shall not tell you anything about it; you will see; go, go; don't waste another minute!"

We took our departure; the institute is close by. As we went along with huge strides, the gardener talked to me, and grew sad.

"Ah, my poor Gigia! To be born with such an infirmity! To think that I have never heard her call me *father*; that she has never heard me call her *my daughter*; that she has never either heard or uttered a single word since she has been in the world! And it is lucky that a charitable gentleman was found to pay the expenses of the institution. But that is all--she could not enter there until she was eight years old. She has not been at home for three years. She is now going on eleven. And she has grown? Tell me, she has grown? She is in good spirits?"

"You will see in a moment, you will see in a moment," I replied, hastening my pace.

"But where is this institution?" he demanded. "My wife went with her after I was gone. It seems to me that it ought to be near here."

We had just reached it. We at once entered the parlor. An attendant came to meet us.

"I am the father of Gigia Voggi," said the gardener; "give me my daughter instantly."

"They are at play," replied the attendant; "I will go and inform the matron." And he hastened away.

The gardener could no longer speak nor stand still; he stared at all four walls, without seeing anything.

The door opened; a teacher entered, dressed in black, holding a little girl by the hand.

Father and daughter gazed at one another for an instant; then flew into each other's arms, uttering a cry.

The girl was dressed in a white and reddish striped material, with a gray apron. She is a little taller than I. She cried, and clung to her father's neck with both arms.

Her father disengaged himself, and began to survey her from head to foot, panting as though he had run a long way; and he exclaimed: "Ah, how she has grown! How pretty she has become! Oh, my dear, poor Gigia! My poor mute child!--Are you her teacher, signora? Tell her to make some of her signs to me; for I shall be able to understand something, and then I will learn little by little. Tell her to make me understand something with her gestures."

The teacher smiled, and said in a low voice to the girl, "Who is this man who has come to see you?"

And the girl replied with a smile, in a coarse, strange, dissonant voice, like that of a savage who was speaking for the first time in our language, but with a distinct pronunciation, "He is my fa-ther."

The gardener fell back a pace, and shrieked like a madman: "She speaks! Is it possible! Is it possible! She speaks? Can you speak, my child? can you speak? Say something to me: you can speak?" and he embraced her afresh, and kissed her thrice on the brow. "But it is not with signs that she talks, signora; it is not with her fingers? What does this mean?"

"No, Signor Voggi," rejoined the teacher, "it is not with signs. That was the old way. Here we teach the new method, the oral method. How is it that you did not know it?"

"I knew nothing about it!" replied the gardener, lost in amazement. "I have been abroad for the last three years. Oh, they wrote to me, and I did not understand. I am a blockhead. Oh, my daughter, you understand me, then? Do you hear my voice? Answer me: do you hear me? Do you hear what I say?"

"Why, no, my good man," said the teacher; "she does not hear your voice, because she is deaf. She understands from the movements of your lips what the words are that you utter; this is the way the thing is managed; but she does not hear your voice any more than she does the words which she speaks to you; she pronounces them, because we have taught her, letter by letter, how she must place her lips and move her tongue, and what effort she must make with her chest and throat, in order to emit a sound."

The gardener did not understand, and stood with his mouth wide open. He did not yet believe it.

"Tell me, Gigia," he asked his daughter, whispering in her ear, "are you glad that your father has come back?" and he raised his face again, and stood awaiting her reply.

The girl looked at him thoughtfully, and said nothing.

Her father was perturbed.

The teacher laughed. Then she said: "My good man, she does not answer you, because she did not see the movements of your lips: you spoke in her ear! Repeat your question, keeping your face well before hers."

The father, gazing straight in her face, repeated, "Are you glad that your father has come back? that he is not going away again?"

The girl, who had observed his lips attentively, seeking even to see inside his mouth, replied frankly:

"Yes, I am de-light-ed that you have re-turned, that you are not go-ing a-way a-gain--nev-er a-gain."

Her father embraced her impetuously, and then in great haste, in order to make quite sure, he overwhelmed her with questions.

"What is mamma's name?"

"An-to-nia."

"What is the name of your little sister?"

"Ad-e-laide."

"What is the name of this college?"

"The Deaf-mute Insti-tution."

"How many are two times ten?"

"Twen-ty."

While we thought that he was laughing for joy, he suddenly burst out crying. But this was the result of joy also.

"Take courage," said the teacher to him; "you have reason to rejoice, not to weep. You see that you are making your daughter cry also. You are pleased, then?"

The gardener grasped the teacher's hand and kissed it two or three times, saying: "Thanks, thanks, thanks! a hundred thanks, a thousand thanks, dear Signora Teacher! and forgive me for not knowing how to say anything else!"

"But she not only speaks," said the teacher; "your daughter also knows how to write. She knows how to reckon. She knows the names of all common objects. She knows a little history and geography. She is now in the regular class. When she has passed through the two remaining classes, she will know much more. When she leaves here, she will be in a condition to adopt a profession. We already have deaf-mutes who stand in the shops to serve customers, and they perform their duties like any one else."

Again the gardener was astounded. It seemed as though his ideas were becoming confused again. He stared at his daughter and scratched his head. His face demanded another explanation.

Then the teacher turned to the attendant and said to him:

"Call a child of the preparatory class for me."

The attendant returned, in a short time, with a deaf-mute of eight or nine years, who had entered the institution a few days before.

"This girl," said the mistress, "is one of those whom we are instructing in the first elements. This is the way it is done. I want to make her say *a*. Pay attention."

The teacher opened her mouth, as one opens it to pronounce the vowel *a*, and motioned to the child to open her mouth in the same manner. Then the mistress made her a sign to emit her voice. She did so; but instead of *a*, she pronounced *o*.

"No," said the mistress, "that is not right." And taking the child's two hands, she placed one of them on her own throat and the other on her chest, and repeated, "*a*."

The child felt with her hands the movements of the mistress's throat and chest, opened her mouth again as before, and pronounced extremely well, "*a*."

In the same manner, the mistress made her pronounce *c* and *d*, still keeping the two little hands on her own throat and chest.

"Now do you understand?" she inquired.

The father understood; but he seemed more astonished than when he had not understood.

"And they are taught to speak in the same way?" he asked, after a moment of reflection, gazing at the teacher. "You have the patience to teach them to speak in that manner, little by little, and so many of them? one by one--through years and years? But you are saints; that's what you are! You are angels of paradise! There is not in the world a reward that is worthy of you! What is there that I can say? Ah! leave me alone with my daughter a little while now. Let me have her to myself for five minutes."

And drawing her to a seat apart he began to interrogate her, and she to reply, and he laughed with beaming eyes, slapping his fists down on his knees; and he took his daughter's hands, and stared at her, beside himself with delight at hearing her, as though her voice had been one which came from heaven; then he asked the teacher, "Would the Signor Director permit me to thank him?"

"The director is not here," replied the mistress; "but there is another person whom you should thank. Every little girl here is given into the charge of an older companion, who acts the part of sister or mother to her. Your little girl has been intrusted to the care of a deaf-mute of seventeen, the daughter of a baker, who is kind and very fond of her; she has been assisting her for two years to dress herself every morning; she combs her hair, she teaches her to sew, she mends her clothes, she is good company for her.--Luigia, what is the name of your mamma in the institute?"

The girl smiled, and said, "Ca-te-rina Gior-dano." Then she said to her father, "She is ve-ry, ve-ry good."

The attendant, who had withdrawn at a signal from the mistress, returned almost at once with a light-haired deaf-mute, a robust girl, with a cheerful countenance, and also dressed in the red and white striped stuff, with a gray apron; she paused at the door and blushed; then she bent her head with a smile. She had the figure of a woman, but seemed like a child.

Giorgio's daughter instantly ran to her, took her by the arm, like a child, and drew her to her father, saying, in her heavy voice, "Ca-te-rina Gior-dano."

"Ah, what a splendid girl!" exclaimed her father; and he stretched out one hand to caress her, but drew it back again, and repeated, "Ah, what a good girl! May God bless her, may He grant her all good fortune, all consolations; may He make her and hers always happy, so good a girl is she, my poor Gigia! It is an honest workingman, the poor father of a family, who wishes you this with all his heart."

The big girl caressed the little one, still keeping her face bent, and smiling, and the gardener continued to gaze at her, as at a madonna.

"You can take your daughter with you for the day," said the mistress.

"Won't I take her, though!" rejoined the gardener. "I'll take her to Condove, and fetch her back tomorrow morning. Think for a bit whether I won't take her!"

The girl ran off to dress.

"It is three years since I have seen her!" repeated the gardener. "Now she speaks! I will take her to

Condove with me on the instant. But first I shall take a ramble about Turin, with my deaf-mute on my arm, so that all may see her, and take her to see some of my friends! Ah, what a beautiful day! This is consolation indeed!--Here's your father's arm, my Gigia."

The girl, who had returned with a little mantle and cap on, took his arm.

"And thanks to all!" said the father, as he reached the threshold. "Thanks to all, with my whole soul! I shall come back another time to thank you all again."

He stood for a moment in thought, then disengaged himself abruptly from the girl, turned back, fumbling in his waistcoat with his hand, and shouted like a man in a fury:

"Come now, I am not a poor devil! So here, I leave twenty lire for the institution,--a fine new gold piece."

And with a tremendous bang, he deposited his gold piece on the table.

"No, no, my good man," said the mistress, with emotion. "Take back your money. I cannot accept it. Take it back. It is not my place. You shall see about that when the director is here. But he will not accept anything either; be sure of that. You have toiled too hard to earn it, poor man. We shall be greatly obliged to you, all the same."

"No; I shall leave it," replied the gardener, obstinately; "and then--we will see."

But the mistress put his money back in his pocket, without leaving him time to reject it. And then he resigned himself with a shake of the head; and then, wafting a kiss to the mistress and to the large girl, he quickly took his daughter's arm again, and hurried with her out of the door, saying:

"Come, come, my daughter, my poor dumb child, my treasure!"

And the girl exclaimed, in her harsh voice:

"Oh, how beau-ti-ful the sun is!"

# JUNE

GARIBALDI

June 3d.

Tomorrow is the National Festival Day.

TODAY is a day of national mourning. Garibaldi died last night. Do you know who he is? He is the man who liberated ten millions of Italians from the tyranny of the Bourbons. He died at the age of seventy-five. He was born at Nice, the son of a ship captain. At eight years of age, he saved a woman's life; at thirteen, he dragged into safety a boat-load of his companions who were shipwrecked; at twenty-seven, he rescued from the water at Marseilles a drowning youth; at forty-one, he saved a ship from burning on the ocean. He fought for ten years in America for the liberty of a strange people; he fought in three wars against the Austrians, for the liberation of Lombardy and Trentino; he defended Rome from the French in 1849; he delivered Naples and Palermo in 1860; he fought again for Rome in 1867; he combated with the Germans in defence of France in 1870. He was possessed of the flame of heroism and the genius of war. He was engaged in forty battles, and won thirty-seven of them.

When he was not fighting, he was laboring for his living, or he shut himself up in a solitary island, and tilled the soil. He was teacher, sailor, workman, trader, soldier, general, dictator. He was simple, great, and good. He hated all oppressors, he loved all peoples, he protected all the weak; he had no other aspiration than good, he refused honors, he scorned death, he adored Italy. When he uttered his war-cry, legions of valorous men hastened to him from all quarters; gentlemen left their palaces, workmen their ships, youths their schools, to go and fight in the sunshine of his glory. In time of war he wore a red shirt. He was strong, blond, and handsome. On the field of battle he was a thunder-bolt, in his affections he was a child, in affliction a saint. Thousands of Italians have died for their country, happy, if, when dying, they saw him pass victorious in the distance; thousands would have allowed themselves to be killed for him; millions have blessed and will bless him.

He is dead. The whole world mourns him. You do not understand him now. But you will read of his deeds, you will constantly hear him spoken of in the course of your life; and gradually, as you grow up, his image will grow before you; when you become a man, you will behold him as a giant; and when you are no longer in the world, when your sons' sons and those who shall be born from them are no longer among the living, the generations will still behold on high his luminous head as a redeemer of the peoples, crowned by the names of his victories as with a circlet of stars; and the brow and the soul of every Italian will beam when he utters his name.

THY FATHER.

THE ARMY

Sunday, 11th.

The National Festival Day. Postponed for a week on account of the death of Garibaldi.

We have been to the Piazza Castello, to see the review of soldiers, who defiled before the commandant of the army corps, between two vast lines of people. As they marched past to the sound of flourishes from trumpets and bands, my father pointed out to me the Corps and the glories of the banners. First, the pupils of the Academy, those who will become officers in the Engineers and the Artillery, about three hundred in number, dressed in black, passed with the bold and easy elegance of students and soldiers. After them defiled the infantry, the brigade of Aosta, which fought at Goito and at San Martino, and the Bergamo brigade, which fought at Castelfidardo, four regiments of them, company after company, thousands of red aiguillettes, which seemed like so many double and very long garlands of blood-colored flowers, extended and agitated from the two ends, and borne athwart the crowd. After the infantry, the soldiers of the Mining Corps advanced,-- the workingmen of war, with their plumes of black horse-tails, and their crimson bands; and while these were passing, we beheld advancing behind them hundreds of long, straight plumes, which rose above the heads of the spectators; they were the mountaineers, the defenders of the portals of Italy, all tall, rosy, and stalwart, with hats of Calabrian fashion, and revers of a beautiful, bright green, the color of the grass on their native mountains. The mountaineers were still marching past, when a quiver ran through the crowd, and the *bersaglieri*, the old twelfth battalion, the first who entered Rome through the breach at the Porta Pia, bronzed, alert, brisk, with fluttering plumes, passed like a wave in a sea of black, making the piazza ring with the shrill blasts of their trumpets, which seemed shouts of joy. But their trumpeting was drowned by a broken and hollow rumble, which announced the field artillery; and then the latter passed in triumph, seated on their lofty caissons, drawn by three hundred pairs of fiery horses,--those fine soldiers with yellow lacings, and their long cannons of brass and steel gleaming on the light carriages, as they jolted and resounded, and made the earth tremble.

And then came the mountain artillery, slowly, gravely, beautiful in its laborious and rude semblance, with its large soldiers, with its powerful mules--that mountain artillery which carries dismay and death wherever man can set his foot. And last of all, the fine regiment of the Genoese cavalry, which had wheeled down like a whirlwind on ten fields of battle, from Santa Lucia to Villafranca, passed at a gallop, with their helmets glittering in the sun, their lances erect, their pennons floating in the air, sparkling with gold and silver, filling the air with jingling and neighing.

"How beautiful it is!" I exclaimed. My father almost reproved me for these words, and said to me:

"You are not to regard the army as a fine spectacle. All these young men, so full of strength and hope, may be called upon any day to defend our country, and fall in a few hours, crushed to fragments by bullets and grape-shot. Every time that you hear the cry, at a feast, 'Hurrah for the army! hurrah for

Italy!' picture to yourself, behind the regiments which are passing, a plain covered with corpses, and inundated with blood, and then the greeting to the army will proceed from the very depths of your heart, and the image of Italy will appear to you more severe and grand."

## ITALY

Tuesday, 14th.

Salute your country thus, on days of festival: "Italy, my country, dear and noble land, where my father and my mother were born, and where they will be buried, where I hope to live and die, where my children will grow up and die; beautiful Italy, great and glorious for many centuries, united and free for a few years; thou who didst disseminate so great a light of intellect divine over the world, and for whom so many valiant men have died on the battle-field, and so many heroes on the gallows; august mother of three hundred cities, and thirty millions of sons; I, a child, who do not understand thee as yet, and who do not know thee in thy entirety, I venerate and love thee with all my soul, and I am proud of having been born of thee, and of calling myself thy son. I love thy splendid seas and thy sublime mountains; I love thy solemn monuments and thy immortal memories; I love thy glory and thy beauty; I love and venerate the whole of thee as that beloved portion of thee where I, for the first time, beheld the light and heard thy name. I love the whole of thee, with a single affection and with equal gratitude,--Turin the valiant, Genoa the superb, Bologna the learned, Venice the enchanting, Milan the mighty; I love you with the uniform reverence of a son, gentle Florence and terrible Palermo, immense and beautiful Naples, marvellous and eternal Rome. I love thee, my sacred country! And I swear that I will love all thy sons like brothers; that I will always honor in my heart thy great men, living and dead; that I will be an industrious and honest citizen, constantly intent on ennobling myself, in order to render myself worthy of thee, to assist with my small powers in causing misery, ignorance, injustice, crime, to disappear one day from thy face, so that thou mayest live and expand tranquilly in the majesty of thy right and of thy strength. I swear that I will serve thee, as it may be granted to me, with my mind, with my arm, with my heart, humbly, ardently; and that, if the day should dawn in which I should be called on to give my blood for thee and my life, I will give my blood, and I will die, crying thy holy name to heaven, and wafting my last kiss to thy blessed banner."

THY FATHER.

## THIRTY-TWO DEGREES

Friday, 16th.

During the five days which have passed since the National Festival, the heat has increased by three degrees. We are in full summer now, and begin to feel weary; all have lost their fine rosy color of springtime; necks and legs are growing thin, heads droop and eyes close. Poor Nelli, who suffers much from the heat, has turned the color of wax in the face; he sometimes falls into a heavy sleep, with his head on his copy-book; but Garrone is always watchful, and places an open book upright in front of him, so that the master may not see him. Crossi rests his red head against the bench in a certain way, so that it looks as though it had been detached from his body and placed there separately. Nobis complains that there are too many of us, and that we corrupt the air. Ah, what an effort it costs now to study! I gaze through the windows at those beautiful trees which cast so deep a shade, where I should be so glad to run, and sadness and wrath overwhelm me at being obliged to go and shut myself up among the benches. But then I take courage at the sight of my kind mother, who is always watching me, scrutinizing me, when I return from school, to see whether I am not pale; and at every page of my work she says to me:

"Do you still feel well?" and every morning at six, when she wakes me for my lesson, "Courage! there are only so many days more: then you will be free, and will get rested,--you will go to the shade of country lanes."

Yes, she is perfectly right to remind me of the boys who are working in the fields in the full heat of the sun, or among the white sands of the river, which blind and scorch them, and of those in the glass-factories, who stand all day long motionless, with head bent over a flame of gas; and all of them rise earlier than we do, and have no vacations. Courage, then! And even in this respect, Derossi is at the head of all, for he suffers neither from heat nor drowsiness; he is always wide awake, and cheery, with his golden curls, as he was in the winter, and he studies without effort, and keeps all about him alert, as though he freshened the air with his voice.

And there are two others, also, who are always awake and attentive: stubborn Stardi, who pricks his face, to prevent himself from going to sleep; and the more weary and heated he is, the more he sets his teeth, and he opens his eyes so wide that it seems as though he wanted to eat the teacher; and that barterer of a Garoffi, who is wholly absorbed in manufacturing fans out of red paper, decorated with little figures from match-boxes, which he sells at two centesimi apiece.

But the bravest of all is Coretti; poor Coretti, who gets up at five o'clock, to help his father carry wood! At eleven, in school, he can no longer keep his eyes open, and his head droops on his breast. And nevertheless, he shakes himself, punches himself on the back of the neck, asks permission to go out and wash his face, and makes his neighbors shake and pinch him. But this morning he could not resist, and he fell into a leaden sleep. The master called him loudly; "Coretti!" He did not hear. The master, irritated, repeated, "Coretti!" Then the son of the charcoal-man, who lives next to him at home, rose and said:

"He worked from five until seven carrying faggots." The teacher allowed him to sleep on, and continued with the lesson for half an hour. Then he went to Coretti's seat, and wakened him very, very gently, by blowing in his face. On beholding the master in front of him, he started back in alarm. But the master took his head in his hands, and said, as he kissed him on the hair:

"I am not reproving you, my son. Your sleep is not at all that of laziness; it is the sleep of fatigue."

MY FATHER

Saturday, 17th.

Surely, neither your comrade Coretti nor Garrone would ever have answered their fathers as you answered yours this afternoon. Enrico! How is it possible? You must promise me solemnly that this shall never happen again so long as I live. Every time that an impertinent reply flies to your lips at a reproof from your father, think of that day which will infallibly come when he will call you to his bedside to tell you, "Enrico, I am about to leave you." Oh, my son, when you hear his voice for the last time, and for a long while afterwards, when you weep alone in his deserted room, in the midst of those books which he will never open again, then, on recalling that you have at times been wanting in respect to him, you, too, will ask yourself, "How is it possible?" Then you will understand that he has always been your best friend, that when he was constrained to punish you, it caused him more suffering than it did you, and that he never made you weep except for the sake of doing you good; and then you will repent, and you will kiss with tears that desk at which he worked so much, at which he wore out his life for his children. You do not understand now; he hides from you all of himself except his kindness and his love. You do not know that he is sometimes so broken down with toil that he thinks he has only a few more days to live, and that at such moments he talks only of you; he has in his heart no other trouble than that of leaving you poor and without protection.

And how often, when meditating on this, does he enter your chamber while you are asleep, and stand there, lamp in hand, gazing at you; and then he makes an effort, and weary and sad as he is, he returns to his labor; and neither do you know that he often seeks you and remains with you because he has a bitterness in his heart, sorrows which attack all men in the world, and he seeks you as a friend, to obtain consolation himself and forgetfulness, and he feels the need of taking refuge in your affection, to recover his serenity and his courage: think, then, what must be his sorrow, when instead of finding in you affection, he finds coldness and disrespect! Never again stain yourself with this horrible ingratitude! Reflect, that were you as good as a saint, you could never repay him sufficiently for what he has done and for what he is constantly doing for you. And reflect, also, we cannot count on life; a misfortune might remove your father while you are still a boy,--in two years, in three months, tomorrow.

Ah, my poor Enrico, when you see all about you changing, how empty, how desolate the house will appear, with your poor mother clothed in black! Go, my son, go to your father; he is in his room at work; go on tiptoe, so that he may not hear you enter; go and lay your forehead on his knees, and beseech him to pardon and to bless you.

THY MOTHER.


IN THE COUNTRY

Monday, 19th.

My good father forgave me, even on this occasion, and allowed me to go on an expedition to the country, which had been arranged on Wednesday, with the father of Coretti, the wood-peddler.

We were all in need of a mouthful of hill air. It was a festival day. We met yesterday at two o'clock in the place of the Statuto, Derossi, Garrone, Garoffi, Precossi, Coretti, father and son, and I, with our provisions of fruit, sausages, and hard-boiled eggs; we had also leather bottles and tin cups. Garrone carried a gourd filled with white wine; Coretti, his father's soldier-canteen, full of red wine; and little Precossi, in the blacksmith's blouse, held under his arm a two-kilogramme loaf.

We went in the omnibus as far as Gran Madre di Dio, and then off, as briskly as possible, to the hills. How green, how shady, how fresh it was! We rolled over and over in the grass, we dipped our faces in the rivulets, we leaped the hedges. The elder Coretti followed us at a distance, with his jacket thrown over his shoulders, smoking his clay pipe, and from time to time threatening us with his hand, to prevent our tearing holes in our trousers.

Precossi whistled; I had never heard him whistle before. The younger Coretti did the same, as he went along. That little fellow knows how to make everything with his jack-knife a finger's length long,--mill-wheels, forks, squirts; and he insisted on carrying the other boys' things, and he was loaded down until he was dripping with perspiration, but he was still as nimble as a goat. Derossi halted every moment to tell us the names of the plants and insects. I don't understand how he manages to know so many things. And Garrone nibbled at his bread in silence; but he no longer attacks it with the cheery bites of old, poor Garrone! now that he has lost his mother. But he is always as good as bread himself. When one of us ran back to obtain the momentum for leaping a ditch, he ran to the other side, and held out his hands to us; and as Precossi was afraid of cows, having been tossed by one when a child, Garrone placed himself in front of him every time that we passed any. We mounted up to Santa Margherita, and then went down the decline by leaps, rolls, and slides. Precossi tumbled into a thorn-bush, and tore a hole in his blouse, and stood there overwhelmed with shame, with the strip dangling; but Garoffi, who always has pins in his jacket, fixed it so that it was not perceptible, while the other kept saying, "Excuse me, excuse me," and then he set out to run once more.

Garoffi did not waste his time on the way; he picked salad herbs and snails, and put every stone that glistened in the least into his pocket, supposing that there was gold and silver in it. And on we went, running, rolling, and climbing through the shade and in the sun, up and down, through all the lanes and cross-roads, until we arrived dishevelled and breathless at the crest of a hill, where we seated ourselves to take our lunch on the grass.

We could see an immense plain, and all the blue Alps with their white summits. We were dying of hunger; the bread seemed to be melting. The elder Coretti handed us our portions of sausage on gourd leaves. And then we all began to talk at once about the teachers, the comrades who had not been able to come, and the examinations. Precossi was rather ashamed to eat, and Garrone thrust the best bits of his share into his mouth by force. Coretti was seated next his father, with his legs crossed; they seem more like two brothers than father and son, when seen thus together, both rosy and smiling, with those white teeth of theirs. The father drank with zest, emptying the bottles and the cups which we left half finished, and said:

"Wine hurts you boys who are studying; it is the wood-sellers who need it." Then he grasped his son by the nose, and shook him, saying to us, "Boys, you must love this fellow, for he is a flower of a man of honor; I tell you so myself!" And then we all laughed, except Garrone. And he went on, as he drank, "It's a shame, eh! now you are all good friends together, and in a few years, who knows, Enrico and Derossi will be lawyers or professors or I don't know what, and the other four of you will be in shops or at a trade, and the deuce knows where, and then--good night comrades!"

"Nonsense!" rejoined Derossi; "for me, Garrone will always be Garrone, Precossi will always be Precossi, and the same with all the others, were I to become the emperor of Russia: where they are, there I shall go also."

"Bless you!" exclaimed the elder Coretti, raising his flask; "that's the way to talk, by Heavens! Touch your glass here! Hurrah for brave comrades, and hurrah for school, which makes one family of you, of those who have and those who have not!"

We all clinked his flask with the skins and the cups, and drank for the last time.

"Hurrah for the fourth of the 49th!" he cried, as he rose to his feet, and swallowed the last drop; "and if you have to do with squadrons too, see that you stand firm, like us old ones, my lads!"

It was already late. We descended, running and singing, and walking long distances all arm in arm, and we arrived at the Po as twilight fell, and thousands of fireflies were flitting about. And we only parted in the Piazza dello Statuto after having agreed to meet there on the following Sunday, and go to the Vittorio Emanuele to see the distribution of prizes to the graduates of the evening schools.

What a beautiful day! How happy I should have been on my return home, had I not encountered my poor schoolmistress! I met her coming down the staircase of our house, almost in the dark, and, as soon as she recognized me, she took both my hands, and whispered in my ear, "Good by, Enrico; remember me!" I perceived that she was weeping. I went up and told my mother about it.

"I have just met my schoolmistress."--"She was just going to bed," replied my mother, whose eyes were red. And then she added very sadly, gazing intently at me, "Your poor teacher--is very ill."

## THE DISTRIBUTION OF PRIZES TO THE WORKINGMEN

Sunday, 25th.

As we had agreed, we all went together to the Theatre Vittorio Emanuele, to view the distribution of prizes to the workingmen. The theatre was adorned as on the 14th of March, and thronged, but almost wholly with the families of workmen; and the pit was occupied with the male and female pupils of the school of choral singing. These sang a hymn to the soldiers who had died in the Crimea; which was so beautiful that, when it was finished, all rose and clapped and shouted, so that the song had to be repeated from the beginning. And then the prize-winners began immediately to march past the mayor, the prefect, and many others, who presented them with books, savings-bank books, diplomas, and medals. In one corner of the pit I espied the little mason, sitting beside his mother; and in another place there was the head-master; and behind him, the red head of my master of the second grade.

The first to defile were the pupils of the evening drawing classes--the goldsmiths, engravers, lithographers, and also the carpenters and masons; then those of the commercial school; then those of the Musical Lyceum, among them several girls, workingwomen, all dressed in festal attire, who were saluted with great applause, and who laughed. Last came the pupils of the elementary evening schools, and then it began to be a beautiful sight. They were of all ages, of all trades, and dressed in all sorts of ways,--men with gray hair, factory boys, artisans with big black beards. The little ones were at their ease; the men, a little embarrassed. The people clapped the oldest and the youngest, but none of the spectators laughed, as they did at our festival: all faces were attentive and serious.

Many of the prize-winners had wives and children in the pit, and there were little children who, when they saw their father pass across the stage, called him by name at the tops of their voices, and signalled to him with their hands, laughing violently. Peasants passed, and porters; they were from the Buoncompagni School. From the Cittadella School there was a bootblack whom my father knew, and the prefect gave him a diploma. After him I saw approaching a man as big as a giant, whom I fancied that I had seen several times before. It was the father of the little mason, who had won the second prize. I remembered when I had seen him in the garret, at the bedside of his sick son, and I immediately sought out his son in the pit. Poor little mason! he was staring at his father with beaming eyes, and, in order to conceal his emotion, he made his hare's face. At that moment I heard a burst of applause, and I glanced at the stage: a little chimney-sweep stood there, with a clean face, but in his working-clothes, and the mayor was holding him by the hand and talking to him.

After the chimney-sweep came a cook; then came one of the city sweepers, from the Raineri School, to get a prize. I felt I know not what in my heart,--something like a great affection and a great respect, at the thought of how much those prizes had cost all those workingmen, fathers of families, full of care; how much toil added to their labors, how many hours snatched from their sleep, of which they stand in such great need, and what efforts of intelligences not habituated to study, and of huge hands rendered clumsy with work!

A factory boy passed, and it was evident that his father had lent him his jacket for the occasion, for his sleeves hung down so that he was forced to turn them back on the stage, in order to receive his prize: and many laughed; but the laugh was speedily stifled by the applause. Next came an old man with a bald head and a white beard. Several artillery soldiers passed, from among those who attended evening school in our schoolhouse; then came custom-house guards and policemen, from among those who guard our schools.

At the conclusion, the pupils of the evening schools again sang the hymn to the dead in the Crimea, but this time with so much dash, with a strength of affection which came so directly from the heart, that the audience hardly applauded at all, and all retired in deep emotion, slowly and noiselessly.

In a few moments the whole street was thronged. In front of the entrance to the theatre was the chimney-sweep, with his prize book bound in red, and all around were gentlemen talking to him. Many exchanged salutations from the opposite side of the street,--workmen, boys, policemen, teachers. My master of the second grade came out in the midst of the crowd, between two artillery men. And there were workmen's wives with babies in their arms, who held in their tiny hands their father's diploma, and exhibited it to the crowd in their pride.


MY DEAD SCHOOLMISTRESS

Tuesday, 27th.

While we were at the Theatre Vittorio Emanuele, my poor schoolmistress died. She died at two o'clock, a week after she had come to see my mother. The head-master came to the school yesterday morning to announce it to us; and he said:

"Those of you who were her pupils know how good she was, how she loved her boys: she was a mother to them. Now, she is no more. For a long time a terrible malady has been sapping her life. If she had not been obliged to work to earn her bread, she could have taken care of herself, and perhaps recovered. At all events, she could have prolonged her life for several months, if she had procured a leave of absence. But she wished to remain among her boys to the very last day. On the evening of Saturday, the seventeenth, she took leave of them, with the certainty that she should never see them again. She gave them good advice, kissed them all, and went away sobbing. No one will ever behold her again. Remember her, my boys!"

Little Precossi, who had been one of her pupils in the upper primary, dropped his head on his desk and began to cry.

Yesterday afternoon, after school, we all went together to the house of the dead woman, to accompany her to church. There was a hearse in the street, with two horses, and many people were waiting, and conversing in a low voice. There was the head-master, all the masters and mistresses from our school, and from the other schoolhouses where she had taught in bygone years. There were nearly all the little children in her classes, led by the hand by their mothers, who carried tapers; and there were a very great many from the other classes, and fifty scholars from the Baretti School, some with wreaths in their hands, some with bunches of roses. A great many bouquets of flowers had already been placed on the hearse, upon which was fastened a large wreath of acacia, with an inscription in black letters: *The old pupils of the fourth grade to their mistress.* And under the large wreath a little one was suspended, which the babies had brought. Among the crowd were visible many servant-women, who had been sent by their mistresses with candles; and there were also two serving-men in livery, with lighted torches; and a wealthy gentleman, the father of one of the mistress's scholars, had sent his carriage, lined with blue satin. All were crowded together near the door. Several girls were wiping away their tears.

We waited for a while in silence. At length the casket was brought out. Some of the little ones began to cry loudly when they saw the coffin slid into the hearse, and one began to shriek, as though he had only then comprehended that his mistress was dead, and he was seized with such a convulsive fit of sobbing, that they were obliged to carry him away.

The procession got slowly into line and set out. First came the daughters of the Ritiro della Concezione, dressed in green; then the daughters of Maria, all in white, with a blue ribbon; then the priests; and behind the hearse, the masters and mistresses, the tiny scholars of the upper primary, and all the others; and, at the end of all, the crowd. People came to the windows and to the doors, and on seeing all those boys, and the wreath, they said, "It is a schoolmistress." Even some of the ladies who accompanied the smallest children wept.

When the church was reached, the casket was removed from the hearse, and carried to the middle of the nave, in front of the great altar: the mistresses laid their wreaths on it, the children covered it with flowers, and the people all about, with lighted candles in their hands, began to chant the prayers in the vast and gloomy church. Then, all of a sudden, when the priest had said the last *amen,* the candles were extinguished, and all went away in haste, and the mistress was left alone. Poor mistress, who was so kind to me, who had so much patience, who had toiled for so many years! She has left her little books to her scholars, and everything which she possessed,--to one an inkstand, to another a little picture; and two days before her death, she said to the head-master that he was not to allow the smallest of them to go to her funeral, because she did not wish them to cry.

She has done good, she has suffered, she is dead! Poor mistress, left alone in that dark church! Farewell! Farewell forever, my kind friend, sad and sweet memory of my infancy!

## THANKS

Wednesday, 28th.

My poor schoolmistress wanted to finish her year of school: she departed only three days before the end of the lessons. Day after tomorrow we go once more to the schoolroom to hear the reading of the monthly story, *Shipwreck*, and then--it is over. On Saturday, the first of July, the examinations begin. And then another year, the fourth, is past! And if my mistress had not died, it would have passed well.

I thought over all that I had known on the preceding October, and it seems to me that I know a good deal more: I have so many new things in my mind; I can say and write what I think better than I could then; I can also do the sums of many grown-up men who know nothing about it, and help them in their affairs; and I understand much more: I understand nearly everything that I read. I am satisfied. But how many people have urged me on and helped me to learn, one in one way, and another in another, at home, at school, in the street,--everywhere where I have been and where I have seen anything! And now, I thank you all. I thank you first, my good teacher, for having been so indulgent and affectionate with me; for you every new acquisition of mine was a labor, for which I now rejoice and of which I am proud. I thank you, Derossi, my admirable companion, for your prompt and kind explanations, for you have made me understand many of the most difficult things, and overcome stumbling-blocks at examinations; and you, too, Stardi, you brave and strong boy, who have showed me how a will of iron succeeds in everything: and you, kind, generous Garrone, who make all those who know you kind and generous too; and you too, Precossi and Coretti, who have given me an example of courage in suffering, and of serenity in toil, I render thanks to you: I render thanks to all the rest. But above all, I thank thee, my father, thee, my first teacher, my first friend, who hast given me so many wise counsels, and hast taught me so many things, whilst thou wert working for me, always concealing thy sadness from me, and seeking in all ways to render study easy, and life beautiful to me; and thee, sweet mother, my beloved and blessed guardian angel, who hast tasted all my joys, and suffered all my bitternesses, who hast studied, worked, and wept with me, with one hand caressing my brow, and with the other pointing me to heaven. I kneel before you, as when I was a little child; I thank you for all the tenderness which you have instilled into my mind through twelve years of sacrifices and of love.

## SHIPWRECK

*(Last Monthly Story.)*

One morning in the month of December, several years ago, there sailed from the port of Liverpool a huge steamer, which had on board two hundred persons, including a crew of sixty. The captain and nearly all the sailors were English. Among the passengers there were several Italians,--three gentlemen, a priest, and a company of musicians. The steamer was bound for the island of Malta. The weather was threatening.

Among the third-class passengers forward, was an Italian lad of a dozen years, small for his age, but robust; a bold, handsome, austere face, of Sicilian type. He was alone near the fore-mast, seated on a coil of cordage, beside a well-worn valise, which contained his effects, and upon which he kept a hand. His face was brown, and his black and wavy hair descended to his shoulders. He was meanly clad, and had a tattered mantle thrown over his shoulders, and an old leather pouch on a cross-belt. He gazed thoughtfully about him at the passengers, the ship, the sailors who were running past, and at the restless sea. He had the appearance of a boy who has recently issued from a great family sorrow,--the face of a child, the expression of a man.

A little after their departure, one of the steamer's crew, an Italian with gray hair, made his appearance on the bow, holding by the hand a little girl; and coming to a halt in front of the little Sicilian, he said to him:

"Here's a travelling companion for you, Mario." Then he went away.

The girl seated herself on the pile of cordage beside the boy.

They surveyed each other.

"Where are you going?" asked the Sicilian.

The girl replied: "To Malta on the way of Naples." Then she added: "I am going to see my father and mother, who are expecting me. My name is Giulietta Faggiani."

The boy said nothing.

After the lapse of a few minutes, he drew some bread from his pouch, and some dried fruit; the girl had some biscuits: they began to eat.

"Look sharp there!" shouted the Italian sailor, as he passed rapidly; "a lively time is at hand!"

The wind continued to increase, the steamer pitched heavily; but the two children, who did not suffer from seasickness, paid no heed to it. The little girl smiled. She was about the same age as her companion, but was considerably taller, brown of complexion, slender, somewhat sickly, and dressed more than modestly. Her hair was short and curling, she wore a red kerchief over her head, and two hoops of silver in her ears.

As they ate, they talked about themselves and their affairs. The boy had no longer either father or mother. The father, an artisan, had died a few days previously in Liverpool, leaving him alone; and the Italian consul had sent him back to his country, to Palermo, where he had still some distant relatives left. The little girl had been taken to London, the year before, by a widowed aunt, who was very fond of her, and to whom her parents--poor people--had given her for a time, trusting in a promise of an inheritance; but the aunt had died a few months later, run over by an omnibus, without leaving a centesimo; and then she too had had recourse to the consul, who had shipped her to Italy. Both had been recommended to the care of the Italian sailor.--"So," concluded the little maid, "my father and mother thought that I would return rich, and instead I am returning poor. But they will love me all the same. And so will my brothers. I have four, all small. I am the oldest at home. I dress them. They will be greatly delighted to see me. They will come in on tiptoe--The sea is ugly!"

Then she asked the boy: "And are you going to stay with your relatives?"

"Yes--if they want me."

"Do not they love you?"

"I don't know."

"I shall be thirteen at Christmas," said the girl.

Then they began to talk about the sea, and the people on board around them. They remained near each other all day, exchanging a few words now and then. The passengers thought them brother and sister. The girl knitted at a stocking, the boy meditated, the sea continued to grow rougher. At night, as they parted to go to bed, the girl said to Mario, "Sleep well."

"No one will sleep well, my poor children!" exclaimed the Italian sailor as he ran past, in answer to a call from the captain. The boy was on the point of replying with a "good night" to his little friend, when an unexpected dash of water dealt him a violent blow, and flung him against a seat.

"My dear, you are bleeding!" cried the girl, flinging herself upon him. The passengers who were making their escape below, paid no heed to them. The child knelt down beside Mario, who had been stunned by the blow, wiped the blood from his brow, and pulling the red kerchief from her hair, she bound it about his head, then pressed his head to her breast in order to knot the ends, and thus received a spot of blood on her yellow bodice just above the girdle. Mario shook himself and rose:

"Are you better?" asked the girl.

"I no longer feel it," he replied.

"Sleep well," said Giulietta.

"Good night," responded Mario. And they descended two neighboring sets of steps to their dormitories.

The sailor's prediction proved correct. Before they could get to sleep, a frightful tempest had broken loose. It was like the sudden onslaught of furious great horses, which in the course of a few minutes split one mast, and carried away three boats which were suspended to the falls, and four cows on the bow, like leaves. On board the steamer there arose a confusion, a terror, an uproar, a tempest of shrieks, wails, and prayers, sufficient to make the hair stand on end. The tempest continued to increase in fury all night. At daybreak it was still increasing. The formidable waves dashing the craft transversely, broke over the deck, and smashed, split, and hurled everything into the sea. The platform which screened the engine was destroyed, and the water dashed in with a terrible roar; the fires were extinguished; the engineers fled; huge and impetuous streams forced their way everywhere. A voice of thunder shouted:

"To the pumps!" It was the captain's voice. The sailors rushed to the pumps. But a sudden burst of the sea, striking the vessel on the stern, demolished bulwarks and hatchways, and sent a flood within.

All the passengers, more dead than alive, had taken refuge in the grand saloon. At last the captain made his appearance.

"Captain! Captain!" they all shrieked in concert. "What is taking place? Where are we? Is there any hope! Save us!"

The captain waited until they were silent, then said coolly; "Let us be resigned."

One woman uttered a cry of "Mercy!" No one else could give vent to a sound. Terror had frozen them all. A long time passed thus, in a silence like that of the grave. All gazed at each other with blanched faces. The sea continued to rage and roar. The vessel pitched heavily. At one moment the captain attempted to launch one life-boat; five sailors entered it; the boat sank; the waves turned it over, and two of the sailors were drowned, among them the Italian: the others contrived with difficulty to catch hold of the ropes and draw themselves up again.

After this, the sailors themselves lost all courage. Two hours later, the vessel was sunk in the water to the height of the port-holes.

A terrible spectacle was presented meanwhile on the deck. Mothers pressed their children to their breasts in despair; friends exchanged embraces and bade each other farewell; some went down into the cabins that they might die without seeing the sea. One passenger shot himself in the head with a pistol, and fell headlong down the stairs to the cabin, where he expired. Many clung frantically to each other; women writhed in horrible convulsions. There was audible a chorus of sobs, of infantile laments, of strange and piercing voices; and here and there persons were visible motionless as statues, in stupor, with eyes dilated and sightless,--faces of corpses and madmen. The two children, Giulietta and Mario, clung to a mast and gazed at the sea with staring eyes, as though senseless.

The sea had subsided a little; but the vessel continued to sink slowly. Only a few minutes remained to them.

"Launch the long-boat!" shouted the captain.

A boat, the last that remained, was thrown into the water, and fourteen sailors and three passengers descended into it.

The captain remained on board.

"Come down with us!" they shouted to him from below.

"I must die at my post," replied the captain.

"We shall meet a vessel," the sailors cried to him; "we shall be saved! Come down! you are lost!"

"I shall remain."

"There is room for one more!" shouted the sailors, turning to the other passengers. "A woman!"

A woman advanced, aided by the captain; but on seeing the distance at which the boat lay, she did not feel sufficient courage to leap down, and fell back upon the deck. The other women had nearly all fainted, and were as dead.

"A boy!" shouted the sailors.

At that shout, the Sicilian lad and his companion, who had remained up to that moment petrified as by a supernatural stupor, were suddenly aroused again by a violent instinct to save their lives. They detached themselves simultaneously from the mast, and rushed to the side of the vessel, shrieking in concert: "Take me!" and endeavoring in turn, to drive the other back, like furious beasts.

"The smallest!" shouted the sailors. "The boat is overloaded! The smallest!"

On hearing these words, the girl dropped her arms, as though struck by lightning, and stood motionless, staring at Mario with lustreless eyes.

Mario looked at her for a moment,--saw the spot of blood on her bodice,--remembered--The gleam of a divine thought flashed across his face.

"The smallest!" shouted the sailors in chorus, with imperious impatience. "We are going!"

And then Mario, with a voice which no longer seemed his own, cried: "She is the lighter! It is for you, Giulietta! You have a father and mother! I am alone! I give you my place! Go down!"

"Throw her into the sea!" shouted the sailors.

Mario seized Giulietta by the body, and threw her into the sea.

The girl uttered a cry and made a splash; a sailor seized her by the arm, and dragged her into the boat.

The boy remained at the vessel's side, with his head held high, his hair streaming in the wind,-- motionless, tranquil, sublime.

The boat moved off just in time to escape the whirlpool which the vessel produced as it sank, and which threatened to overturn it.

Then the girl, who had remained senseless until that moment, raised her eyes to the boy, and burst into a storm of tears.

"Good by, Mario!" she cried, amid her sobs, with her arms outstretched towards him. "Good by! Good by! Good by!"

"Good by!" replied the boy, raising his hand on high.

The boat went swiftly away across the troubled sea, beneath the dark sky. No one on board the vessel shouted any longer. The water was already lapping the edge of the deck.

Suddenly the boy fell on his knees, with his hands folded and his eyes raised to heaven.

The girl covered her face.

When she raised her head again, she cast a glance over the sea: the vessel was no longer there.

# JULY

THE LAST PAGE FROM MY MOTHER

Saturday, 1st.

SO the year has come to an end, Enrico, and it is well that you should be left on the last day with the image of the sublime child, who gave his life for his friend. You are now about to part from your teachers and companions, and I must impart to you some sad news. The separation will last not three months, but forever. Your father, for reasons connected with his profession, is obliged to leave Turin, and we are all to go with him.

We shall go next autumn. You will have to enter a new school. You are sorry for this, are you not? For I am sure that you love your old school, where twice a day, for the space of four years, you have experienced the pleasure of working, where for so long a time, you have seen, at stated hours, the same boys, the same teachers, the same parents, and your own father or mother awaiting you with a smile; your old school, where your mind first unclosed, where you have found so many kind companions, where every word that you have heard has had your good for its object, and where you have not suffered a single displeasure which has not been useful to you! Then bear this affection with you, and bid these boys a hearty farewell. Some of them will experience misfortunes, they will soon lose their fathers and mothers; others will die young; others, perhaps, will nobly shed their blood in battle; many will become brave and honest workmen, the fathers of honest and industrious workmen like themselves; and who knows whether there may not also be among them one who will render great services to his country, and make his name glorious. Then part from them with affection; leave a portion of your soul here, in this great family into which you entered as a baby, and from which you emerge a young lad, and which your father and mother loved so dearly, because you were so much beloved by it.

School is a mother, my Enrico. It took you from my arms when you could hardly speak, and now it returns you to me, strong, good, studious; blessings on it, and may you never forget it more, my son. Oh, it is impossible that you should forget it! You will become a man, you will make the tour of the world, you will see immense cities and wonderful monuments, and you will remember many among them; but that modest white edifice, with those closed shutters and that little garden, where the first flower of your intelligence budded, you will perceive until the last day of your life, as I shall always behold the house in which I heard your voice for the first time.

THY MOTHER.

THE EXAMINATIONS

Tuesday, 4th.

Here are the examinations at last! Nothing else is to be heard under discussion, in the streets in the vicinity of the school, from boys, fathers, mothers, and even tutors; examinations, points, themes, averages, dismissals, promotions: all utter the same words. Yesterday morning there was composition; this morning there is arithmetic. It was touching to see all the parents, as they conducted their sons to school, giving them their last advice in the street, and many mothers accompanied their sons to their seats, to see whether the inkstand was filled, and to try their pens, and they still continued to hover round the entrance, and to say:

"Courage! Attention! I entreat you."

Our assistant-master was Coatti, the one with the black beard, who mimics the voice of a lion, and never punishes any one. There were boys who were white with fear. When the master broke the seal of the letter from the town-hall, and drew out the problem, not a breath was audible. He announced the problem loudly, staring now at one, now at another, with terrible eyes; but we understood that had he been able to announce the answer also, so that we might all get promoted, he would have been delighted.

After an hour of work many began to grow weary, for the problem was difficult. One cried. Crossi dealt himself blows on the head. And many of them are not to blame, poor boys, for not knowing, for they have not had much time to study, and have been neglected by their parents. But Providence was at hand. You should have seen Derossi, and what trouble he took to help them; how ingenious he was in getting a figure passed on, and in suggesting an operation, without allowing himself to be caught; so anxious for all that he appeared to be our teacher himself. Garrone, too, who is strong in arithmetic, helped all he could; and he even assisted Nobis, who, finding himself in a quandary, was quite gentle.

Stardi remained motionless for more than an hour, with his eyes on the problem, and his fists on his temples, and then he finished the whole thing in five minutes. The master made his round among the benches, saying:

"Be calm! Be calm! I advise you to be calm!"

And when he saw that any one was discouraged, he opened his mouth, as though about to devour him, in imitation of a lion, in order to make him laugh and inspire him with courage. Toward eleven o'clock, peeping down through the blinds, I perceived many parents pacing the street in their impatience. There was Precossi's father, in his blue blouse, who had deserted his shop, with his face still quite black. There was Crossi's mother, the vegetable-vender; and Nelli's mother, dressed in black, who could not stand still.

A little before mid-day, my father arrived and raised his eyes to my window; my dear father! At noon we had all finished. And it was a sight at the close of school! Every one ran to meet the boys, to ask questions, to turn over the leaves of the copy-books to compare them with the work of their comrades.

"How many operations? What is the total? And subtraction? And the answer? And the punctuation of decimals?"

All the masters were running about hither and thither, summoned in a hundred directions.

My father instantly took from my hand the rough copy, looked at it, and said, "That's well."

Beside us was the blacksmith, Precossi, who was also inspecting his son's work, but rather uneasily, and not comprehending it. He turned to my father:

"Will you do me the favor to tell me the total?"

My father read the number. The other gazed and reckoned. "Brave little one!" he exclaimed, in perfect content. And my father and he gazed at each other for a moment with a kindly smile, like two friends. My father offered his hand, and the other shook it; and they parted, saying, "Farewell until the oral examination."

"Until the oral examination."

After proceeding a few paces, we heard a falsetto voice which made us turn our heads. It was the blacksmith-ironmonger singing.


THE LAST EXAMINATION

Friday, 7th.

This morning we had our oral examinations. At eight o'clock we were all in the schoolroom, and at a quarter past they began to call us, four at a time, into the big hall, where there was a large table covered with a green cloth; round it were seated the head-master and four other masters, among them our own. I was one of the first called out. Poor master! how plainly I perceived this morning that you are really fond of us! While they were interrogating the others, he had no eyes for any one but us. He was troubled when we were uncertain in our replies; he grew serene when we gave a fine answer; he heard everything, and made us a thousand signs with his hand and head, to say to us, "Good!--no!--pay attention!--slower!--courage!"

He would have suggested everything to us, had he been able to talk. If the fathers of all these pupils had been in his place, one after the other, they could not have done more. They would have cried "Thanks!" ten times, in the face of them all. And when the other masters said to me, "That is well; you may go," his eyes beamed with pleasure.

I returned at once to the schoolroom to wait for my father. Nearly all were still there. I sat down beside Garrone. I was not at all cheerful; I was thinking that it was the last time that we should be near each other for an hour. I had not yet told Garrone that I should not go through the fourth grade with him, that I was to leave Turin with my father. He knew nothing. And he sat there, doubled up together, with his big head reclining on the desk, making ornaments round the photograph of his father, who was dressed like a machinist, and who is a tall, large man, with a bull neck and a serious, honest look, like himself. And as he sat thus bent together, with his blouse a little open in front, I saw on his bare and robust breast the gold cross which Nelli's mother had presented to him, when she learned that he protected her son. But it was necessary to tell him sometime that I was going away. I said to him:

"Garrone, my father is going away from Turin this autumn, for good. He asked me if I were going, also. I replied that I was."

"You will not go through the fourth grade with us?" he said to me. I answered "No."

Then he did not speak to me for a while, but went on with his drawing. Then, without raising his head, he inquired:

"And shall you remember your comrades of the third grade?"

"Yes," I told him, "all of them; but you more than all the rest. Who can forget you?"

He looked at me fixedly and seriously, with a gaze that said a thousand things, but he said nothing; he only offered me his left hand, pretending to continue his drawing with the other; and I pressed it between mine, that strong and loyal hand. At that moment the master entered hastily, with a red face, and said, in a low, quick voice, with a joyful intonation:

"Good, all is going well now, let the rest come forwards; *bravi*, boys! Courage! I am extremely well satisfied." And, in order to show us his contentment, and to exhilarate us, as he went out in haste, he made a motion of stumbling and of catching at the wall, to prevent a fall; he whom we had never seen laugh! The thing appeared so strange, that, instead of laughing, all remained stupefied; all smiled, no one laughed.

Well, I do not know,--that act of childish joy caused both pain and tenderness. All his reward was that moment of cheerfulness,--it was the compensation for nine months of kindness, patience, and even sorrow! For that he had toiled so long; for that he had so often gone to give lessons to a sick boy, poor teacher! That and nothing more was what he demanded of us, in exchange for so much affection and so much care!

And, now, it seems to me that I shall always see him in the performance of that act, when I recall him through many years; and when I have become a man, he will still be alive, and we shall meet, and I will tell him about that deed which touched my heart; and I will give him a kiss on his white head.

FAREWELL

Monday, 10th.

At one o'clock we all assembled once more for the last time at the school, to hear the results of the examinations, and to take our little promotion books. The street was thronged with parents, who had even invaded the big hall, and many had made their way into the class-rooms, thrusting themselves even to the master's desk: in our room they filled the entire space between the wall and the front benches. There were Garrone's father, Derossi's mother, the blacksmith Precossi, Coretti, Signora Nelli, the vegetable-vender, the father of the little mason, Stardi's father, and many others whom I had never seen; and on all sides a whispering and a hum were audible, that seemed to proceed from the square outside.

The master entered, and a profound silence ensued. He had the list in his hand, and began to read at once.

"Abatucci, promoted, sixty seventieths. Archini, promoted, fifty-five seventieths."--The little mason promoted; Crossi promoted. Then he read loudly:

"Ernesto Derossi, promoted, seventy seventieths, and the first prize."

All the parents who were there--and they all knew him--said:

"Bravo, bravo, Derossi!" And he shook his golden curls, with his easy and beautiful smile, and looked at his mother, who made him a salute with her hand.

Garoffi, Garrone, the Calabrian promoted. Then three or four sent back; and one of them began to cry because his father, who was at the entrance, made a menacing gesture at him. But the master said to the father:

"No, sir, excuse me; it is not always the boy's fault; it is often his misfortune. And that is the case here." Then he read:

"Nelli, promoted, sixty-two seventieths." His mother sent him a kiss from her fan. Stardi, promoted, with sixty-seven seventieths! but, at hearing this fine fate, he did not even smile, or remove his fists from his temples. The last was Votini, who had come very finely dressed and brushed,--promoted. After reading the last name, the master rose and said:

"Boys, this is the last time that we shall find ourselves assembled together in this room. We have been together a year, and now we part good friends, do we not? I am sorry to part from you, my dear boys." He interrupted himself, then he resumed: "If I have sometimes failed in patience, if sometimes, without intending it, I have been unjust, or too severe, forgive me."

"No, no!" cried the parents and many of the scholars,--"no, master, never!"

"Forgive me," repeated the master, "and think well of me. Next year you will not be with me; but I shall see you again, and you will always abide in my heart. Farewell until we meet again, boys!"

So saying, he stepped forward among us, and we all offered him our hands, as we stood up on the seats, and grasped him by the arms, and by the skirts of his coat; many kissed him; fifty voices cried in concert:

"Farewell until we meet again, teacher!--Thanks, teacher!--May your health be good!--Remember us!"

When I went out, I felt oppressed by the commotion. We all ran out confusedly. Boys were emerging from all the other class-rooms also. There was a great mixing and tumult of boys and parents, bidding the masters and the mistresses good by, and exchanging greetings among themselves. The mistress with the red feather had four or five children on top of her, and twenty around her, depriving her of breath; and they had half torn off the little nun's bonnet, and thrust a dozen bunches of flowers in the button-holes of her black dress, and in her pockets. Many were making much of Robetti, who had that day, for the first time, abandoned his crutches. On all sides the words were audible:

"Good by until next year!--Until the twentieth of October!" We greeted each other, too. Ah! now all disagreements were forgotten at that moment! Votini, who had always been so jealous of Derossi, was the first to throw himself on him with open arms. I saluted the little mason, and kissed him, just at the moment when he was making me his last hare's face, dear boy! I saluted Precossi. I saluted Garoffi, who announced to me the approach of his last lottery, and gave me a little paper weight of majolica, with a broken corner; I said farewell to all the others. It was beautiful to see poor Nelli clinging to Garrone, so that he could not be taken from him. All thronged around Garrone, and it was, "Farewell, Garrone!--Good by until we meet!" And they touched him, and pressed his hands, and made much of him, that brave, sainted boy; and his father was perfectly amazed, as he looked on and smiled.

Garrone was the last one whom I embraced in the street, and I stifled a sob against his breast: he kissed my brow. Then I ran to my father and mother. My father asked me: "Have you spoken to all of your comrades?"

I replied that I had. "If there is any one of them whom you have wronged, go and ask his pardon, and beg him to forget it. Is there no one?"

"No one," I answered.

"Farewell, then," said my father with a voice full of emotion, bestowing a last glance on the schoolhouse. And my mother repeated: "Farewell!"

And I could not say anything.